D1243693

Island Songs

Island Songs

ALEX WHEATLE

This edition first published in Great Britain in 2006 by
Allison & Busby Limited
13 Charlotte Mews
London W1T 4EJ
www.allisonandbusby.com

Copyright © 2005 by ALEX WHEATLE

The moral right of the author has been asserted.

A catalogue record for this book is available from
the British Library.

10 9 8 7 6 5 4 3 2 1

ISBN 0 7490 8243 7
978-0-7490-8243-7

Printed and bound in Great Britain by
Bookmarque Ltd, Croydon, Surrey

ALEX WHEATLE was born in South London. He is currently working with Booktrust to introduce literature to the dispossessed. He organises and holds workshops in prisons and young adult institutions. He is the author of four previous novels: *The Seven Sisters*, *East of Acre Lane*, *Brixton Rock* and *Checkers* (co-written with Mark Parham).

Prologue

South London
July 2003

Two bridesmaids sporting matching pink dresses, white socks and pink ribbons in their hair, danced the last waltz. They were at their uncle Royston's wedding reception. Giggling and holding hands, they had the floor to themselves. They enjoyed the polite applause that rippled around the decorated hall from the remaining guests as they mimicked poses and dance steps that they had seen enacted by their elders earlier in the evening.

Watching the girls from the top banquet table was their grandmother and great aunt, pride glowing. They were both in floral dresses, white shoes and white hats and their expressions told of rich experiences and lost dreams. The scene before them reminded them of their own childhood and they could almost hear the gentle Jamaican breezes curling and weaving through the leaves of the Blue Mahoes in the Claremont valley.

"Dey look so beautiful out der," gushed the grandmother, Hortense, clapping enthusiastically. She was thinking of her own wedding day many years ago. It was in rural Jamaica and she wondered what her mother would have thought of the plush surroundings. Today, she spotted an old man nursing a paper cup full of rum punch sitting alone in a corner. He was staring vacantly at the remains of the wedding cake. Irritated skin framed his eyes. He looked like a rejected male lion.

"Jenny," Hortense called. "Yuh nah gwarn to say hello to Jacob? Yuh two 'ave been avoiding each udder all evenin'."

Jenny's brow hardened. She shot Jacob a dismissive glance. "We 'ave not'ing to say to each udder."

"But yuh were married to each udder fe over twenty years," stated Hortense. "Yuh cyan't be civil to each udder?"

Jenny inhaled deeply, attempting to master some dark emotion. Her eyes flicked between her sister and Jacob and a sense of guilt weighed heavily on her mind. Why did *he* have to turn up, she thought to herself. Maybe he wanted to say his last piece before she and Hortense flew back to Jamaica for good in a week's time. Well, she for one would not entertain him.

"Hortense," Jenny said softly, leaning over to speak in her sister's ear. "People divorce an' live dem separate lives. We don't need to talk to each udder every time we pass. Me don't know why yuh invite him."

Draining the last of her champagne, Hortense stood up. "Well, me gwarn to say hello to him. Me don't see him fe fifteen years now. We was all so close one time."

"*Hortense!*" Jenny protested, panic coursing through her veins.

Ignoring her sister, Hortense walked across the varnished wooden floor to where Jacob was sitting. Jacob seemed not to acknowledge her presence. He gazed at the crumbs and lumps of icing as if they offered some kind of meaning to his life.

"Jacob," Hortense greeted, trying to raise a smile while sensing her sister's eyes boring into her back. She offered Jacob her hand but he refused it. She studied his face and noticed the curved lines of bitterness marking his forehead. The tufts of hair around his ears and clinging on the back of his head were coloured stress-white. "It's been ah long time," Hortense resumed. "Me glad dat yuh did accept me invitation to me son wedding. Yuh two were close. We was all so..."

Sipping from his cup again, Jacob looked over Hortense's left shoulder. He spotted his ex-wife's anxious looks and summoned up a cruel smile.

"I'm not here fe ya benefit, Hortense. I come to give ya son, *my* nephew, my blessing."

"Jacob, me cyan't understand why ya like dis to me. Wha' did me ever done to yuh?"

Jacob grinned again, his cheeks unmoving. He enjoyed

Hortense's discomfort but his eyes still betrayed a sour memory. "Yuh know, Hortense, my fader did ah warn me about ya family. Him used to tell me stories about ya devil papa. I never believed him at de time. An' he did never waan me to marry Jenny. Him tell me de whole lot ah yuh was cursed by de devil himself. But like ah fool I married into ya godforsaken family. An' me will regret it 'til de end ah my days. My fader died cursing ya papa's very name."

Placing her hands upon her hips, Hortense leaned in closer to Jacob and glared at him. "Yuh lucky dis is me son wedding an' me don't waan to cause nuh fuss. It's not me fault why yuh an' Jenny divorce an' its about time yuh get over it! It's been fifteen years now. Me could never understan' it anyway becah der was nuhbody else involve."

Jacob locked Hortense in an intense stare. He paused before breaking out into a manic chuckle. "Wasn't der?" he asked, almost mockingly.

Hortense could hear the clip-clip of Jenny's heels approaching. She returned Jacob's gaze with interest. The music was fading away and Hortense, conscious of people around her, lowered her voice. "Yuh implying dat me sister did 'ave relations wid ah nex' mon?"

Reaching Hortense's side, Jenny immediately tried to usher her away. "Come, Hortense," she whispered, looking about her. "Don't waste ya time wid dat fool. He's all bitter an' twisted."

Downing his drink, Jacob stood up unsteadily. He turned to Hortense. "An' she call me bitter an' twisted! Hortense, I cyan't tell yuh de trut' becah it would kill yuh an' I truly love yuh as ah friend. As de Most High is my witness! My marriage was ah sham. Ah fraud! Yuh better believe it. Becah Jenny only did ah love two mon in dis world. One was her pagan fader an' de udder was *not* me."

Feeling her heartbeat accelerate and sensing that the other wedding guests were taking an interest, Jenny pulled Hortense's left arm and walked her away. Jacob, not finished and slurring his words, yelled, "Hortense, why yuh don't ask ya so-called sweet sister who she really did ah love!"

Jenny closed her eyes in mortification, gratefully dropping into a nearby chair. With a handkerchief she wiped away the sweat that had collected upon her temples. She finally turned to her sister who took a seat beside her. She took Hortense's left hand and held it tightly within her own trembling hands. "Don't lissen to him, Hortense. Jacob ah talk pure fart. Me cyan't wait 'til we get 'pon dat plane to carry us home fe good."

Shocked by what Jacob had said, Hortense replied, "ah change has come over him. Me don't know why. Him even call Papa ah devil. Wha' is ah matter wid dat mon? Wha' do him mean dat de trut' coulda kill me?"

Feeling a weight pressing upon her conscience, Jenny thought of the other man. Then she thought of her father, as she always did in time of crisis. She could see him in the picture of her mind, tall and proud. He was strapping on his size thirteen boots, slinging his crocus bag full of tools over his broad shoulders and setting off to work, his long strides eating up the ground.

Chapter One

Claremont, Jamaica
October 1945

Joseph Rodney rubbed his hands to free the clingy particles of soil, lifted his head and surveyed the distant hills that were shrouded in mist. He could see the faint light-brown traces of footpaths and goat byways that snaked upwards and faded into the horizon. The dense vegetation was a rich green, peppered with the vibrant colours of fruits and plants. A stream sliced its way through a lush valley of tall Blue Mahoe trees. The Claremont valley offered only meagre patches where the folding, rolling lands met on a rise.

Joseph could see Mr Welton DaCosta's livestock grazing upon the sloping field above the village. Although he was grateful to his father-in-law, Neville, who presented him with the strip of good soil he now laboured on, Joseph hoped of owning and breeding livestock one day, the dream of all Jamaican country folk.

The cooling breeze that drifted in from the Caribbean sea was still and Joseph guessed that the seasonal wind and rains would surely come soon; he sensed it in the balmy aroma of the soil. He looked up again and wondered if the terrain he was studying locked away as many secrets as he did, nightmarish memories that he had yet to even tell his wife. He turned slowly to view the ramshackle dwellings of villagers who had constructed their homes precariously on steep hillsides and astride grassy escarpments, the patchwork of corrugated zinc roofs reflecting the light. A hot Jamaican sun was setting, but on this secluded part of the north of the island, two thousand feet above sea level, the yellow eye didn't rage as it did on the flat southern plains, where most of the sugar plantations were located and where the crocodiles swam silently in swampy rivers thick with reeds.

Joseph thought of a white man he had once seen and how he seemed so uncomfortable sweltering under the sun, forever dabbing his reddened, peeling face as he rode by. Joseph was unaware that the man was employed by the British colonial government to 'oversee' the Crown Lands (of which the Claremont valley was a part) and report any undue incidents; it was whispered in these parts that the man had fathered three children in Browns Town and there, locals stole questioning glances at caramel-skinned children.

"Madness!" Joseph laughed. "Dat white mon face did ah look like spoil red pepper!"

Taking off his wide-brimmed, straw hat, Joseph swabbed the sweat off his brow with a huge mud-stained hand, replaced it so that it covered his eyebrows and muttered to himself, "dem neva learn. When Massa God decide to blow him cruel wind as he surely will, den de people der ah mountain side will be tossed to de sky like ah John-Crow feader."

Joseph had finished his work for the day and he was satisfied that the callaloo, lettuce, yams, tomato and hot peppers would be ripe for picking before the next full moon. He knew that the pumpkins and sweet potato were not quite ready. Joseph felt he could probably get away with it if he decided to include the pumpkins and sweet potato in his harvest offerings to the church, but that would be cheating. He also didn't want the preacher man, Mr Forbes, to offer his fellow villagers any gossip or 'susu' talk of how the Rodney family did not give of their best.

"Him t'ink him so special wid him big house an' him big talk," Joseph thought. "Me'd rader cross crocodile river inna flimsy broad leaf dan gwarn to dat mon church every Sunday. Him lucky him getting any harvest from me becah me only do it fe Amy. Me don't waan nuhbody to look wid bad eye to her or me family."

Joseph recalled the preacher's reluctance to perform the wedding ceremony for him and Amy twenty years ago. The wedding feast had consisted only of ardough bread, chicken, rice and peas, and Amy was dressed in her mother's simple white frock, the same garment in which she had been baptised. Many villagers boycotted the festivities. "Why is sweet pretty Miss Amy marrying dat black, devil mon?" they asked out aloud. "She is ah nice Christian girl. An' dis devil mon mus' ah put spell 'pon Misser Neville to get dat land!"

It was a Sunday and sometimes Joseph hated the solitude that he felt working on the Sabbath. Despite having his own family he felt a loneliness that would never leave him alone. Everybody else was taking their rest or singing their praises to the Most High in Mr Forbes's church – the biggest building in the village that also doubled as the school. Joseph's youngest daughter, Hortense, loved the singing there and her sister, Jenny, excelled in her lessons. Jenny looks so much like my own mother, Joseph thought. Bless her tears.

A strong pang of guilt wracked Joseph. He hadn't seen his mother for thirty years, having left home amid total devastation at fifteen years of age. He always pictured her in his mind weeping. Always weeping. "Ah, pure madness!" Joseph muttered to himself, shaking his head. He didn't even know if she was still alive or indeed if any of his siblings were. A disturbing image of his older brother, Naptali, chilled his bones; the broken expression, the complete loss of a long-held dream and those crazy eyes! He had only seen him once, for just one day of his life, in the fall of 1914. A day that he could recall in minute detail from the time he blinked sleep from his eyes to the sound of the debating crickets of *that* night when Joseph tried but failed to sleep.

A call interrupted Joseph's recollections. "Moonshine! Moonshine!" Looking down the hill where the voice was coming from, Joseph knew it could only be one person. Kwarhterleg. For nobody else in the village dared to call Joseph by this nickname, although they felt free to do so when Joseph was out of earshot. The inhabitants of this tiny hamlet were immediately struck by Joseph's blackness and his intimidating physique. Fearful of him, they thought he was some kind of disciple of the devil, they referred to Joseph as him black 'til him shine an' Old Screwface mus' ah sen' fe him to turn we away from praising de Most High'. As years passed by this description was shortened to the moniker 'Moonshine'.

Joseph knew he was descended from the Maroons, a fierce tribal people who would not yield to slavery and fought their oppressors with everything they had. Many of them had won their freedom from their Spanish captors upon arrival on Jamaican soil at a place that is now called Runaway Bay. From there the Maroons made their way to 'Cockpit Country', the mountainous interior of the island. The Spanish conquistadors, fearful that the legendary Coromanty curse might well strike them down if they dared to pursue the runaway slaves, let them be. The British, after assuming control of Jamaica, decided to send in waves of red-coats to hunt the Maroons down, ignoring the local warnings of house slaves who spoke of the mighty deeds of the Maroon warrior queen, Nanny. Hardly any of these forces would look on their homeland again and the ones that did never did so with sane eyes. The British imperialists even resorted to shipping over fierce Indians from the Mosquito Coast in Central America, promising them lavish rewards for quelling the Maroons' spirit of resistance. They fared no better, never to be seen or heard of again.

Born in Accompong Town, the first Maroon settlement in Jamaica, not more than a fifteen minute John-Crow journey from the bony wastelands of Cockpit Country, Joseph was unfortunate that when he arrived in Claremont, in the northern parish of St Anne, that very few people there had ever seen Maroons or knew about them, save a handful of old wizened folk who spent their time teaching their grandchildren the art of tilling and telling fireside tales of ghosts and demons. They offered Joseph vague and knowing nods whenever he walked by, never revealing what lay behind their polite greetings.

A few of the Claremont elders knew that the land they had tilled and lived on for two hundred years or so was gained after a colonial government agreement with African ex-slaves, who were once owned by the Spanish and later roamed free following the Spanish withdrawal from the island. It was decided that these former slaves would be granted land if they hunted and captured newly-escaped slaves from the profitable plantations. Even a number of Maroons complied with this contract. Feeling a deep sense of guilt, aged Claremontonians carried the secret of their inheritance to the grave.

"Don't ask nuh question an' me cyan't tell yuh nuh lie," they would say.

The people of the Claremont valley kept to themselves, worked their land and praised the God of the King James Bible. Most believed that any malady or handicap that visited a man was God's punishment of his sins. Many Jamaican rural folk were even unaware that a year ago, in 1944, their colonial masters had granted voting rights to every male or female over the age of twenty-one. Those who were not ignorant of this shrugged their shoulders and said, "it'll will nah effect me if me crops nuh ripe an' sweet. Wha' good is ah blasted vote!" The people who lived here preferred the devil they knew.

Kwarhterleg employed a crutch hewn from a branch of a tree, its shoulder shaped by his left armpit due to constant use since he was seventeen. The left leg of his stained, torn khaki pants was tied up in a knot just below the knee. He hobbled up the goat's path to Joseph's small plot of land, holding a soiled plastic bag full of something that had a potent aroma. In his late sixties, Kwarhterleg didn't have much hair, but made up for it with his untamed grey beard. He was a foot shorter than Joseph, and leaner, and his hooded eyes spoke of some distant betrayal.

Stumping his way to Joseph's patch of land, Kwarhterleg threw away his crutch and sat down. While he caught his breath, he seemed apprehensive, fearful of the news he had to deliver.

"Yuh bring me de yard of tobacco me sen' yuh to get?" Joseph asked casually, taking out a homemade pipe from his pocket. He had named his smoking pipe Panama. "Misser Patterson satisfied wid de pear, plum and strong-back leaf me give him?"

"Yes, mon. Him well pleased wid de strong-back leaf. Him son ketch ah fever an' has ah serious need fe it," replied Kwarhterleg, his tone full of reverence. "It's inna de bag."

"Well, bring it come den," demanded Joseph impatiently.

Kwarhterleg emptied the contents of the bag on the ground. Joseph, in his trouser pockets, found a pair of rusty scissors and proceeded to snip the tobacco leaves into a fine cut before generously stuffing his pipe; if he had had more patience he would have sweetened it with sugar water and left it out to dry. As Joseph lit himself what he thought was a well-earned smoke, Kwarhterleg watched his long-time friend with concern.

"Moonshine," he began with caution, "somet'ing serious happen ah church today. Me affe tell yuh. Serious t'ing. Long time yuh tell me to inform yuh if de Preacher Mon trouble any of ya family."

Exhaling his smoke, Joseph turned to look at his friend and scolded, "Kwarhterleg! Yuh love mek big bull outta young goat! Tell me wha' happen, mon! Me don't 'ave nuh time fe long journey around broad bush."

"Jenny get ah serious beating today, mon," Kwarhterleg revealed. He went on to tell Joseph of what happened today at church. Jenny was playing tag with her sister during the singing of a hymn and had squealed when Hortense had pinched her. The preacher slammed his hymn book closed, looked upon his congregation in disbelief that a child had interrupted the singing and walked slowly over to Jenny. His eyes fixed upon the girl's petrified expression, he struck her twice with an open palm, the sound echoing in the church hall. Jenny fell off her chair and banged her head upon the dusty wooden floor but she was determined not to cry. Still glaring at the child and looming over her, the preacher recognised Joseph's defiance. He offered Jenny a dismissive glance before returning to the pulpit. Amy, Jenny's mother, helped her daughter to her feet as fury rose within her. Amy was about to protest when she spotted her father, Neville, who was gesturing with his hands to calm down. She could read his lips. "Nuh cause bangarang inna God's house."

Not betraying an emotion, Joseph toked twice on his pipe and peered into the mists. He said nothing for ten minutes, until he had finished smoking. Kwarhterleg was filling his own wonky wooden pipe when finally Joseph spoke. "Amy say anyt'ing?" he asked innocently.

"Nuh, mon. Yuh know so she won't say anyt'ing to de Preacher-Mon. Who would? Ah mon of God dat. Serious t'ing! If yuh cuss de Preacher-Mon den Old Screwface will set his mark 'pon yuh an' yuh will surely ketch ah fire."

"Me nah 'fraid of nuh Preacher-Mon or de devil himself or Old Screwface as yuh like to call him," said Joseph defiantly. He stood up and examined his cutlass that was resting six feet away from him on the ground; the cutting edge of the blade stained brown from the soil. "Come Kwarhterleg! Amy should 'ave dinner ready an' me sure ya belly ah tickle yuh like hog sniffing him tripe dat he cyan't see. An' me affe talk to Preacher-Mon."

Collecting his tools, pick, spade and cutlass, Joseph placed them inside an old crocus bag, slung it over his shoulder and started off. Kwarhterleg hobbled behind him, trying to keep up with Joseph's long strides, his unlaced black boots making clear imprints in the rich soil. Refusing to walk more than thirty paces in a straight line, Joseph would suddenly zigzag to confuse any malevolent spirits that he thought could be pursuing him; even Old Screwface himself might take matters in hand after his recent comments, Joseph thought.

They went downhill, following the goat's path through a forest of palm trees before passing groves of bamboo, tambarine and ackee. It became hotter as they declined further, the mosquitoes becoming more numerous, energetically skitting through the dust. They soon saw the first corrugated zinc roofs of the sparse dwellings of their village.

Most of the homes had only two tiny rooms – one for sleeping and the other for storing farming tools, cooking utensils, brushwood and water urns. A kerosene lamp, hooked on a wooden beam near the front door, provided light. Everybody had an outside kitchen – a corrugated aluminium roof set upon wooden stilts and a low fireplace. Some villagers kept their fires going all day to ward off the mosquitoes. Between the home and the kitchen was a patch of rock-hard ground where the chickens scratched, bare-footed children played, goats strayed and skinny yapping dogs – if they were bold enough to risk a thrashing – snouted for scraps. The village itself was sheltered by green-cloaked hills on all sides.

The Rodney dwelling was similar to many of the others in Claremont except for the water lillies, tulips, Croton green and other flowers that Joseph had planted around his domain; Amy's mother, Melody, named the ring of flowers Joseph's Coat Of Many Colours. Joseph had also planted an avocado and a bambay mango tree which were now reaching their maturity; from one of their branches hung an old tyre, attached to a rope, still in the late afternoon calm.

Jenny, Joseph's ten-year-old daughter, was the first to see her father returning home. She halted the game she was playing with her eight-year-old sister, Hortense, and ran up to him, smiling. Joseph put his crocus bag on the ground, dropped to his knees and received Jenny into his tight embrace, returning his daughter's happy greeting. Hortense came running behind her sister but Jenny was not about to loosen her firm hold around her father's neck. Both girls had their hair braided for church but Hortense had thrown away the green Croton flower that had decorated her head. She had teased Jenny about the slaps she suffered from the preacher and aped the preacher's actions by smacking her with the flower. Jenny had still kept her bloom, wanting to hold onto the gift that her father had given her.

The two sisters were dressed in simple white knee-length cotton dresses. Kwarhterleg knew that Joseph only genuinely smiled when greeting his eldest daughter after a hard day's toil. He didn't even reserve this special greeting for his wife. Amy emerged from the house wearing a white head-scarf; it was clear she had passed on her looks to Hortense. Jenny was darker and much taller than her sister. Amy, thirty-seven years of age, looked no older than twenty-five. Her brown skin glowed like freshly melted milk chocolate and there was a proud fire in her warm caramel eyes. "Dinner soon ready," she informed her husband. "Why don't yuh tek off your boot dem an' res' yaself before me give yuh dinner. Jenny, leave ya fader alone an' give him space!"

Jenny reluctantly unwrapped her arms from her father's neck. Hortense grinned mischievously then ran up behind her sister, slapped her upon the back of her neck and bolted away, shouting, "ya it!"

Joseph's eyes followed his two daughters. "Me cyan't tek me res' now," Joseph told Amy as a chicken strolled in front of him, unaware that it might well be next Sunday's main course for dinner. "Me affe sort out ah liccle somet'ing wid Preacher-Mon."

Amy glared at Kwarhterleg, crossing her arms. Kwarhterleg, feeling uncomfortable under her fierce gaze, stumped away to his favourite seat against the bambay mango tree. He took out his pipe and hoped Amy would bring him a drink after her vexation had subsided. Joseph collected his crocus bag, slung it over his shoulder and set off again. He turned to his wife after ten long strides. "Amy, where David der-ya?"

"Him gone walking. Yuh know how him love to walk around strange bush when de fancy tek him. Or mebbe him find ah girl to court wid dat him don't tell we about. Nuh fret, Joseph. David never late fe him dinner. Especially if it chicken."

Joseph started off again leaving the yard. Jenny caught sight of him departing. "Papa! Papa!" she called. "Cyan me come wid yuh? Please Papa."

"Nuh, Jenny. Nah dis time. Play wid ya sister. Ah madness me 'ave to deal wid."

Jenny stomped off into the field behind her home, outrage marked her expression. Hortense set about teasing her, a game she loved to play whenever her father slighted Jenny. "*Papa don't waan to walk wid yuh becah ya face look like wrinkle-up plum,*" she sang. Jenny picked up a spoiled mango and threw it at her sister, just missing her target. Hortense ran off complaining to Amy as Jenny went deeper into the field.

Once Joseph's face was out of his family's view, it changed to an uncompromising fury. As he walked through the village, Claremontonians offered him cautious greetings and bade him well but none paused for a conversation to discuss the matters of the day as Claremontonians loved to do. He passed a farming tools repair shop where a grey-haired man was mending a broken plough. Mr Cummings, the proprietor of the crop-seed store, waved to Joseph but Joseph didn't see him.

He marched on, weaving through soiled fruit, rotting vegetables and garbage that the marketers had left behind from the morning market. Joseph saw that most of the liquor bars that lined the market square were shut, observing the Sabbath. However, Mr Johnstone's 'rum joint' was open for business and a man sitting on an unsteady bench was enjoying a glass of milk and rum, his donkey tied to a tree nearby. "Good evening, sa!" the man said. Joseph, not recognising him, guessed he was a travelling businessman heading for the north coast, and ignored him.

His stride lengthening, Joseph passed the DaCosta family dairy. He paused and took off his hat to greet Mrs DaCosta, a long time friend of his wife, who was milking a goat. He also greeted Mrs Walters, another friend of his wife; she ran a small dressmaking concern and journeyed weekly into St Anne's Bay to purchase textiles. The dusty, pot-holed road sloped and curved downhill, coconut trees and five-fingered plant fronds skirting its edges. Women went by balancing jugs of water upon their heads with ridiculous ease. A dozen or so elderly women, all dressed in perfectly white, ankle-length frocks and white headscarves, were returning from a baptism at the river. They were singing heartily while clapping their hands. Joseph kept his distance from them and guessed that if Isaac conducted the service, he would be heading home too.

Joseph's mind was fixed on revenge. He passed a group of young men playing cricket in a field; their ball was a round piece of raw chocolate bound with elastic bands and their bats were hewn from broken-off branches. Bowlers aimed at sticks speared into the hard ground. In their playing field, stray goats snuffed and nibbled, and at the boundary stray hungry dogs hunted in small packs, searching the refuse for a meal but keeping their distance from the players. On rare occasions, Joseph had seen a wheezing Ford car struggling up the hill, its suspension wailing. Villagers would pause from whatever they were doing and gawp at the driver, wondering how rich he was.

Joseph didn't bother to acknowledge the families who lived in not-so-square wooden huts on either side of the road as he got to the edge of the village, although he once knew them all. Inside the sparse homes, mothers were braiding the hair of sobbing daughters; older girls were hanging clothes, nylon, cottons and crimpolene, on washing lines, resisting the temptation to wring them free of water for they owned no clothes-irons. They hoped the breeze would blow out the creases. Tough-footed children threw sticks at mango trees and played pirate and sword-fencing games. Matriarchs sat outside on wonky stools reading their Bibles aloud while simultaneously slapping the children who misbehaved in front of them. No misdemeanour escaped their quick eyes. Other young boys fed the fowls and swept backyards with coarsed-grass brooms while men rested their backs against unstraight walls, smoking and chewing raw tobacco, staring blankly ahead. It seemed they were asking God, Why yuh mek we suffer so?

In Joseph's mind, Mr Forbes's body morphed into a rusty nail.

The smell of boiling rice and chicken, cooked in coconut and goat's milk, wafted from the outside kitchens from blackened cooking pots; many Claremontonians never enjoyed the Sunday traditional Jamaican dish of 'rice and peas', for the red kidney beans that were mixed with the rice proved too expensive. A few bread-winning adult males in Claremont, including Mr DaCosta, had the luxury of a 'watchmon' – a chunk of salt pork added to their generous portions of rice, 'peas' and chicken.

Mr Forbes, the Preacher Man, lived a two and a half mile trek from the centre of the village. His church was even further away but no villager queried the madness of having to perform a six mile round trip to praise their Lord. Although his formal duties were with the church, Mr Forbes was also a part-time agony aunt, counsellor, clairvoyant, Godfather to almost every child born in Claremont and, on one occasion, an exorcist to a villager who had stolen food from a man's plot of land and who swore that Old Screwface ordered him to perform this heinous deed.

It took forty minutes for Joseph to reach Mr Forbes' home, his long strides making the journey fifteen minutes shorter than it was for most men. An almond tree was planted near the entrance of the house and Joseph took shelter in its shade, his legs weary from his long day. He took off his hat and palmed the sweat off his forehead. Two goats eyed the visitor.

"Preacher Mon!" called Joseph replacing his hat, his deep baritone snarling through the warm, late afternoon air. "Preacher Mon."

A boy came running out. It was Jacob, Mr Forbes' thirteen-year-old son. He was wearing long grey shorts and a white shirt. His hair was centre-parted and Joseph thought that he looked ridiculous. He reckoned that Jacob's Sunday prayers probably hadn't yet stopped for the day. Too much blasted praising fe de Lord inna dese parts, he said to himself. But will de Most High ever come down an' help me plant me field? Nuh sa!

"Good afternoon, Misser Rodney," Jacob greeted, his manners immaculate. "Papa soon come. Him jus' changing him clothes from church. Yuh waan ah drink, Misser Rodney? We 'ave all kinda juice drink an' ah liccle rum if yuh waan it?"

"Nuh, mon," Joseph bellowed, not even looking at the boy and keeping his eyes trained on the entrance of the house. "T'ank yuh kindly."

"Is dat yuh, Joseph?" Mr Forbes called from within the house as Jacob skipped inside. "I'll soon be wid yuh. I really wanted to talk to yuh anyway becah I never see your son, David, at church today. So it's ah good t'ing yuh come down to see me. I t'ought dat we did agree dat yuh would not stop any of ya family from coming to church. So it troubles me dat I never saw David in de congregation dis marnin. Maybe David feels dat if his fader don't attend church den him don't 'ave to. So I waan talk to yuh about dat an' set t'ings right. Also, I was forced to strike Jenny today. Dat chile need some discipline. Fussing an' fighting inna God's house! Unruly she is! Yuh 'ave to discipline her an' tek ah big hand to her backside. Joseph, yuh know I cyan't tek dat kinda behaviour in my church."

Mr Forbes finally emerged from the house. He was wearing a black felt hat that covered his round head. A white shirt restrained the overflow of his stomach, his smart velvet black jacket ending just above his knees. Grey slacks hugged his stocky legs and Joseph could see the braces that held them up. His lace-up, brown brogue shoes were recently polished and he wore a gold ring on his left hand. Joseph thought that someone who dressed like this in this part of the country was crazy. He guessed that Mr Forbes was able to afford his 'uppity' clothes because of the offerings he received every Sunday from his flock.

Striding towards Joseph with the countenance of a man who knew he was superior, Isaac's back straightened as his thumb and index fingers held the lapels of his jacket. But Joseph's lack of response to his earlier comments slightly disturbed him; he had expected some kind of explanation or an apology. Before the preacher could add anything else, Joseph dropped his crocus bag, swung back his right fist and levered a punch with devastating ferocity. It struck and lifted Isaac clean off the ground, propelling him backwards. He hit the earth with a solid thud and by the time he had blinked away his momentary concussion, he could only focus on a cutlass, poised an inch away from his left eye. Joseph's frame loomed above him. "Lay one finger 'pon me girl chile once more an' me will skin yuh wid me cutlass like fat-bellied goat skinned 'pon Christmas eve. Den me will hang yuh over Crab Foot Gully an' mek de buzzard dem peck ya eye dem!"

Glancing at Joseph's intense expression, Isaac knew that he meant every word. The preacher closed his eyes for two seconds believing that Joseph might just kill him now. When he re-opened them saw Joseph strolling off, flinging the crocus bag over his left shoulder. Joseph paused, turned around and regarded the preacher once more. To Isaac his eyes were inhuman, unfeeling, like those soulless duppys who preyed on unbelievers at night.

"Come harvest time," Joseph added, "nuhbody will bring ah better basket of offerings dan I. Dat's as sure as mountain goat find safe route 'pon dangerous hillside." Joseph tipped his hat with a flourish. "May tomorrow mek yuh wizer."

On his return journey, Joseph found that no villager was abroad, save a couple of silver-headed men who offered Joseph vague nods of greeting as they sat outside their homes, peering at the stars.

Joseph laughed to himself, not understanding why the villagers were so afraid of the dark. But he still walked in curves and bends, the kerosene lamps guiding his steps.

The moon had risen over the eastern hills by the time Joseph finished his dinner. In this remote corner of Jamaica, its silver light in a navy-blue sky reflected off the tree tops, creating a kaleidoscope of dark greens, browns, greys and blues that blurred the horizon. Joseph was sitting on a sawn-off tree trunk, shaped and smoothed by countless backsides. Two of his dogs were waiting for the bones from the pot. Amy was boiling water in a pot over the fire, about to wash the dishes and cutlery. Jenny, using the fire's glow, read from the family Bible, the pages dog-eared and yellowed. She took extreme care when turning over the pages and her forehead was locked in concentration. Hortense sat astride her brother David's back, the two of them playing some horse game, and Kwarhterleg, satisfied, smoked his pipe, sitting against his tree.

Having fed the dogs with the bones, Joseph passed his empty plate to Amy. "Joseph," Amy called sternly, "yuh sure yuh never cause ah fuss an' ah bangarang der ah preacher yard?"

Searching in his pockets for his pipe, Joseph replied, "nuh, mon. Nuh worry yaself. Preacher Mon will never box Jenny nuh more. Me mek him agree to dat."

Using a cloth to protect her hands, Amy poured the steaming water into a plastic bowl where she had placed the dishes. Employing a palm-sized block of wood that had the coarse hairs of many coconut shells glued to it, she proceeded to wash up. "Me don't waan to hear nuh susu talk from neighbour how me husband ah cuss cuss wid preacher. Me was about to strike Hortense an' Jenny meself fe dem unruliness inna church." Amy also feared that her father would learn of any incident that might have occurred.

Exhaling his first satisfying smoke, Joseph returned, "dat is ya right. Preacher Mon don't 'ave *any* right. None at all."

Cursing and tutting under her breath, Amy carried the bowl inside the house. Jenny looked up at her father and smiled. Joseph stroked her head. "Nuh worry yaself, liccle angel. Papa would never let any mon give yuh pain. Come, de moon is coming out to play.

Yuh better gwarn to ya bed before Mama get too gripy." They didn't see Hortense who was staring at them with jealous eyes.

"Hortense," Joseph called. "Time fe ya bed."

"But, Papa. Me an' David playing ah game."

"Don't boder let me ask yuh twice."

"Yuh never sen' Jenny to bed when she don't waan to go."

"Don't argue wid me chile! Go to ya strikin' bed before me box yuh!"

"Papa, yuh always t'reaten to box me but yuh never t'reaten to box Jenny. An' she could do wid ah mighty box! Her crooked smile deserve it."

"Gwarn to ya bed!"

Hortense knew it was an idle threat, for her father had never struck her in anger throughout her life, but she stomped into the house and found her sister was already inside. Joseph could hear them quarrelling until Amy rebuked them. David, seventeen years of age, emerged from the pit toilet and walked towards his father. He noticed that Kwarhterleg was falling asleep, pipe still in his mouth. Joseph recognised his own dark eyes in his son's gaze and the same complexion. But there was no anger there, no haunting loss in his forehead, no loneliness shrouded around the eyes. Just a simple love of life, patience and respect. Joseph envied him.

"Papa," David called gently. "Yuh box de Preacher Mon fe true? Mebbe me shoulda walked down to Preacher Mon plot an' talked to him. Mama said when yuh gone dat she'd bet her last flour dumpling dat Papa woulda raise ah storm."

Joseph sucked his pipe for two minutes before answering. "Me box him yes. Trut' ah de matter is Preacher Mon never like me an' me never like him. From de day me arrive inna Claremont me realise dis. Him t'ink me don't know dat him spread rumour about me ah devil chile. So it was bound to happen one day. Preacher Mon know where me stan' now."

"Don't trouble ya head, Papa. Yuh nah de only one who waan to strike Preacher Mon down. Der are udders who feel de same way."

Joseph wondered who these others could be. David changed the subject. "Papa, Mama affe gwarn to de river tomorrow to wash clothes. So me t'ought dat me should control de shop inna de marnin. Dat's wha' yuh waan me to do, Papa?"

Smiling, Joseph realised that at least the Most High blessed his traumatic life with godly children. "Yes, mon. Me don't waan to ask Kwarhterleg becah him 'ave nuff trouble pushing de cart. But if Miss Jo come ah shop ah marnin den don't charge her. She inna mad money trouble. An' if Misser Patterson wife come give her discount. Dis tobacco smoke nice. Madly strong but him dry it out good dis time."

"Yes, Papa. Me remember. Papa, me gone to me bed now. Goodnight."

"Wait up, David. Preacher Mon tell me yuh nah der-ya ah church today. Where yuh der?"

David took his time in answering. "Jus' walking, Papa. Yuh know, de Most High mek ah beautiful country around dese parts, Papa. Sometime me jus' like to tek in de air, walk ah hilltop, y'know. It mek me feel good."

Joseph smiled. "Ya mama t'ink yuh find girl to court wid."

"Nuh, Papa. Me don't ready fe dat yet. Me waan me own yard before me t'ink about dem t'ings."

David went inside. Joseph nodded. "Ah good bwai dat."

An hour and a half later, Joseph awoke Kwarhterleg with a glass of goat's milk containing two drops of rum.

"T'ank yuh sa," Kwarhterleg accepted. "Mon, me getting seriously weary dese days, Joseph. Me bones creaking like dead wood when fatty woman ah sit down 'pon it!"

Joseph took a sip from his own glass. "Yes, Kwarhterleg, age ah catch up 'pon yuh. Res' yaself inna de marnin. David will look after de shop."

Kwarhterleg downed his drink and Joseph helped him to his feet. He led him to his sleeping quarters in a corner of the kitchen. A pile of empty crocus bags formed Kwarhterleg's pillow.

Before Joseph retired he made a cross with the toes of his right foot in the dusty ground immediately outside the front door. He sprinkled his drink on the cross before draining the last of it and could hear the shrill cicadas from the surrounding fields. "Aaaahhh.

Yuh t'ink me would ever forget, Screwface?"

Entering the bedroom, Joseph could just make out in the dark Jenny and Hortense fast asleep coupled together like two spoons, Hortense was snoring into the nape of Jenny's back. They were sleeping on a mattress full of straw. David was curled around his sisters' feet. Joseph kissed both his daughters on the forehead, taking his time to tenderly stroke Jenny's left cheek. Jenny twitched, her subconscious feeling a warmth of familiarity. Joseph studied the contours of her face for thirty seconds as if he was remembering something from long ago.

He made his way to his own bed where he found Amy in her usual position against the wall. Not making a sound, he undressed to his shorts and vest, folded his clothes and placed them on a wooden chair beside his bed. He ran his fingers over the rippled, flaky black skin upon his left shoulder; a knife wound. He wondered if he would be hated even more because of his striking of Preacher Mon. As he lay down he felt the comfort of Amy's hand upon his chest.

Closing his eyes, Joseph saw an indistinct image of his mother form in his mind. It was the end of 1907. She had just reached home from a seven mile round trip to the post office. A letter was gripped tightly in her left hand like a wad of dollar bills. The seven-year-old Joseph, who was feeding guinea fowl at the time, heard his mother's call and ran to the house with his four sisters, brother and father. His mother looked the happiest she had been for a very long time and she felt the pages of the letter. It was a letter from Joseph's brother, Naptali. Inside the envelope were two American bank notes.

'Dear Mama,' she started reading. Everyone was silent.

Joseph opened his eyes and wondered if his recurring nightmares would ever end. "Madness!"

Chapter Two

Rising with the first herald of roosters, Amy went outside to view her homestead. The sun was already creeping over the eastern groves and hillsides, creating a reddish-green glow. The air was cool at this time of the day and Amy yawned extravagantly, stretching her arms and filling her lungs with cool Jamaican air. She dressed quickly for she knew that time was against her. She collected two clay water urns and started the one and a half mile trek on foot to the nearest stream, a tributary of the White river. Amy washed her face here, the fresh water energising her body. She then filled the jugs so that her family could swab away the night and sip coffee on her return. She didn't say much to the other women, just the occasional 'good marnin'. She knew they all had work to do and there was little time for 'susu' talk.

Balancing one of the urns on her head on her way home, Amy grimaced for she knew she would have to make a longer journey to scrub her family clothes in the river later on. When she reached home she placed the vessels on the hard-baked apron of ground before her front door and set about waking her family. Hortense and Jenny were the first to use the water, freshening their faces from the same plastic bowl using a small cake of carbolic soap bought from Mrs Clarke's tiny shop in the market. They then dabbed their fingers into the ashes of the dead fire, spread it across their teeth and cleaned their molars with a shared toothbrush, rinsing out their mouths with water. Coconut gratings were melted so that Jenny and Hortense could moisten their skin; they didn't want to be teased at school for having 'grey knees'. They dressed quickly and braided each other's hair. Jenny had learned to 'corn roll' her own hair when she was only five years old. Amy went off to start work in the kitchen, frying eggs, slicing ardough bread and preparing mugs of coffee with goat's milk. She presented her two daughters with a mango each to supplement their breakfast, all the time careful not to disturb Kwarhterleg who was still snoring a rasping snore.

David was the last of the family to take his 'marnin fresh' and by the time he did so, his mother was ready with his breakfast. Although he felt it was his duty to help out with the family business, he wanted to inform his parents soon that he needed to make his own way in life; a nagging restlessness had besieged him for the past few months. David watched his father preparing and sharpening his tools for his working day ahead and he thought to himself that however honourable work in the fields might be, the wider world must have more to offer than planting vegetables and selling them in the market-place in the centre of the village.

He knew that his father hoped that in time he would take over the farming duties and remembered Joseph's habitual phrase, 'if yuh put nuff work inna de soil den de soil will put in nuff work fe yuh'. But he heard from travellers and merchants who were passing through the village of gigantic boats dropping anchor in Kingston harbour, big loud towns where so many people lived that it was impossible to greet everybody with a hearty 'good marnin', and red-faced white people who lived in double-decker houses of seven rooms or more.

Meanwhile, as a weekly treat, Amy was preparing for her husband and son a cake that the locals called 'Bluedraws'. She kneaded and folded cassava, flour and sweet potato, pressing it hard with her thumbs and fingers. She cut the dough into four round portions and fried these tasty concoctions until brown. She then wrapped the four cakes in banana leaf to keep them fresh and shared them equally between Joseph and David. She was rewarded with a kiss on her cheek from her son. Joseph offered her a warm smile, sniffing the dish. "Amy, yuh is one ably cook! Yes sa! Nuhbody else ah compare."

David watched his sisters receiving money from their mother to buy lunch at school; vendors pushing carts would jostle and cuss-cuss each other for business outside the church-come-school. Sometimes fights would develop and Isaac and the teachers would have to rush out to keep the peace. The vendors sold cartoned juices, citrus fruits and a variety of snacks that included fried dumplings. "Hortense," Amy warned, "if yuh lose ya money once more me gwarn lick yuh wid chicken bone 'pon ya head top when yuh reach home. Yuh hear me chile?"

Hortense nodded then ran up to her brother. "David yuh nuh walk me to school? Me cyan't remember de last time yuh walk me to school. Yuh don't love me nuh more?"

David laughed and picked up his sister, twirling her about. He put her back down and for a short second, Hortense was dizzy. "Hortense. Yuh ah big woman now. Yuh don't need me to walk yuh ah school nuh more."

"Me know me ah big woman but since yuh stop walk me ah school, Jenny jus' run gone an' lef' me wid de older girl dem. Me cyan't keep up wid her long foot an' mon stride!"

"Dat don't mean Jenny nah love yuh, Hortense," said David. "She jus' getting ah liccle older an' she waan her own space."

"Yuh t'ink Papa waan him own space from me, David? Him don't love me. Him don't really talk to me. Mebbe me should call yuh papa, David."

Taking Hortense's words in jest, David chuckled, knowing that when the time came to leave home, he would sorely miss Hortense's unique charm. He glanced at Jenny kissing her father goodbye and whispered to himself, "Dat girl chile don't need nuhbody else apart from her papa. De mon who tek ah fancy to Jenny when she come ah age will affe mek Papa feel very sweet!"

Hortense and Jenny set off and by the time Jenny had reached the bottom of the hill, Hortense was already fifty yards behind her. "See if me don't tell David yuh run gone an' lef' me!" yelled Hortense. "When me sight yuh ah school see me don't lick yuh wid me shoe corner!" Jenny ignored her sister. Now far ahead of her, she slowed down to a walk, enjoying her own company.

At the side of the house was the wooden cart off which the Rodney family used to sell their groceries. It had been patched up many times and had been through many sets of wheels; the village wheel-smith, Mr Price, was Jenny's godfather. David smirked as he recalled his father promising the family a donkey two years ago. David sucked on the cool, amber-coloured flesh of a mango before setting off to work, pulling his brown cloth cap over his head. He tossed the mango skin to the dogs and paid no attention as they fought over the scraps. As he pushed the cart of limes, grapes, oranges, water-melons, jackfruits and coconuts downhill, he considered visiting Levi after his shift. Levi was a man he had befriended in the hills one afternoon four months ago. David smiled to himself as he recalled his first encounter.

After a morning's toil on his father's plot of land, instead of taking a high-noon nap beneath a palm tree as was usually his custom, David decided to set off for a stroll. He headed uphill to where the stubborn mists had settled; they couldn't be shifted by the scorching sun and no breeze was forthcoming. David's father always looked up in fascination at this lofty terrain but was too superstitious to investigate this area himself. David discovered that jackfruit, sweet-sop, hard chocolate, breadfruit and ackee grew freely here. He climbed a tall jackfruit tree that afforded him a generous view of the lush green valley below, the ugly dwellings of Claremont blemishing the beauty of the scenery. The horizon shimmered in the heat and David wondered what lay beyond the swerving hills. Using a machete that hung from his belt, David cut down a jackfruit that was more than a foot long and seven inches wide. As he descended back to earth he saw a most remarkable sight.

A man, or at least something that resembled a man, was standing at the base of the tree. His hair, if it could be described as such, seemed to David like thick clumps of blackened wool that stood erect on the head as if this being had just set eyes on Old Screwface himself. His beard was of a similar appearance, like that of an old fat-bellied goat, only blacker. He was holding the jackfruit David had just cut down and through the matted hair, David could see his white teeth; he wasn't sure if this something was snarling or smiling. He was bare-backed and bare-footed, dressed only in a soiled pair of blue cotton pants that were roughly cut just above the knee.

Cautiously, David leapt down, not sure whether to scarper or offer his surrender. He thought of his mother's words. "Nuh stray or wander inna foreign land becah yuh don't know wha' might happen to yuh. Old Screwface has many crooked an' crafty ways to tempt de foolish an' unwary."

He studied this wild man with wary eyes, not even thinking about disputing the ownership of the jackfruit in his hands.

"May Akhenaten bless ya morning, sa," the man greeted warmly. He presented the jackfruit to David who was wondering who Akhenaten was. "Me don't sight too many mon up here ah hillside so me glad to see yuh. Me name Levi an' me live up jus' ah liccle furder more." He pointed to the direction of his abode. "De jackfruit taste nice up here, mon. Why yuh don't follow me steps up to me strikin' plot an' join me to nyam ah liccle somet'ing? Me about to fry some grunt fish an' me gwarn roast some breadfruit. Me 'ave sweet-sop too. Wha' yuh ah say, mon? Long time me don't 'ave company an' it seem dat fate carry yuh here 'pon de breeze."

His curiosity overcoming his fear, David followed Levi to his hillside encampment, transfixed by the tangled hair upon Levi's head.

Trading went well for David in Claremont market. Many of his customers were his mother's friends, whom David had known all his life, or passing wayfarers who paused in Claremont on their way to the north coast; they proved to be the best customers. Others, who lived in the shanty huts down the hill, only offered fierce glares and aggressive mutterings, but David simply smiled at them, adding to their vexation. The people David knew warned of the perils of sin and how he should be looking for a wife now and setting up home, releasing the burden on his 'ably mudder'. Mrs Grogan even introduced her daughter, Debbie, to David, asking her to do a twirl to showcase her 'healthy body' while she waxed lyrical about Debbie's cooking prowess and her 'strong breedable pickney hips'. Debbie, only fourteen years old, didn't utter a word. She simply stared at the ground in mortification.

Mrs Clarke, who owned the nearby shop, informed David of the happenings and occurrences in St Anne's Bay. She inspected David's wares as she spoke, picking up those she liked. "Some of de fishermon affe move from de beaches becah de people wid money ah buy up land to buil' hotel. It *nah* right, David. Dem get nuh money to relocate an' dem cyan't tek dem shanty hut wid dem. Me talk to one fishermon an' him tell me him 'ave not'ing so him gwarn try him luck inna Kingston. Same t'ing happen to some farm worker who ah toil 'pon land t'irty mile from here. Some ah de soil red, so de farm owner decide to sell him land to ah bauxite company. De farm worker lost dem job. Most ah dem packing up an' heading fe Kingston. It nah right! It seem dat everybody 'pon de move an' even up here inna Claremont where some people forget about we, tribulation will finally reach we. It nah right!"

When Amy's friends paused from counselling David they shrilled the praises of Jenny and Hortense and how mightily Hortense sang in church last Sunday. Miss Jo scolded David for his absence from church but haggled over the price of limes even though David offered her half-price discount. Hardly any of his patrons referred to Joseph, just the occasional, "ya fader alright? Amy finally teach him how to smile?" Then they changed the subject, mostly complaining about the lack of a bus service. "Browns Town 'ave ah bus service! An' Alderton! Why dem leave we out? Don't dey know dat people who live ah Claremont need to travel too?" Others moaned about their sons going off to the 'sin city', Kingston, and relinquishing their responsibilities to their families. "Yuh ah good bwai, David, trodding in ya grandparents footsteps!" Mrs Coleman said inspecting the peppers. "*Don't* forward ah Kingston like me eldest son where Old Screwface 'ave him backyard."

David had learned not to disagree with his elders and humoured them with generous smiles and nods. He kept to himself the knowledge that there wasn't enough good top-soil in the Claremont valley to serve all of its sons.

For those fortunate enough to own patches of land, business had been brisk for the Claremont farmers throughout the war years. Farmers with bigger lands beyond the Claremont valley were obliged to aid the war effort and they found that as soon as they plucked their crops from the soil, someone was waiting to take them to Montego Bay or Kingston for shipping to the motherland: England. German U-boats harassed and targeted these ships, sinking many. Subsequently, there were food shortages in most of the major towns throughout Jamaica for it was deemed that shipping foodstuffs to the motherland carried much more importance than feeding the Jamaican population.

To make matters worse, many Jamaican farm workers were dispatched to the citrus groves of Florida, to aid the war effort there. However, none of this affected Joseph and his family who inhabited such a remote area that the authorities seemed not to acknowledge their existence or had simply forgotten. A few well-journeyed, tough-footed men knew of the fertile lands around Claremont and they paid a fair price for the groceries on offer, taking it back with them to places like St Anne's Bay or the blossoming tourist town of Ocho Rios on the north coast where rich white people paid inflated prices for their wares. Claremontonians, despite their unease in the presence of Joseph Rodney, had no reason to dislike his produce and had to admit it was of a very high quality.

David reached home by 1.15 p.m. He was glad to finish his shift for the constant cuss-cussing of the other 'higglers' had grated his nerves. He found that his mother had hooked a string line from the kitchen to the house where the family's clothes were hung out to dry. Kwarhterleg was lipping a mango by his tree; he hadn't many teeth to bite with. "Afternoon sa," he greeted David. "Ya mama, Hortense an' Jenny are ketching dem sleep. Yuh waan to rest up an' smoke ah liccle tobacco wid me?"

"Kwarhterleg! Yuh know me don't smoke. Where Papa? Still ah work der ah him field?"

"Yes, sa. David, yuh waan go up der an' tell him to rest himself. Harvest time ah come soon, by de end of de week. Tell him to save him energy fe dat. Serious t'ing."

"Nuh trouble ya head, Kwarhterleg. Sometime Papa ketch him sleep under de palm grove up der."

Parking the cart, David then looked in on his mother and sisters. They were blissfully asleep. He placed two coins each by his sisters' heads, knowing that once they wake up they will both skip into the village and buy themselves 'box juices'. He emerged again into the hot sun and approached Kwarhterleg, fingering in his pockets for more loose change. He tossed the old man two coins. "Hold dis, Kwarhterleg. Go buy yaself ah Red Stripe or somet'ing. Me gone to look fe Papa to give him ah money we earn today."

"T'ank yuh, sa," Kwarhterleg accepted gratefully. Before he had time to consider what drink he would buy for himself, David was gone.

Twenty-five minutes later, David found his father snoozing under a palm tree. "Papa. Papa. Wake up now mon. Me 'ave ah money to give yuh."

Joseph focussed his eyes and saw his son counting out notes and coins on the ground. "Me sell nuff today, Papa. See de money der."

Sitting up, Joseph found his straw hat and placed it on his head. "David, me trus' yuh y'know. Yuh don't affe walk up to me plot to give me ah money. Dat is madness. It coulda wait 'til me reach home."

"Nuh trouble ya head, Papa. Me jus' teking ah liccle walk ah hillside up der ah yonder."

"Alright. But don't boder get yaself lost. Yuh know ya mama don't like it when yuh plant ya foot ah strange land."

David picked up a mango from a collection huddled around Joseph's feet. He took a generous bite, not bothering to peel the skin. "Papa, cyan me ask yuh somet'ing?"

"Yes, sa. Wha' is it?"

"Papa, de Bible say dat de Most High made mon in him own image, y'understand?"

"Yes, dat true. Ya mama swear by de good book an' she teach yuh good."

"Den if dat true de Most High mus' be ah black mon. Nuh true?"

Fidgeting with discomfort, Joseph didn't know how to answer David's question. "Well. Me nah sure. But when me once sight Preacher Mon old picture Bible, Jesus Christ always white an' him 'ave blue eyes. So me feel so dey mus' show dat fe ah reason."

Not convinced by his father's reasoning, David shrugged. "Papa, yuh t'ink black people inna de old days had mighty Kings and Queens like de royal family dat live inna mighty palace inna England? Yuh t'ink dat coulda be true, Papa?"

Searching his son's face, Joseph wondered why David was quizzing him like this. "Nuh, mon. We come from slaves. Well, most of we. Me cyan't see how slaves coulda ever be King or Queen. David, yuh been talking to mad Miss Blair inna market square? People say she one ah dem mad Garveyite. Marcus Garvey born inna dis land but people say Garvey talk pure fart. Even Preacher Mon say dat inna him service so Amy tell me. Yuh know Miss Blair? De old woman wid ah long mout' an' knock knock knees? Her husband pass away many moons ago an' she live out near ah Crab Foot Gully where de grass grow long an' holler wid de wind."

David nodded. "She is one strange woman," Joseph added. "Me feel so she coulda be inna de obeah t'ing."

"Nuh mon," David laughed. "Papa, Miss Blair 'ave her strange ways but she ah nice old woman. Me don't know how yuh cyan accuse de poor woman of witchcraft. Papa, yuh been lissening too much to de higgler dem."

"She talk madness, mon. Me don't trus' her. Me tell Amy dat if she come to buy anyt'ing den she mus' give it to her free of charge."

Laughing again, David enjoyed his father's superstition. He then composed himself with another bite of the mango. "Papa, me talk to ah man de udder day who is well educated. Him know him letters an' him cyan read mighty. Him tell me dat back inna de days of de never never der was dis African king who call himself Prester John. Dis Prester John was well mighty an' him ah rule nuff people all over Africa an' ah place call Asia Minor. An' him wise like Solomon. Papa, yuh ever hear ah dis mighty mon?"

Joseph shook his head. "David, who ah tell yuh dis mad talk an' loose words? Don't lissen to dem, David, for dey waan lead yuh astray. Who ah tell yuh dis foolishness?"

"Jus' ah mon who was passing t'rough," David lied. "Me cyan't even remember wha' dis mon look like. But me generation is learning new t'ings dat ya generation cyan't tolerate." Rising to his feet, David attempted to mask his unease and disappointment. "Papa, me ketch yuh later. Mebbe we cyan share ah liccle rum when de moon ah shine bright an' de cricket dem start quarrel."

"Yes, sa." Joseph looked at the money his son made for the day. "Yuh deserve it mon. Mebbe yuh coulda tek ah liccle money to court girl wid," Joseph smiled.

Joseph's last words were wasted for David was already climbing the field.

Hunched over his fire, Levi was lunching on a lobster, crab and callaloo when David emerged from the thicket. "Afternoon, brudder," he greeted. "Yuh come jus' in time. Yuh waan ah portion ah dis lobster?"

Levi's makeshift home was situated on a sharp slope between two cedar trees surrounded by Blue Mahoes. Scraps of dead wood and warped sheet-metal formed the walls and a ragged length of corrugated aluminium acted as a roof. There was just enough room inside for a straw and almond leaf bed. A nearby smaller hut contained Levi's cooking items, a selection of books, food, various sundries that a man required to live in the bush and brushwood.

"Nuh mon," David finally replied, sensing his refusal might injure Levi's feelings. "Me jus' nyam ah liccle somet'ing. Where yuh get your lobster an' fish from anyway?"

"From dis good brudder who live 'pon de coast. Him come check me from time to time. Me give him chocolate, ackee, sweet-sop an' him give me any fish dat him ketch."

Feeling the cooling hillside breeze that threaded through the trees, David sat down. "Why yuh don't sell ya t'ings ah Claremont market?"

Levi rocked back in laughter, his mane of hair dancing in the air. "David! Look 'pon me! Yuh t'ink Claremont people would give me dem custom? Nuh, brudder! Dey would never understand dat me ah Nazarene. Dem would t'ink me was born from de seed of Old Screwface himself."

"So yuh don't 'ave nuh family?" David wanted to know.

"Yes, brudder. Of course. Me come from ah good well intentioned family. Dem sen' me ah school in Montego Bay an' der is where me learn to read."

Looking inside the stores hut at the selection of books, David remarked, "yes, yuh mus' read well mighty".

Smiling, Levi said, "but education is ah dangerous t'ing. An' de education me receive outta school prove even more deadly."

"How is dat?" asked David, already feeling a dull ache in his backside.

Mimicking the countenance of a professor, Levi explained, "from when me learn dat Moses was ah black mon who did ah waan re-introduce de praising of de One God, jus' like Akhenaten an' him first wife, Nefertiti."

Recalling that Levi had once related the tale of Akhenaten and Nefertiti, David couldn't remember the finer points of the story. He nodded and faked understanding and allowed Levi to continue.

"Yuh see, David, Moses quarrel wid Pharoah was never about de freeing of de slaves. It was about Moses' intention of establishing de praising of de One God – de God of Akhenaten."

Still not grasping what Levi was saying, David nodded his head again. Levi resumed, enjoying his attentive pupil.

"Moses had many followers an' Pharoah affe treat Moses intentions serious becah him know dat Moses was ah High Priest an' ah Alchemist. He did know de high arts an' sorcery dat dem both learn inna Heliopolis. It was ah High Priestess dat collect Moses from him bankra from de Nile."

Raising his hand excitedly David exclaimed, "me know dat! Me know dat. Mama teach me dat from de Bible."

Not liking David's interruption, Levi resumed, his face now stern. "Moses grow up inna Pharoah house an' learn everyt'ing dat Pharoah learn. But some call dese facts blasphemous. Even educated black mon will chant yuh down if yuh speak it. Even me own fader chant me down. Me decide to live ah simple life living by me own means. Me family disown me from dat. Me don't waan to work fe nuh white mon an' mek him belly get fatter, y'understand? An' read *der* interpretation of de Bible. ME REFUSE TO CARRY DE

CURSE OF *HAM*!"

David recognised Ham as the black son of Noah, but didn't want to be led into a discussion. He had eavesdropped on his Grandfather Neville, who spoke of such things in secret gatherings and the subject had caused much controversy. David wanted to address his own circumstances. "Me waan to lead me own life, Levi," he stated, his tone full of determination. "Me waan to travel far an' see t'ings. Living ah Claremont cyan't satisfy me. But me don't know how to tell me Papa. An' telling Mama would be worse dan dat. It would truly trouble her sweet head. But me 'ave made up me mind. Me will forward to Linstead first, mebbe find work ah bauxite place, an' tek t'ings from der."

Pondering his answer, Levi was fully aware of his growing influence on his new friend. "David, yuh live ah good clean life, an' ya family too. Yuh live de way de Most High intended ah brudder to live. Me respect dat to de fullest! Yuh know, David, me been living up here ah hillside fe more dan ten years now. Sometime me don't see people fe untold moons. Sometime me come down to look 'pon ya fader working him plot of land. An' me see dat ya fader treat de soil like it ah gift from de Most High. Yuh tell me ya fader never go church all de time, but him still live Godly. Yuh see, David, we all come from de dirt an' we shall return to it. So it's Godly dat ah mon like ya fader live off de land. An' yuh tell me yuh don't waan to follow ya fader mighty footsteps?"

"Nuh mon!" David's voice grew louder. "Yuh talk jus' like me Papa! Levi yuh lucky becah yuh 'ave seen different places an' different land. Yuh tek one step inna de big wide world an' decide to live like ah bushmon. But inna me seventeen years me see not'ing apart from de pure hills dat surround Claremont. Me waan to tek ah mighty step inna de big world an' mek ah decision meself!"

Standing up, Levi went inside his storage hut and emerged with a water coconut in his right hand; the top was scalped to allow drinking. "Tek dis, brudder. Nice an' cool. It will quench ya temper. Dey say dat Maroon blood is mighty quick to boil."

David accepted and drank, tipping the juice into his mouth.

"David," Levi continued. "Me don't waan to tell yuh to do dis an' dat. Yuh affe follow yuh own destiny an' mek up ya own mind about de problem. But me affe tell yuh dat de big wide world out der is dangerous."

Suddenly, David laughed, causing the juice inside his mouth to dribble over his chin. He wiped his mouth with his left palm and said, "living inna Claremont cyan be dangerous too. De udder day poor Miss Mavis get run down by mad cow."

Fixing David with a stare that spoke of disapproval, Levi continued. "Inna de big universe out der yuh affe rely 'pon de corrupt minds of mon. For example, mon an' mon will mek decisions about ya life dat yuh 'ave nuh control over. Ah job or ah opportunity fe example."

Raising his arms and showing his palms, David remarked, "but isn't dat how de world go?"

"Not if yuh waan it to. If yuh follow ya fader's footsteps den de only t'ing dat 'ave control over yuh is de soil dat grow ya food an' de sun dat ah shine bright, giving everyt'ing life. Soil cyan't lie an' soil cyan't never be corrupt. An' living off de land yuh mek yaself ya own king. Me don't 'ave nuh shoes an' nuh shirt but nuh mon ah control me or corrupt me. Now, nah even de King of England cyan't say dat wid ah honest heart."

David bowed his head and stilled his tongue. He did not want to disagree with Levi. But the desire to bless his eyes on new pastures was something that could not be denied. He decided to inform his parents of his intentions after harvest; his father would need him that day. Following that he would leave and his father or Levi could throw no words at him to make him change his mind. Once gone he'd grow his hair like Levi, be a Nazarene like John the Baptist. Last week he had so enjoyed Levi's tale of Jesus' disciples warning him off approaching 'the dirty, matted hair wild one'. As he read when Levi showed him a passage of the Holy Piby, no scissors would trouble his hair again. He'd walk into far lands and see the world but keep that black pride that Levi instilled in him. Yes, he told himself. Me time ah come.

Chapter Three

Two days until harvest Sunday. Amy, shaded by the zinc roof, was nursing a mug of rum and goat's milk while sitting on an unsteady stool outside her kitchen, the choking smoke of burning tyre strips from her neighbours' yard irritating her; Miss Panchita, who lived twenty yards away, was breastfeeding her three-month-old baby and wanted to ward off any mosquitoes and other insects; she had yet to register the birth of the infant in the parish capital, St Anne's Bay, but hardly any Claremontonians ever did – the long trek put them off, notwithstanding the illiteracy that most Claremont folk shared and the subsequent fear of embarrassment.

Sighing wearily, Amy was much relieved that her morning chores were over; sweeping out the yard, scrubbing the cooking vessels in the stream, collecting wood for the fire and mending a pair of Joseph's old cotton pants. She looked forward to this time of the day. Her daughters, meanwhile, were learning how to sing *Rule Britannia* at school and reading about the acts of bravery of Nelson at Trafalgar and the red-coats who thwarted the Zulus at Rourkes Drift. Amy thought it was a mockery for Jamaican children to sing the lines, '...*Britannia rules the waves, Britons never never never shall be slaves...*' She felt her daughters should be taught to rely upon what the soil offered them rather than educated about the deeds of men who lived in a world her kin couldn't comprehend. "*Rule Britannia* cyan't mek de yam grow sweet," she whispered to herself. "An' *Rule Britannia* cyan't mek me daughters be dutiful wives."

Snoozing with his back against the mango tree, Kwarhterleg had earlier volunteered to decapitate, pluck and cook a chicken but Amy could not afford the luxury of stretching her own rest. She had yet to call on her sister, Jackie; buy a prize goat from Mr DaCosta, the local goat-herd; and then call in on her parents: she received a message while she was in the market that her father wanted a 'strong word' with her. She guessed it had to be about Joseph. It was always about Joseph.

Amy drained the last drops of her cocktail and for a short second, considered refilling her mug. "Aaaahhh! Joseph. Where ever did yuh come from?"

She reminisced to when she was eight years old. One quiet evening in the fall of 1915 Amy's father heard a gentle tap-tapping upon his creaky front door. He opened the door cautiously and there was the fifteen-year-old Joseph, standing up straight with the setting red sun slowly dropping behind his right shoulder. The contours on the right of his head seemed to be glowing. He was nervously holding his tatty straw hat with both hands. His feet, apart from the blisters and sores, were the same colour as dried mud. His ragged, soiled vest and pants clung to him like an outer skin. His hair was dry, browned by over-exposure to the sun. Amy laughed when she recalled her father's description of her future husband. "Lord me God, wha' ah crazy sight me see dis balmy evening! Come look here family, der's ah long bwai outside me door who black 'til him cyan't black nuh more! Moonless night mus' be him fader. Him ah dressed up inna him smelly reg-jegs dat even de curious dog dem would nah sniff." Despite his words, Neville, Amy's father, knew he was looking at a Maroon and he suffered a sharp pang of guilt; he knew that one of his forefathers had been conscripted by the English to spy on the Maroons.

Bowing slightly, tipping his head, Joseph greeted, "goodnight, sa. Me really sorry to trouble yuh dis fine evenin'. Me walk far an' wide an' me liccle weary. Me jus' waan to ask yuh, sa, if yuh 'ave any work to give me. Me 'ave ah strong back an' de midday sun don't trouble me strengt' inna me shoulder dem. Me cyan plant, sow an' reap anyt'ing, sa. Me know how to pluck fowl, skin goat an' chop off ah pig head top. Me well ably, sa. Me don't waan nuh money, sa. Jus' somewhere to lie me head when de moon ah shine bright an' me don't care if me 'ave to ketch ah sleep wid de dog an' fowl dem. Me used to dem smell an' it don't trouble me."

Inspecting the poor wretch, Neville gave him a strong 'eye pass'. Neville's family, Amy included, peeped from behind his back.

"Where yuh come from, bwai? Where ya mama an' papa? When de las' time water ah rinse ya armpit? Where ya shoes? 'Pon ya travels yuh never t'ought to moisten ya skin wid coconut? Ya elbows are grey like vexed rain cloud!"

Joseph's eyes dropped to gaze at his scored feet and he emitted a sense of shame. "Me don't 'ave nuh family, sa," he lied. "Tell me where de river der an' me would forward to it, sa."

"But yuh mus' 'ave ah strikin' plot somewhere," Neville insisted. "How cyan yuh born widout family. If yuh is ah trickster or ah t'ief me gwarn lick yuh wid me piece ah breezeblock 'til de crab louse come outta ya dutty hair!"

Refusing to answer, Joseph continued to stare at the floor. Amy, wrestling free from her mother's grip, stepped to her father's side. She took a lingering look at the visitor. He was different from anybody she had ever seen. So dark! So tall! And the eyes! So pitiful. But he looked strong, his shoulders barely fitting within the door frame. Amy compared Joseph's jawbone to a Blue Mahoe branch that she sometimes sat upon.

Seeing himself as a Godly man, Neville considered that if he offered this young beggar some food and a place to rest his bones for the night, it would only enhance his reputation, especially if he told the aged preacher man about it. Yes, old Mister Forbes would have to talk about this good deed in church, he thought. Maybe if I play my cards right, the good people of Claremont might want *me* to sermon them when the preacher man passes away and rises to heaven to get his reward. Wise Mister Forbes bones are getting creaky and his crazy son, Isaac, spends him time trying to sway pretty girls to follow him to the bush. "Alright, bwai," Neville decided. "Yuh know ya name?"

"Joseph," muttered the stranger, his words aimed to the floor.

"Come in, Joseph. We will give yuh ah liccle supper an' somewhere to rest ya mosh-up foot...Amy, start up de fire an' boil some water an' mek de bwai ah coffee. Don't use too much coffee bean!"

In the morning, Neville emerged out of his house and found that the yard had been swept by Joseph already, wood had been collected for the fire and Joseph had located the stream to wash himself in; his hair now looked a rich black texture. Neville, mightily impressed, asked his wife, Melody, to cook Joseph's breakfast and while smoking his pipe, pondered Joseph's future. He decided to give him a trial run working on one of his two fields. Joseph dropped to his knees in thanks, his eyes filling with tears.

Neville discovered that Joseph was indeed industrious and knew the ways of tilling and farming. At length he discussed Joseph's fate with Melody, and one night he said to her, "sometimes de Most High give yuh ah chance to right ah wrong. Mebbe if we do right by Joseph de Most High might finally bless we wid ah son. So long He has cursed my seed."

After two weeks he decided to take Joseph on permanently; his wages were food, an outside straw bed and a drop of rum to wash down the ackee and salt-fish supper that Neville insisted upon on Friday nights. Amy, Neville's youngest daughter, was delegated to bring Joseph's meals to him in the evenings; Jackie was asked initially but she cried off, saying, "de black stranger wid de wolf eyes look like de angel of deat'". Joseph never said much upon receiving his dinner, just a "t'ank yuh liccle Amy, ya mos' kind". He never did reveal where he hailed from, despite Amy's mother prompting him and, in the end, she shook her head, muttering under her breath, "hear me Lord, praise is ya very name. It easier to t'read ah long belly goat t'rough de eye of ah needle dan getting dat long bwai Joseph to talk about him past."

"Amy! Amy. Wha' happen to yuh? Yuh ketch inna daydream?"

Shaking the memories out of her head, Amy composed herself and looked at her sister, Jackie, who was carrying a long piece of rope in her hands. Jackie was shorter and fatter than her younger sister. Her eyes looked fearsome and her bunched calf muscles well defined from treading miles every day since she could remember. She could also cuss-cuss with the best higglers in the market. She was wearing a simple light blue frock and a white, cotton headscarf that exposed her silvering temples.

"Yuh forget we 'ave to go up to Misser DaCosta to buy fat goat fe harvest night."

"Nuh, Jackie. Me don't forget. Cool down ya fire an' stop fret! Me jus' ketching ah liccle res'."

The two sisters set off and took the winding goat's path uphill, through water coconut and pimento groves that led to Mr DaCosta's land. Sometimes the terrain was treacherous and unstable underfoot but years of experience allowed them to find a true path, Amy using long, elegant strides while Jackie employed short, hurrying steps.

"Amy," Jackie called, her tone over dramatic. "Preacher Mon come up to talk to Papa las' night. When me sight him tie up him donkey, Preacher Mon face look like fiesty higgler slap him face wid wet callaloo. Him was vex me ah tell yuh."

"Isaac fussing?" Amy queried casually. "Wha' is wrong wid him now? Him wife der 'pon her mont'ly cycle? Him donkey run away becah de poor beast cyan't tek de beatings nuh more? Somebody t'ief de collection money?"

"Why yuh always call Preacher Mon Isaac?" Jackie wondered. "Nuh Isaac him name?"

"Yes, but yuh should nah call him dat. Anyway, Amy, yuh well an' truly know why Preacher Mon vex. Joseph, ya brute of ah husband, ah lick him down. Me hear Preacher Mon ah tell Papa. Papa ah lissen an' shake him head 'til him head get loose. An' den Papa frown an' frown 'til him face look like ah crushed old plum. Dis gwarn cause one mighty bangarang an' de Most High himself might set curse 'pon ya family! De poor people dat live down ah hillside hate Joseph already an' wid dis latest news some ah dem might seek der revenge. Mebbe dey will chop off more of Joseph's finger dem!"

"Jackie, yuh jus' like dem leather-neck higgler ah market who cyan't sell dem wares an' dem spend dem time ah create rumour an' susu while dem head top ah turn grey! Foolishness de higgler dem ah talk, but ya susu, Jackie, is ah whole heap worse. Cyan't Isaac defend himself? Why him ah ride to Papa yard an' start bawl like girl chile who cyan't find her pretty dress to go ah church 'pon Sunday. Isaac mus' fight him own battle an' don't drag anybody else inna it. Isaac like fowl who run away from craven dahg."

"Yuh know, Amy," Jackie cooled her tone, not wanting a cuss cuss with her sister for her tongue was no match for hers. "Yuh t'ink Preacher Mon still ah feel it becah yuh turn him down all dem years ago?"

Amy's eyes betrayed a sour memory and she switched her gaze in front of her. Jackie seized on the opportunity and went on. "Him even ask Papa fe permission to marry yuh before yuh know anyt'ing about it. Amy, yuh coulda live inna Preacher Mon big house. Me remember dem time an' Preacher Mon ah bawl 'til him tears run dry. Dat's why him coulda never like Joseph."

The last remark cut Amy like a sharp stone on a bare-footed child. But she wasn't about to display any hurt to her sister. "Well, if Isaac still ah feel it den me don't care," Amy shrugged, remembering the marriage proposal that came when she was only fourteen years of age. "All of yuh did ah laugh after me when me tek up wid Joseph an' Isaac did ah t'ink dat me turning fool like fowl who lose dem head. So him only feel it becah Joseph prove him an' everybody else wrong."

"But, Amy, yuh affe admit dat sometime Joseph gwarn strange. Him use to frighten me when me ah girl chile wid him wolf eyes. An' yuh still don't know where him ah come from after all dese years."

Coming to a halt, Amy caught Jackie with a fierce glare. "Dat is *me* business, nuhbody else's!"

The two sisters looked at each other for more than thirty seconds, both of them realising that they jousted verbally with each other as long as they could remember. Jackie wanted to win this particular battle. She went on. "As him turn up dat night outta nuhwhere any day him coulda tek up him long foot an' disappear to nuhwhere. Some people inna town still call him *Black Duppy.*"

Resuming her trek, momentarily leaving Jackie yards behind, Amy countered, "yuh woulda like dat, Jackie. Den yuh coulda spread rumour dat Old Screwface ah kidnap me husband an' tek him down to work inna hell fire."

Jackie opened her mouth but no words came out. Old Screwface had never appeared in a cussing joust with her sister before. Amy continued, her tone full of injustice, her voice raised. "Jackie, me don't understan' yuh becah me never blaspheme or slur ya husband. Although me always sight him down ah liquor bar near ah market wid ah drink of somet'ing inna him hand, talking pure fart to anybody who care to pass while him crops ah wonder where him der."

Now grinning, Amy went for the kill, knowing if it would come to a fight she always had the upper hand. "Lazy him ah lazy. Licky licky ya husband licky. Me surprise de rum him ah drink nuh turn him into sugar cane. Him coulda grow ah new sugar plantation if him piss 'pon de land. Even people who suffer from cold fever an' ah live inna St Anne's Bay cyan smell de rum offa ya husband breat'! Jackie, ya de one who should start *fret!*"

Priming her tongue for a reply, Jackie thought better of it. The remainder of their trek was completed in silence.

Mr Welton DaCosta, a lean light-skinned man, owned a sizeable plot of sloping land where he raised cows, bulls and goats; one of his forefathers was the child of a Spanish captain and a slave. To quell the gossip and the scandal, when this child reached his teenage years, he was dispatched with his mother to the backwoods of Claremont, accompanied by a bull and four cows. The days leading up to harvest time was Mr DaCosta's busiest and most lucrative of the year; there was no red soil staining his land so he hadn't been tempted by the corporate cash wads like other farm owners had been. He saw Amy and Jackie approaching him. They had a fearsome reputation in the village. Welton knew there was no way he could tempt the harsh-mouthed sisters into purchasing one of his cheap 'maaga' goats.

The sisters left Mr DaCosta's land with a fat-bellied goat walking dejectedly behind them, as if it knew of its fate. A noose was around its neck and Jackie gave it no time to nibble on grass or inspect anything with its nose. The siblings reached their father's home forty-five minutes later; Jackie paused at the post office where she collected her father's mail. Neville lived just outside the village near a tambarine grove, a mile away from Amy and her family. The location offered a grand view of the descending hills that led to the sea. On fine mornings, Neville and his family could detect a shimmering horizon tinted with shades of light blue.

His house, containing three rooms, was impressive by Claremont standards. It was made of white-washed breeze blocks. Jackie lived with her immediate family in a small hut on the same plot separated by a chicken coop and a pig pen. They all shared the nearby kitchen. Four of her other sisters were now married and had moved away from Claremont. Many shrieking children, whom Neville was babysitting, formed a circle playing some game in the yard that involved a rotten mango and a water coconut. *"Brown girl in de ring, tra la la la la!"*

Wearing an unbuttoned cotton shirt of check pattern that revealed tight grey curls upon his chest and brown three-quarter length pants, Neville was sitting on a wooden chair outside his front door. A beige, cloth cap hid his silver hair and the thick smoke from his pipe was soon lost in the hot afternoon sun. His forehead was lined and appeared wise and his countenance commanded respect. Some Claremontonians said he had 'spirit' in his eyes and called him 'Custos' – a title of deep respect. But he seemed weary of his exertions keeping the 'kidren' in line. He pulled his pipe from his mouth and gave Amy a stern eye pass. Jackie tied the goat to the trunk of an avocado tree and passed two letters to her father. The goat set about exploring the ground, checking if there was anything worth nibbling.

"How is David, me one gran'son?" Neville asked calmly. "Why him don't come look fe me 'pon ah Friday evenin' like him used to do? Me still have so many t'ings to teach him."

"Him busy y'know," Amy answered, wondering when her father would discuss Joseph.

"An' Hortense an' Jenny?" Neville queried. "Dem alright?"

"Yes, Papa. Dem fine."

Neville's eyes narrowed, like a slowly-closing oyster shell. "Amy! Wha is wrong wid ya swift-tempered mon?" he barked. "Preacher Mon ah come down to me yard an' ah complain 'til me ears start burn! Him tell me dat he was giving ah mighty welcome to Joseph becah him ah t'ink dat Joseph come to settle dem differences. But

Joseph ah strike him down before Preacher Mon coulda offer him ah liccle rum an' ah handshek. Don't Joseph realise dat him affe be careful? Some people who live down ah hillside still waan to string him up. People aroun' here don't forget not'ing!"

"Nuh believe everyt'ing Isaac ah tell yuh, Papa," Amy defended her husband. "Isaac always love to mek long-tail alligator outta small bullfrog."

"Amy, Preacher Mon show me him bruise. Him face swell up like water melon wid too much water. Yuh affe talk to Joseph, Amy. Him cyan't jus' lick down everybody who ah vex him. Me like Joseph but him *too* crazy."

"So, Papa. Yuh never see de swelling 'pon poor Jenny's face. She never stop bawling 'til she reach home an' me give her ah box juice. Isaac don't 'ave any right to strike down pickney dat him seed nah produce."

Giving himself a further toke from his pipe, Neville had long ago realised that Amy would always stand up for her husband, no matter if he was in the wrong. He would never reveal it to anyone but when Isaac stormed into his house, complaining about his son-in-law, he felt a certain satisfaction, wishing he had struck a blow on Isaac's jaw many seasons ago when he decided that Isaac didn't deserve the prominence and respect his role as preacher afforded him. He would also never admit that he still felt like a failure for only producing daughters. But now he secretly admired Amy's 'talk-back' ways and she was now his favourite. She had ah 'mon tongue'.

"Alright, Amy," Neville dropped his angry tone. "Not'ing cyan change now but when me sight Joseph me will say some strong words. Me will deal wid de goat inna while an' chop off him head. Ah fine goat dat. It well an' truly should feed many mout'. Me woulda leave de work for Jackie husband, but only de Most High or Old Screwface know wha' crazy time him reach home from liquor bar ah night time."

Kissing her teeth, Jackie made a mocking sucking sound, stormed off and barked at her children, ordering them to halt their game and start their chores. Amy, stifling a snide grin, remarked, "me always say Reuben too licky, licky."

"An' ya Joseph ah wear him skin too t'in," retorted Neville, pointing at her with his pipe. "One day ya husband will find himself inna mighty trouble wid him quick-fire temper. Him like crazy bull inna blood-grass field. So before yuh laugh after ya sister, t'ink about dat."

"Joseph don't trouble anyone who nuh trouble him," Amy replied.

"Yes, dat true. But der is somet'ing inna Joseph dat ah eat him up from de inside. Sometime me sight dis inna him dark eye. Somet'ing dat is deep inna him soul. De African spirits 'ave told me dis inna me dreams. So me know fe certain. Yuh know dis fe true, Amy. Me been asking yuh fe long time now, but yuh affe find out about him past. Becah dat is de key to Joseph. If yuh waan to know de secret of ah mon yuh affe study him childhood. Me tell yuh dis before, Amy. Fe years an' years me mind been concentrating on dis very t'ing an' it ah drive me crazy wid frustration."

"Papa, yuh love to repeat yourself. Every day me see yuh ya say de same t'ing. Everyt'ing will be alright. Nuh fret, Papa. Me give up long time to try an' dig de deep soil ah Joseph mind. It mek nuh sense to trouble him about it nuh more."

"Amy, me hope yuh is right," Neville replied, intimidating his daughter with unblinking eyes. "But me warn yuh! De same tribulation dat Joseph run away from will look fe him an' knock 'pon him door."

Sensing her father was right, Amy didn't want to admit it openly. Discomfited by her father's hard gaze, she walked off to find Jackie.

"Amy," Neville called. "*Don't* speak ah me dreams to *anyone*! Yuh know wha' people ah like in dese parts but der are udder powers dan de Most High inna dis world. Powers dat uneducated people cyan't understan'."

"Yes, Papa. Nuh fret yaself."

An hour later, Amy and Jackie had stripped the headless goat free of its coat and suspended it from a tree, prepared for seasoning; the head was buried by Neville in a field a mile away. Lifting his face to the heavens he offered a quick prayer of thanks. Meanwhile, the children looked on the goat's carcass and licked their lips.

Kwarhterleg, who had plucked, gutted and chopped up a chicken, was tasting his cooking in the pot when Amy arrived home, the steam carrying a seasoned, mint and pepper aroma that made everybody hungry. The old man was stirring the pot with one hand and with the other, used his crutch to fend off the dogs who were yapping at his one heel. Jenny was sitting down in the kitchen quietly reading the Bible and Hortense was trying to catch a ride on David's back but David, not at his most playful, kept shooing his younger sister away. Drawing on his pipe in another corner of the kitchen, Joseph sat deep in contemplation. Hortense spotted her mother's return. "Mama! Mama! Cyan me stay up fe harvest night? De rest of de girl dem ah school are staying up, Mama. An' dey will tease me if me don't reach, Mama. An' yuh know dem kidren tek any chance to cuss me an' Jenny. Please, Mama. Papa tell me to ask yuh."

"Yuh behave yaself inna school dis week, Hortense?"

"Yes, Mama. Miss Mary even stroke me head top when me finish me spelling an' write essay about de English empire. Dis week we learn about Queen Elizabet' de first an' how she mosh up, cramp an' paralyse de Spanish Armada. Mama, Miss Mary show me England 'pon ah map an' me did ah wonder how ah land so small coulda 'ave king an' queen dat rule half de world. An' Miss Mary smile wide like ah piece ah long, golden corn when me sing de English national anthem – me know all de words. Liccle after dat she give me ah sugar water fe me pretty work an' singing. De udder girl dem ketch red eye. Jealous dem ah jealous. An' Mama, two of de bwai dem did ah cuss cuss Papa's name. If dem carry on see me don't tell Gran'papa an' he will set curse 'pon dem dirty behind!"

"Yes, dat true, Mama," added Jenny, her fury obvious in her expression. "Sometime it mek me mad an' me waan to do dem ah evil somet'ing. Like giving dem poison cassava to nyam. Beast dem bwai ah beast, Mama an' may dem burn inna hell-fire!"

"Jenny, mek sure dem t'oughts get outta ya head," rebuked Amy. "An' yuh too, Hortense."

Jenny turned to Hortense. "Ya tek all day to write de strikin' essay," she revealed. "An' when Miss Mary turn her back yuh rush come to me an' copy wha' me write."

"*Lie* she ah tell, Mama! Me pretty work was all by meself!"

"Alright, Hortense an' Jenny. Me don't waan nuh contention tonight! Me sick an' tired of it. Jenny, yuh should be helping ya younger sister anyway. Hortense, yuh cyan stay up 'pon harvest night, but yuh affe help out wid chores tomorrow."

"Nuh problem, Mama," grinned Hortense, cutting her eyes at her sister. "Anyt'ing yuh ask."

Amy turned to Jenny who returned to reading her Bible. She felt no need to ask her if she was good at school. Praise de Lord, Amy thought. De Virgin Mary herself coulda never behave better when she ah girl chile.

"Mama," Jenny called softly, her voice much more fragile than her sister's. "Cyan me wear me pretty pink frock fe harvest night, Mama? De same frock me wear to Auntie Virlinger wedding. Nuh worry, Mama. Me would never dutty it. An' even if me did dutty it me would carry it over to river meself an' scrub it 'til it cyan't clean nuh more."

A smile curled around Amy's mouth. "Yes, Jenny. But yuh too affe help out tomorrow an' rise up inna de marnin wid de rooster call."

"Nuh worry yaself, Mama. Me will rise fe true even before sweet Papa ah pull on him mighty boot an' drink him first marnin rum when he t'ink nuhbody ah look."

Joseph had to yank his pipe from out of his mouth in order to laugh.

Observing her father chuckling at Jenny's remark, Hortense darted off to sit in the tyre hanging from the mango tree. She called on David to push her and thought of ways she could make David laugh.

"Kwarhterleg, yuh well ably inna de kitchen," Amy said gratefully. "It smell nice." She went over to the pot and tasted the boiled chicken; the dogs suddenly shied away as if greatly alarmed. "Yes, sa. Kwarhterleg, yuh waan me put on de rice?"

"Nuh, Miss Amy. Go an' res' yourself. Me 'ave t'ings inna serious order."

Amy went off into the house to fetch herself a drink of goat's milk and rum. She returned with a stool and set it beside Joseph. "Yuh look tired, Joseph," Amy greeted. "Or is der somet'ing else 'pon ya mind?"

"Nuh, Amy. Not'ing 'pon me mind. Jus' restin' me bones."

Amy decided to tackle her husband later, when Jenny, Hortense and Kwarhterleg were asleep. She steeled herself for another attempt to get to the root of Joseph's mysterious past. In quiet moments she could detect a pain in Joseph's eyes. It was this that had instilled a certain fascination all those years ago. That mystery, those repressed memories, what was going on in the back of his mind. When they became intimate during their courting days, Amy would question Joseph about his past. But he would just shrug, saying. "It don't matter, Amy. De past is der inna de past. It's de future dat me look forward to."

Three hours later, Joseph was sprinkling rum upon the threshold of his dwelling. Amy watched him intensely. Unseen by both of them, David, who was in the yard, stood very still and looked out to the dark contours of the hills that lay to the south.

"Joseph," called Amy, using her most diplomatic tone. "Don't yuh ever get lonesome? Y'know, being 'pon ya own in dis cruel world. Widout nuh brudder, sister, mama or papa? Me family live all around dese parts an' sometime dem get 'pon me nerves. But me woulda surely feel it if dem nah der. Y'understand? It mus' be ah mighty burden... Yuh don't wonder sometime where ya family der? Gran'papa always used to tell me dat de twig is mightier an' wizer when him know where de root of de tree lay."

Taking his time in answering, Joseph could not turn around and face his wife. He took a swig from the rum bottle, thinking that yes, Amy deserved an explanation, but after thirty years, he had still not come to terms with the horror of it. He couldn't even understand himself why he had walked out on *that* day. But he had had to get away. If Amy knew the truth he would surely lose her respect. Ah good mon woulda never leave him distressed family,

Joseph said to himself. But he had. Guilt had been a constant companion ever since. Guilt was with him when he rose in the morning and guilt spoke to him in the moments before he fell asleep. "Me alright, Amy," Joseph finally replied. Nuh worry yaself. Ya family me tek fe me own so me don't need anybody else. Yuh is me root now."

Allowing the matter to drop, Amy decided that she would keep on chipping away in the hope that Joseph would one day lower his guard. "David, where yuh der?" Amy called. "Me an' ya papa gone to we bed now. Nuh stay outside an' let de duppy dem play wid yuh."

"Nuh trouble ya head, Mama. Ghost or duppy never trouble me. Me jus' ketching de night breeze an' ah lissen to de cricket dat ah talk. Me soon gone to me bed, Mama."

Fifteen minutes later, Joseph stretched out on his bed alongside his wife. As soon as Joseph's eyes closed he found himself back in 1908. He was feeding the chickens when he heard his mother's excited call.

Chapter Four

Harvest Sunday morning. An arch of the sun had just crept over the eastern hills, showering light on the green Claremont valley and glittering the stream that hurried through the bush-banked ravines of the uplands. The flowing water rushed down and filled the clay and limestone gulleys, nourishing the vegetation of the lowlands. There wasn't a cloud in sight and only a single Doctor bird gliding through the heavens, showcasing her full span of wings and her long, multi-coloured forked tail, surveyed the Eden-like land beneath her.

The cooling breeze and rains that had moved away from the Caribbean sea during the night and swept through the higher places of Claremont and the surrounding districts, were now, in the uncompromising face of the rising sun, losing their potency. The damp leaves in the tree tops were now calm but Levi's lofty domain remained cloaked in a stubborn mist, only the uppermost leaves of the Blue Mahoes visible to a bird's eye. Mosquitoes, liking the dewy conditions, multiplied around shaded, still waters and muddy gulleys. On the ground, roosters challenged one another and the dogs tried to match them with their barks.

But they had no need to sound their early morning alarm calls for the people of Claremont had already risen and had their 'marnin fresh'. Indeed, the dogs in the village looked at each other, wondering when they would be thrown their next bones and why their owners had set off en masse, leaving them behind. Another morning in the 'land of springs'.

Along a squelchy mud path with steep grassy banks that curved and wriggled almost every step of the way, a long stream of Claremontonians were trekking downhill to Isaac's church, intermittently shaded by palm leaves. Everyone was dressed in their Sunday best. All who were able carried a basket or what the locals called a 'bankra' of harvest offerings that contained the fruits and vegetables of the Claremont valley; the firm-backed men, including David, were burdened with bigger baskets that they called 'cutacoos', the woven shoulder straps made of hemp.

Donkeys, blinking away the flies buzzing around their eyes, made up the rear, carrying crocus sacks full of crops on their hind legs, their masters poised with sticks in case of disobedience. Other donkeys transported the elderly and infirm. At the head of the train was Neville, who was leading the people behind him in passionate song. He was striding out flamboyantly, dodging the puddles and denying his sixty-four years, his steps timed to an ancient drumbeat.

"Hear me Lord!" Neville sang, almost bursting his voice-box.
"HEAR ME LORD," the followers echoed.
"We gwarn give to de poor."
"WE GWARN GIVE TO DE POOR."
"De fruits of our harvest."
"DE FRUITS OF OUR HARVEST."
"An' hunger shall be nuh more."
"AN' HUNGER SHALL BE NUH MORE."
"We reap wha' we sow."
"WE REAP WHA' WE SOW."
"Inna de field an' we soul."
"INNA DE FIELD AN' WE SOUL."
"An' we hope de Lord bless our land."
"AN' WE HOPE DE LORD BLESS OUR LAND."
"So we cyan come again an' bless ya mighty hand."
"SO WE CYAN COME AGAIN AN' BLESS YA MIGHTY HAND."

Walking with his family ten yards behind Neville, Joseph didn't sing with the same faithful heart as his fellow villagers. Instead, he shifted his eyes to glance upon the people who he thought still despised him. Hortense had none of her father's concerns, her shrill voice rising above the congregation's roar. Earlier, the excitement had proved too much for her and she wetted her drawers. Amy had given her a spanking but even this could not quell her joy for the day ahead. She was the first of her family to join the march and she made sure everyone heard her voice. Although Jenny's spirit was uplifted by the lively call and response led by her grandfather, she still stole dismissive glances at the children who lived in the shanty huts and wore the same frocks they always did, only today their dresses were a little brighter. Sporting her favourite pink outfit, she said to herself, "yuh say me Papa ah devil mon but at least he cyan buy me ah pretty frock! Wha' cyan ya penny-ketching papa buy yuh?"

Dressed in his most striking dark suit and white shirt, Isaac stood outside his wooden, stone-built church and clapped his hands when he sighted his flock sluicing down the hillside. He bade a special welcome to those who attended church rarely, shaking the men's hands firmly and kissing the women upon their cheeks. "Praise de Lord!" he bellowed.

The donkey owners secured their beasts to tree trunks and when everybody was ready, Isaac ushered them inside the sparse building. The food bearers laid their baskets around the plain altar which displayed a single flaming candle in a brass holder and an old leather-jacketed Bible on its bare wooden top; local legend had it, eagerly fanned by Isaac and his father, that the Latin Bible was the only personal belonging a Spanish priest had left behind before fleeing from the English in the 17th century. Isaac didn't know of anyone who could read it.

There were three clay basins on each side of the church, sitting below open windows. Neville, his face solemn, filled them with blessed water, bowing his head as he did so. Then from a crocus bag he was carrying, he dropped mint leaves, grapefruit halves, quarters of watermelons, sliced limes and dandelion flowers into the bowls. When he had finished, Neville turned around and saw that the church was packed and everyone had taken to their simple wooden chairs; women, some of whom had kicked off their muddied footwear to stretch their toes, were cooling themselves with home-made fans, the men using their white handkerchiefs to dab their brows. The church was beginning to emit a fresh, fruity aroma that the flock were grateful to inhale.

Looking at his most proud, Isaac stepped up to the pulpit and gazed out upon his congregation, offering them a broad smile. Mouthing a silent prayer while closing his eyes, he blessed the food. He then raised his arms and prompted, "let us sing!"

"We plant de fields an' scatter de good seed 'pon de land..."

The service lasted two hours and even the birds nesting in far-off tree tops heard the joyous singing and praise of the Most High. Before worshippers were given license to leave, Jacob, Isaac's son, walked respectfully among the flock, accepting donations.

Standing straight-backed outside his church, Isaac shook hands with everyone as they filed out, offering thanks and the good grace of the Lord to protect them. He even seized a surprised Joseph's mighty right paw with both hands, grasping it hard and seeming somewhat reluctant to let go. Joseph, feeling mightily abashed, for he only ever attended church for harvest time, weddings or christenings, smiled weakly, looking around for Amy to save him; she was purchasing box juices from a vociferous vendor who had suddenly appeared outside the church door with his creaking cart. Hortense and Jenny soon quenched their thirst with guava juice while someone nourished the donkeys with crushed sugar cane and water.

Following half an hour of susu sessions, where the good people of Claremont huddled in groups of sixes and sevens, commenting on their neighbours' dress sense, cleanliness of shoes and other matters they felt important to remark upon, they set off home, carrying their empty bankras and cuttacoos, the donkeys plodding along the path more happily and freely.

When they all reached home, the women set about cooking the goats, spicing and jerking the pork, making fish fritters and fried dumplings, roasting varieties of fish, preparing the vegetables and fruits for the forthcoming feasts. The men drifted off to the liquor bars that dominated the market square where they bought the finest Appleton rum and the local homemade port while lipping bottles of Red Stripe beer; Mr Patterson was winning healthy trade selling yards of tobacco, hemp and a herb that he called 'lambs bread'. The young children, legs weary from the long walk and tired from rising early, took an afternoon siesta.

Expressing exhaustion, Kwarhterleg was slumped on a stool outside an open bar next door to the post office, nursing a beer. He was flanked by Joseph and David. Across the road, a young woman was admiring the new crimpolene frock she had just purchased from Mrs Walters, the local seamstress. She held it tight against her chest before carefully placing it inside her bag. She then set off quickly for home, excited as Cinderella preparing for the ball. The bartender, who had been eyeing the woman, was arranging bottles on a warped shelf; the constant *clink clink* irritated Kwarhterleg. "Mon, wha' ah serious tribulation!" Kwarhterleg gasped. "Believe me, dat might be de las' time me hobble down to Preacher Mon church."

"Well me did ah tell yuh dat yuh should nuh boder," rebuked Joseph. "An' David tell yuh de same t'ing. Kwarhterleg, yuh stubborn like mad mule. Even Preacher mon affe understan' dat yuh cyan't mek long walk nuh more. Him don't know dat Alligator ah nyam off ya leg?"

"Of course Preacher Mon know! Me never miss ah church harvest fe fifty years," Kwarhterleg stated proudly. "As long as me ably me will tek de walk."

"Den why yuh ah complain! David, try an' talk some sense into dis mad fool. Nex' year me don't waan carry dis old peg-leg down ah hillside 'pon me shoulder."

David, looking at the southern hills preoccupied about something, hadn't been paying attention to what was being said.

"David!" Joseph called, his tone deeper, louder. "Wha' de matter wid yuh bwai? Yuh lost ya tongue today? Yuh been too quiet fe me liking an' yuh look like yuh inna daydream."

The bottle of drink in David's right hand was still full. He brought the lip of the bottle to his mouth but only to moisten his cracked lips, using his tongue to spread the beer. Joseph looked at him curiously. David gently placed his drink down on the wooden table, pulled out a handkerchief to wipe his forehead and took a sharp intake of breath. "Papa," he said, his tone full of regret, "me affe leave dis place."

Swapping fretful glances with Kwarhterleg, Joseph's shock denied him any quick response.

"Papa, it's ah long time me been feeling dis need. Yuh provide me wid ah good life. Me never hungry. Me go ah school, learn many t'ings. But me waan see de outside world, Papa. It's like ah calling. Me affe go an' rely 'pon me own hand. Stan' up 'pon me own foot."

Joseph fished in his trouser pockets for his pipe. He soon stuffed it with tobacco and gave a leaf to Kwarhterleg for his own use. He took three tokes before saying another word. "David, yuh cyan't jus' leave widout nuh plan. When yuh plan to leave anyway?"

Kwarhterleg wondered why Joseph was taking this startling news so casually.

"Papa, me leaving tomorrow," David announced. "Me plan to go to Kingston but before me go der me heading to ah place near Linstead. Dem 'ave ah aluminium bauxite place der so me could get ah liccle work. Dat's wha' me waan do, Papa. Travel, see place, work an' den move on. Many ah me friends who me go school wid 'ave lef' Claremont. Me feel it inna me bones, Papa. Ah calling."

"David, yuh don't hear of de serious labour strikes inna dem cane field?" Kwarhterleg warned. "Some time ago dem affe sen' in police an' roughneck to mek people go back ah work. Nuff mon dead."

Kwarhterleg had heard from travellers passing through Claremont that the indentured Indian workers received more pay than blacks in the cane fields, and this was despite the British only making a fraction of the financial rewards from sugar as they used to, and from a number of over four hundred sugar plantations there were now less than forty. Aluminium bauxite was found in Jamaican soil and country folk, desperate for work, arrived at bauxite sites in great numbers. Opportunist employers paid minimal wages for those who were willing to work and this caused much contention and fights. A man called 'Busta' set up the first recognised union in Jamaica but the employers had the police on their side, breaking up strikes with uncalled for violence. Many strikers were bludgeoned to death.

Kwarhterleg looked at Joseph expecting him to state further

warnings. Joseph's mind flashed back to when he left home and he had to admit to himself that at least David announced his intentions like a man. No stealing away in the middle of the night as he had done. He wondered whether this calling was a family trait. Naptali, his eldest brother, had left home before Joseph was even born. Joseph himself had a great urgency to leave home, build a new life. "Every mon affe do wha' him affe do an' go where him destiny ah tek him," Joseph said finally.

"But yuh cyan't jus' go jus' like dat," Kwarhterleg argued. "Who gwarn to tek over de plot ah land when ya fader bones get too creaky? Yuh t'ink about dat, David?"

"Who ah say me gone fe ever?" David asked calmly. "When me see wha' me waan see an' when me experience de mighty t'ings dat de world affe offer me, den me come back. Me will come back an' work me fader land 'til me laid to rest. Me swear to de Most High dat dis true. But right about now, me affe go, becah de itch inna me foot cyan't be scratched."

Seeing that his son hadn't troubled his beer, Joseph asked the barman for two more. He passed one on to Kwarhterleg. Joseph's bottle was three-quarters empty before he spoke again. "David, me give yuh me blessing fe ya journey in dis life but me waan yuh to promise me somet'ing."

"Anyt'ing yuh ask, Papa," David replied, now drinking his beer.

"Nuh tell ya mama 'til marnin come. Let her and ya two sister enjoy harvest day widout ya mad news. Tell dem inna de marnin."

"Nuh trouble ya head, Papa. Me will tell everyone inna de marnin. Me don't waan to spoil dem day."

Kwarhterleg shook his head, sure that Amy would not be so understanding of David's calling. And Hortense? It could prove a sore loss for her.

As the last golden rays of the sun dipped below the western ranges, the fires of harvest night lit every beacon, crook, hillside and dwelling throughout Claremont and districts beyond. Songs of praise filled the valley and Mr Welton DaCosta had even hired a mento band to entertain his family and guests on his plot of land, the musicians equipped with improvised banjo instruments and quick-witted lyrics of country life and rural proverbs.

"Nuh tease alligator before yuh cross de river
Put ah cross before ya door an' Old Screwface cyan't mek yuh
shiver
Heed dese warnings or yuh end up like Old Mama Jeebah
She live inna de wood ah work 'pon spells she deliver
Mama Jeebah is older dan de spine of Jamaica
She even know de old pirate Captain Morgan an' where him hide
him treasure
She was once ah good girl very kind to her mudder
Her fader run away from him brutal slave master
She used to speak wid de same tongue as her African ancestor
Some say her family come from de Gold Coast or it coulda be
Ghana
But one day she skip church go ah forest full of wonder
Nuh even de Maroons or Anancy would step der inna adventure
Old Screwface set up him net an' he did ah ketch her
She lost her soul an' not'ing she cyan remember
Now her back is bent like de mountain der ah far off yonder
Her face so full of wart, more dan de feaders 'pon ah rooster
Her nose is so long dat John-crow coulda perch, res' him wing an'
loiter
Now she work 'pon spell to ketch anoder good sister
So children beware yuh nuh stray an' sight Old Mama Jeebah
Fe yuh could be roastin' 'pon ah spit ah Old Screwface fire."

Armed with two bottles of rum, Joseph and his family had ambled over to Neville's bonfire, which was fifty yards away from the patriarch's home. They had left Kwarhterleg who had complained of a sore throat but Joseph knew he had drank too much warm beer in the afternoon.

They were accompanied by their neighbours, Miss Panchita, who was carrying her baby in a brace upon her back, and her husband Matthew. About forty-five adults were ringed around the fire, plus twenty or so excited children running here and there, most of them related to Neville in some way.

Food was already being served and Hortense and Jenny enjoyed their starter of 'star-apples'. This was followed by curried goat and rice, roasted snapper fish, ardough bread, all the fried dumplings they could eat, and, if there was any space left in their stomachs, a whole range of ripe fruits. Rum was flowing, loosening tongues and prompting courting couples to steal kisses. Elders paraphrased Biblical tales, adding their own spin and extravagances for dramatic effect and those who won the silent attention of the audience were rewarded with coins and rum toasts.

Neville, the heart and soul of the party, looked upon his oldest grandson, David, with watering, red eyes. He burped rather loudly. "David! Nuh girl ah Claremont ah tickle ya fancy? Yuh is ah mighty fine looking young mon! Come tell me, David. Which fine Christian girl yuh 'ave ya eye 'pon? An' don't worry about wha' ya mama an' papa might say becah ya gran'papa is asking yuh. Now tell me, David. Why me don't see yuh wid ah nice girl to embrace dis fine night? Me don't waan to dead before yuh present me wid many great-gran'sons. Ah mon's wealth is calculated by de amount of great-granson's him seed produce. Don't yuh know dat?"

Hoots of laughter filled the red-night air. David, mortally embarrassed, struggled to find words. Joseph flashed him a fretful eye pass. Teenage girls feasted their eyes upon David's handsome looks with relish, praying they wouldn't be childless by the time they reached eighteen and branded a mule by their peers; most of their male counterparts had left Claremont so they felt David was a prize catch.

"Gran'papa!" David finally answered. "Yuh know me well busy working me fader plot. Me don't 'ave any time to court nice girl. An' anyway, de girl who live ah Claremont dem so nice an' sweet dat ah mon like me don't really know how to choose! Mon, wha' ah cruel tribulation fe ah humble young mon!"

David's courteous response was met with cheers, wolf whistles, claps and a clinking of rum bottles. Joseph smiled, realising his only son would handle himself well in the wide world. Yes, sa, he thought. David well ably wid him tongue.

Three hours later Amy roused her husband from his dozing. Joseph forced open his heavy lids and in his blurred vision, saw that many of Neville's male friends were laying horizontal amid the empty rum bottles upon the ground. The fire was flickering into death here and there. Women were taking their children home. Courting couples had already stolen away to the woods. Those who lived in warped wooden huts and had no land to till, carried away the left-over food. They didn't have to ask for it.

"Joseph! Joseph!" Amy called. "Wake up now mon! Yuh been too licky licky tonight wid de fire-water! Come mon. Yuh affe carry Hortense home."

Joseph focused his eyes. He saw Hortense blissfully asleep on the ground, her head resting upon a hacked-off branch. Joseph went to pick her up, slinging her over his shoulder. "Where Jenny der ya?" he asked.

Amy looked around. Under the leaves of Neville's avocado tree, using the light of the kerosene lamp that was hooked on the side of the house, Amy's mother, Melody, seated on a stool and using her hands to express herself, was telling African Anancy stories to seven captivated children. Jenny was one of them. "...An' Anancy was well crafty an' from ah spider, turn himself into ah long-belly goat but he was still speaking to de terrified white mon inna African tongue. De white mon ah scream an' scream 'til he could nah scream nuh more..."

"Jenny!" called Amy. "Come chile. Time fe bed."

"But Mama. Gran'mama nuh finish her story yet!"

"Jenny! Nuh let me come up der an' tan ya backside."

"Tan me backside? Papa never tan me backside yet so why yuh waan tan me backside, Mama?"

"*Don't* get wise! *Come*, chile!"

Melody kissed Jenny upon the forehead, stroked her head and said, "gwarn to ya mudder, chile. Me don't waan *Man-tongue* fussing to me inna de marnin becah me waan to preserve me ears. Nex' time yuh come me will tell yuh de res' ah de story. Goodnight an' don't let nuh bugaboo bite."

Skipping to join her family, Jenny was perturbed to see her father carrying Hortense. She was soon filled with a burning jealousy, sulking behind her parents, dragging her heels. She looked up occasionally, firing a fierce stare into Hortense's back.

"Wha' happen to David?" Joseph asked, looking about him. "Him gone to anoder fire? Mebbe to Misser DaCosta plot?"

"Yes," Amy replied, not revealing that David had simply vanished into the night and hadn't informed anyone where he was going. "Me sure him gone ah Misser DaCosta. Him mus' waan to hear de mento band dat ah play up der."

For a few seconds, Joseph doubted this news but he soon reassured himself that David wouldn't shy away from bidding farewell to his mother and sisters.

"Ooowww, me leg," Jenny howled in pain. "Me leg, Papa. Blood ah run!"

Joseph and Amy turned around and saw Jenny lying on the ground, blood trickling from a gash in her knee. "Me cyan't walk, Papa," Jenny cried. "Me walkin' an' me stumble."

Joseph roused Hortense. "Come, Hortense, wake up. Yuh affe walk. Ya sister hurt her leg."

Joseph helped her down to the ground. Hortense, focusing her sleepy eyes, shot a look of utter scorn at her sister before reluctantly holding her mother's proffered hand. Joseph picked up Jenny, kissed her on the cheek and set off once more. Jenny sobbed all the way home.

"Papa, Jenny ah bawl crocodile tears!" shouted Hortense. "She mus' ah pain her leg by herself. *Lie* she ah lie. Don't trust her, Papa! Jenny crafty like Anancy when she ready. Yuh don't see de red glow inna her eye?"

"Now, Hortense," said Joseph. "Why woulda Jenny mek blood run from her own leg? Nex' time me promise me will carry yuh wherever yuh waan go."

"Nex' time me will nuh boder ask yuh, Papa," Hortense sulked. "*David* will carry me. Me don't even 'ave to ask him. *He's* me true papa!"

"*Hortense*!" Amy rebuked. "Quiet ya mout' or me will stick ah jackfruit inna it!"

Joseph felt an ignition of guilt burning his conscience and decided to ignore Hortense's accusing eyes.

When they finally reached home, Hortense kicked Jenny's supposedly injured leg. "Now yuh cyan bawl fe real," snapped Hortense, rage in her expression. "Yuh dutty *liar*. Jezebel yuh ah Jezebel! See me don't fling rockstone after yuh if yuh do dat trick again."

David had not attended Mr DaCosta's party like many of the other young men and women who resided in Claremont, but had hiked up the hillside to pay Levi a final visit. Numerous bonfires that stretched to the horizon and lighting up the night sky offered a spectacular view behind him.

Roasting a fish on a sharpened stick over his own small fire, Levi smiled warmly when he saw his visitor. "Me suppose yuh don't waan anyt'ing to nyam?"

"Nuh, sa," laughed David, palming his stomach in a circular motion. "Me jus' come to say goodbye. Me gone tomorrow."

"Oh! Yuh tell ya family?"

"Me tell Papa today. It kinda surprise me becah him never fuss about it. But me affe tell me mama inna de marnin. Me hope she don't trouble her head too much."

Satisfied that the fish was cooked, Levi placed it in a charred frying pan where his fork was waiting. He went over to David and embraced him. "May de Most High protect yuh. An' if t'ings don't turn out good, don't be too proud to come back."

"Yes, sa. Levi, yuh look mighty strange to me eye but yuh been ah good friend. Me will never forget yuh an' de t'ings yuh teach me will stay inna me mind."

The friends regarded each other for a long, silent second, then parted. Sadness crept into Levi's eyes for David's company had proved a comfort to him and his departure would be a sore loss. No man is an island, he thought. Although David first looked upon Levi with fearful eyes, he had never passed judgement on him, accepting him for what he was. A rare thing in Levi's world. Godly him ah Godly, Levi muttered to himself.

"David," Levi spoke softly. "De t'ings dat me teach yuh, y'know, about de Bible an' de true words from de Holy Piby. Don't speak of it to anyone. Keep it to yaself. Jus' let it guide yuh. Come back when yuh 'ave time to visit an' keep honouring ya mudder an' fader. Yuh know, ya fader come from ah mighty people, de Maroons dem. Never forget dat. In fact, all of we come from de seed of kings."

"Levi, who ah teach yuh dese t'ings yuh ah teach me?"

Levi paused, not sure if he had the authority to answer. "Me will tell yuh, David, becah me trus' yuh. From Montego Bay me go to ah school inna Kingston fe furder study. Me fader ah sen' me der to learn about de ways of de church an' study de Bible. As any good fader inna Jamaica, him did waan me to follow him footsteps. Anyway, one fine night inna Kingston, when me 'ave not'ing fe do, me met ah mon who call himself Kwabena. He was ah well educated mon, know nuff t'ings dat happen in de world. T'ings dat European mon conceal from we. As me get to know him, Kwabena ah tell me dat him belong to dis order call de Coptic Masons. Dem very secretive but very wise. Der duty is to pass on vital information dat 'ave passed t'rough nuff generation all de way back from Africa. But dem affe be very careful to who dey pass on dese facts." Levi looked upon David as if he was warning him.

Understanding the legacy that Levi had given him, David smiled warmly, then set off down the hillside, emerging out of the mist like a living silhouette. He hummed one of the songs his maternal grandmother always sang, happy that at last he'd become a man, plotting his own path in life and allowing himself to praise the One God of Moses, Akhenaten and Nefertiti.

Early next morning, Amy rose with the rooster's first call. As was her custom, she looked down at her sleeping children, silently giving thanks to the Most High for a new day. David wasn't in his usual place at the bottom of the sisters' bed. Amy dashed outside, thinking her son had come to harm up at Mr DaCosta's last night – his parties usually concluded with fisticuffs. She found David in the back yard, splashing his face with water that he had already collected from the stream.

"David! Why yuh rise so early? Yuh brute, David! Yuh stop me heartbeat when me rise an' me don't see yuh sleeping."

David walked over to the kitchen where he had already placed a pot of water over the fire; Kwarhterleg, coched in the corner, had one eye open, feigning sleep. "Mama, sit down an' let me mek yuh ah coffee."

Perching herself on the unsteady stool, Amy eyed her son with suspicion. David presented an uneasy Amy with a mug of coffee. "Mama, me leaving Claremont today," he said gently.

"Wha' yuh mean ya leaving Claremont today? Ya fader ah sen' yuh 'pon errand ah Brown's Town to pick up seed or somet'ing?" Amy ignored her coffee.

"Nuh, Mama. Me leaving to find me own way, see de world."

"But, David! Yuh cyan't leave. Yuh 'ave ah good life here an' yuh me only son! Only ah few weeks ago ya papa an' me was talking how we gwarn give yuh ah liccle money to buil' house nah far from we. Now yuh tell me yuh intend to leave? Ungrateful yuh ah, ungrateful! Wha' gwarn happen to we plot ah land if ya fader tek sick or old age ah ben' him back? Who give yuh life after mighty pain? Who bathe yuh? Who feed yuh? An' now yuh 'ave de damn cheek to say yuh leaving. Jus' like dat? If it wasn't so damn early me woulda lick yuh wid me washing line. Ungrateful yuh ah, ungrateful!"

"Mama, me nuh gone fe ever. An' when me 'ave liccle time, look fe me come harvest or Easter time. Becah me would come to visit wid de Most High's blessing. Me jus' get dis calling dat is mighty hard to ignore."

"Wha' yuh mean yuh get ah calling? Me get ah calling every marnin dat me shoulda stay inna me bed an' res' meself an' mebbe de duppy will cook fe me an' fetch water an' do all de t'ings me affe do every day. But me cyan't stay inna me bed! Me affe do wha' me affe do! Don't de good book ah say dat ah chile mus' honour him fader an' mudder? Me cyan't believe dis! Gwarn an' leave us if yuh 'ave to, but me *don't* give yuh me blessing!"

Closing his eyes, David hung his head in exasperation. Amy tutted, turned away from her son and stormed back into the house, cussing loudly. Five minutes later, Hortense came running out and made straight for David, throwing her arms around his waist. Tears were running down her cheeks. "David! David! Why yuh leaving? Yuh don't love me nuh more!"

Dropping to his haunches, David palmed away Hortense's tears and gazed at her as only a loving elder brother can. "Nuh cry, Hortense. Nuh cry. Of course me love yuh. Love yuh t'rough to me bone, all of yuh. But me ah mon now. Me affe look fe ah wife, stan' up 'pon me own foot, rely 'pon nobody but meself. In time yuh will understan' but *never* t'ink dat me nuh love yuh."

"But, David. Who? Who me gwarn to play wid now yuh gone an' lef' me? Yuh nuh love me, David. YUH NUH LOVE ME!" She began to throw punches and kicks at her brother, tears flowing from her eyes. David grabbed Hortense's arms and pulled her close to his chest.

"Hortense, me t'ought dat yuh was ah big woman? If yuh ah big woman den why me sight eye-water 'pon ya cheeks? Nuh cry Hortense becah when yuh get me outta ya mind den yuh will sight me once more. Nuh cry. In time when yuh grow yuh will find someone to love an' yuh will look 'pon dis day an' laugh."

"Nuh me won't," protested Hortense. "Me will never do dat!"

"Den carry me inna ya heart," said David. "Remember our good days. Even Jesus had to leave his family to start him work. Never doubt dat me t'inking of yuh every day. Never doubt me return an' most important of all, learn to love an' live wid yaself. For dat is our gift to Massa God."

"David," Hortense sobbed. "Me nuh understan' ah word yuh ah say."

"Yuh will. Me promise yuh dat. Yuh will."

Hugging his youngest sister, David could see Jenny slowly approaching him. In striking contrast to Hortense, Jenny was very subdued, cold almost. David released his hold on Hortense, stood up and opened his arms to receive Jenny. Jenny walked up to her brother, stood on tip-toes and kissed him formally on the cheek. "David, me will miss yuh. May de Most High bless ya every step."

David stroked Jenny's head. "Look after ya sister fe me, becah she need yuh more dan yuh ever know. Remember dat. Keep studying de Bible, for de stories inna it hold de key to de soul. An',

Jenny, let ya heart sing so everybody cyan hear. Don't restrain it! For dat will cause yuh damage like over-cooked yam inna cooking pot wid de lid pressed down tight."

"Nuh worry yaself, David. Me nuh understan' wha yuh say but me love de Bible an' me will learn from dat. Hortense ah sometime full ah stingin' nettle but me will cool her fire. See if me don't."

Deeply upset and still sobbing, Hortense ran towards Jenny and pushed her over before bolting away. Jenny didn't bother to chase her. She just got up to her feet, brushed herself down and said, "ya see, David, she full ah nettle."

David watched Jenny pour herself water into a bowl for her morning fresh. Dat chile is old before her time, he thought.

Jenny then sought out Hortense, who was crying uncontrollably under the leaves of a Blue Mahoe tree about half a mile away from the family home. "Hortense, David affe go," Jenny said softly.

"Go away, Jenny! Becah yuh don't care fe David, he *don't* love yuh. Go'long! Run to Papa."

"Nuh him *don't*! David love everybody."

"Lie yuh ah tell," snarled Hortense. "Dis is how it go. Papa only love yuh an' David only love *me*. Yuh only come here to brag an' boast becah David gone. If Papa ever gone me gwarn to laugh after yuh an' tease yuh every strikin' day!"

"*Don't* say dat, Hortense! Yuh will bring bad luck 'pon we."

Laying face down upon the grass, Hortense began to sob. Jenny knelt down and stroked her hair. "Come, Hortense, nuh cry. Me still love yuh. Sometime yuh get 'pon me nerves wid ya fire-nettle ways an' yuh snore ya mighty snore inna me head-back. But me still love yuh. Me promise me will play wid yuh liccle more now David gone."

"Yuh promise?" Hortense wanted confirmation, still burying her face into the turf.

"May de Most High strike me down if me bruk me promise. Stop cry, Hortense. Me will look after yuh."

Rolling over, Hortense sat up and stretched out her arms. Jenny stepped into her embrace and the two sisters remained under the whispering leaves of the Blue Mahoe until the sun reached the western sky.

A change of clothes and fruits packed into a crocus bag that hung from his shoulder, David followed his father to the family plot. Earlier he had sought out Neville and bade a tearful farewell to him; Neville kissed David's feet and anointed his soles with rum while praying for the spirits to protect him. Then, David had looked for Hortense to say a final goodbye, but called off his search, thinking he would inflict more damage than good.

Once they had reached Joseph's plateau, Joseph, inexplicably, started to dig with a shovel in a spot a few feet away from where sweet potatoes were growing. David looked on curiously. "Papa, wha' yuh ah dig for? Yuh find old pirate treasure?"

Joseph didn't answer, his eyes fixed on the soil.

David lifted his head and looked into the sky. "Papa, me don't 'ave much time. Me waan to set off before de sun put on its crown an' start blaze."

Ignoring his son, Joseph threw his shovel down and started to forage with his hands. David walked over to him to satisfy his curiosity. He found that his father was pulling out pound notes and coins from the earth. He shook and thumbed the cash free of its soil and turned to David, laughing. "If only money coulda grow like coconut, eehh? Den we'd be rich like anyt'ing. Anyway, from de time we start sell our crops der ah market, me been putting ah liccle somet'ing by. It nah much but it will give yuh ah liccle start in dis mad world. At first me an' ya mudder were planning to give yuh ah liccle money to buil' ya own place. But me don't see nuh reason why yuh cyan't 'ave it now. Besides, David, yuh work mighty hard fe dis. Tek it, mon."

Accepting the money gratefully, David embraced his father. It amounted to a little over seven pounds. "Papa, sometimes when me look 'pon yuh its like yuh is ah mon wid nuff untold stories to tell. But me coulda never expect ah better fader. May de Most High bless yuh. Papa, jus' one t'ing me affe tell yuh. Don't be offended. But Hortense would like to feel ya mighty hand 'pon her cheek too."

Joseph nodded. "Yuh know ya two sister more dan me know dem meself. It's nah dat me don't love Hortense."

"Me know, Papa," David reassured.

"Ah mon don't pick an' choose him favourite chile. It kinda happens. It's like somebody already set it."

"Me realise dat, Papa."

Pocketing the money, David set off down the hill, leaving his father standing alone. Unseen by both of them was Levi, looking down from a tree about half a mile away. "May Moses bless him every step," he muttered to himself.

In the weeks following David's departure, Hortense only spoke when spoken to. She would arrive home from school, dutifully and silently perform her chores and sit under her adopted Blue Mahoe tree, most of the time accompanied by Jenny. From there they would simply gaze out towards the southern hills, wondering what David was up to. Sometimes Amy could hear them singing a gospel song, Hortense's pained, shrill voice betraying her bruised heart. Kwarhterleg voiced a concern about Hortense's behaviour but Amy shrugged it off, saying, "Give her time. She'll be alright. Jenny's wid her."

Jenny took it upon herself to bring her sister out of her melancholy, walking her to school, performing chores that were designated to her sister, whispering to her at night. Every evening she asked Hortense if she wanted her to braid her hair. Hortense would offer a forlorn look, replying, "but David nah here to see it!"

Relenting after the seventh week of David's departure, Hortense allowed Jenny to braid her hair into a 'corn row' style under the Blue Mahoe. When Jenny had finished, she said, "yuh look pretty, Hortense. Very pretty. When yuh grow yuh will attract nuff mon fancy. Me nah tell nuh lie. Why yuh don't come wid me to Gran'papa Neville so yuh cyan look inna de looking glass?"

A faint hint of a smile caressed Hortense's cheeks. Her first smile since David left. "Yuh sure me look pretty? Me wish me coulda show it off to David."

"Nuh worry, Hortense. David soon come 'pon ah visit. An' when him come back him cyan see yuh pretty like today. Becah from now on me will braid ya hair like dis. Come, let we look fe Gran'papa!

An' if we behave good, Gran'mama might tell we Anancy stories."

Hortense's face opened into a broad grin. They set off together, arm in arm. The sisters called in on him on their return from school every day. Neville, who shared Hortense's sadness, would place Hortense on his donkey and would lead her in country walks, teaching her old songs and slave spirituals. Jenny would occupy Melody's time, always laughing and being delighted in the crafty and secretive ways of the Anancy character of Melody's fairytales. In school drawing lessons, Hortense would sketch trees and landscapes, she always named the area beyond the horizon as 'David's place'.

Jenny covered her text pages in myriad doodles of spiders, some with human heads and some with human legs. She loathed to show any of her classmates her artistry and when the teacher displayed her work upon the classroom wall, Jenny refused to sketch again. At home, Amy noticed that her daughters' long battle for Joseph's attention had ceased. If there was a victor, Amy thought it was Jenny, who still enjoyed the intimate affection that her father offered her. But she found it strange that Hortense seemed to give up on her father's love. Sometimes she blatantly ignored Joseph's coming home from work despite his attempts on giving her his attention.

Instead, Hortense began to crave attention from elsewhere – any passer-by, new person in town or distant cousin she had yet to know. She was always first to the door when a visitor called and never too shy to enter an adult's conversation.

Chapter Five

Claremont
Late July, 1951

Standing upon his wooden verandah, Isaac, in grey pants that were held up with braces, threw chicken bones and left-over slops to his dogs. Their coats dripping with rain-water, the skinny mutts fought each other for the best scraps. Isaac, the kerosene lamp making a crude shadow of his generous bulk, ignored the intense frenzy below him and looked up to the dark, threatening heavens, wondering when the persistent drizzle that had begun in the morning would end. "Jamaica funny," he whispered to himself. "When de sun ah shine, Jamaica like God's garden, providing nuff shade ah beautiful green but when rain ah fall an' de sky dark, I cyan imagine Lucifer an' Beezlebub dancing inna de gulleys an' 'pon mountain top."

In Isaac's role as preacher man for the Claremont valley district, he had just given counsel to a man who had just seen his eighth child being born. The man wanted to know if God provided any natural contraception for he could not afford a ninth child. Isaac advised him to sleep outside when he felt a stirring within his loins. Thinking about the man's predicament, Isaac was about to go back inside when something caught his eye. Emerging from the grey murk at the bottom of the hill was a horse and cart approaching slowly around a bend; the man who held the reins gave the horse no respite with his stick. Isaac was curious. *De light soon fail so why is ah mon making fe wid him wares at dis hour,* he thought.

As the cart neared, Isaac heard the distinctive sound of a wailing baby. His curiosity piqued, he stepped off the verandah to meet the travellers, the rain pitter-patting upon his black felt stetson. Crowned by a black cloth hat, the man driving the old horse was a lantern-jawed, thick-set fellow; he was chewing tobacco in the left corner of his mouth, the few teeth he had were stained brown and his expression reflected the mood of the heavens. He presented Isaac with a threatening eye-pass before turning around and shouting at his passenger. "Dis is ah far as me ah go! Me don't waan go any furder becah me waan reach home an' me hear some strange tales about Claremont – obeah business, pagan business an' all dat. De village ah der up ah yonder, one hour walk if ya feet nuh bruise! An' may de Most High protect yuh!"

Not liking the defamation of his home village, Isaac returned the eye-pass with interest, thinking that this man probably lived in a major town for him to carry on in such a loose-tongued manner. Then, a young woman, her head wrapped in a black head-scarf, sat up in the cart, obviously weary. Tribulation was etched on her forehead and her eyes betrayed a grievous loss. She looked ahead at the rising hills before her and wept silently, closing her eyes for a few seconds.

Wiping her baby's face free of the rainwater, she climbed off the cart, collected her two crocus bags and offered thanks to the man wielding his stick. The weary horse turned around obediently and set off again. "Ya lucky me come dis far," the man said to the woman in a contemptuous tone. "Dis ride usually cos' one shilling more."

The woman's child was wrapped in a tatty blanket and for a moment she was unsure of what to do next as the cart trundled haphazardly down the uneven hill; the two wheels were buckled, unable to run true. Only dressed in a printed blue frock and a white cardigan, she finally realised that Isaac was watching her. "Please, Misser. Me looking fe de Rodney family," she said. "It's very important."

"De Rodney family?" Isaac asked. "Yes, me know dem well. Dem live inna Claremont, t'ree miles away. May I ask wha' is ya business wid dem?"

The woman paused, looked upon her baby and replied, "him need feeding. Please, Misser. Cyan me come inside fe ah liccle while an' feed me pickney? Before me set off again? Me foot well tired an' me head wet up."

Seeing the young woman's distress, Isaac helped her with her bags and led her inside. He ushered her into the tiny room where he received guests and performed his counselling duties for his parishioners. Sparely decorated, it only had three wooden chairs set around an old desk with a hand-carved fruit-bowl upon it next to a well-thumbed Bible; a collection basket, full of coins, was resting on a small table in a corner. The Bible lay open at the book of Psalms; certain passages were highlighted with coloured pencils. The young woman noticed a white-painted, wooden cross that was nailed to the wall. A portrait of what the young girl guessed was a bishop or a high ranking official of the catholic church hung from, and dominated, another wall. It was signed in black with a Latin signature.

"Jacob! Jacob!" Isaac called.

Footsteps could be heard from the back of the house. Seconds later, Jacob, now a handsome young man of nineteen with a cheerful expression, appeared in the room. Dripping wet, he was wearing nothing on his feet and his clothes, hands and face were smudged with mud. Isaac glared at him. "Wha' happen to yuh, Jacob? Yuh been bathing inna de wet soil?"

"Nuh, Papa. De gate 'pon de pig pen bruk an' one ah de hog dem escape. Me affe chase after it an' I did ah slip an' slide. Dem hog really rapid an' swift when dey waan to be. Nuh boder yaself, Papa, I never come inna de house wid me dutty shoe dem. I know Mama woulda curse me 'til nex' year after she strike me wid de Dutchpot!"

A faint hint of a smile caressed the young woman's eyes as Isaac shook his head in embarrassment. "Jacob, cyan yuh mek dis good lady ah mug ah coffee an' mek ah liccle somet'ing fe de young chile. Mebbe yuh cyan mek some cornmeal porridge. If der is any t'ing lef' inna de cooking pot, warm it up an' bring it come. Don't wake ya mama – she well tired from going ah river."

"Yes, Papa. Me soon come."

Jacob closed the door. Isaac turned his attention to the young woman, steepling his hands together. "Now, me chile. Mebbe yuh cyan tell me ya name?"

"Carmesha."

"Now, Carmesha. It very late fe travelling 'pon dis hour an' if yuh never did ah see me an' try to mek ya own way to Claremont, if God don't guide yuh, den yuh woulda surely find yaself los'. I see inna ya tears dat ya pickney is not ya only burden yuh ah carry. So why yuh don't tell me wha' is bodering yuh an' I will try to help. I is ah mon ah God an' good people come to me to unburden der worries."

"Yuh know David Rodney well?"

"Yes, of course me know David Rodney. Amy's son. Ah good bwai from ah saintly mudder. Him usually come home fe harvest an' Easter but I don't see him dis year or de las'. Him family well looking forward to see him come October."

Dropping her head, Carmesha cried new tears. She embraced her baby close to her chest. "David dead," she muttered, barely forcing the words out. "An' de pickney me ah carry ah him son. Daniel is eight mont's old."

Isaac opened his mouth but no words came out. He could only visualise Amy, shuddering at the pain she would surely feel. He stood up, turning his back on Carmesha, his eyes locked on the cross. He wished that he could be the one, not Joseph, to comfort Amy in her dark hour of loss. *Why* did she ever take up wid black-heart Joseph? Isaac wondered. Becah I'm sure dat God has cursed Moonshine and his seed. Ungodly dat mon ungodly! "How? How did dis grievous t'ing happen?" Isaac finally asked.

"Police ah Spanish Town aress' David an' batter him 'til him dead," Carmesha replied automatically, her voice tinged with great bitterness.

"But David never ah criminal?" Isaac said, trying to compose himself. "Why would de police arress' him? He regularly attended my church when he was ah bwai."

"Becah David ah grow locks 'pon him head," Carmesha answered; her sobbing had ceased but the anger in her voice grew.

Not knowing what to say, Isaac marched to the door, opened it and shouted, "Jacob! De chile an' de lady nearly dead fe hunger. Hurry up now mon!"

"Yes, Papa. Soon come!"

Closing the door, Isaac regarded Carmesha again. Her shaking head was half buried in the blanket wrapped around her child. But what he had seen of her, he felt an immediate attraction. If only he was twenty-one again, he thought. He placed his right arm upon her shoulder. "May de Most High bless yuh, chile. Yuh come wid grievous news, for David was much loved. Especially by his mudder, Amy. Ah Godly woman. Tell me Carmesha, so how long yuh been married to David?"

Carmesha shook her head, unwilling to lift it to meet Isaac's eyes.

Patting Carmesha's shoulder, Isaac didn't allow his distaste for Carmesha's unmarried status to show itself. "Anyway, ease ya worries. I will tek yuh up to de Rodney place meself, after yuh 'ave ah liccle somet'ing to eat. Yuh know how to ride donkey?"

Carmesha shook her head once more. Isaac lifted his head and muttered to the ceiling, "Lord, wha' ah cruel tribulation to strike de Rodney family. Give me strengt' to deal wid dem mourning."

After Carmesha had suppered and Daniel had dribbled most of the cornmeal porridge down his fleshy chin and onto his cotton gown, Isaac led Carmesha outside to his donkey. He fixed the rope reins around the donkey's neck and helped Carmesha to mount, lifting her from the waist. He passed Daniel to her when she was comfortable. The heavens had called off its deluge but night was closing in rapidly; no stars had managed to penetrate the overcast conditions and the surrounding hills appeared stark and menacing. They set off in silence with Isaac grim-faced and fearful as he led his beast of burden. He tried not to show his dread of the dark to Carmesha. He recollected the last time he had set eyes on David and his hair was combed and clean – just like a good Christian boy, he thought.

Meanwhile, Jenny and Hortense were sitting on the dirt floor in the small back room of their home, an extension that Joseph had built in 1949 to house crops, herb jars, bottles of kerosene, a spare wooden plough and other household sundries. Under the light of a kerosene lamp, they were stripping the raw, hard kernels from corn cobs with a corkscrewing, crunching motion that had blistered and reddened their palms. They had managed about thirty each, throwing the ears of naked corn into crocus bags.

Now sixteen, Jenny had grown tall and had developed her father's square jaw-bone. Her forehead was curved and prominent and her dark eyes didn't seem to reveal what she was thinking. The corn-row plaits of her hair were as neat as she could make them and her lips were not generous, almost severe. Her chin was proud and defiant and she never allowed herself to slouch, even when sitting down. Hortense, now fourteen, was much prettier. She had round, doe eyes, full lips and a certain cocksure confidence in her expression. She favoured loose braids rather than corn-row. Unlike her sister, she had curves where most Jamaican men liked them; a slim waist, full breasts and a generous backside. Vitality marked her every movement and her head never remained still, as if she was worried that she might miss something to the side of her or behind her. Neville, remarked to Amy on many occasions, "Amy, yuh coulda never disown Hortense fe ya daughter, she look more like yuh dan yuh look yaself!" Hortense knew how to use these assets when she walked through the village, knowing that every young man's eyes were on her. She had long ago perfected the 'screwface' glare to anyone who vexed her but she secretly loved the moniker that villagers had given her –Fire Nettle.

"Me telling nuh lie, Jenny," Hortense insisted. "Yuh ah tickle Jacob fancy! Me see de way him look 'pon yuh ah church yesterday."

"Hortense, hold ya tongue, becah me know how yuh love to susu an' spread rumour like de long-mout' higgler ah market. Carry on dem way an' see if de Most High nuh curse yuh to be ah old cranky mule fe de res' ah ya days."

"Old Mule! As sure as chicken ah cluk an' t'irsty donkey drink water, me will find ah husband before yuh! Anyway, dis time me nah lie! Jacob look 'pon yuh like him waan to carry yuh off to bush an' grine yuh like mad bull ah grine lazy cow!"

"Hortense! Mind ya tongue! If Mama ah hear yuh talk like dat she gwarn lick yuh wid de yard broom."

"Jenny, it's like yuh don't waan to admit it to yaself. Mebbe yuh cyan hide ya secrets from everybody else but *not* me. De fact ah de matter is Jacob waan to jiggle an' wriggle him rod ah correction inside yuh an' mek ya belly swell."

"Mek me belly swell? How coulda yuh say such ah t'ing, Hortense Rodney! Yuh t'ink me coulda ever breed pickney before me get married? Yuh t'ink me ah bluefoot?"

"Jenny, wid ya innocent smile an' nice talk ways, yuh might be ably to fool Mama an' Papa, but me sight yuh look 'pon de mon who ben' over while working 'pon Misser Banton's land. An dey 'ave nuh marina or vest 'pon dem back. Der muscle ah glisten beneat' de afternoon sun. Yes, Jenny. Me sight yuh ah lick ya lips like craven dahg looking 'pon cooking pot full ah chicken leg!"

"Me was jus' looking at de way dem ah work de land! Hortense Rodney, ya mind full of imagination! Me never get sexy t'oughts inna me head! Yuh don't see how me read de Bible every night?"

"Rubbish yuh ah talk!" reproved Hortense. "Me know yuh, Jenny. Remember, me know all ya secret. Me don't know why yuh ah complain anyway. Jacob ah handsome mon! Yuh better go wid him to de bush before him find anoder fancy. But de only problem is, der is ah curse 'pon sinful preacher mon. If Jacob did vex de Most High an' him place him hand 'pon ya *business*, ya *business* will heal an' close up. An' dat mean Jacob coulda never jiggle an' wriggle him rod ah correction inside yuh. Higgler woman ah market tell me dis. So before yuh lie down inna bush an' get ready fe Jacob to grine yuh, mek sure him heart pure an' he's widout sin."

"Hortense! How many time me affe tell yuh to stop lissening to higgler talk? Nonsense yuh ah talk! An' yuh better mind ya blasphemous talk or de Most High might tek notice."

"Oh, Jenny, stop ya noise! It's me ya talking to, not some old, white-top lady inna church who is two fat moons away from de grave. Me know yuh t'ink about sex. All de time. When yuh dream yuh mek ah whining sound as if ah handsome mon is feeding 'pon ya breast. Me cyan read ya dreams, Jenny. But yuh try an' give de impression dat yuh de virgin Mary! An' me don't believe dat Mary ah virgin anyhow! Joseph mus' ah wriggle him t'ird leg inna Mary to mek Papa Jesus born."

Unable to restrain her laughter, Jenny hurled a cob of corn in Hortense's direction, striking her on the chin. "Ah good shot dat," Jenny exclaimed, throwing her arms in the air. "Ha Ha!" Outraged, Hortense picked up four cobs but before she could retaliate, Amy appeared under the door frame; her temples were a little greyer but for a woman in her mid-forties, her face was remarkably unlined. "Yuh two nuh finish yet?" she barked. "When me was ah girl chile me use to strip untold corn fe me fader, t'ree times as much as me give yuh tonight. It only used to tek me two hour. Anyway, yuh cyan stop now an' mek ah coffee fe ya fader an' meself. Nuh fret about Kwarhterleg becah ya fader ah boil up some herb fe him. Tomorrow yuh cyan both wash de callaloo an' strip de scallion. Water affe fetch inna de marnin too an' *don't* forget to feed de fowl."

Running to the kitchen, Jenny and Hortense passed their father on the way who was carrying a pot of steaming water; he had just turned fifty-one but no silver had yet to trouble his pitch-black hair; a few God-fearing villagers took this as evidence that Joseph was in league with Old Screwface. Joseph had boiled strongback leaf, grated orange skin, coconut and lime peel, ginger, sersee leaf and a rare herb that he called 'lion-tail'. The remedy emitted a powerful aroma that cleared every bunged-up nostril in a twelve-yard radius. Indeed, Joseph's fever remedies had proved to be a good source of income during the past few years.

Kwarhterleg was laying on Amy and Joseph's bed, his face – lit by a kerosene lamp situated by the door – sweating like an Englishman demonstrating how to cut cane on a plantation. A mug was beside the bed and Joseph filled it with his medicine, a concoction that he had learned from his mother. Before giving Kwarhterleg the potion, he wetted a handkerchief with over-proof rum and dabbed Kwarhterleg's neck and chest with it. The strong smell of rum and herbs soon filled the room. Kwarhterleg's tired eyes seemed to yearn for a peaceful death.

"Now, Kwarhterleg," Joseph instructed. "Yuh affe drink all-ah it.

Den fill it up once more. Me will leave de pot beside de bed. De somet'ing will mek yuh breathe more easier an' cool ya mad fever, drawing it out. Now drink like how yuh drink ya Red Stripe beer inna Misser Robinson's bar."

"T'ank yuh, sa," Kwarhterleg panted. "Moonshine. Since me know yuh, yuh 'ave been mighty good to me. Ah true brudder. When yuh first come ah Claremont dem used to say yuh is de angel of deat', but yuh 'ave proved to be de child of light. May de Most High bless ya soul. Me jus' waan to tell yuh dat before me pass away an' greet me ancestor. Serious t'ing."

"Kwarhterleg, stop chat ya mad foolishness!" rebuked Joseph. "Ya nah about to dead 'pon me. Yuh only ketch ah liccle fever. Ya soon better so cease ya mad deat' talk!"

They both heard a loud knock upon the door. "Who de backside ah come to me door at dis late hour?" Joseph complained.

"Nuh fret yaself, Joseph," Amy called from the storage room. "Tend to Kwarhterleg an' mek sure him ah drink him remedy. Mebbe de remedy will quiet him labba labba mout'! Me never know ah mon dat cyan talk so much when him sick! Me will see who ah come."

Amy went outside and was surprised to see Isaac securing his donkey to a tree. Carmesha stood still, as if afraid to take a step. Puddles were around her feet. Daniel was sleeping, snuggled upon his mother's shoulder. Isaac found it difficult to meet Amy's eyes. "Isaac," she called. "Why yuh bring strange girl wid pickney to me door 'pon dis hour?"

Carmesha stepped back a pace but Isaac, supporting her back, brought her forward. Tears were welling up in Isaac's eyes. "Isaac, why yuh ah start bawl?" Amy wanted to know. "Is it yuh de fader ah dis young girl pickney? How many times me affe tell yuh to keep away from de young girl dem. Ya black bamboo don't satisfy yet? Me don't know how ya poor wife put up wid yuh. Talk to me mon! Old Screwface ah tie knot inna ya tongue?"

"It's David," Isaac stuttered. "David dead."

Isaac bowed his head. Carmesha began to sob once more. Amy stood perfectly still, just gazing ahead at nothing in particular as if trapped in some kind of surreal world. Joseph emerged out of the house. He looked at the head-bowed Isaac, the crying Carmesha and then at his shocked wife; she remained rooted to the spot but her lips were trembling violently. "Preacher Mon?" Joseph asked. "Yuh never come here so. Is it me one son?"

Isaac answered with his watering eyes and a slight nod.

"Yuh better come inside," Joseph offered after a pause. Gently taking Amy by the arm, he led her into the house. Isaac and Carmesha followed him. They all sat down on the girls' bed. Kwarhterleg, whimpering, tried to raise his head to discover what was happening but Joseph's potion was having its powerful affect. Jenny and Hortense appeared from the kitchen.

"Papa! Wha' ah gwarn?" Hortense demanded. "Wha' wrong wid Mama? Who de strange lady wearing de dutty frock wid pickney? Why Preacher Mon come to we house?"

Joseph, who was about to answer, peered into Hortense's eyes, but couldn't bring himself to do so. He dropped his head and searched for Amy's right hand, grabbing it tightly. Carmesha was now in utter turmoil, rocking herself back and forward, letting out an agonising wail.

"Papa! Tell me mon," Hortense urged. Jenny was behind her and she placed an arm around her sister's shoulders, frightened to discover what might have happened.

Isaac took it upon himself to pass on the news. "Hortense. Jenny. May de Lord God protect yuh. Ya brudder David 'as passed away to de eternal life. Police ah Spanish town arress' him an' apparently batter him 'til him dead. I'm really sorry. May de Most High bless him soul."

Summoning every last drop of power in her lungs, stretching her neck tissues and straining her vocal chords, Hortense screamed. She rushed towards Isaac, shaking her head and began to assault him with wild punches. "IT NUH GO SO! IT NUH GO SO. LIE YUH AH TELL! LIE YUH AH TELL. IT NUH GO SO, IT NUH GO SO! COME OUTTA ME YARD PREACHER MON WID YA SERPENT'S TONGUE!"

Pulling Hortense off a shaken Isaac, Joseph lifted and carried her outside but her shouts and shrieks grew more intense. Joseph suffered scratches and slaps to his face. She began to curse Isaac, using foul words that shocked the preacher. "Preacher Mon place obeah spell 'pon me sweet brudder becah him nuh like yuh, Papa! Him kill David fe true! Let me go, Papa! Me waan *kill* Preacher Mon."

Amy offered no flicker of a reaction to her daughter whatsoever. She just sat still, staring vacantly ahead. Jenny went to her mother, placed her arms around her neck and buried her head into her bosom, sobbing silently. Amy didn't seem to notice. Amid all of this, Daniel slept silently, only caring for his next meal.

"Preacher Mon kill me sweet David," Hortense raged on. "*He* truly hate yuh, Papa. Yuh mus' kill him, Papa!"

Embarrassed, and with guilt preying on his mind, Isaac dropped his head.

"Isaac, nuh fret yaself," whispered Amy. "Hortense don't know wha' she ah say."

Three hours later, Joseph had managed to sedate Hortense with some bush tea; he had used a stalk of sinsimilla as part of his potion, an extremely potent variant of the cannabis plant. Joseph never revealed where he had found it, not even to Kwarhterleg. Sometimes he had found use for the herb as a pain killer and Amy, who suspected that Joseph was growing it somewhere near his plot, would secretly boil it with her coffee to quell her period pains. But Joseph would never smoke it, unlike some men in the village who swore the herb presented them with 'stamina fe grine woman'.

Now sound asleep, Hortense lay perfectly still. Daniel was at rest snuggled up next to her. Jenny, sitting up beside her sister, was stroking Hortense's hair, lost in her own thoughts. She looked upon her sister tenderly, only hearing Kwarhterleg's rasping snores – he having been knocked out by the concoction he had drunk. "Nuh worry yaself, Hortense," Jenny whispered. "Me will look after yuh. See me don't keep me promise to sweet David, until de end of we days."

Isaac had departed an hour ago, informing the family that he would do anything they asked of him. Over-dramatically, with tears running down his fleshy cheeks, Isaac bowed and then kissed a stunned Amy's hand as he left. Amy, Joseph and Carmesha had relocated to the kitchen; Joseph had lengthened it over a period of time and now there were stools for everyone to be seated around a small homemade table. They were all sipping goat's milk and rum from chipped mugs. The unseen owls outside, or 'Patus' as the locals called them, hooted desolately. A low fire was flickering, flashing erratic light upon everybody's pained expressions.

"Carmesha," Joseph said softly. "Me waan to tek home me son's body. Where it der?"

"Inna de police station ah Spanish Town. Dem would nah let me tek it becah dem say me nuh married to him an' me cyan't prove David ah fe me relation. Yuh affe go der an' present papers ah identification."

"Joseph," Amy said in a whisper. "Me waan me only son home."

Joseph nodded, filling his pipe. "Yes, me too. Me gone when de first light ah shine. Yuh two should try an' get some res'. Carmesha, yuh is family now. Never forget dat. Me cyan't believe me ah gran'papa. Me cyan't believe me one son dead..."

Carmesha helped Amy into the house, leaving Joseph alone with Panama and his thoughts. He sucked the tobacco mightily, blowing smoke into the kitchen's ceiling. He watched the wisps disappear and thought his family was cursed. Maybe he had brought the curse with him and had unknowingly blighted David with it. Perhaps he should leave, he thought, and take the curse with him.

A new day. The sun had barely risen when Joseph secured the straw-filled cart to his donkey. He had already eaten his breakfast but the cool water that cleansed his face couldn't rinse out the dreadful feeling in his stomach. He stuffed a crocus bag with two mangos, a water coconut, plums and an avocado for provisions and some mint leaves. He then set off for the near seventy mile journey to Spanish Town – the old Spanish capital of Jamaica.

He first went through Walker's Wood, where the fronds of the trees that fringed the path shielded the sun and young bare-footed children pushed vendor carts of green banana and plaintain. They lived in ramshackle dwellings that clung on for dear life to the tangled hillsides. For a moment Joseph considered walking in a straight line deeper into the wood, waiting for nightfall and allowing Old Screwface to claim him.

The village of Moneague owned a beautiful small-spired church with white stucco walls. A burial ground lay behind the building and Joseph felt a chill in his heart. David appeared smiling in the forefront of his mind. Innocence marked his expression. Joseph dropped his head and wept silently, only hearing the creak and rhythm of the wheels and ignoring passer-bys who offered him good mornings.

Joseph finally reached the outskirts of Spanish Town just after six thirty in the evening. He had been journeying for nearly thirteen hours. He asked someone for directions to the police station and twenty-five minutes later was showing a surly policeman his marriage certificate that was signed by Isaac; Joseph didn't reveal that he was unable to read what was written on the document, apart from his own name that Amy taught him to write.

David's body was in a corner of what seemed a forgotten stone cell. The tough, dirt ground was specked with blood. Joseph presented his two police escorts with such a hard baleful stare, that they feared that they had just been cursed. The officers, one of whom had scratch marks upon his face, soon left Joseph to his own devices, saying they had errands to perform. Joseph, parting the locks on David's head, noticed the back of his head had sustained a blow from a blunt instrument. Congealed blood was spotted around the neck and upon his bare shoulders and back.

Lifting up his son very carefully, Joseph carried him over his right shoulder. He took him to the police station's back yard where he cleansed David's fatal wound with water from a stand-pipe. He then carried him to his cart, laying him gently upon the straw. Before he set off once more, he wetted and sprinkled mint leaves over the body. He threw the police station another vengeful glare and then grabbed the hemp reins of his donkey, leading him on. He ignored the gawps and whispered comments from passer-bys. His lasting memory of Spanish Town was of the many, many people occupying such a small area and how none of them seemed to care about his grief.

Fourteen hours later, Joseph was glad to see his home village. His legs were almost failing him and twice he considered parking the cart and joining his son in everlasting sleep. Seeing nobody about, he parked the cart by the side of the house and stole inside the storage room seeking a plastic sheet. He rummaged around for thirty seconds when he heard footsteps behind him. He turned around and found Amy, standing with arms folded, a compassionate look upon her face. "Joseph," she whispered. "Tiredness mus' be killing yuh. Me never t'ink yuh woulda come back so quick! Go to ya bed, mon. Me an' Carmesha will wash David's body. *Gwarn!* Let me tek de burden now."

Nodding wearily, Joseph slipped away to the bedroom. As soon as he lay down, he fell into a troubled sleep. Amy found Carmesha, who was sitting in a nearby field, rocking her baby. She was staring vacantly ahead. "Carmesha! Joseph come back wid David."

They both headed outside to the cart. Amy swept the mint leaves away from David's face with her hands. Then using all of her fingers, felt the contours of David's face and wiped away the specks of dirt upon his forehead. She looked at him adoringly, making no sound. She kissed him upon the forehead. "Please forgive me, David," she whispered. "When yuh lef' me six years ago me tongue was full of nettle. Me deeply sorry fe dat. How could me ever doubt ya devotion to me? Everybody know dat yuh 'ave de most pure heart inna dis family. Even me papa know dat fe true. Sleep peacefully me liccle bwai. Me favourite chile. Sleep peacefully."

Biting her lips, Carmesha watched Amy with overwhelming pity. She could hardly bear to stand there so she went to collect two jugs of water. When she returned she found that Amy had pulled off David's pants and undergarments. He lay naked under the morning sun. Amy handed David's clothes to Carmesha. "Burn dem, Carmesha, becah dem clothes 'ave de stench ah deat'."

Using a clean cloth, Amy began to wash David's body from the waist to the feet. She then bathed him from the waist to the head, remembering the death rituals taught to her by Neville. She flipped

David over onto his belly and for a short second, was shocked at the sight of the ugly wound at the back of his head. She repeated the cleansing process, knowing that not to purify ever pore upon David's skin could have dire consequences for his afterlife. When she concluded her task, she and Carmesha carried David into the house. They instructed Jenny and Hortense, who hadn't gone to school, to rise from their bed in order to lay David down. They made sure his head was as far away from the door as possible, for Amy had learned that evil spirits could be lurking near the threshold of a home if they detect the aroma from a dead person's head. To conclude the formalities, Amy dropped a little fresh water into David's mouth in order to cleanse his soul. They then covered his body with a plastic sheet that Joseph had used to shield vulnerable crops. Carmesha, Hortense and Jenny looked on silently; Hortense could only watch David's lifeless body for a minute before bolting away. Kwarhterleg wanted to go after her but Amy said, "Let her be. Let her grieve."

Brooding under her Blue Mahoe tree, Hortense repeated to herself in a mantra-like chant, "nuhbody ah love me now, nuhbody ah love me now, nuhbody ah love me now."

Wanting to console her sister, Jenny, instead, was sent to Neville to inform him of the tragic news. Neville, showing no emotion, went outside alone to a nearby field. He looked up to the sky and raged in a coarse voice, "WHY YUH TEK ONE OF WE SONS? ME DAUGHTER'S *ONLY* SON. IS DAT YA REVENGE? MUS' OUR SONS PAY FE DE SINS OF DE FOREFATHERS. YUH HAPPY NOW?"

Until twilight claimed the afternoon, Neville remained abroad, accompanied only by his Bible. Angry with God, he resorted to his grandfather's secret custom that he had observed as a child. Neville, checking that nobody was spying on him, sacrificed a chicken, held it aloft to the heavens and as the blood ran down over his hands and arms, prayed to the west African river Gods to protect any future males of his family that might come into the world.

Two mornings later, Isaac led the mourners up to the burial plot, a short walk away from Joseph's agricultural plateau. Half of the village had turned out and the other half did not go about their work, deciding to take a day off. Claremontonians were superstitious like that. Isaac read aloud from the Book of Psalms. Behind him, Neville, Joseph, Jacob, Reuben and two more male members of the extended family, carried the simple coffin made by Mr Collins, a miserly carpenter from Browns Town whom Kwarhterleg knew. Kwarhterleg, now recovered from his illness, stumped behind them. Although Isaac had advised the Rodney family to host the customary nine nights of mourning where friends and family turned up at all hours to pay their respects, toast David's life with fine rum and eat good food, Joseph declined. This decision went much against the grain and even Neville rebuked Joseph for it, but Joseph just couldn't see how he was supposed to be celebrating David's life. He had no life, he thought. He was just starting out.

When the long line of mourners had finally reached David's last resting place, they made a ring around the graveside and began to hum hymns; Joseph and Jacob had already dug the grave. Turning the pages of his Bible, Isaac was looking for a certain psalm to read out to conclude the service. He noticed a few heads turning around and looking up to the misted hillside. Levi, walking stick in hand, although he didn't seem to require it, strode down to attend the funeral. He was only dressed in his stained cut-off trousers. Astonished by the matted brown locks that fell below Levi's waist, some mourners crossed themselves while others were outraged. "Who de wild mon wid de Medusa head?" someone whispered.

"Lord protect us!" another said. "De legend ah de blackheart mon fe real!"

Joseph looked upon Levi curiously while Amy tried to restrain the disgust in her eyes.

Levi reached the graveside. Mourners backed away from his presence. "Me jus' waan to pay me respect," said Levi. "David was ah Godly mon an' did 'ave ah true heart. An' he was ah true friend."

Levi's statement didn't satisfy anyone but nobody was willing to challenge his presence fearing that he could be an ambassador sent by Old Screwface. Levi flashed a glance at Isaac and Isaac seemed to shiver, as if a demon was fighting to penetrate his soul. The Bible in his hands was shaking and sweat was pouring down his temples. He tried to compose himself but was obliged to lift the rum flask from out of his inside jacket pocket. He took a generous gulp, ignoring the amazed glances from the mourners who thought that the preacher was overwhelmed by the reality of David's death.

But Isaac was in a state of shock because he had just laid his eyes upon his eldest son, Levi, whom he had christened Joshua. He couldn't believe that the young boy who had read passages aloud from the Bible, impressing his parents and well-to-do visitors at the Forbes home, was now a wild-looking, serpent-haired vagrant.

Managing to pull himself together, Isaac concluded the formalities. The coffin was lowered into the grave. Suddenly, the mourners heard someone singing in a foreign tongue. It was Joseph. The language was of the Akan districts of Ghana but Joseph didn't know this. He simply felt that it was appropiate to sing a song he had learned from his mother. He never asked her what the lyrics meant. Everyone gaped at Joseph in astonishment but nobody could doubt his sincerity, hearing his heartfelt deep baritone delivery.

The incidents and drama of David Rodney's funeral proved a good source of material for the higglers. In places as far as St Anne's Bay, Browns Town, Alderton and Rhoden Hall, country folk gossiped about how this blackheart man came down from the hills with a nest of serpents upon his head and using the dark forces of the underworld, inserted a demon into the soul of Mister Rodney, causing him to speak the language of Old Screwface himself.

Following the funeral, Levi marched back to his hillside dwelling. He never spoke or acknowledged his father. Isaac watched him disappear into the mists, tears falling freely down his cheeks. Amy studied Isaac, utterly bewildered.

Later that night, laying down to rest under the roof of the kitchen, having just given Hortense another dose of the sinsimilla potion to help her sleep, Joseph thought of his mother. He couldn't help but think of *that* dreadful day. It had started like any other day, Joseph recalled. It was in the fall of 1914.

Chapter Six

Seven days had passed since David's funeral and Amy decided it was about time that she questioned Carmesha about the last year or so of David's life. Having finished her morning chores, she placed a pot of water over the fire and then washed two mugs, preparing to make coffee. She noticed that the wind had picked up and the clothes on the washing line were blowing horizontal. Clouds above were moving swiftly. Kwarhterleg, strands of tobacco on his lips, was taking his afternoon siesta.

Spread across his face to shield his eyes from the sun was a yellowed edition of the *Daily Gleaner* where, on the front page, framed by reports of the assassination of King Abdullah of Jordan and the anti-British riots in Iran that had left nine dead, was a headline detailing the dwindling sugar cane fields in Jamaica and the fact that banana was now the nation's most lucrative export crop; only the most desperate of men were prepared to bend their backs from sun-up to sun-down wielding a cutlass in a cane field. Written on the back page was an article about the newly crowned world boxing middleweight champion, Randolph Turpin, who had savagely out-pointed the overwhelming favourite, Sugar Ray Robinson. Inside the house, Carmesha was rocking Daniel to sleep; Daniel, not yet accustomed to his new surroundings, had slept fitfully during the night.

"Carmesha!" Amy called. "Yuh waan coffee?"

"Yes please, Amy. Ya well kind. Daniel sleeping at las', so me coming."

"Carmesha, how many times me affe tell yuh! Yuh mus' call me Mama now. Yuh give birt' to me first gran'chile!"

"Sorry. Mama. Me keep forgetting."

Carmesha joined Amy in the kitchen, seating herself on a stool. Amy looked upon Carmesha with compassionate eyes, guessing that she was no older than nineteen. The cares of life had yet to etch itself upon her forehead but they soon would, Amy thought. For that is the lot of Jamaican women. While the men were fussing, fighting, drinking or working, Jamaican women had to raise families, ensure that everybody was fed, fetch the water, scrub the clothes in the river and lay down uncomplaining in the bush as their men satisfied themselves. No excuse of tiredness or a headache would suffice and the pleasure was always for the man to enjoy.

Joseph wasn't guilty of most of these charges, Amy concluded, but he would only cook dinner if she was ill or Kwarhterleg was indisposed. She wondered what kind of world she had brought her two daughters into – the tedious cycle of rural Jamaican life. No chance for them to set off upon adventures and see the outside world. Ah well, she thought. Hortense cyan look after herself, although she will affe get over de loss of David. At least me cyan guess how she is feeling by her open expression. So full of life. But Jenny? Me never know wha' she really t'inking. She hasn't grieved at all. She jus' tek everyt'ing inna her stride.

"Carmesha," Amy began. "Me still don't understand why de police arress' David. Yuh tell me dat David ah never involve himself wid any rebel dem."

"Dat is right, Amy," Carmesha said. "De problem was dat untold rastamon come down from de hills from above Spanish Town." Carmesha went on to reveal the events that led to David's death.

Led by a self-proclaimed prophet named Leonard Howell, who enjoyed the company of many wives, many rastafarians rejected the normal customs of Jamaican life and lived in a remote hillside commune called Pinnacle, north of Spanish Town. Discovering that the dreads cultivated marijuana, the police raided Pinnacle whenever they felt the urge. They were never shy to employ their long batons.

Not wanting to be a practise dummy for the unforgiving arm of the law, forty or so dreads escaped from the commune and made their way down to Spanish Town. Unsure of what to do next, the rastas walked around in confusion, attracting complaint and scorn. The police soon confronted the dreads again and thrashed them mercilessly.

Returning from his work at a government farm that bred Hereford cows, David spotted the brutality of the police in Spanish Town's main square. He ran to the scene, confronted officers and voiced his grave concerns about the unnecessary force being used. He said, "ah brudder should nah beat 'pon him fellow brudder mon." But a policeman spotted the infant locks upon David's head, cracked him with his baton upon the back of his skull and frog-marched him to the police station. Meanwhile, the rastas who had remained up in Pinnacle were arrested and thrown in jail – many of them didn't survive their beatings.

Pinnacle was set ablaze and as the smoke drifted over the northern parts of Spanish Town, Leonard Howell was committed to an asylum.

A few years earlier, David had been working upon the docks at Kingston harbour. Carmesha, who had one day journeyed to Kingston with her mother to visit relatives, couldn't tolerate the heat and renk conditions of the downtown area so she went for a walk upon the harbour road, relieved to breathe in the sea air. She spotted David who was lifting boxes from a cargo ship. She had never seen such a handsome man, David's rich black skin glistening beneath the hot sun. His smile was broad and welcoming but the attribute that set him apart from any other man was that he walked and stood like a king. "Hey, pretty girl," he called.

Warned by her mother about the reputation of men who worked on the docks, Carmesha strolled on. "Hey, pretty girl," David called again. "Me like de way yuh walk! An' ya face coulda light up any dark night! Yes, sa! Yuh remind me of me future wife. De Most High know dat fe true! Yuh mus' be ah nubian princess."

"But yuh don't even know me," replied Carmesha, a smile escaping from her lips.

"So yuh better wait 'til me come down an' introduce meself."

"But me live inna de country," revealed Carmesha. "Me only inna Kingston fe de day, so we path will only meet dis one time."

"An' wha' ah time! Fate bring yuh down dis road. Yuh mus' give me ya address. Me will look fe yuh. See if me don't!"

Writing her address on a used envelope, Carmesha didn't imagine that she would bless her eyes on David again. But three weeks later, David arrived at her home in the tiny hamlet of Churchpen. He tipped his cloth hat to Carmesha when she answered the door, his eyes sparkling. "Good marnin, Mrs Rodney! Wha' name should we choose fe we first son?"

A year later, David and Carmesha moved into a rented room in Spanish Town. When Carmesha discovered she was pregnant, David took the decision to work abroad in a cotton field in Georgia, north America. He wanted to accrue enough money so he could get married and build his own home. Papa and Mama would be proud of him and Hortense and Jenny would make fine bridesmaids. Yes, sa, David thought. It would be a sweet day.

Fear stalked David every night and day whilst he toiled under the Georgian sun and slept under her stars. He learned of lynchings and murders of black folks for sometimes nothing more than a glance at a white woman's ankle. Unlike Kingston, where a number of white people would sometimes engage in conversation and socialise with black folks, David was shocked to see the separation of the races in the American south. At work his opinion and views meant nothing to white ears. He was expected to be subservient at all times. White men addressed him as 'boy' and white women refused to talk to him at all. He noticed that many of the black men walked 'bent' with invisible weights on their shoulders and some black women seemed to want to shrink within themselves, never lifting their chins from their collarbones and they moved as if every step was an apology.

David noticed that many young black men from the American south, only carrying an extra change of clothing, were heading to cities like Chicago and New York. They hoped they could find work and then send for their sweethearts. Most of them spoke bitterly of the white man's promise of forty acres and a mule. On many occasions David watched the packed trains disappear – some men who couldn't afford the fare, ran and jumped aboard the moving train. David likened it to the migration of country folk in Jamaica heading for Kingston. Only here in America it was on a grander scale.

Although he tried to live like a Nazarene, David felt it would be too dangerous for him to grow locks. He was attracted to the black American church. The soulful and heartfelt singing he had heard there led him to the conclusion that black people the world over were essentially the same. They struggled the same struggle, fighting for equality and justice and gaining strength from their faith. He observed it was all they had to cling onto – some distant hope that their wretched lives will be rewarded once they reached heaven. He recalled one of the lessons of Levi when he affirmed, "we *are* the lost tribe of Israel. An' if yuh doubt it, look 'pon de expressions of our brudders an' sisters. Look in der eyes."

He attended secret gatherings of Garveyites in church halls after the midnight hour. He was introduced to books and pamphlets that the white man banned. Being born from the same parish as Marcus Garvey, David soon gained much respect from his fellow activists. They looked after him whenever he was sick, fed him when David couldn't afford a meal. They discussed their strategies of ressurecting Marcus Garvey's dream of a 'Black Star' shipping line. Members of Garvey's old 'back to Africa' movement came from as far afield as Harlem, Detroit and Chicago to visit. They left before the sun rose. Then the gathering would return to their labours picking cotton and growing peanuts, feigning ignorance, stupidity and docility to any white man they met.

David was instructed in self-empowerment and the pride of the black race and he learned to hide his new-found intelligence from his employers – others who were not so discreet went missing or their homes were set on fire.

Writing to Carmesha every week, David revealed that there was an unwritten curfew for black people. He dismayed that he couldn't take the chance to walk the fields at night and take in the cool air, smell the plants and admire nature at its most serene. *America has ah deep stain, Carmesha*, David wrote. *De stain of slavery. Even inna Jamaica ah black mon is free to ah certain extent. But over here, ah mon jus' cyan't tek him foot to de mountain side an' live off de land like ah mon me used to know. Nuh, sa! An' dey say dat slavery carry on fe 400 years. Me fear dat it will tek anoder 400 years to remove de stain. Carmesha, almost every young black mon is leaving here. Dem cyan't tek de white mon's anger nuh more. Me don't understan' der hatred becah wasn't it we who cut dem cane an' pick dem cotton when de white mon ah sit inna de shade watching him wallet get heavy. Jus' de udder day dem kill off ah sharecropper's son. Ah good, proud mon. Too proud an' him tongue run away from him. He could nah hold back him temper nuh more. Ah frien' of mine said 'dey came inna de night'. His fader did own ah liccle land but him always cry an' gnash his teet' becah of debt. Dem old mon work so hard but still 'ave not'ing. Debt shadow every old black mon me know who own ah liccle piece of land. Me own papa is lucky becah him owe de white mon not'ing. Carmesha, de land of de free is not'ing but de land of black mon misery. De curse of Ham ring very true inna dis broad land. Me will soon come back home. De wider world is ah ugly world an' me nuh waan nuh part of it. Dat's why me say NUH when ah nex' frien' invite me to go Chicago wid him. Nuh, sa! Me cyan't wait 'til me reach home an' live de simple life. Kiss de baby fe me an' pray fe me deliverance.*

Returning home in March, 1951, David won a job with a Spanish Town farmer only because he could read the government instructions and invoices that were sent to the farm. He could also understand the 'uppity' words of the businessmen who occasionally visited the establishment. David could see a bright future for his family – until the dreads came down from their mountain.

Carmesha concluded her tale with a knowing smile, as if she was reliving a pleasant memory. Amy rose to her feet. "Carmesha, yuh waan ah liccle rum inna ya coffee? Joseph ah t'ink me only drink de fire-water ah nighttime after me dinner, but me cyan't see why woman cyan't enjoy de good t'ings ah life when de sun high inna de sky. Come, Kwarhterleg sleeping so him cyan't say not'ing, an' if him do me gwarn fling away him crutch!"

"Yes, Mama, if yuh don't mind."

Amy went into the storage room and returned with a bottle of Appleton's rum in her hands. She topped up the two mugs of coffee with it. Carmesha looked upon the sleeping Kwarhterleg, shaded by the mango tree. The leaves rustled loudly above his head. "So wha' is Kwarhterleg's story?" she asked.

"Kwarhterleg!" Amy sighed. "Kwarhterleg born ah Brown's

Town. Him say him inna de sixties but de trut' is Kwarhterleg seventy plus, nearly eighty; don't tell him me tell yuh so. Kwarhterleg's papa was ah farmer, jus' like Joseph an' de intention was dat Kwarhterleg woulda work 'pon him papa plot. When him reach sixteen him fall in love wid ah girl. Kwarhterleg cyan't never forget her name, Joanne Lindus. Ah red skin girl wid pretty, pretty curly black hair dat cyan't be blacker. Her glow beautiful like de twilight red sun ah set over de mighty Blue Mahoe as Kwarhterleg used to describe her. Me t'ink Kwarhterleg used to say dat she did 'ave Spanish blood inside her; Carmesha, yuh will notice dat in dese parts, nuff people 'ave Spanish blood inside dem but dem don't admit it.

"Anyway, Kwarhterleg an' de pretty Joanne was about to marry, but t'ree weeks before de wedding, Kwarhterleg ah tek off to Black River inna St Elizabet' wid him frien' fe ah weekend. Yuh know, like ah liccle vacation. Dem never know dat alligator ah loiter an' wait fe foolish people inna de river fe dem supper. Dem nyam off Kwarhterleg foot an' him nearly dead from loss ah blood. Dey had to use fire to stop de bleeding. When him come back ah Browns Town now, Kwarhterleg girl look 'pon him stump ah leg an' decide dat he coulda never provide fe her an' work 'pon de land. So she lef' him. Kwarhterleg was devastated, especially years later when him see Joanne wid ah nex' mon wid her belly nearly ah burst wid pickney. Him decide to leave Browns Town an' come ah Claremont. Him used to beg inna de market; some mon would fling bruise mango after him. Unruly kidren would fling rockstone after him. People never easy wid him."

"Oh Lord!" Carmesha exclaimed. "Wha' ah cruel tribulation."

"Yes," Amy nodded. "But de Most High work inna funny way. Becah dem time, when Kwarhterleg was begging inna de market an' sleeping ah bush an' inna de gulley, Joseph an' meself were jus' setting up we own place. Becah Joseph work so hard 'pon me papa land, him decide to give de land to we as ah wedding present – me cyan tell yuh dat dis cause nuff fuss from de mon who used to work fe me papa, but dat's ah nex' story. Joseph was de only one inna de village who did ah tek time an' talk to Kwarhterleg, sometime t'rowing him ah few penny fe ah Red Stripe beer. One day Joseph turn up wid Kwarhterleg all drunk up from fire-water. It was ah harvest night an' dey jus' come back from Misser DaCosta party, dat is Welton's papa. Joseph ask me if Kwarhterleg coulda stay fe de night. Me set up ah sleeping place fe him inna de corner ah de kitchen. Him been wid us ever since."

"Ah nice story dat," Carmesha nodded. "It funny. Me mudder use to say all Jamaican mon ah t'ink about is dem fire water!"

Amy laughed. "An' dem black bamboo stick or dem rod ah correction!"

Carmesha nearly choked with laughter, realising that life would be humorous with the Rodney family.

"So wha' is ya plan fe de future?" Amy asked.

"Well, me don't waan go back ah Spanish Town. Der is nutten fe me nuh more down der. If yuh would 'ave me den me would like to stay wid yuh. Me will help out any way me cyan."

"Nuh fret yaself, Carmesha. Yuh is family now an' me tek ah mighty liking to me one gran'chile. Him favour David inna big way an' me see de Maroon inna him. It's in de eyes. See how dem shiny black?"

"Yes, me notice it de day him was born," agreed Carmesha. "Me would like to live here wid yuh. De hillside look so pretty."

Cupping Carmesha's jaws with her hands, Amy kissed her upon the forehead. "Ya welcome."

As Carmesha and Amy drained the last drops of their rum coffees, Joseph was climbing the hills above his plot of land. He felt the freshening winds cool his face and wondered why he was reluctant to set foot here before. He was surprised to see that jackfruit trees grew tall here and the ackee was plentiful. Breadfruit grew freely too. Joseph wished he had brought a crocus bag with him so he could take home these fruits and discover if they tasted any different to the fruits that ripened further down in the valley. "Jamaican soil fertile like Miss Coletta wid her t'irteen pickney," Joseph laughed to himself. "Miss Coletta husband shoulda tek to fishing inna de night-time. Becah all him affe do is kiss her 'pon de forehead an' she breed like sex mad mosquito!"

Through a gap in the trees, Joseph saw smoke threading itself through the leaves before disappearing under the greying sky. He walked towards its source. Hunched over his fire, Levi was roasting grunt fish; he didn't even hear Joseph creeping behind him.

"Afternoon, sa," Joseph greeted.

Turning around in alarm, Levi wondered how anyone could steal so close to him without detecting a presence. "Joseph! Er, yuh waan some roast fish?"

"Nuh, sa. Me jus' t'ought dat me should come look fe yuh. Yuh see, me used to wonder why David ah wander inna de mist to dis hillside but of course, me shoulda known. To see yuh."

"So. Yuh know me here all de while?"

"Yes. Joshua."

Levi hadn't been called that name for over sixteen years and the sheer shock of hearing it had drained the gloss from his cheeks.

"Amy used to wonder wha' happen to Preacher Mon eldest son. She know dat him sen' yuh ah different school inna Montego Bay. Nobody used to see yuh. An' den we learn dat yuh gone ah Kingston fe furder study. By dem time everybody forget wha' yuh look like. But nuh me!"

Levi could do nothing but laugh and when he composed himself, offered Joseph a share of his lunch. Joseph, although not really hungry, finally accepted.

Picking out the tiny bones of his fish, Joseph asked. "So why yuh live up here so, all alone? Wha' happen wid yuh an' ya family?"

Pausing, Levi stared into the woods with a hint of a sore memory. "Ah long story dat. Basically, me an' me papa coulda never agree wid wha' de Bible say."

"Oh," Joseph chuckled. "Sometime me glad dat me cyan't read ah word. Except me very name. Dat book, me sure, cause nuff fussing an' fighting dan de writer ever t'ought possible."

Levi found himself nodding. The two men talked for over an hour, relating to each other's particular experiences. Indeed, Joseph regretted not seeking out Levi before. As they shared a jackfruit, a sudden gust of wind blew out the fire. Startled, Levi quickly climbed a tree to view the heavens. The grey, cumulus clouds were moving swiftly and Levi felt spots of rain upon his face. In the distance it was like night had already claimed the day and Levi could hear the faint echo of thunder. He was aware that the equatorial sea had been cooking all summer and now the rising warm air had finally met the dense cold air, the classic ingredients of the seasonal winds, and Levi sensed this was much more foreboding than the usual gales at this time of the year. He leaped down from the tree, a fretful expression upon his face.

"Mighty storm ah come! De branch inna tree already start bend!"

Standing up, Joseph strained his ears. He could hear the rapidly strengthening wind whistling above his head. Birds were flapping here and there and gusts that weaved through the intricate woodland, began to disturb the soil, throwing up dust and twigs. Joseph looked up. "De Most High decide to blow him cruel breat' today. Levi, yuh cyan't stay up here so. Dis place too expose. Yuh better come wid me down to Claremont. Mek pace to grab anyt'ing yuh need."

Not having to be told twice, Levi quickly stuffed his crocus bags with his books and picked up his cutlass. "Ah shame," Levi laughed. "De first time inna sixteen years dat yuh look fe me an' mighty storm start brew. Some people would say dat's ah curse."

By the time they were running down the exposed hillside, the temperature had plunged dramatically and they were being slammed with horizontal rain; Levi ran past a dead bird that had fallen to the ground after being drowned in mid-flight. Tree trunks were belly-dancing and Levi and Joseph only saw a grey, greenish blur before them. It seemed as if the storm was about to claim the island as Levi and Joseph held up their hands to protect their faces from the sting of cold rain, the snarling wind currents forcing them to crouch and crawl. Joseph just about recognised his plot of land.

"Me mus' tek out me corn!" he yelled.

Turning around, Levi saw Joseph battling against the wind on his knees, trying to find a digging implement. "JOSEPH! Come, mon. Yuh affe leave it!"

Now covered in mud, Joseph had found his fork and had proceeded digging. A huge blast of wind toppled him over but he picked up his fork again as if in a trance – utterly determined.

"Joseph!" Levi called.

Slipping and sliding, Levi scrambled over to the farmer. He put his arms around Joseph's waist. "Yuh cyan't stay here!"

"Me corn! Me corn!"

Using all his strength, Levi dragged Joseph off his plot. Suddenly, a river of mud swept them downhill next to an arching palm tree. They could hear the felling of trees all around them. The light of the day was rapidly diminishing as lightning streaked across the unforgiving heavens. They tasted saltwater upon their lips and it seemed that the rain had become a huge blanket of water, devouring everything in its path. Echoing booms of thunder battered their ear-drums, shaking the liquifying ground. Joseph, despairingly, held his head within his palms. Levi knew that they had to move fast to lower ground. He grabbed Joseph's arm and hauled him up on his feet. "COME MON!" Levi had forgotten his cutlass and his books.

They stumbled down to the fruit groves which offered them a brief respite. Joseph tripped over a fallen coconut. Other fruits lay scattered all over the mired earth. Ravines and gulleys were soon filled with galloping rain-water, carrying all before it. The baked earth had turned into a quagmire, making progress arduous. Countless chickens lay dead in newly formed ponds. Goats were circling about on the spot as if madness had struck them. Their survival instincts guiding them, cows made for any tree cover they could find but many perished under fallen branches. The howling and whining of dogs led villagers to believe this was the work of Old Screwface.

An hour later, an exhausted Joseph and Levi stumbled inside the storage room of Joseph's home covered from scalp to toe with dripping mud. The walls were built of stone. Water had seeped inside, now developing into a widening pool. It was only mid-afternoon but blackness reigned outside. Amy, holding the kerosene lamp in her right hand, was not too bothered about the presence of Levi. She closed her eyes in relief, thankful for Joseph's safe return. Carmesha, Daniel, Hortense and Jenny were huddled up in one corner. Kwarhterleg, Matthew, Miss Panchita and her child, the next-door neighbours, were gathered in another. Everybody looked up to the ceiling, hearing the natural elements do their worse, praying silently that the sun would rise again. Jenny compared the sound of the wind to some kind of deathly church organ playing in a low key with no distinctive melody. Old Screwface's music, she concluded. "De Most High vex wid somet'ing," she said. Trembling, Hortense had her arms tightly around her sister's neck, her face pressed into her back. "Yes," Hortense answered. "Him vex wid Preacher Mon an' de people dat live down ah hillside becah dem put obeah 'pon sweet David an' mek him dead. Me hope de breat' of de Most High will toss dem liccle house inna de air an' put it down inna mighty deep river!"

"Hortense!" Amy rebuked. "Mind ya tongue."

"Nuh worry yaself, Hortense," whispered Jenny. "Hold on tight to me. De Most High's mighty breat' cyan't hurt yuh if yuh stay close. *An' de shanty people get wha' dem deserve.*" Hortense grinned and tightened her grip.

"Dis is de end! We all gwarn to die! Dis storm worse dan 1907!" Kwarhterleg insisted, his eyes opened wide with panic. "Me live me life but it's de pickney me ah cry for. Oh Lord protect us! Serious t'ing dis wind!" He started to mumble the Lord's prayer.

"Kwarhterleg!" Amy scolded. "Stop ya noise an' stop scaring me pickney!"

Many shanty dwellers, who lived either side of the road through Claremont, could only stand and watch their wooden huts being collected and slammed into trees by the violent gales like a spoilt child throwing away his toys. They held on tight to their young and made their way down to Isaac's church where they found shelter.

Kingston was almost flattened, suffering thirty foot waves that smashed and breached the harbour front and covered the entire downtown area in three feet of sea-water. Small boats and yachts were reduced to timber scraps and a few cargo ships were damaged beyond repair. Those unlucky enough to have built their homes on the seafront could only watch their property break into pieces and dissolve into the raging, marble-coloured sea. At the apex of the hurricane, waves were smashing into the harbour every seven seconds. Those who were swept away near the harbour front couldn't tell whether it was the horizontal rain or a mighty wave that had claimed them. Ghetto dwellers watched their shanty homes being torn asunder and drifting and flying to all parts of Kingston. Many drowned. Scores were killed by cartwheeling, jagged sheets of corrugated zinc, shards of concrete and severed lumps of masonry. Five miles inland, in the hills of St Andrew where the well-heeled dwelled and drank afternoon tea, they woke up the next morning to discover that seaweed and the rubble that had laid upon the ocean bed was now dumped and scattered over their ruined lawns. The North coast fared no better. Many poor fishermen, who lived in barren huts beside the sea-front and who always parked their canoes on the golden beaches, had failed to seek adequate cover. A few of them were sandblasted to death, their nostrils and mouths filling with wet sand, cutting off their supply of oxygen. A state of emergency was declared.

Two mornings later, holding a pitch fork in his right hand and his feet sinking into the soil, Joseph stood still upon his land and surveyed the damage. In the surrounding hills, he could just make out odd figures searching for the timbers that had made up their blown-away house-fronts and walls or perhaps their kitchen roofs. Joseph took out Panama, stuffed it with tobacco and lit it with a match. Following his second toke, tears welled up in his eyes. He looked up to the clear, calm blue sky and muttered, "De poor always bear de harshest brunt. Yuh is ah cruel God."

Standing beside Joseph, Levi nodded his agreement. "Come, Joseph! We affe try an' drain away all de water. Come!"

His eyes defeated, Joseph turned to Levi. "Don't yuh affe look about ya place? Yuh know, fix it up an' rebuil' it?"

"Dat cyan wait. Besides, me be lucky if me cyan find one strip ah wood. Me hear dat even Misser DaCosta's Delco generator find itself being tossed inna de wind."

"Yes, me hear dat too. One heavy piece of somet'ing dat. Misser DaCosta finally find it inna de gulley. All mosh up. Now de people ah Claremont cyan't go up to Misser DaCosta plot an' lissen radio.

Ah shame. Becah even Amy an' Jenny did ah like to go up der an' lissen sermon broadcast from Kingston 'pon ah Sunday night. But at least Welton providing shelter fe de poor people who ah live up der... Me pass ah mon today who could nah bear to look 'pon de place where him place once stood. Him family der wid Isaac but dis mon, proud he is, don't know where to go. Me give him ah liccle money to buy ah Red Stripe. Me cry fe dem kind ah mon. Me cry fe everyt'ing. Massa God tek away me only son an' now him tek away me land. Me feel like joining dem whole heap ah mon who are travelling to Kingston to look fe work – any kind ah work."

"Not all ah dem forwarding to Kingston," said Levi. "Me sight ah few ah dem trekking up ah hillside. Dem say dem gwarn to plant ganga becah dat's all dem cyan do. Ganga grow quick an' rapid. Me cyan't really blame dem."

"Nuh, sa. Desperate time need desperate measure. Dem affe be careful though, becah de police burn down ah ganga field near ah Orange Valley ah while ago an' beat an' mosh up de cultivator dem."

Levi paused, for secretly he was wondering whether he should cultivate cannabis. He decided to change the subject. "Joseph, me will help yuh clear de water," he offered. "We cyan till de land once more an' plant new seed. Me know so if David alive him woulda help yuh, so me offer me labour."

Placing his right hand upon Levi's shoulder, Joseph squeezed it and managed a smile. "Isaac don't know him 'ave ah Godly son."

For six weeks, Levi and Joseph worked tirelessly from sun-up to sun-down. At first they forked the land, enabling the excess water to escape. When it was dry, employing the family donkey and a re-built plough, they grooved new channels for the seeds that were carefully placed. Levi always sang his favourite spiritual as they toiled. Following a few days of hard graft, Joseph joined him in song.

"We till de land an' plant we corn
We 'ave liccle res' from dust to dawn
Nuh slavemaster ah crack him whip every morn

Nuh back ah get lash an' nuh flesh ah torn
Like we forefader, teken from der land 'pon one African dawn
An' dey were set to work 'pon de white mon lawn
So we pray to de Most High to bless dis land
Cyan yuh bless de work of de humble black mon?
Fe too long we 'ave been under ah burden, an' we need ya mighty
hand
Mek we rise up an' tek we stance again
Blow away de heavy clouds an' de rains ah pain
Cyan't Yuh do dis fe we?
Fe de people still inna bondage, de mighty cutters ah ya cane
Mek we seed ah grow ripe an' sweet
Nuh let we forget we ancestors drum beat
Give strengt' to our bodies inna de blazing heat
Mek we. rise again an' take we seat
An' nuh let de tiredness ketch we bare blistered feet."

In the evenings, by the light of a kerosene light, they rebuilt Levi's home with wood, mortar and stone. During this time they only slept for four hours a night. Amy sensed a dogged, urgent determination in Joseph's eyes. In the little time he spent with his daughters, he asked them what they had learned at school. A first for him. Jenny immediately went into a long detailed description but Joseph cut her short, saying, "yuh two ah big woman now an de time will come when yuh affe look after ya parents instead of we looking after yuh. An' yuh will affe learn to be responsible fe we land."

"Papa, why yuh ah say dat?" Jenny asked. "Yuh don't reach old age yet an' ya back nuh ben' yet."

"Fate has strange t'ings in store fe we. Who knows wha' madness might bring tomorrow?"

"Me alright, Papa," Hortense grinned. "Jenny will look after me if Fate bring ah nex' badness. Besides, wha' cyan Massa God do to me now? *Him* tek away sweet David already."

Smiling, Joseph ruffled the hair of both his daughters before marching off to his plot of land. Hortense thought nothing of the conversation and returned to feeding the guinea fowl, but Jenny remained rooted to the spot until her father disappeared from her vision. She sensed a dark foreboding.

Even though Joseph slept little, Amy would sometimes wake up in the dead of the night and discover that Joseph wasn't beside her. She would find him in the kitchen, sometimes talking with Kwarhterleg but mostly smoking his pipe, staring ahead blankly, lost in some past terror that he dare not speak of. Amy put it down to David's passing, thinking that Joseph, like her, had a tortuous time getting over the tragedy.

As the first sproutings of the new corn leaves appeared upon Joseph's plot, he turned to Levi and said, "Levi. Me woulda never know wha' to do if yuh never did ah help me. Me will be t'ankful 'til me laid to res'. But now me gwarn ask yuh fe ah even mightier favor. Me hope yuh don't t'ink it's ah liberty me teking. But me affe ask becah me affe do somet'ing. Me nuh know how yuh gwarn to judge me but me mind made up. De time has come. Levi, come sit down, mon, so me cyan tell yuh me story so yuh understand. Wha' me tell yuh mus' never escape to ah nex' mon ears – especially ya fader Preacher Mon. It cyan't even escape to Kwarhterleg or even Amy's ears. Not yet anyhow. Me 'ave ah liccle rum fe yuh an' some tobacco. Mebbe ya wise head coulda understand de troubles inna me mad head."

Seven hours later, Amy was serving out a dinner of boiled beef, callaloo, yams, scallion and sweet potato. Carmesha was mashing the evening meal for Daniel as Hortense and Jenny waited patiently for their drinks of guava juice. For nearly a minute, Levi watched the family scene silently, remembering his own childhood. He saw his own mother in his memories. "Miss Amy! Miss Amy! Me affe talk wid yuh most urgent."

Amy presented her two daughters with their plates and told them to pour their own drinks. She walked over to Levi with a wooden ladle in her left hand. She looked beyond Levi. "Where Joseph?" she asked.

Levi shook his head.

"*Don't* tell me yuh don't know! Now tell me where him der! It's about time him spent more time wid him family!"

"Him gone," Levi answered. "Him gone to do somet'ing him shoulda do t'irty six years ago. Dat's all me know. Him did ah feel too guilty to tell de news fe himself. Him say one day him will come back but don't know when. An' also him did say him don't 'ave de strengt' to tell yuh himself de reason why. Like David did. Me sorry to tell yuh dis, Miss Amy."

Dropping the ladle, Amy crossed her arms and looked out to the southern hills. There she gazed for the next ten minutes as Levi explained to her that until Joseph's return, he would gladly work the land. Half an hour later Amy calmly told the rest of her immediate family what had occurred. Hortense rushed up to Levi. "Wha' yuh do wid me papa? Yuh kill him? Me never did ah trus' yuh! Blackheart mon yuh are blackheart mon! Move away from we house before me pick up rockstone an' fling it after yuh!"

Levi dropped his head, turned around and walked away. He knew there was no sense in trying to reason with Hortense at this time.

Meanwhile, Jenny, her composure intact, simply walked away into a nearby field where she sat down amid the long grass. There was a controlled expression upon her face, refusing to yield to any emotion. She began braiding her hair while humming a hymn. She only returned when the three-quartering moon was high in the sky. Amy was sipping coffee at the kitchen table, sitting beside Hortense. A dog was snoozing by her feet.

"Ya alright, Jenny?" Amy asked. "Me don't really know wha' we do to de Lord to mek Him t'row tribulation inna we face. Me really don't know."

Picking up a mango, Jenny took a small bite and gazed at her mother in such a way to make her feel uncomfortable. "David dead an' now Papa gone," she said calmly. "Me surprise dat yuh nuh gone wid him an' leave Hortense an' meself 'pon we own. Me an' Hortense are orphans now."

"Jenny! How coulda yuh say such ah t'ing?"

"Becah yuh care more about family reputation dan Hortense an' meself! Remember dem time Preacher Mon would give me licks inna church? Yuh jus' ah sit down an' say not'ing! Only when Papa ah lick Preacher Mon down him ah stop trouble me. Now Papa gone. As me see it only Hortense ah care fe me."

"Jenny, ya upset," said Amy, her eyes incredulous. "Yuh don't know wha' ya saying. Everybody's brain inna mangle an' mebbe when de sun shine inna de marnin we could t'ink more clearly. Why yuh don't gwarn to ya bed an' res' yaself? Everybody has had ah cruel day ah tribulation."

Displaying a perfect poise, Jenny eyed her mother coldly, like a boxer meeting his opponent for the first time at the weigh-in. "When de las' time yuh come ah school an' talk wid de teacher dem?" she asked. "When de las' time yuh kiss me goodnight? When de las' time yuh say t'ank yuh after Hortense an' meself strip corn fe yuh? Ya heart made of rockstone! Ya feelings cool like de water dat ah flow down up where Levi live. Ya eyes still only see David. Me cyan't remember yuh ever frying fe me an' Hortense Bluedraws an' yuh don't like we going to Gran'papa Neville. But David did enjoy all dem t'ings der wid ya blessing... It's like yuh never like breeding two daughter. Sometimes me t'ink me don't 'ave nuh mama."

Looking on wide-eyed, Hortense thought her mother would surely beat Jenny but Amy was too shocked to do so. Instead, Amy tutted, stood up and went to feed the guinea fowl, although she had fed them an hour previously. She secretly admitted to herself that David was her favourite. '*Love de bwai chile an' prepare de girl chile dem to love her mon*,' Amy recalled her father telling her when she was a teenager.

Offering her mother a dismissive glare, Jenny joined her sister at the table.

"Why ya start 'pon poor Mama?" Hortense asked.

"Me don't care wha' Levi affe say," answered Jenny. "Papa mus' ah run away becah Mama mus' ah do somet'ing to vex him."

"How yuh know dat?"

"Becah Papa don't even like laying down wid Mama. After de midnight hour me see Papa ah rise up an' go 'long to de kitchen where him ah spend de res' ah de night whispering wid

Kwarhterleg. So dey mus' ah been going t'rough some kinda contention."

"But yuh cyan't say dat fe true. Sometimes Papa behave inna him funny ways an' me see it dat if Papa gone fe good, den nuhbody ah push him out. Mebbe Mama was right dat ya upset an' don't know wha' ya saying. Well, she upset too. Ya t'ink dat all becah yuh never see eye-water 'pon Mama face dat she don't feel it?"

Biting another chunk of her mango, Jenny thought about it. Tears were forming in her eyes. "Now me know how yuh feel when David gone," she revealed. "Me jus' pray dat de Most High will nah offer sweet Papa de same fate."

Hortense took Jenny's face into her palms and kissed her upon the forehead. She then embraced her. Jenny was now crying uncontrollably, her tears dampening Hortense's frock. Amy looked on from the chicken coop, feeling helpless.

"Now it's just de two of we," sobbed Jenny. "We against everybody else. We cyan't rely 'pon nuhbody to love we. Nuh, Hortense! Better dat we jus' care fe each udder. Promise me dat yuh will be always standing beside me. *Promise* me!"

"Of course," whispered Hortense, not wanting her mother to hear. "Of course."

The next morning, Amy fried Bluedraws for everybody. As Jenny accepted her dish she kissed her mother formally on the left cheek in a gesture of sorrow. Her eyes expressed no emotion and Amy found Jenny's lips almost cold. Amy hugged her eldest daughter with the realisation that she couldn't remember the last time she had held Jenny in this manner. Her embrace wasn't returned and Jenny quickly walked away.

Over the following months Amy watched her daughters form an unbreakable bond. They walked to school arm in arm together and their school friends soon realised they only had time for each other. Hortense and Jenny maintained their daily visits to Neville, taking Daniel with them; sometimes Neville would ignore Jenny's and Hortense's presence and take Daniel for long walks into the fields, just as he had done for David when he was a child. Melody's Anancy story-tales no longer captivated Jenny, she was only interested in what Melody thought about her father and where he might have disappeared to. Although Jenny enjoyed her grandparents' company, she would refuse to stay over for the night when invited to do so. "Nuh, sa," she would protest. "If Papa come back inna de middle of de night me waan to mek sure me der to see him."

To Jenny's dismay, Hortense would happily accept sleeping over at Neville's and whenever she did so, Jenny would return home in a sulky mood and start rows with her mother on the slightest of whims.

During one early morning, comforting Hortense after a nightmare when she imagined Jenny being murdered and buried beside David, Neville hugged her close to his chest and said, "love is nah de one t'ing dat define de human condition. Nah, sa. For animals an' creatures cyan display love also. Nuh, Hortense. Wha' defines we is we reaction to ah love lost or ah love never felt. Yes, Hortense! From ah love lost or never experienced is bred vengeance, jealousy, rage, sorrow, guilt an' so many udder t'ings. One of de first sins was committed becah ah mon never felt he was loved. Me know yuh miss David but remember dis. Yuh would nah feel so much pain if he never loved yuh so greatly. So rejoice in dat fact. An' be kind to ya sister, for she don't know if she has lost her fader's love for ever or if it will come back. An' her soul will bruise from dat."

Wiping her tears away, Hortense asked, "why don't Papa love me like him love Jenny?"

Neville looked away from Hortense, as though he was remembering something from long ago. "De decision was made fe him by ah higher being. He had nuh choice. Yuh woulda affe understan' ya papa childhood to truly find de reason. But becah ya fader's love to Jenny was great, she will suffer now he's gone. Now go back to sleep."

When the sisters were at home together, they shared the cooking and washing duties. At night they sat up in bed whispering into each other's ears. They giggled at jokes in church and shared secrets to each other while strolling in the fields. They washed each other's hair in the river and journeyed home upon their donkey's back, Jenny always in front and Hortense clinging around her waist as she sang a song her grandfather taught her. If a school girl wanted to fight one of the Rodney sisters, and they often did, they also had to combat the other. Unable to tolerate taunts like, "ya papa must' ah gwarn to Old Screwface backyard!" and "David dead becah him fader de son of Jezebel!" no quarter was given. Hortense would often say before combat, "if ah blood appear den mek it run, if yuh 'ave ah piece of wood, den me will pick up rock, if yuh pick up rock, den me will find me gran'papa cutlass. Now, who waan come, come!"

Despite Amy having to explain her daughters' actions to irate parents, she thought Jenny's and Hortense's close attachment was a positive outcome, borne from testing family circumstances. But as she watched her daughters arrive home from school arm in arm, only to acknowledge Amy with a quick nod before they changed clothes and disappeared into the surrounding fields, Amy couldn't help feeling excluded.

Chapter Seven

Friday evening. The setting sun shone through the gaps of the far-off trees, creating amber rays that forced the people in Claremont market to squint. They were soothed by a freshening breeze that drifted off the Caribbean sea. The liquor bars that fringed the market square were soon full of thirsty men who had just returned from the fields, happy that their working week was over, happy they had work. They now wrapped their earth-soiled hands around warm bottles of beer and Dragon stout. Their women were at home, cooking the traditional Jamaican Friday supper of fish, ackee and ardough bread. Those who were well-booted sank shots of rum and pulled hard on foreign cigarettes that had recently become available: keen-eyed shanty girls would sometimes accept the offer of a drink from a man toking on an Embassy Filter.

The front of the post office was now blackened by the emissions of country buses. Three cars were parked outside the bakery, Mr DaCosta's dairy and Mrs Walters' dressmaking concern; she now had three sewing machines and had built a small extension to her home. Wide-eyed children peered through the windscreens. Recently married men constructed their new homes on the knolls above Claremont; many of them worked in the bauxite quarries twenty or so miles away, and shanty dwellers were still repairing or rebuilding theirs. Even Levi now had neighbours. Most of them grew marijuana for an income on any strip of land they could find up in the hazy hills. Stalks of sinsimilla could pay for a child to attend school for a month. The marketers saw new faces every day. There was now a bustle and a bangarang in the market square that the Claremont elders frowned upon; they especially disliked the Chinese family who were the proprietors of a new grocery shop near the market.

As the men drank, smoked their raw tobacco and played contentious games of domino, they watched the young women saunter by, and sometimes offered up their remarks. "Sweet girl inna de pink frock! Yuh waan to rinse an' clean me bamboo inna ya tunnel ah love? It will tek nuff time becah me bamboo long like fishermon rod an' broad like cedar trunk. But me 'ave nuff stamina!" The men's comments were answered swiftly with raucous put-downs and fierce finger-jabbing, questioning, amongst other things, the man's sexual technique, sexual orientation and who his real mother was. "Go away liccle bull-bottom-face bwai to ya strikin' plot! An' ask ya fake mama who ya real mama is an' beg Massa God fe ah nice girl to court wid! An' dutty rooster wid mosh-up claw an' mouldy feader is ya real papa but ya fake papa don't know!" These men rarely chanced their crude courting skills with Jenny, for they had learned from their embarrassing experiences with her sister, Hortense. Maybe Jenny has the same 'whip' tongue, they feared.

Now eighteen and as tall as most men, Jenny insisted on wearing one of her best frocks whenever she worked the family stall; her figure had filled out and she found it uncomfortable whenever a man presented her with amorous looks. She found it even more unsettling whenever a handsome man lavished her with praises. She loathed the bartering in the market, having to raise her voice to compete with the other vendors and higglers. But, as always, she kept her thoughts to herself, accepting her duties in her father's absence. Sometimes, Carmesha and Hortense relieved her, but Hortense, her skin not thick enough to absorb the whispered comments about her 'devil papa', cursed and offended many. Indeed, on two occasions, Levi and Jenny had to come down and rescue her from a beating. That should have been Papa's job, thought Jenny. She asked the question she had asked every day since he disappeared. How could he vanish jus' like dat? Me was his favourite. His liccle angel. Why has he done dis to me?

Carmesha and Hortense had grown close and whenever Hortense had the opportunity, she barraged Carmesha with questions about Kingston. "Do de people live mighty? How big are de ships dem? How many rooms do de white people 'ave in dem house? Wha' kind ah music dem lissen to? How do de young girl dem dance? How dem dress? Any black mon der rich an' drive big car? Yuh t'ink ah handsome, polish-booted Kingston mon would say me pretty?"

Travelling on the odd occasion to Kingston visiting relatives, Carmesha did her best not to paint an idealistic picture of Jamaica's capital. Kingston spat at the weak and laughed at the good-natured, Carmesha told Hortense many times. People live upon each other's toes in sprawling government yards. A dozen or more families had only the use of one source of water – a standpipe in the middle of the courtyard. These yards were built after the 1951 hurricane and Carmesha, upon visiting her uncle who lived in Jones Town, could not believe the concept of an inside kitchen. So unhygienic, she thought.

Running parallel to the yards was an open sewer system that even the stray goats baulked at. It was an ideal habitat for flies and mosquitoes. Barefooted children suffered from horrific foot disfigurements, caused by blood-loving, burrowing insects laying in wait upon the dusty lanes that networked downtown Kingston. Gangs of bad men walked up and down flashing their ratchet knives but even they kept their distance from the Kingston lunatics who at night spoke and quarrelled with the moon. Kingston wasn't a place for a nice country girl, Carmesha thought.

Not dissuaded by Carmesha's descriptions, Hortense would reply, "But it mus' be mighty exciting living inna Kingston. David survive it an' me waan to see it fe meself. Carmesha, nex' time yuh go ah Kingston, me beg yuh to tek me."

Ready to leave the market now after she had stuffed the notes in her drawers and placed the coins into her small, cowhide purse, Jenny heard someone calling her. "Angel! Angel!"

Turning around, Jenny saw that a young man was running up to her. He was wearing a white Fred Perry T-shirt, cream-coloured slacks and polished, brown brogues. A blue flannel was protruding loosely out of his back pocket, his 'sweat-rag'. His beer-dampened moustache was full but his sideburns and beard were wispy, not fully developed. He was sporting a brown, pork-pie hat with a black feather sticking out. He was tall and athletic with an easy smile but his eyes promised romance and an adventurous spirit. Behind him, two dogs were scrapping over spoiled green bananas.

"Yuh calling me?" Jenny asked, not impressed by the smell of beer, thinking this man was a cocksman.

"Do yuh see any udder pretty girl dat me coulda call?" replied the young man, displaying a clean row of teeth.

Giving her admirer a lingering eye-pass, Jenny had to admit the young man was handsome. Very handsome. But there would be rainbows in Old Screwface's domain before she told him this. "Who is yuh to call after me? Yuh t'ink me any bluefoot girl who tek off wid any mon? Yuh t'ink yuh coulda carry me off fe ah grine-ah-bush? If yuh come wid dat intention me will fling rockstone after yuh. *See* if me don't. An' me name is *not* Angel!"

"Cool ya temper, sister! Me only trying to be friendly. Me was jus' cooling wid ah Red Stripe an' me sight yuh ah sell food der ah market. An' me say to meself, Lord! Me sight ah pretty girl dis fine day! Me had to talk wid her. Me name Cilbert. Cilbert Huggins. Some mon call me Wire. Yuh cyan't tell me ya name?"

"Wha' for? We 'ave any business? Come outta me way becah me waan reach home. Me don't 'ave nuh time to chat wid strange mon looking to sweet-talk ah nice girl to de bush. Why yuh nah go down der ah hillside where dem bluefoot girl will grine any mon fe ah single red cent!"

"Bloodfire! Yuh nuh easy, sister!"

"*Don't* talk bad word to me!"

"Alright, alright. Cool yaself, sister. Look, me tell yuh wha'. Mek me buy some ah ya yam an' breadfruit an' give me some ah dem tomato too."

Catching Cilbert with a stern glare, Jenny warned, "yuh better give me de right money becah me nah give credit."

"Nuh worry yaself, sister."

"Me is *not* ya sister!" Jenny rebuked before handing over the vegetables.

"Alright," Cilbert winked, still flashing his molars. "We 'ave ah business now. Me one ah ya customer. So yuh cyan tell me ya name now?"

Almost succumbing to a smile, Jenny managed to stop herself. She felt her heart beating. He was devilishly beautiful, she admitted. And confident. The kind of man Preacher Mon raged against in his sermons about the temptations of the flesh before marriage. But Jenny wanted to learn more about her potential suitor. "Alright," she agreed. "If yuh promise yuh nuh boder me nuh more."

"Me promise," said Cilbert, thinking he was getting somewhere.

"Jenny," she revealed, accepting the cash.

"Well, dat is ah mighty fine name," returned Cilbert. "Look, Jenny. Misser DaCosta holding ah party tonight. It's him daughter, Elvira, birt'night. Music will be playing, yuh know, New Orleans jump-up music from de radio an' yuh coulda lissen to mon like Amos Milburn. Me wire Misser DaCosta radio so we cyan tune into dis station dat broadcast *direct* from de jump-up city. Dem play nuh boring Frank Sinatra or dem kinda boring singer white mon. So, Jenny, yuh waan escort me dis fine night?"

Her curiosity aroused, Jenny wanted to hear for herself what her peers had been talking excitedly about for months. But she thought she would invite gossip from the market higglers if she stepped to Mr DaCosta's with a stranger. And what would Hortense think? Maybe she wouldn't like it if she had a *bwai-frien'*. It would upset things. No matter how princely a man looked she would never let him come before her sister. *Nuh*, sa! "Do me look like de kinda girl dat tek off wid stranger wid ah blue-swee smile? Yuh only know me for two seconds an' yuh waan tek me out go rave? Me 'ave to know ya intentions first! Yuh know where me work so if yuh see me yuh see me!"

"Me not ah stranger nuh more," Cilbert protested. "Me one ah ya prize customer!"

"Yuh t'ink yuh cyan sweet me wid ya sugar-talk? Like sugar inna chocolate goat milk? Go 'long, mon, becah me don't 'ave nuh time to waste!"

Cilbert's confidence was waning and his face betrayed the injuries to his ego. "Alright, look, Jenny. Me sorry dat me charge in like hungry bull. At least allow me to help yuh push de cart. Dat t'ing look like ah mighty struggle fe ah fine girl to handle."

Jenny thought about it. Her legs were tired from standing up all day. "Alright. Yuh cyan walk wid me jus' ah liccle of de way. But *don't* get any ideas inna ya pants becah me nah 'fraid to fight any mon."

The broad smile returned to Cilbert's face. Jenny relinquished her hold on the cart and stood still with her arms crossed, waiting for Cilbert to take over. He flashed her a smile and started pushing. Jenny ambled beside him with a prissy grin. "So where yuh come from?" she asked, momentarily taking down her guard.

"Me family live ah Orange Valley, down below Walker's Wood," revealed Cilbert. "We're related to de DaCosta's 'pon me mudder side. Me training to be an electrician. Nex' year me gwarn to learn at de University ah de West Indies der ah Kingston; me sponsored by Misser DaCosta – ah good mon dat. Me cyan fix anyt'ing, Jenny. Any radio an' dem t'ing der. Me even fix Misser DaCosta generator after it get mosh up inna de fifty-one storm."

"So yuh know about wire! Yuh waan me to clap me hand?"

"Nuh, Jenny. Me jus' telling yuh wha' me do. Me 'ave nuff ambition. When me finish me learning me waan leave Jamaica, go ah England an' mek nuff money an' den come back an' buil' mighty house. Some mon say der is gold to be found inna de London streets."

"Me would *never* go ah foreign land. Me prefer to live de simple life an' help out me family. An' de only gold to be found is inna heaven."

Cilbert paused and stood up. "Yuh tell me dat all yuh waan' do wid ya life is to sell food ah market? An' push dutty cart?"

"Me papa buil' dat cart so *tek* back ya slander! An' me family don't strive fe de riches 'pon eart'. We jus' live simple, praising de Most High. Living off de land dat de Most High provide we."

Cilbert resumed shoving the cart; it proved difficult because of the wonky wheels. "But Jenny, our parents toil inna de land an' work dem finger to de bone to give we ah better life. So de least we cyan do is show nuff ambition."

Jenny thought of the strutting, cocksure men who always frequented the bars in town and who never attended church. "Ambition lead to vanity. Vanity lead to greed. Greed lead to sin an' sin lead to deat'."

"Yuh cyan't really mean dat," replied Cilbert. "Yuh talk like dem old preacher."

"Better to talk like old preacher dan talk like ah fool who crave material t'ings."

Regretting her last words, Jenny didn't mean to offend Cilbert – he seemed nice enough, she thought. But maybe not the marrying type. And even if he did ask for her hand, how could she leave for England and leave Hortense? How could she even consider marrying him? Hortense still needed her. But he was so damn handsome!

Jenny had been drilled at church not to seek riches and be glad to live off the land where she walked. Isaac had reinforced this message on his twice-weekly visits to her house, which had started with the disappearance of her father. Hortense would always run off when Isaac parked his donkey but Jenny didn't want to further embarrass her mother and listened to whatever Isaac preached to her.

Sensing that Jenny would not be an easy catch, Cilbert accepted defeat. "Jenny. It's been nice walking wid yuh an' getting to know yuh. But me affe gwarn to Misser DaCosta's an' help him set up t'ings fe de night. Mebbe we will see each udder again an' we cyan talk some more. Until dat time."

Cilbert waved, forcing a polite grin. Jenny wanted to smile and wave back but something stopped her from doing so. She watched him disappear over a hill and felt the gathering tempo from her heart. She rebuked herself for having carnal thoughts.

Reaching home fifteen minutes later, Jenny could smell the roasted mackerel and the steaming rice and ackee as she walked passed the kitchen; Hortense was seeing to the cooking with a sour expression upon her face. Kwarhterleg was aiding her, poised over the rice pot with gratings of coconut in his palm. "Afternoon, liccle

Jen," he greeted. "Afternoon, Kwarhterleg, Hortense," returned Jenny. Hortense shot her a grumpy look. Jenny avoided her sister, not in the mood for what her mother called Hortense's 'horse dead an' cow fat': the irrelevant details of her day. She should have been helping me in de market! Jenny thought. Leaving me all alone to deal wid all de shouting an' bangarang! She approached her mother who was unpegging clothes from the washing line. "Mama, ah good day fe selling. 'Pon Friday we mek as much money as de res' ah de week. But, Mama, sometime me cyan't tek de rudeness ah dem new people who now live ah Claremont. Ungodly dem ah ungodly! Yuh waan me to go up to Levi an' give him ah money?"

Now showing her exhaustion under her eyes and the lasting pain of a mother who has lost her first born, Amy smiled at her eldest daughter. "Nuh fret yaself, Jenny. Res' yaself. Carmesha already promised me she would go up to Levi. An' as fe de new people who talk wid nuh manners. Pay dem nuh mind. Dey don't know de ways of country living an' dey 'ave to learn manners."

Presenting Amy with the day's takings before entering the house to find her comb, Jenny then took the donkey's reins and led him into the nearby field to graze while she braided her own hair. She hummed her favourite hymn, trying to rid the sexual image of Cilbert from her mind.

Having just changed Daniel's undergarments, Carmesha passed her son into Amy's arms. "Yuh know," said Amy, peering at Jenny in the field. "Anyt'ing me ask her she don't complain. It seem she finally forget about her fader an' de contention she did ah give me liccle after dat. Levi used de donkey dis marnin but Jenny keep her mout' quiet. Me surely been blessed wid Jenny. But sometimes me wonder if she alright, yuh know. Me feel dat me affe tip-toe around her becah yuh never know when she vex. Me affe remember dat she did feel it de most when Joseph gone."

"Me did ah *feel* it too!" sniped Hortense from the kitchen. "An' stop chat behind me sister back!"

"An' me did ah feel it too!" interjected Kwarhterleg, his eyes lost in some memory of Joseph. "Serious t'ing!"

"Nuh trouble yaself, Mama," Carmesha replied, turning her

attention to Amy. "Jenny well ably. She sort out an' deal wid t'ings inna her own way. She 'ave ah wise head 'pon her shoulder."

Amy passed on some money to Carmesha. "Tell Levi dat him 'ave to grow more pepper. We running out. Me wonder wha' dat mon ah spend him money 'pon?"

"Him probably ah plant it," laughed Carmesha. Him coulda at least t'row away him smelly reg-jegs an' buy new pants! An' when me talk to him Levi talk back in riddles. Yuh woulda 'ave to be King Solomon to understand dat mon."

"Yes," Amy nodded. "But don't jest wid him! Yuh know, Levi come like ah saviour to we since Joseph gone an' lef', although him look like de reincarnation ah Medusa 'pon ah bad day. So never vex him. Always talk to him nice. Lord give me strengt'! To t'ink dat Preacher Mon papa used to warn me when me ah girl chile, 'beware of de blackheart mon becah dem 'ave serpents 'pon dem head an' dey look fe children to mek dem dead.' An' now de so-called blackheart mon ah help we. Why yuh don't find Levi ah pair ah Joseph pants?"

"Yes, ah good idea dat. But of course! Me know me affe talk sweet wid him. Me know dat, Mama. But sometime yuh don't wonder where him ah come from? Where him family ah der?"

Recalling the first months when Joseph appeared in her life, Amy offered Carmesha a knowing smile. "Jamaican *mon*!" she chuckled. "So damn secretive an' funny inna dem ways."

"Jamaican *women*," Kwarhterleg retorted. "So full ah talk dat de brain cyan't work an' reason. Massa God never tek him res' 'pon de sevent' day, him start work 'pon de vocals of de Jamaican women an' him *don't* finish 'til de patu dem hoot in de midnight hour. *Ha ha ha*! Serious t'ing."

The Rodney women looked upon Kwarhterleg with sideway glances and angled brows.

"Amy?" Carmesha called, dropping her tone, ignoring Kwarhterleg's histrionics. "It's been over two years since Joseph gone an' me affe say dat yuh seem to handle it well ably. Sometime ah nighttime me cry fe yuh when me sight yuh ah stan' up outside de yard an' look out down de road. Me know so it ah Joseph yuh look for. But most of de time it's like yuh behave like him never exist?"

Considering her reply, Amy looked out to the southern hills; her expression was blank. "Yuh know, Carmesha. From de day me marry dat mon me was 'fraid dat him would leave me one day. Jackie did ah always tell me so, but now she don't talk about it becah she t'ink me would box her down. An me would fe true! Me sister too free wid her opinion. Me papa keep quiet about de matter too; him know wha' is good fe him! Papa used to tell me somet'ing when me was ah girl chile. *Ya lose one, yuh gain one.* And dat is certainly true wid David an' Daniel. Carmesha, me papa love ya son it's ah shame! Him always begging me to bring Daniel to him. But anyway, de trut' ah de matter is dat me never feel dat bad when Joseph lef' an' gone. Me was expecting it. Of course me miss him but me don't 'ave nuh time to pine an' wail an' bare me teet' like hillside farmer who get up inna de marnin an' cyan't see nuh water inna him well. Water affe fetch. Dinner affe cook, corn need to be stripped. Work never stop. But yuh know, Joseph *will* come back. Me sure ah dat."

Facing Carmesha, Amy presented her with a warm smile. "Carmesha, me well glad me 'ave yuh to talk to, udderwise me feel dat me would be talking to de Blue Mahoe tree dem."

"Sometime yuh talk to de fowl," joked Hortense. "An' dem cyan't tek ya cuss-cuss neider!"

Carmesha laughed before entering the house to find a pair of Joseph's old cotton strides. She departed, leaving Amy staring in wonder at the southern ranges that were now looming, shapeless grey shadows in the oncoming Jamaican night. Kwarhterleg was still chuckling to himself.

Despite the night devouring the day, Levi was still toiling in the fields when Carmesha arrived. His mane of hair seemed to impede him as he bent his back, his fingers a blur as they worked the land. "Levi!" Carmesha called. "Levi!"

Levi stood up and turned around, offering a smile. He had to resist sexual thoughts as he looked at Carmesha. He couldn't remember the last time he had been with a woman and the emergence of Carmesha, Jenny, Hortense and even Amy in his life had sorely challenged his Nazarene oaths. He had asked himself many times if he was stubbornly refusing to 'be' and 'act' like a man with a man's faults and vices. Who was he to deny his manliness? While asleep in his lofty retreat he had frequently dreamed of having sex with them all.

"Levi. Me waan yuh to tek off ya dutty pants so me cyan wash dem down ah river. Here's ah pair ah Joseph old pants. Put dem on becah me cyan't tek ya smell an' every time me stan' up close to yuh me affe hold me nose tight like virgin holding on to her lover."

Mildly offended, for he had bathed himself in the river two nights ago, Levi yielded to Carmesha's orders without complaint. He pulled off his muddied, unlaced boots, then turned around so not to expose his genitals and whipped off his soiled, blue pants. He stood naked under the red-setting sun. Carmesha never saw his abashed face. She let her eyes feast on Levi's body. His calves were bunched and well defined. His thighs were honed from many years walking up to his hillside home, the hamstring muscles clearly formed in a perfectly set arch and the small details of his back muscles rippled whenever he performed the slightest moves.

"Levi, isn't it about time dat yuh come down from ya hillside an' live wid de living?" asked Carmesha.

"Nuh, Carmesha. Me content where me der. Living me life wid nature. Lissening to de Natural Mystic. Nature cyan't lie to me an' dat's where me get me fulfilment."

"Don't give me dat foolishness, Levi! Yuh know, Amy t'ink ya Godly but yuh know wha' me t'ink? Me t'ink ya 'fraid ah living wid de living! Of course, yuh 'ave it easy up here so. Yuh don't affe talk to anybody apart from we family. Yuh don't affe sell food ah market an' put up wid de higgler susu. Yuh jus' keep yaself to yaself. David had his beliefs but him never hide himself like yuh. Him never live like ah small island. Nuh, mon! Me don't t'ink ya Godly. Becah if yuh truly Godly den yuh will nah fear nuhbody susu talk an' live life nuh 'fraid ah scandal an' dem t'ing der. Yes, Levi. Yuh 'ave it easy. *We* 'ave to deal wid people, reason wid dem an' accept or try to ignore wha' people say about yuh. It's about time yuh defend yaself."

"Why should me affe defend meself? Argument an' contention is de devil's talk an' when mon come togeder dat's all dem do."

"Even Jesus Christ walk fe forty days inna de wilderness an' had to resist Old Screwface temptations, but him come back to de living," snapped Carmesha. "So, Levi. Sometime me wonder to meself if yuh too 'fraid to resist temptation if yuh live wid de living. Why yuh so 'fraid? Yuh t'ink dat if yuh live wid us dat yuh cyan't be so damn pure an' Godly? Mebbe yuh will find dat yuh jus' like any udder mon."

Finding himself nodding, Levi was unable to think of a retort. Carmesha, grinning triumphantly, approached him. "Why yuh tek dis family burden, Levi? Why? Becah yuh 'ave nuh obligation?"

Levi glanced at the spot where David was buried. "Becah when me hear dat David dead, me t'ought dat me was responsible. Him use to come to me fe guidance, yuh know, we used to reason an' talk. An' Carmesha, yuh say yaself dat de police kill him becah de locks 'pon his head. So me affe accept some part ah de responsibility fe David life. Me 'ave to honour him memory."

"Foolishness yuh ah talk!" sniped Carmesha. "David had his own mind. David do wha' him waan to do an' believe me, nuff mon try an' influence him wid dem talk but David formed him own opinions. So, Levi, yuh nah responsible fe anyt'ing! Understan' dat mon."

Levi could do nothing but nod again, thinking to himself that Carmesha was a mighty impressive woman. She walked up to him, offering his share of the takings. "Levi, wha' yuh do wid ya money?"

Levi shrugged. "Not'ing."

Now laughing, Carmesha turned and started down the hill. Levi watched her disappear into the coconut groves. His mind was forming a vision of making wild love to her under the palm fronds, tearing off her frock and running his hands over her generous breasts, rolling around on the grass, both of their naked bodies soiled by the dirt. "Yes," he admitted to himself. "Me not nuh Nazarene. Me jus' ah simple mon. Like any udder." He heard Carmesha shout. "Levi! Me forget to tell yuh, yuh affe plant some pepper! An' one more t'ing. De good book say dat mon affe multiply. Levi, yuh cyan't multiply wid scallion an' sweet potato! Until de nex' time, see yuh!"

Levi laughed but now felt more alone than ever, only the birdsong and the rustling of the leaves above his home to look forward to. He couldn't even read his books for the 1951 storm had washed them away. He hoped Carmesha would come up and see him tomorrow. He hoped one day he would live with her.

As Carmesha was returning home, glad that she had finally won a verbal battle over Levi, Jacob, Levi's brother, was nervously knocking on the door of the Rodney household. He was holding his black, felt stetson with both hands while shuffling his feet, trying his best to be presentable. Amy opened the door. Jacob bowed slightly, smiling. "Good night, Miss Amy," his words of greeting following the best polite Jamaican tradition. "I waan to ask ya permission if I coulda escort Jenny to Elvira's birt'night party up der ah Misser DaCosta."

Biting her lip to stem her humour, Amy replied. "Yes, of course. Me will jus' call her. Jenny! Jenny!"

Jenny came trudging to the door, looking disinterested. She was holding the family Bible in her right hand. Jacob bowed elegantly again. "Good night, Jenny. Mighty fine to see yuh dis fine night an' as ever, ya face shame de most elegant flower." A stifled laughter could be heard from a back room but Jacob continued. "Jenny, yuh remember me tell yuh las' Sunday inna church about Elvira's birt'night? Well, de day has come an' me here to escort yuh."

Jenny offered a false smile, running her eyes over Jacob who was soberly dressed in a blue suit and red tie. Not as dangerous as Cilbert, she concluded. No way near as handsome. Ah nice pleasant mon but dat is all. "Yes, me remember, Jacob. But me 'ave blister 'pon me foot from standing up ah market all week an' me well, well tired. Me was flattered dat yuh ask me an' if me coulda come me would. But me don't waan yuh to carry me home if me cyan't walk an' me don't waan to be nuh burden. Me sweet sister, Hortense, is looking after me. Liccle earlier she place some herb inna bowl full ah hot water to mek me soothe me foot dem. Mebbe de nex' time."

Amy presented Jenny with an accusatory glare as Jacob dropped his head. He placed his hat back upon his head and sighed. He was just about to say farewell when Hortense appeared at the door. "Yuh cyan't tek me?" she offered, smiling broadly, her eyes sparkling. "Me foot nuh bruise or blister. Besides, Jenny never love to dance. She woulda jus' sit down an' sip her box juice all meek an' quiet. So, Jacob, wha' yuh say?"

Sensing an argument might develop, Amy bid farewell to Jacob before leaving to tend to her grandson. Jenny scowled at Hortense with utter disdain before marching off. Hortense presented an anxious Jacob with another sexy grin that hit the target; Jacob inched backwards, staring at his feet. "I. I cyan't see nuh reason why I cyan't escort yuh. It. It would be ah pleasure, Hortense."

"Yes, it would," returned Hortense, quick as a flash. "Sorry about me sister, sometime she 'ave her funny ways. She always come back grumpy when she work alone in ah de market. An' she cyan't expect me to be wid her all de while. But, Jacob, yuh deserve dat me look me best dis fine night so me jus' gwarn to change. Soon come." She offered Jacob a wink as she about-turned. Jacob closed his eyes, anticipating a bad night ahead with *Fire Nettle*.

Hortense was dressed in a light blue, knee-length frock that she had bought from Mrs Walters; Amy negotiated a discount with the dressmaker that involved a sackful of yams, peppers and sweet potatoes. She offered Jacob her arm. Jacob, smiling nervously, accepted and led her uphill to Mr DaCosta's land through the pimento groves.

Although he had lost many of his livestock in the 1951 hurricane, Mr Welton DaCosta, who had learned from his father the science of selective breeding, had since prospered, selling his livestock not just in Claremont but to surrounding hamlets as well.

Mr DaCosta had built a two-room extension to his original six-room home and upon his wide verandah there were now four circular tables with striped blue and white umbrellas sprouting out of them; Mrs DaCosta gave afternoon teas following church on Sundays to the likes of Isaac and his wife and other well-booted folk. In the corner of the verandah stood a radiogram, its height challenging Mr DaCosta's tallest goat and its width similar to that of one of his brown cows. It was connected with a cable to a vibrating generator behind the house that was next to an outside kitchen with three hearths.

Thirty yards to the right of Mister DaCosta's home, underneath the shelter of water-coconut trees, sat the cockpit, ringed by corrugated sheets of metal and warped lengths of wood. Two squawking cocks were held aloft in the air by a red-skinned man; Welton DaCosta's son, Enrique. He invited a baying crowd of young men who had their hands raised clutching cash, to place their bets. Wagers were taken by Enrique's younger brother, Luis. The cocks were tossed into the pit, their claws reinforced with tacks, and fought each other under the light of kerosene lamps to wild cheers and curses.

In moon-shadowed clearings beyond the cockpit, men chanced their luck by rolling poker dice and those merry with fortune purchased cannabis and lambs bread from Mr Patterson's son, Samuel, who stealthily crept here and there, his eyes on the alert for any member of the DaCosta family. His customers rolled their herb in brown gummed paper and smoked it raw. Others watched perched in trees the proceedings of a domino tournament, played out on two tables by the left of the house next to Mr DaCosta's small pick-up truck. The contest was a sober affair with men stroking their chins as they flicked their eyes from the dominos that were played to those in their hands. Elders shouted out their advice freely and wasted no time in yelling their disapproval if they saw bad play. "Wha's ah matter wid yuh bwai? Yuh sure yuh ever attend school? Ya papa never give yuh any sense? Ya brain inna ya black bamboo?"

As they approached the party, Hortense and Jacob could hear the alley-cat piano play of Jelly Roll Morton sounding from the cranked-up radiogram that was broadcasting one of New Orleans' more lively radio stations. Young men and women were dancing deliriously upon the apron of hard ground in front of the verandah. Older men, their wide-brimmed hats concealing their silver-topped heads, slouched around eyeing the young women while toking raw tobacco. They complained that the Yankee DJ from New Orleans wasn't playing any blues or big band music.

Mr DaCosta's female kin were serving hot curried goat with rice, fish fritters, fried and heavily seasoned chicken legs, and the family rum punch that no outsider knew the recipe of. It was served in paper cups and its lethal effect was soon apparent judging by the unsure steps and silly grins of many guests. Red Stripe beer was piled in crates in a corner of the verandah and cool-looking men, crowned with pork-pie hats, sporting clipped moustaches and pulling on Craven A cigarettes, posed with two bottles between their fingers, sipping each in turn. Children ran here and there, sucking on sugar cane and lipping box juices, enjoying their freedom from parental control. The night air was filled with chat-up lines, put-downs, laughter and cussing, and, although many of the guests were dirt poor, nobody could party quite like them.

Intoxicated with the excitement before her, Hortense unwrapped her arm from Jacob's, ran up to where the rum punch was being served, downed a whole cupful in one take and before Jacob realised what had become of her, she proceeded to jig wildly to the liquor-house boogie-woogie of Kid Stormy Weather, hitching up her dress to give her legs more freedom. Men's heads turned immediately and as Jacob was asking for a beer, Hortense found herself being encircled by whistling, clapping men. She raised her dress to reveal her thighs, laughing as she did so, and this act was met with hollers of approval. A commercial break interrupted Hortense's energetic dancing and she was bombarded by offers of a drink. She opted for another cup of punch, downed in time to skip to Champion Jack Dupree. Jacob, his fears realised, caught sight of her and shook his head. Hortense's female peers, including Elvira, looked at her from the corners of their eyes in silent admiration and envy.

Greatly appreciating Hortense from his position next to the radiogram was Cilbert. His bottle of beer poised just below his mouth, his eyes refusing to blink as he blessed his eyes upon Hortense's dance moves. "Hey, Wire," a friend called him. "Yuh t'ink yuh coulda control dat. Lord bless me poor mama knee-bone! Wha' ah pretty, bamboo-stiffening sight!"

"Yes, mon, ah fine sight." Cilbert agreed licking his lips, not diverting his gaze. "Fe true! Ah great prize she is an' any mon who capture her heart would feel mighty wid her 'pon him arm."

An hour later, while Amos Milburn was complaining about '*Bad Bad Whiskey*', Cilbert saw Hortense slumped on a chair upon the verandah, fanning herself with a piece of cardboard. Cilbert asked his cousin to look after the radiogram and walked up to her. He put on his best blue-swee smile and adjusted the angle of his hat. His heart was pounding inside his chest and he couldn't remember ever feeling so nervous before 'fishing fe ah pretty girl'. "Me. Me been watching yuh dance fe de last hour an', er. Me. Me come to de conclusion dat yuh mus' dance professional like! Yuh mek de udder girl look like. Like dem 'ave splinter. Yes. Like dem 'ave splinter inna dem foot!"

Hortense laughed out loud while giving Cilbert a complete eye-pass, even craning her neck to check how his backside fitted his slacks. "Well, me hear better compliments dis fine night so before yuh talk to me once more, wash out ya mout' to clear out de goat-shit dat wrap around ya tongue! Yuh like ah rooster dat find ah small rockstone inna him mout' before him start sing to signal de marnin. Ha ha! Lord me God yuh mek me laugh."

Quickly turning around to see if any of his friends had witnessed his embarrassment, Cilbert smiled away his obvious shame. "Sorry. Sorry to boder yuh, sister. Me. Me jus' did ah waan to applaud yuh on ya fine dancing." He was about to return to the radiogram while thinking up excuses to tell his friends.

"Where yuh go!" barked Hortense. "Yuh give up so easily? Yuh sen' out one fishing line an' me mek ya feel shame so yuh go 'long an' lef' me? Bring me ah drink an' come mon an' loosen ya tongue! Don't give me nuh half-full cup. An' clean off de sweat 'pon ya forehead."

Unsure if he could handle Hortense's jousting and remembering his failure with Jenny, Cilbert paused momentarily, thinking of further possible injuries to his ego. He looked at her again, losing himself in her eyes and decided she was worth the risk.

"Give me some ah dat rum punch," Hortense ordered. "An' nuh worry yaself. Me don't bite."

On his way to fetch the drinks, Cilbert gave a thumbs-up sign to his friends. Upon his return, he found Jacob sitting beside Hortense. "Er, excuse me, sa," he addressed Jacob, his excitement of the chase checked. "Me don't waan to intrude. Me jus' ah bring drink fe de young lady."

Jacob, who wanted to depart the riotous party as soon as Hortense was ready, looked bewildered. "Nuh, mon," Hortense replied. "Me nah wid him. Let me introduce yuh. Dis is Jacob, ah mighty fine mon. Yuh don't know him? He's de son of Isaac, de preacher mon who wag him tail at anyt'ing inna frock. But Jacob nah like dat. Him love off me sweet sister very deeply but she don't know wha' is good fe her."

Cilbert gave Hortense her drink and pulled up a chair to sit beside her. He tipped his hat in greeting Jacob and the preacher's son wished for a hole to appear in the verandah floor and swallow him. "So, does loveliness 'ave ah name?" Cilbert asked, displaying a clean row of front teeth.

Before Hortense could answer, a young woman marched up to Cilbert, hands on her hips, her fury obvious.

"Almyna!" Cilbert called, his eye-brows rising near to his hair-line. "Wha'? Wha' yuh doing here?"

Almyna leaned towards Cilbert, nearly headbutting him. "Ah surprise, Cilbert! Me come all de way from Orange Valley wid me sister, Myrna, fe ya benefit, an' when me reach me find me very mon ah carry drink fe ah nex' girl! Me don't even get ah welcome!"

"Almyna. Me jus' serving drink. Dat is all. Cool ya fire!"

Hortense ran her eyes over Almyna and saw that she was indeed pretty. But she had never liked the '*I'm better than you ways*' of 'red-skin' women, so she offered Almyna an evil look. She then turned her attention to Cilbert, giving him a fabulous smile. "Well, Cilbert. If yuh was *my* mon me would always keep yuh in sight. T'ank yuh kindly fe bringing me drink. Enjoy de res' ah de night! Mebbe we will meet again under de sweet moon one night?"

Almyna glared at Cilbert and he ushered her away with sweet words and poured her some rum punch. She didn't see Hortense's eyes following her. "Red skin bitch!" Hortense muttered under her breath. "Yuh t'ink ya so nice. Well, me nicer! An' me don't 'ave nuh white mon blood to stain me. Me gwarn tek away ya mon!"

An hour later, Jacob was walking Hortense home. The crickets and cicadas were in full cry and the stars shone brightly above their heads. Two roosters, whose internal alarm clocks had gone awry, could be heard in the distance announcing the morning five hours early. The breeze had gone and the land was still. The formless shadows towards the horizon were now at an unguessable distance but the invisible Natural Mystic remained, a feeling and a presence that Jacob and Hortense could both sense. It was soothing for the soul and they believed it protected them from Old Screwface whenever the sun took its rest.

"T'ank yuh, Jacob fe teking me out dis fine night," Hortense said. "Yuh know, me realise me full ah nettle an' fire but sometime me feel dat me life ah nah go nuhwhere. Y'understand?"

"Yes, I understand. Claremont don't 'ave too much to offer. But as fe meself my family been inna de service of de Most High fe generations. An' I feel it is my duty to serve de people who live an' work 'pon dis land."

"Dat is admirable," replied Hortense. "But yuh don't waan ah life fe yaself? Dat's wha' me always tell Mama, me waan to live me own life, yuh know. Go far away from Claremont an' let me kidren see somet'ing different to de far-off mountain an' plenty, plenty tree. Me know people ah susu behind me back an' say Hortense too wild an' Hortense mout' too labba labba. Even Jenny sometime tell me to quiet me mout'. But me jus' letting off frustration, yuh know. Dem expect ah young girl to praise de Lord every day, do dem chores an' be polite to we elder. But it seem to dem dat ah young girl cyan't have fun. Me love her dearly, but even if me try me coulda never be like me sister. We're too different. We 'ave been very close but she cyan't understand dat me need me space, yuh know, live me own life."

Jacob paused, forming an image of a smiling Jenny in his mind.

Hortense read his thoughts. "Yuh really love her, isn't it? Nuh worry yaself, Jacob. In time you'll win her love. Me know Jenny. She 'ave plenty fire inna her belly an' she full of emotion. She like one ah dem new fizzy drink can dat's been shaken. Storm ah grow inside de can but de outside remain cool. She still dealing wid Papa disappearance an' even Mama don't know how much she really feel it. Mama don't know many t'ings about me an' me sister. When nuhbody about apart from me, she talk about Papa all de while. Yuh see, she 'fraid of ah mon bruising her heart once more. Y'understand? Give her time an' ya devotion will be paid in full. But yuh affe realise dat her waters run deep like lake wid nuh bottom."

"Yes, Hortense. Yuh well fiery but yuh cyan read my mind. Jenny tek my heart fe ah long time now but I never know wha' she t'inking becah she don't say too much."

"She don't even say too much to her own mudder but believe me, deep down she respect yuh an' *will* love yuh. Me promise yuh dat."

"Don't yuh miss ya papa?" asked Jacob.

Hortense paused, her eyes staring blankly ahead. "Papa never love me. Me don't know why. Me gran'papa say him have nuh choice. So me learn to deal wid it. It's funny, yuh know. Jenny t'ink dat Mama never love her an' me t'ink Papa never love me, but me nah worry about it nuh more. Yuh see, me still miss David. It's David me talk to inna me prayers. He was de only one who me really an' truly love." Hortense trailed off, her expression betraying her loss. "It's David foot dat me waan to follow. *Not* Papa or Mama."

Fifty yards ahead, Hortense and Jacob both saw a figure standing outside the family home. It was Amy, standing still with arms crossed, peering down the road. Hortense went up to her. "Mama? Yuh nuh tired yet?"

Producing a welcoming smile, Amy ignored Hortense's question. "Yuh 'ave ah good time? Jacob, t'anks fe escorting me daughter home. Me sure Jenny's foot will heal an' nex' time she cyan go sporting wid yuh."

Hortense turned to Jacob. "Well, t'ank yuh again. Me gone to me bed now. Don't let de bugaboo bite yuh 'pon ya way home an' *don't* give up 'pon me sweet sister."

Hortense went inside. "Yuh don't 'ave to trod home yuh know, Jacob," Amy said. "Yuh cyan stay wid us fe de night. Me will mek up ah bed fe yuh inna de store-room."

"Nuh, Miss Amy. I'm nah 'fraid of de dark like my papa an' him generation. T'ank yuh fe de offer. But I affe look about me papa business inna de marnin an' I waan ah early start. Goodnight, Miss Amy."

Watching Jacob disappear into the night, Amy thought he would make a fine son-in-law. When he was out of sight, Amy poured a little rum in a mug and sprinkled it over the threshold of her home. "Old Screwface," she smiled. "Me don't know why yuh ah wait an' loiter becah me will *never* forget."

Then she returned to her vigil of peering down the road, her arms crossed.

Chapter Eight

Six days after Elvira's birthday party. Hortense had volunteered to work the family stall all week – much to Jenny's surprise, for in the past she had always described it as 'work fe woman who cyan't find nuh mon'. Jenny was glad to take a break from the market and busied herself helping out her mother while hoping to see Cilbert at church the coming Sunday; Amy noted Jenny's new obsession in how her mother met her father and how he courted her. At last! Amy thought, a thawing of their relationship. "Me eldest daughter come back to me," she whispered at night before sleep claimed her.

Jenny had dreamed of Cilbert every night since she met him and at quiet moments prayed to God, pleading forgiveness for her fleshly desires. It was the only intimate secret she had kept from her sister. He would surely come to church if him waan to claim me heart, Jenny thought. Mebbe he would ask Mama fe permission to tek me out? Hortense had none of her sister's qualms, however. So one morning, when she saw Cilbert walking through the market carrying a broken transistor radio, she hailed him. "Wire! Wire!"

Recognising the battered cart, Cilbert realised that Jenny and Hortense were sisters. "Ya red skin girl ah still pull ya rope?" Hortense opened with, pushing out her chest, striking a pose like a Kingston madam.

"Nuh, Hortense," Cilbert strongly denied, disliking the jest. "She jus' ah girl who me grow up local wid, yuh know. Mebbe she t'ink we 'ave ah future togeder."

"Is dat so?" asked Hortense. "Almyna too maaga anyhow. She don't 'ave chile-bearing hips an' she waan put chain 'pon ya ankle. An' her eyes are full of deceit. Remember dis, Cilbert, de blacker de plum de sweeter de juice." Hortense flashed Cilbert a sexy smile so he could be in no doubt of her meaning.

Two days later, they arranged a liaison in an isolated spot near

Crab Foot Gully; a patch of narrow sloping land that ran parallel to a dry, clay gulley where the grass grew long and the crickets multiplied. Under the leaves of a Blue Mahoe, lust overcame Cilbert as Hortense allowed him to paw and suck her breasts, his hands sliding over her toned midriff before diving between her legs. Titillation overcoming him, his fingers intruded under her knickers. Hortense slapped Cilbert's face, abruptly stood up and adjusted her under-garments. With a sideways grin, she commented. "Ya hungry! An' mighty *firm*. But me have me family reputation to t'ink about! Yuh nuh know me's an innocent Christian girl?"

They next met in secret after Sunday church; Jenny was desperately scanning the flock for Cilbert, wondering when she would see him again, while Jacob was staring at her, distracted from his altar-boy duties. Hortense, who knew Cilbert would be waiting for her in a jackfruit grove half a mile away, sang her heart out. This time Hortense allowed Cilbert to pull her drawers off and, as she moaned with pleasure as he stroked her crotch, he wondered if indeed she was a virgin as she claimed to be. Sensing her excitement as well as his own, he mounted and prepared to enter her. Hortense punched him, man-like, in the forehead, causing a welt to appear over her suitor's left eyebrow. "Wha' kind ah girl yuh t'ink me is? Me know so yuh 'ave one woman already an' yuh waan to grine me! Nex' time dat red piece ah shit, Almyna, come up to see yuh from de wild bush she ah live, tell her yuh *done* wid her. Sen' her back to her liccle shanty hut where de fowl neck are scraggy, de dahg dem maaga an' de women 'ave tough toe like tree root!"

Hastily pulling on her clothes, Hortense marched off cursing Almyna's very existence, leaving Cilbert still aroused. He shook his head as he watched her leave. "Mon! Wha' ah blasted nettle ah tease but me affe grine her even if it kill me! Yes sa."

On her next weekend visit to Cilbert, who was lodging with Mr DaCosta's family, Almyna learned that Cilbert harboured no plans for them to get married. She cussed him for giving her promises and taking her virginity, but Cilbert, fazed only by the prospect of making full love to Hortense, ignored her shrieks and pleas and flailing arms. He offered to walk her to the bus stop. Almyna walked daintily with her head held high as if she was born from aristocratic stock, but the curses that spewed from her mouth betrayed her poise.

Cilbert, embarrassed whenever a passer-by offered disapproving glances, looked upon Almyna with wearisome eyes. "Almyna, t'ings change from we parents time. Ah mon don't affe marry de girl nex' door or de girl him ah first court wid. Ah mon now cyan marry anyone him please – even if him parents don't give dem blessing."

"Cilbert! Ya words were different when yuh tek me virginity," stormed Almyna. "Yuh don't remember how yuh feel so sweet when yuh push yaself inside me? Yuh forget how yuh kiss me behind an' all over? Saying yuh been to heaven. Becah ah yuh, me affe lie to me papa, who ah wonder if me having 'relations' wid yuh. Everybody inna we village pass dem remark how we look so nice togeder. How me gwarn to tell dem dat we bruk up? Cilbert, yuh mek me look like ah damn fool an' me know wha' some ah me girl friends will say. Dey will say dat Almyna gwarn to be ah chileless mule! Me nineteen now an' still nuh marry! So don't try to sweet me wid any words becah yuh spoil me life fe true."

"But Almyna, ya still very pretty an' nuff black mon me know go fe ah red skin girl. So me cyan't see nuh problem ketching ah nex' mon. It's jus' dat me nuh ready to settle down jus' yet."

"Mebbe me shoulda stick to me own complexion!" Almyna roared, aiming to injure Cilbert's self esteem. "Me nuh know why me ever tek up wid yuh! How cyan yuh treat me so? De blacker de mon de more uncivilise dey behave wid woman. Dey don't possess manners an' respect. Dat is wha' me gran'mama used to say an' me shoulda lissen to she more keenly when me grow. Me cyan't believe ah *black* mon refuse me!"

The cursing never stopped until Almyna had informed everybody in her village of Cilbert's refusal to marry her. She secretly regretted not becoming pregnant and trapping Cilbert but she had always shoved Cilbert off her as he was about to climax, fearful of what her father and other villagers would say if she had fallen pregnant before marriage.

Mr DaCosta, counselling his young relative, asked Cilbert, "Hortense, 'ave yuh by ya seedbag an' madness ah claim yuh wid dis girl. Yuh sure yuh mek de right choice?"

Cilbert paused before answering. "Yes, me sure, uncle. She different from Almyna. She 'ave ah fire. She only follow her own mind. She never tek nuh shit from anyone. Me love de way she walk! We both waan ah betterness in we life. We both waan to move on from de country, start afresh somewhere else. An' she is de prettiest girl me ever see. Wid Almyna, becah of her red skin, me always feel...below her, yuh know. Like she done me ah privilege by courting wid me. Her family? Dey used to look 'pon me wid de corner ah dem eye. Sometime me used to t'ink dat me woulda be better off if me tek me mudder's complexion. Wid Hortense me is her equal; me nuh feel inferior. Yes, sa, she is de one."

A week later, Hortense invited Cilbert for Sunday dinner. She had risen early and swept out the front and back yards. She cleaned out the chicken coop and even sponged down the walls of the house as she sang gospel hymns. Jenny watched her suspiciously. Amy's eyes followed Hortense with a smile, glad to hear song around the house once more. Realising it was a big day for her youngest daughter, Amy bought a goat from Mr DaCosta – he offered it to her at quarter price following Amy's gift of prize pumpkins, avocados and all the scallion she could carry. Hortense, only thinking of Cilbert, ignored the stares from her family and put on her best dress for church.

Jacob conducted the service on this day as his father was ill. His eyes kept seeking out Jenny but she only responded with a listlessness that he couldn't understand. Her mouth kept firmly closed at the singing of hymns and it seemed that Jenny couldn't drag her eyes from the floor. Meanwhile, Hortense sang with vigour and heart, impressing the elders. Upon the return home, Amy scolded Jenny for her indifference. "Sorry, Mama," Jenny said in her defence. "Me don't feel too well today an' me t'roat ah liccle dry. Me never mean to embarrass yuh, Mama. Me mek sure it don't happen again."

"Yuh shoulda say somet'ing!" replied Amy, looking concerned.

"Me will boil up some ginger an' lime when we reach home."

"T'ank yuh, Mama. Dat would be Godly. Yuh know, Hortense woulda usually do dis t'ing fe me an' look out fe me when me sick. But she too wrap up wid dat cocksman, Cilbert. By de sound ah him me don't trus' him, Mama. Me hear some wild stories about dis Cilbert. Some say him 'ave woman here an' der. Mama, yuh sure yuh waan give ya blessing to Hortense an' Cilbert relationship? Sweet Hortense is fragile an' me don't t'ink she could ah cope if ah mon bruise her heart. She still missing David so she vulnerable. If somet'ing go wrong wid dem it will be *me* who would 'ave to repair Hortense's loving heart."

"Well, him coming today so we cyan all check out him intention."

Dressed in a grey hand-me-down suit and a brown stetson that he had borrowed from Mr DaCosta, Cilbert arrived at the Rodney home at four o'clock in the afternoon. He was bearing a gift of a bottle of finest Appleton's rum; Amy was quick to mix the spirit with goat's milk and shared it out to all in mugs, Kwarhterleg hobbling in assistance.

"T'ank yuh, Miss Amy, fe inviting me 'pon dis fine Sunday afternoon," began Cilbert, wary of the dogs who were yapping around his ankles. "It's an honour to be here."

Amy collected Cilbert's hat and hung it up inside the house. Hortense was strangely subdued as she introduced Cilbert to her family. Cilbert tensed up as he proffered his hand to greet Jenny. "Hortense, wha' ah fine looking family yuh come from. An' dis is Jenny? Mighty fine to meet yuh, Jenny."

Cilbert was unable to meet Jenny's eyes but Jenny herself smiled warmly. "An' mighty fine to meet yuh too. Hortense ah me younger sister so if yuh don't look after her right yuh will 'ave *me* to answer to!"

For a stretched second there was a certain tension in the air but it faded when Jenny laughed. "Cilbert," Jenny chuckled. "If yuh gwarn to be wid ah Rodney woman den yuh mus' learn to tek joke!"

"Me will drink to dat," interjected Kwarhterleg, raising his mugful of rum, wondering if a top-up would be permitted.

"Cilbert, yuh 'ave any cigarette yuh cyan give me?"

"Yes, of course."

Cilbert went over to Kwarhterleg and gave him two cigarettes. Kwarhterleg was eager to chat to Cilbert for a while for since Joseph's departure he had been denied conversations with fellow men; Levi would only drop by for a few minutes. Hortense went to assist Carmesha with the cooking while Jenny, no eyes upon her, shot baleful glances in her sister's direction, her breathing becoming heavier.

Managing to compose herself by the time the family had settled down to dinner, Jenny indeed proved to be the perfect hostess, serving drinks and food to everybody with a ready smile. Cilbert talked of his ambitions and dreams. Hortense grinned girlishly beside him, laughing at his jokes. "Yes, sa, me soon off to de big city, learn me trade, an' wid Hortense by me side, live ah good life."

Amy and Carmesha responded by clapping their hands and embracing Hortense. They assumed that they had just heard a clumsy proposal. Jenny stood up and complained of an upset stomach. She excused herself and walked rather theatrically to the pit toilet where she remained for half an hour.

During Jenny's absence, Levi arrived on the family donkey. He was wearing Joseph's old clothes that were much too big for him and the family tried hard to stifle their laughter, save Hortense who collapsed in giggles. "Sorry me late," Levi said. "Me hope dat some dinner still lef'. Me bless yuh all 'pon dis fine day."

Securing the donkey's reins to a post, Levi then went to greet everybody at the dinner table; Cilbert regarded him with unblinking eyes. "Carmesha," Levi said. "Cyan me jus' steal yuh fe ah minute. Ah delicate t'ing me wish to discuss wid yuh."

"Carmesha!" Hortense laughed. "Ya wild mon finally find courage."

"Hortense! Quiet ya mout'," Amy rebuked.

Blushing, Carmesha walked away with Levi to a nearby field. "Wha' about ya dinner!" Amy called.

"Me will soon come fe it," returned Levi who was fishing in his pockets.

His left hand emerged with a beautifully carved wooden hair clip that had the image of a Doctor Bird engraved on it. Shyly, he looked into Carmesha's eyes. "Fe yuh, Carmesha. Fe many t'ings yuh do fe me."

Accepting the gift, Carmesha pressed it to her chest. "T'ank yuh, Levi. Me will treasure dis."

Smiling, Levi said, "yuh always accuse me of talking in riddles. Well, dis nah nuh riddle. Me waan to live like ah mon. Becah me is ah mon first before anyt'ing else. Y'understand?"

Nodding, Carmesha grinned broadly.

"After me 'ave me dinner," Levi continued. "Me waan to show yuh de place where me live. It beautiful up der. An' ya presence will mek it complete."

Fixing the hairclip into her hair, Carmesha replied, "only if yuh fry me some grunt fish fe ah late night supper."

Looking on from fifty yards away, Amy remarked, "dis romantic t'ing mus' be ketching!"

Three hours later, Kwarhterleg was smoking his pipe under his favourite tree. He was peering into the heavens, reflecting on some long-held memory. He couldn't make out Cilbert and Hortense's whispered conversations, who were thirty yards away in a field, snuggled up to each other. They too studied the star-lit sky, thinking of their futures.

"Cilbert," Hortense called affectionately. "Yuh really mean wha' yuh say today? Dat yuh waan we to live togeder side by side? As mon an' wife?"

"Of course! But me affe go ah Kingston an' study fe de nex' t'ree years. Me 'ave family inna Papine me cyan stay wid. Den when me get me papers we cyan invite everybody an' get marry."

"Me don't waan to wait dat long! Nuh, sa! Me waan to get married *now*. Who knows wha' might happen to yuh while yuh study inna Kingston. Anoder red skin bitch might tek ya fancy an' yuh will forget about me! An' look 'pon poor Carmesha! She was waiting fe de day to marry me sweet brudder, David. But dutty police batter an' kill him fe not'ing inna stone cell. Nuh, mon. Yuh better mek me ah honest woman *now* or forget de whole damn t'ing!"

Cilbert pulled Hortense back to him and reassured her by stroking her face. "Hortense! As if me could look fe anoder when me 'ave yuh. Nuh boder yaself! T'ings will work out jus' fine. Me will come back to Claremont every weekend to see yuh. An' also me will come back when me der 'pon vacation. Den, when me get me trade papers we cyan 'ave ah big wedding an' set up home somewhere nice. Or even go ah foreign land. Yes, sa. *England.*"

Wrestling herself free, Hortense stood up and placed her hands on her hips. "*Nuh.* Dat cyan't go so! Yuh nuh lissen to me when me talk about David?"

"Yes, Hortense, me understan' ya tribulation but me promise it will nah strike again."

"Cilbert! *Don't* tempt de will of de Most High. Who knows wha' him 'ave in store fe we. Marry me now before fate come down crushing 'pon we!"

As Cilbert walked back to the DaCosta home that night, he pondered Hortense's sudden display of vulnerability. He took it as a good sign, reasoning that she needed commitment. It had also dampened his own fears, for he dreaded that while he might be away studying in Kingston, a well-booted man could take Hortense's fancy. It had been a great worry, especially as Cilbert had yet to make full love to Hortense. He recalled his father saying to him once, "yuh cyan never be sure of ah woman's love 'til ya mek her sweet wid ah mighty climax an' de moon juices run like plenty, plenty rain filling dry gulley. When yuh give dat pleasure to her, she will nah look anoder. Fe true!"

Reaching the DaCosta home, Cilbert roused his uncle from sleep. He poured a rum for his uncle and himself and offered him a cigarette. They sat in chairs upon the verandah, listening to the eerie and mysterious sounds of the Jamaican night and peering into the blackness. Cilbert emptied half his mug in one gulp. He grimaced from the burning sensation he felt in his throat and then announced cheerfully, "me an' Hortense gwarn to marry inna de nex' few weeks." Cilbert's smile had never been so broad and his eyes sparkled with excitement. "Cyan yuh believe dat? Me gwarn to marry de prettiest girl ah Claremont."

Mr DaCosta, his eyes not fully open, replied, "de prettiest an' de loudest."

Early next morning, Jenny was washing the family clothes in the river. She came across the light blue frock that Hortense had worn to Elvira's birth-night party. She held it to her chest and closed her eyes. She imagined Cilbert forcing himself upon her, pulling at her clothes. She managed to free herself and was running through a mango grove, trying to escape. But Cilbert's pursuit was swift. He caught up with her and tore off her frock, exposing her breasts. Jenny fought him off ferociously but when his hand slid down and pressed upon her crotch, Jenny yielded, allowing Cilbert to do whatever he wanted. Her flesh was screaming with excitement as Cilbert roughly palmed her genitals, breasts and buttocks. He forcibly pushed her down upon the ground and Jenny felt the soil grazing her stomach. Jenny then felt Cilbert's manhood penetrating her, a powerful thrust that resonated throughout her body. A weird, excruciating pain but deeply pleasurable. She wrapped her legs around his waist, urging him on.

Opening her eyes, Jenny saw that she was still holding Hortense's dress and in a fit of pique, ripped it from the collar to the sleeve. Seconds later, she offered a quick prayer to God, asking for His forgiveness.

Riding the family donkey home, Jenny thought of explanations for what had happened to Hortense's dress. Hortense was absently feeding the guinea fowl when her sister returned, humming some hymn. "Hortense! Hortense!" Jenny hailed mournfully. "Tribulation ah strike me today! Me cyan't believe wha' happen."

Ignoring the frenzied feeding in front of her, Hortense replied, "wha'? Ah tall fine strange mon bid yuh good marnin? Donkey ah shrug yuh off becah yuh nah rinse ya armpit? De sex crazy one-eyed bull inna Misser Dawkins plot mistake yuh fe cow?"

"Nuh. Me was scrubbing ya favourite dress an' all of ah sudden it jus' tear up. Me cyan understand it. Mrs Walters mus' ah made some kind ah mistake. Me very sorry. It jus' tear up jus' like dat."

Suspicion upon her face, Hortense walked towards Jenny. Jenny dismounted from the donkey and went to look for the washing line to hang the clothes upon. Hortense caught up with her just outside the storage room. "Wha' yuh mean it jus' tear up?"

"Me cyan't explain it! Mebbe de stitches were loose or somet'ing like dat. It jus' come apart."

Hortense went to retrieve the dress. She studied it like a juror scrutinising a murder weapon. She found that the dress wasn't just torn or coming loose from the stitching. "*Lie* yuh ah tell, Jenny! Me bes' dress! An' yuh tear it up to spite me about somet'ing. Mebbe becah me look so *nice* inna it. Mebbe becah me don't spend so much time wid yuh nowadays."

"*Hortense*! How yuh coulda say such ah t'ing?"

Hortense threw the frock down to the ground in disgust. "Why yuh tear up me dress? *Tell* me before me strike yuh down as de Most High is me witness!"

"Me *nah* tell nuh lie! Mek de Lord strike me down if me nuh tell de trut'! It jus' come apart as me washing..."

Before Jenny could finish her sentence, Hortense clenched her right fist and swung a right hook that connected with Jenny's left cheek, knocking her to the ground. Chickens scattered and the dogs began barking. Fine dust scattered in the air as Jenny found herself sprawling on the dirt. Hortense sprang and straddled her sister's back, proceeding repeatedly to cuff the back of Jenny's head, forcing her to taste the dry earth. Reacting ferociously, Jenny, with a mighty shrug, managed to force the heavier built Hortense off her and began to kick her about the head.

Hortense spread her palms across her face to protect herself, not quite believing the intensity of Jenny's assault; in their previous fights Jenny had always been the first to cry off complaining to Amy that Hortense had been too rough. The kicking had paused, enabling Hortense to peer through her fingers. Her eyes widened in fear of what she saw next. Jenny had picked up three stones and with an untamed rage, ran up to Hortense and hurled one. It struck at the small of Hortense's back. Hortense grimaced and writhed in pain, trying to scramble away for Jenny was readying herself to hurl another missile, levering her right arm behind her. "Yuh Old Screwface loving Jezebel! See me don't cramp an' paralyse yuh – yuh dutty bitch!"

It was Carmesha who stayed Jenny's arm. "Wha' yuh doing? Yuh waan *kill* her? Me cyan't believe me eyes!"

Still furious, Jenny looked upon Carmesha for a tense second with rigid brows. She then tossed the stones behind her and stormed off into a field, mouthing choice Jamaican expletives. Carmesha tended to Hortense and later in the evening, Amy, who had returned from her stint in the market square, boiled her some bush tea that included a stalk of sinsimilla, to 'fling away de pain'; Levi bought it for her from his neighbours in the foggy hills. Amy fiercely scolded Jenny, demanding what had ever come over her, but Jenny ignored her, remaining tight-lipped. Hortense stared at her sister throughout the evening, concluding that perhaps the dress *did* come apart in her hands. Why would she ketch such a fierce rage? It was only after midnight that Jenny felt remorse seep into her heart. Sleeping beside Hortense, she snuggled up to her and began to stroke Hortense's head. Hortense didn't hear Jenny whisper, "me so sorry, Hortense. Me nuh know wha' come over me. Me cyan't believe me strike de one me love de bes'. David tell me to look after yuh an' look wha' me do. Me will ask de Most High fe him forgiveness. Sleep well." Although fast asleep, Hortense seemed to sense a comfort with her sister's touch that she had known since birth. Instinctively, she manoeuvred herself into her sister's embrace, sighing pleasurably. Amy, secretly looking on, smiled.

In a simple ceremony in March, 1954, attended by family and close friends, Cilbert and Hortense married in Isaac's church; Jenny was the chief bridesmaid. The reception, held at Mr DaCosta's plot, was a subdued affair with Cilbert's father, Constantine, still sore about the Almyna issue. He begrudgingly sank his wedding punch drink while constantly eye-passing Hortense, finally realising that the black-skinned Cilbert's opportunity of climbing the Jamaican social ladder by marrying the lighter-complexioned Almyna, was now denied. When Constantine wasn't studying Hortense, he stole glances at his own caramel-skinned wife, wondering what possessed her to marry him.

Blissfully unaware of the politics that surrounded her wedding, Hortense was the happiest she had ever been. Mrs Walters had adjusted and embellished Amy's old, white baptism dress and Hortense appeared radiant in it; Mrs Walters left no doubt as to who had customised the dress. She named it 'de Angel's Frock'.

Looking forward to his wedding night, Cilbert had to almost drag his new bride away from her dancing, much to the amusement of the guests. The couple spent their first night of marriage in the home of Mr DaCosta's nephew, Hernando, who lived in isolation three miles to the west of Claremont; his family remained at Mr DaCosta's for the following week.

Even Levi, now coupled with Carmesha, attended the wedding; he wore Joseph's old marriage suit that Carmesha had fashioned and shortened for him. Daniel, now accustomed to living in the country, ran around with his new friends but received a beating for staining his new pants with guava juice; Neville, picking up his errant great-grandson, rebuked Carmesha for her assault.

It was only Jenny who seemed to register her father's absence. Jacob, her escort, felt a certain pride linking arms with Jenny all the way from the church to Mr DaCosta's home, but when he found her alone in Mr DaCosta's backyard, reflecting sorrowfully on whatever grievance she bore, Jacob couldn't even hazard a guess on what was troubling her. "Jenny," he called softly. "Look how long we know each udder. Yuh cyan't tell me of de mighty burden dat seem to lean 'pon yuh?"

Jenny didn't even meet Jacob's questioning eyes. "Jacob, ya sweet like sugar inna milo, becah only yuh ah sense me bruise soul. Me lose me sweet sister today. Me bes' frien'. Me never did t'ink either of we coulda ever marry. Y'know, becah we so close. Me t'ought dat we would be togeder fe ever. Y'know, Hortense an' meself against de world. Everyt'ing happen so fast. Me lost Papa an' Hortense soon gone. Not even yuh cyan help me now. Dis is between me an' de Most High. He's been very cruel to me. Papa always said He's ah spiteful God. Yuh know, me try an' live me life good, de way de Most High waan we to live. But der mus' be somet'ing inside of me. Somet'ing bad fe Massa God to treat me dis way. Me cyan't understand it."

"Jenny, He don't expect we to be perfect an' nuhbody ah expect yuh to be so. Least of all me. He will understand dat ya feel dat ya sister abandon yuh. He knows how close yuh two is, especially after ya papa run an' gone. An' wid de grievous loss of David. Ah long time I 'ave been watching yuh try an' be de perfect Christian girl. Why yuh don't try an' be yaself? Living ya own life. Hortense had to grow up one day. An' she don't depend on yuh so much as before. Yuh affe let her go."

Jenny momentarily shot Jacob a cancerous glare, thinking how dare he tell her to let Hortense go, but she soon recovered her composure. "Go'long Jacob, me will be fine inna short while. Gwarn an' enjoy yaself."

Hortense had only five days to enjoy her honeymoon, for Cilbert bade her a tearful farewell before he set off to Papine. He promised he would return every weekend and he kept to his word, catching the first Saturday morning 'bungo bungo' bus from Crossroads, Kingston and arriving in Claremont just before noon. He would collect Hortense from her family home and they would spend most of their short time together in a spare room at Mr DaCosta's, only emerging for meals and lazy rambles in the surrounding hills and groves. When they were not making love, Hortense barraged her husband with questions about the big, bad city.

Unable to capture a good night's sleep whenever Hortense was away, Jenny loathed the prospect of weekends, despite offering her brief opportunities to bless her eyes upon Cilbert. She also found herself pining for Hortense's larger-than-life company, her cantankerous ways and her dawn singing. It felt as if some part of her being had been ripped away forever. On weekdays, she craved Hortense's attention feverishly; walking with her to the river when it was Hortense's turn to wash the clothes, learning gospel songs together, washing and braiding Hortense's hair even when she didn't require it and occasionally surprising Hortense with questions about her love life.

"Jenny!" Hortense would rebuke. "Yuh gwarn so innocent an' everybody ah say how ya nice like de virgin Mary herself. But me know better. Ya tongue ah betray yuh! Lord me God! Jenny, yuh cyan't expect me to talk about dem kinda t'ings when me ah married woman. It nah right. We're nah nuh two foolish teenager who ah talk stupidness while we're stripping corn! Go look Jacob! It's time yuh 'ave ah mon friend, becah yuh cyan't spend ya time ah follow me around like puppy dahg dat lose him mudder. An' Jacob love yuh more dan yuh ever realise. Why yuh t'ink him don't find ah girl yet? Jacob waiting fe yuh! Mebbe he's de answer to ya problem becah yuh start to get 'pon me nerves wid ya company."

Her smile rapidly evaporating, Jenny stormed off in a rage. Hortense muttered under her breath. "An' dey call *me* full ah nettle! An' wha' is so wrong wid Jacob? He would look after Jenny so nice."

Isaac kept faithfully to his twice-weekly visits to Amy and it was on a Thursday in June, 1954, that he found his son, Levi, sitting around Amy's kitchen table. Securing his donkey, he saw Amy approaching him with a mug of coffee and a freshly-picked avocado. "Now, yuh lissen to me, Isaac," Amy ordered. "Ya gwarn talk to ya son! Nuh excuse! An' me waan nuh argument! Me will leave yuh be becah me 'ave ah liccle shopping to do. *Don't* drink off me rum!"

Amy marched off, muttering something under her breath about the stubbornness of Jamaican men. Isaac neared Levi cautiously, debating whether he should trouble the rum flask inside his jacket pocket. Levi looked on his father's timid approach blankly, as if he was waiting for a bus to stop. The onlooking Jenny, her mind whirring with some notion, ran up to Isaac. "Preacher Mon! Mighty good to see yuh. Praise de Lord!"

"An' good to see yuh too! Bless yuh chile."

"Yuh staying fe dinner, Preacher Mon?"

"Yes, ya mudder so kindly invite me."

"Den cyan me borrow ya donkey? Me waan ride somewhere. Carmesha 'ave we own up der ah family plot. She ah toil 'pon we land while yuh ah talk wid Levi."

"Yes, of course me chile. Nuh go too far an' give him ah water an' mek him munch 'pon de sugar cane."

Mounting the donkey, Jenny set him on a course to Isaac's home. It was Jacob who answered the door and surprise struck him like a Jamaican yard dog being tossed a generous portion of prime beef.

"Ya mudder der-ya?" Jenny asked, looking over Jacob's shoulder.

"Nuh, Jenny. She der ah market shopping. Did yuh waan see her?"

"Nuh, sa. Me come to see yuh."

Jacob looked puzzled. "Yuh waan to study de Bible wid me, Jenny?"

Smiling with a confidence that she never knew she had, Jenny walked into the house. "How long yuh been waiting to court me?"

"From time 'pon time," Jacob replied, trying to read Jenny's intentions.

Striking a pose and pushing her chest out, Jenny recalled, "remember ya tell me dat me mus' be meself an' stop trying to be de perfect Christian girl?"

"Well, yes, Jenny. But I cyan't see ya reasoning."

Jenny grinned devilishly. "Well, see me here. Wha' yuh gwarn to do wid me?"

Without hesitation, Jacob took Jenny by the hand and led her to his tiny bedroom. His bed was two mattresses placed on top of each other. A wooden broom handle, secured at each end inside an alcove, held his two pairs of suits and shirts. Church pamphlets, hymn sheets and service schedules were resting upon an aged wooden desk. Propped up on this, against the wall, was Jacob's Bible. It was opened at the book of Proverbs.

Jenny, feeling her heartbeat accelerate, walked towards the Bible, picked it up and placed it face down upon the table. It was now or never, she thought. Me cyan be jus' as sexy as Hortense. Me pretty like she. She then turned to Jacob, linking her arms around his neck. Without uttering another word and looking down at the floor, she began to unbutton Jacob's shirt, kissing his chest as she did so. Jacob immediately responded by frantically pulling at Jenny's clothes. They laughed at each other's clumsy efforts to undress one another. Jenny refused to meet Jacob's eyes.

Naked, they dropped onto the bed, pleasuring each other for the next fifteen minutes until Jenny pulled Jacob on top of her. She braced herself for the pain she thought she would have to endure but as Jacob entered her, she closed her eyes and the image of a smiling Cilbert filled her mind. Jacob, withdrawing at the last moment, climaxed within a minute, leaving Jenny to wonder what all the fuss was about.

An hour later, she made love to him once more, shutting her eyes tight, attempting to induce a dream-like state with Cilbert. Jacob managed to endure a little longer and Jenny found that she enjoyed it more than the first time. But embarrassment was now warming her cheeks. She dressed quickly and before she departed, returned Jacob's Bible to its original position. As a satisfied Jacob watched her leave, he wondered why she didn't even say farewell or arrange their next liaison. Indeed, Jenny hadn't said a word of affection or of anything else since she first entered his room. But these thoughts were soon discarded by his glad heart.

Informing Hortense of her secret trysts with Jacob, Jenny went into every detail. "Is it de same feeling yuh get wid Cilbert?" Jenny wanted to know. "When yuh lose all control of ya body an' yuh get dis sweetness dat ripple inside of yuh? It mek me laugh when Jamaican mon advise we dat yuh should not 'ave sex before marriage. Becah dem *love* it! Yuh waan to see de look 'pon Jacob's face when him juices ah rush t'rough him black bamboo! Cilbert's face ever look so crease up an' mad wid excitement?"

Hortense fell about laughing. "If Papa could hear yuh now! Nuh sweet liccle Jenny any more! Jenny, of course mon love it. But *we* love it too. Dat's why me don't lissen to de cranky woman who go to church. *Don't 'ave sex, don't do dis, don't do dat*, dem say. But me bet me last red cent dat dem love sex an' probably did ah love it before dem marry. Yes, Cilbert gwarn de same way. Him face ah crease an' crease up 'til it cyan't crease nuh more, an' when him shot him juices it's like relief mek him eyes close an' him t'anking de Most High fe de pleasure. It's ah cruel God to deny anybody dat pleasure."

Holding onto Hortense's every word, Jenny nodded. "Yes, me affe agree, but *don't* tell nuhbody! Everybody t'ink me ah nice Christian girl."

"But yuh affe tell Mama one day, Jenny. Yuh cyan't keep dis secret. An' yuh doing not'ing wrong. Yuh an' Jacob are jus' two people who love each udder. Fe true? Me truly glad dat yuh two come togeder. Jacob will never leave yuh, Jenny. He will never cheat 'pon yuh an' he will do *anyt'ing* to mek sure ya happy. Yuh find ah good mon."

Jenny hesitated before breaking out into a plastic smile that Hortense didn't detect. "Yes, me do love him," she said. "Jacob is ah sweet mon."

"Den marry him," insisted Hortense.

Why not? Jenny thought. It might make Cilbert jealous.

Jacob and Jenny married under an overcast sky in mid-May, 1954. Refusing to wear her mother's baptism dress for her wedding, Jenny insisted that Jacob should find the money for a new dress. After much pleading, Jacob finally received the cash from his father. A more than happy Mrs Walters designed and made the ankle-length, laced-white dress. She named it 'the wisp of the north'. Isaac, who guessed that his son was a virgin before courting Jenny, reluctantly conducted the service. He believed that a man only understood the ways of women after bedding plenty of them.

Everyone saw the disappointment in Isaac's eyes when Jacob said, "*I do!*" As Jacob kissed his new bride, only Amy, observing Jenny's undemonstrative body language towards Jacob, sensed something that was troubling. The photographer that Isaac hired had to work hard and tell a few jokes to coax Jenny's smile out of her and it was Hortense who explained to guests that her sister was 'mighty nervous' about being the centre of attention.

Neville, who had given his grand-daughter away, whispered to Jacob, "me soon expect ah nex' great-grandson!" Happy as any man could be on his wedding day, Jacob replied to Neville, "nuh fear, Custos. My dream come true an' me an' Jenny will provide nuff great-grandsons!"

The wedding reception was held in the church hall and Jenny danced longer with Cilbert than she did with her new husband who was busy accepting handshakes and slaps on the back. Cilbert, unaware of the pounding of Jenny's heart, kissed his new sister-in-law upon the cheek at the conclusion of the dance as a gesture of congratulation. This act meant more to Jenny than the love-making with Jacob upon her wedding night, where she simply pulled Jacob on top of her and said, "me sweet darling, Jacob. Let we get dis over wid. It's been ah long day an' me well tired. An' de rum punch gone to me head!"

During the summer of 1954, Amy found that she more often than not cooked only for Kwarhterleg and herself. Jenny was now living with Jacob, rarely visiting her mother's home and Cilbert, enjoying a break from his studies, had Hortense with him at Mr DaCosta's. Becoming bored of Kwarhterleg's endless tale of woe about the love of his life, Joanne Lindus, Amy would trek up to Levi's place where she was entertained by Carmesha; she would bear the gift of a bottle of rum. While Carmesha and herself drained the fire-water, becoming merry and jovial, Levi, who thought that women deserved a break from the monotony of country life, would cook a delicious fish supper. Indeed, Amy found Carmesha's company more stimulating than her own daughters. Carmesha had no cause to question Amy's love for her and she imagined how special the relationship was that Amy had with David.

It was a Friday night in August when Amy, tipsy and bleary-eyed, had just returned from a visit to Carmesha's. Not able to sleep, she made herself a coffee. She decided to sit just outside her front door and take in the nocturnal sounds of the chirping insects and catch the night breeze upon her face, hoping it might well induce sleep.

Through her reddened eyes, Amy thought that she saw someone approaching from the crest of a hill – a towering, black silhouette. She blinked rapidly, trying to focus and indeed, there was a man coming towards her. He was tall and wore a straw hat. A crocus bag was draped over his left shoulder.

His long strides reaching Amy before she could express her

surprise, Joseph offered a warm smile. He raised his right arm and cupped Amy's jaw with his hand. Amy clasped it and closed her eyes for a long second, pressing Joseph's hand into her face. "Me here to stay," whispered Joseph. "Nuh longer me foot yearn fe travelling. Me 'ave so much to tell yuh."

Amy let go of Joseph's hand and picked up her coffee. She drained half of the mug. "Joseph, ya hungry?" she asked.

"Yes, Amy. But de midnight hour pass an' yuh sure yuh waan cook dis time ah night?"

"Nuh, sa! Yuh know where de kitchen der-ya an' besides, me drink too much fire-water dis night. Me gone to me bed! Clothes affe wash ah river inna de marnin an' me affe go up to Levi to give him ah money. Yuh cyan tell me wha' yuh affe tell me when de rooster start holler. Nuh mek too much mess inna de kitchen an' *don't* drink off me rum! An' furder more, before yuh start chat me ears off about ya disappearance, yuh cyan tell me where yuh grow ya sinsimilla. We run out an' me need it! De people who ah live up near Levi charge plenty, plenty money. *Goodnight.*"

Joseph shook his head in admiration and laughed, sure in his mind that everything was going to be just fine.

After listening to Joseph's full tale, Amy insisted to her husband that he must repeat it to the whole family. So a week after his return, Joseph let it be known that he would tell his tale in a 'story-time' session around Grandpapa Neville's fire.

So eager and fascinated was Mr DaCosta by the prospect of hearing Joseph's story, he sold one of his prize goats to Amy at half price for the occasion. Neville had to entertain fellow Claremont elders who knocked upon his door at all hours. They all wanted to attend his 'story-time' session, despite the warning he had given out that it was strictly for family. Even those who had hated Joseph for years found that their curiosity was provoked and wanted to attend. The least they wanted to do was to pour scorn on Joseph's storytelling skills. After constant irritation and Neville concluding that it was about time Joseph confronted his accusers, he yielded and gave them permission to attend but warned them of interruptions.

Jenny, who had spent the entire week at home, worked the market stall with her chin held high, the return of her father giving her a huge boost. A spring was in her step and the men who frequented the bars had noticed in Jenny a blossoming sexuality. She walked by them and offered them sideway grins. A man would rise and say, "come here sister! Mek me buy yuh ah drink so me an' yuh could talk an reason an' mebbe forward ah bush to get to know one anoder."

Grinning mischievously, Jenny would reply, "yuh t'ink yuh coulda satisfy me? Me don't deal wid nuh t'irty second mon an' besides, while yuh ah sit down drink ya beer an' look 'pon me pretty self, Joe Grine is grining ya wife! Me *not* available. Me married now to Jacob so look an' *don't* touch." She would flash her wedding ring and thought not even Hortense could cuss like her.

Jenny dismissed those Claremontonians who doubted that her father would ever return and she enjoyed doing so. Hortense, who was residing at Mr DaCosta's, only came down on just the one evening to introduce her husband to her father; a nervous Cilbert was careful to be perfectly polite as his hat trembled in his hands. On their departure, Hortense confided to Cilbert, "dis story-time t'ing *nah* necessary. Me don't waan people to know we business."

As an appetiser to the main event, Amy's mother, Melody, told Anancy tales to the children while the men fuelled themselves with rum, curried goat, fried grunt fish, bammys and rice. All eyes were upon Joseph who was quietly stoking the bonfire. Whispered conversations and sceptical eyes made Joseph wonder if this was indeed a good idea. He glanced at Amy for reassurance. Amy nodded.

Up to a hundred and fifty adults were ringed around the fire and a few gained a vantage point in the surrounding tree branches. Even a couple of market vendors had caught news of the event but they were soon sent packing by Neville. Hortense was laying down with her head in Cilbert's lap, her eyes displaying apathy. Jenny was sitting beside Jacob, gazing proudly at her father's every move. Isaac, parking his donkey at a tree, surprised all by his presence, for the more conservative of his Claremont parishioners thought that story-time sessions were bordering on paganism. The fire danced in the Jamaican night, illuminating everyone's captivated brows.

"Everybody quiet!" shouted a gruff-voiced Neville, holding out his arms. "Story time dis ah story time! An' tonight, fe ya consumption, Joseph will reveal himself to we. *Nuh* lie mus' come outta him mout'! Mek him swear 'pon de Bible."

Neville placed his old Bible upon the ground in front of Joseph. Joseph paused for a moment before placing his left hand on the book and closing his eyes. "Me swear nuh lie will come outta me mout'."

"Alright, sa. Let ya story begin!"

Joseph cleared his throat, scanned the eager faces all around him and closed his eyes momentarily. "Some ah yuh t'ink me mad," he began. "Mebbe rightly so. Becah madness ah shadow me life. But me waan to explain meself. So me waan to start wid de beginning. De Alpha as Neville call it. An' dis Alpha start nearly two hundred year ago. Born ah free mon in 1765 in Accompong Town, near to Cockpit country where de bones of de very earth rip t'rough de dry ground, was me ancestor, Kofi. He was named inna de Akan tradition of ah chile born 'pon ah Friday. Pure Coromanty blood ah flow t'rough him veins. An' Africa is de land of we forefaders. Some call his people Maroon but dat was de name de Spanish give we. Kofi's story was told to me by me mudder an' her mudder before her."

Joseph could sense the hush as he paused. He could only hear the chinking of rum bottles against mugs and the patus hooting from the trees. He began to recite Kofi's tale.

Tall like his father before him, Kofi was curious and headstrong. Disregarding the warnings of his elders who told him that on no account was he permitted to come within three miles of any plantation, Kofi violated this law on countless occasions.

Weary of trying to capture hogs in the wild and his curiosity getting the better of him, Kofi, roaming south into the parish of St Elizabeth, always trespassed within the forbidden areas of the plantation at dusk. Concealing himself behind bushes, Kofi sighted slaves at work cutting cane, defeated expressions upon their faces.

Pauses were punished with cracks of a forked whip and at nightfall he witnessed women tending to the scored backs of their menfolk with soiled rags. Kofi learned that the slaves called these cloths 'blood-claats'. He saw the overseers tossing the slaves chicken claws and cow foot; the women placed them inside a pot, mixing it with corn and scallion to boil a broth. On one occasion he witnessed a woman, sobbing uncontrollably, plunge the spike of a sickle deep into her belly, killing herself and her unborn baby. She was soon dumped into a sewage pit.

On another nearby plantation, Kofi couldn't but be affected by the mournful song of the men who were ordered to chop down the giant silk-cotton trees; a handful of these slaves chanced execution by stealing mug-fulls of rum and sprinkling it over the felled trees while humming a lament. Kofi knew that to cut down a living tree would provoke demons and malevolent spirits. Why are they doing this? he thought. He could never understand why the slaves wouldn't stir themselves into bloody revolution.

One afternoon, while lying in the long grass just outside the fenced perimeter of the plantation and refreshing himself with a water coconut, Kofi heard a melodic humming. He went to investigate and was struck by its source – a beautiful brown-skinned girl of about fifteen years of age. She was collecting felled sugar cane and placing it in two baskets that were balanced upon her shoulders with a piece of stick; her back bent beneath the burden. He watched her for many days, trying to capture her attention but couldn't get close enough without being detected by the overseers.

Kofi decided to risk using his Abeng horn, hewn out of a cow's bone. It was nightfall and Kofi had inched as near as possible to the perimeter fence. Seeing her, he blew softly so only she could hear. Startled and not detecting Kofi's presence, she dropped her baskets and screamed, believing she had heard the agonised wail of a tree demon.

The next day, Kofi concluded that he would have to show himself. In the morning he had hunted and killed a boar with more energy and determination than he usually exerted; he sustained a wound in his side and treated it with a smoking, charred ember and herbs. He roasted the boar on a spit before carving it up and placing slices of the meat in cowhide pouches that were strapped around his waist; he suspended the remaining carcass from a tree for further use if he cared for it; the boar's tusks were hanging from his necklace of twined reeds. He journeyed to the plantation, reaching it only when the sun was falling. He bided his time until he seized the opportunity when the girl he so much admired was isolated and no danger was in sight. He clambered over the fence, ran towards the girl and hurriedly presented his hard-fought game to her. He said nothing but gazed into her eyes for a long second, thinking if he uttered something she wouldn't understand his Coromanty words. Stunned and before she could nod a thank you, Kofi was already climbing over the fence, his lithe legs and sculptured torso glistening in the moonlight. The girl smiled as she watched him disappear into the Jamaican night.

And so it continued for many days, Kofi waiting for nightfall before stealing cherished seconds with the girl he believed would carry his children, giving her ring-tail pigeons, land crabs, slices of hog meat and other game he had hunted in the wild. He would only half-smile at her, touching her cheeks and lips with his long coarse fingers, marvelling at her brown skin. Then he would scarper away without whispering a sound.

One moonless night, Kofi was finally seen by an overseer. Someone trained the barrel of a musket upon his back but the aim was untrue and Kofi escaped. Thanking the spirits of old African rivers for protecting him, Kofi decided he would have to think of a plan to free his girl. Two nights later, taking more care upon his approach to the plantation, Kofi was aghast at what he saw. Laying down outside her hut, which she shared with three other families, was Kofi's girl. Kyeisha was her name. She was in acute pain for her master had cleaved off her ankle and achilles tendon, totally disabling her. The back of her leg, treated with fire to stem the bleeding, was a seared, dry, bloodied mess. An overseer with a musket at hand was patrolling nearby. Kofi, twenty yards away, blew on his horn softly, signalling to her that he would return, although he doubted if she understood. Kyeisha looked up, spotted Kofi and shook her head in despair, her cheeks smudged with tears.

In the next two days, Kofi roamed the wild, blowing his horn, using a tone and pitch that promised war to Maroon ears. It was a summons that no Maroon within hearing range could ignore. Twelve fellow compatriots from his settlement answered him, each responding with their own unique calling sound, each armed with spears, machetes, cleavers and sickles, all of them well apprenticed by their fathers and grandfathers in guerrilla warfare, ambush and covert raids. Two men raised doubts over Kofi's proposed revenge, arguing that they were about to dishonour an agreement following the last Maroon war with the white planter class. Kofi talked them around, reasoning that the lands they had received as part of the contract were not bountiful.

Following the sacrifice of a hog, they invoked the spirits of the obeah underworld. Kofi and his band then marched barefoot and silently to the plantation in the dead of the night, their faces daubed with blood drawn from one another's palms and their bodies covered in leaves and twigs. Only the patus, the gossiping crickets and the rasping cicadas saw and heard them coming.

The warriors found that four house-slaves were sleeping in hammocks on the master's verandah. Oil lamps showered light upon the mosquitoes who buzzed around their faces. Awoken by the creak of timber, one of the house slaves was about to raise the alarm but before he could do so, his throat was neatly slit from ear to ear. The Maroons didn't take any chances with the other house slaves. They covered the slaves' mouths with their hands while severing their heads with three powerful swishes of their cleavers. The house-slaves were left to swing gently in their places of rest. Mosquitoes gorged on their blood.

Gaining entry to the mansion via a window, Kofi left six of his men to stand guard outside as he and the rest of his brethren crept upstairs, their minds fixed on revenge. Overseers were still asleep in their own homes dotted around the plantation; some of them sleeping with female slaves of their choice. Before the master was aware what was happening, a rough black hand was held tight over his mouth. Many other hands grabbed his body and he found himself being carried down the stairs. He could only watch from the base of the stairs as other raiders dragged his wife from bed, ripped off her night-gown and hacked off her head with five swings of a meat cleaver. The slavemaster's two children, too afraid to scream, were hauled before their father. Their eyes spoke of a dread that Kofi was unable to dismiss from his memory to his last waking day. The boy was aged nine and the girl was no more than seven years old. They were soon efficiently decapitated. Blood dripped down from the bare staircase and was forming in a pool that was staining the slavemaster's knees. Slivers of human tissue smeared the bannisters. Kofi then hacked off the slavemaster's feet before chopping off his head. The headless bodies were dumped in a nearby pit toilet.

His thirst for vengeance satisfied, Kofi ran to collect Kyeisha and made good his escape. His brethren only followed him after they had daubed the front of the slavemaster's house with the family's blood. They placed four grisly heads upon the verandah, their faces angled in such a way as to face the morning sun.

Kyeisha, who was named 'Firefoot' by the Maroons, produced nine children for Kofi. She never walked again. Bent with age and after the passing of Kofi, she told the story of her rescue to her many grandchildren – one of them included Joseph's great grandmother. Joseph's mother, Panceta, had heard the tale from her mother and she had passed it on to all of her children. They were left in no doubt that it was Africa where they came from and they swore that they would never allow themselves to be enslaved again.

It was only after hearing this revelation that Amy and Carmesha guessed that David must have put up a great resistance in his Spanish Town jail – it was in his blood.

Finishing his mother's tale, when he revealed that he was given the name of Kojo at his birth, Joseph paused and studied the eyes of his audience. He spotted Preacher Mon stealing away, shaking his head. Neville, sitting beside Joseph, took out a pound note from his pants. He held it aloft theatrically so everybody could see before slamming it against Joseph's forehead – an African tradition that meant Joseph had told the story well. The audience raised their bottles and clapped their hands, shouting their approval. Joseph, relief flushing through him, told the remaining tale of his family's history. Meanwhile, Amy looked on with a satisfied smirk, her pride recovered. Joseph concluded the story-time session by detailing his whereabouts for the last two years.

Following his disappearance, Joseph had returned to Accompong Town where he found that his mother was living alone and ill. Only one of his sisters, Shimona, had remained in the town and she had her own family but she looked in on her mother every day.

Seeing that the house needed repairing and that the land that his family toiled on was now barren, Joseph set to work. Daylight hours were spent ploughing grooves for new seed. He decided to plant corn and scallion because they quickly agreed with the soil. He also planted flowers around the home. At night, by the light of the kerosene lamp, Joseph patched the roof with long grass, dried mud and straw. He would then sit by his mother's bedside and feed her with herb teas mixed with rum, but watched the strength of her body slowly depart. Trauma was still in her eyes and Joseph recognised the same loss of children that Amy bore.

Panceta revealed to Joseph that Abraham, his father, had always felt uneasy with the fact that his own father had died a slave and was owned by the white man. Abraham couldn't offer heroic tales of his forefathers 'putting up a mighty resistance'. He was unaware of what part of Africa his family hailed from and with the knowledge that Panceta could trace her roots back to the Akan districts of Ghana, Abraham banned all talk about Kofi and Kyeisha in his household. Panceta had to choose her moments carefully to inform her children of their heritage.

Every evening Shimona arrived with the evening meal – neither Joseph nor anyone else wanted to cook dinner in the outside kitchen. She continually rebuked Joseph for leaving at the family's greatest moment of need but she finally forgave him. Breaking down in tears, Shimona said that she had thought Joseph was dead. She had imagined that his skeleton was hanging from a tree somewhere in the wild.

Bedridden and with the knowledge that in the Maroon tradition it was the women who worked in the fields while the men hunted game, Panceta's final wish was for her to bless her eyes upon the family's plot of land. Joseph carried her out and she saw rows of golden corn, scallion, yam hills, lettuce, pumpkin, sweet potato and callaloo. She managed a smile and kissed Joseph's forehead. She said, "tomorrow me will bless me eyes 'pon Naptali an' Menelik again at last. It's been ah long time. Now, Kojo, yuh affe return to ya family. Give dem me blessing an' nuh let nuh curse worry ya head. Like me yuh 'ave lost ya first born but yuh still 'ave ah wife an' two daughter. Yuh 'ave fe live fe de living. Don't worry ya head about de dead. Even when dey used to chop down de giant, silk cotton tree, de seeds find ah way to born ah new sapling. Remember dat. Now it's time fe me final rest."

Panceta died the next day. Joseph buried her in the family grave. Feeling safe with Shimona's promise that her family would continue working the plot, Joseph returned to Claremont.

Claremontonians, satisfied with the night's entertainment, went up to Joseph to congratulate him on his storytelling skills. Whether his tales were embellished or not didn't matter to them. As long as they had 'ah long peep inna Moonshine's soul' they were content. Joseph was now one of them.

Hortense was preparing to depart but Cilbert insisted that they should both congratulate Joseph. They approached Joseph who was still accepting handshakes and pats on the back. "Papa," Hortense called. "Me an' Cilbert gone now."

"So soon?" Joseph answered. "Yuh don't waan to stay here fe de night? Neville waan de family togeder so we cyan talk an' reason about t'ings. Me so glad! Me don't affe look over me shoulder when me walk down de hill where de poor people 'ave dem hut."

"Papa, Cilbert affe leave Sunday marnin. So me don't waan to waste any time. Me place is by him side. Cilbert me first priority. Yuh affe understan' dat now."

Embarrassed, Cilbert shook Joseph's hand before leading Hortense away. In contrast, Jenny wouldn't leave her father's side. She was smiling at him in adoration as Jacob looked on at a distance. He finally decided to walk home, realising that Joseph's return had brought him down a notch in Jenny's estimation.

Chapter Nine

Kingston, Jamaica
July 1957

Shaken by the bus driver's refusal to slow down when he negotiated corners and bends, Hortense peered out of the dirt-stained window as the bus approached the junction of Half Way Tree. Through the city haze, she saw a multitude of bobbing heads, heading this way and that. Hortense saw unsmiling faces that were coloured from light-honey to midnight-brown. They had uncompromising expressions, almost threatening. Now and then Hortense spotted the odd pink dot but when she tried to look again at these white faces, they were lost like a grain of white sugar in a jar of demerara. Hortense scanned the bruised shop fronts and peeling buildings as the bus inched forward and wondered why the capital of Jamaica was not glossed in brilliant white as in her dreams.

Hortense watched men of leisure, their palms wrapped around warm bottles of Mackesons and Red Stripe beer. They were standing outside rum bars, sucking on their Four Aces, Buccaneer and Camel cigarettes while eyeing the young women who went by. A select few, most of them caramel-skinned, peered through their sunglasses, sporting pastel-coloured jackets and silk-banded, straw boaters. Hortense glared as they looked down at the chaos below them from rooftop terraces, sipping cocktails served to them by black waiters wearing ultra-clean white jackets and black bow ties. Thick Havana cigars slid between the corners of the diners mouths, arched by delicately trimmed moustaches. Her eyes returning to road level, Hortense could see shoe-shine boys, their heads almost drowned by cloth caps, waiting patiently with their buffers and boxes at the exits of drinking clubs and fine restaurants, their palms as dark as the back of their hands. Taking off her own shoes, Hortense spat on them and gave them a quick rub with her handkerchief. Slipping on her footwear again, Hortense resumed looking out of the window.

She could see many men idling, walking in no particular direction while scanning the passing traffic with defeated expressions. "Lazy good fe not'ing people dem!" she muttered under her breath. A few of these men chanced their luck by beseeching the shiny-shoed and the clean-shirted, pleading for a shilling. They were ignored. Topless, grey-footed scavengers came into Hortense's vision. They unashamedly searched the refuse bins for half-eaten snacks and discarded cores of fruit. The clientele of the bars paid them no mind. "Dey shoulda go ah country an' do some hard work," Hortense whispered to herself.

Hortense studied the filthy streets, grimacing as she did so. Garbage was packed tight against the kerbs, spilling onto the pavements; squashed tin cans, crushed cartons, flattened cardboard boxes, smashed bottles, yellowed newspapers, fowl bones, goat carcasses, broken household appliances, unusable push carts, warped wheels, tyre strips, rotting vegetables, stains of soured milk and failed Chinese betting slips.

Hortense's view was intermittently disrupted by cyclists playing Russian Roulette with the traffic. They were transporting and selling all manner of produce, the ninety-five degree Kingston sun bouncing off their reflectors and the wing mirrors that they had retrieved from the many abandoned cars that lay strewn throughout the city, all stripped bare of anything remotely usable. Other pedal-pushers advertised their religious beliefs in the form of flags, badges, stickers and any other means they could think of as they hollered their religious convictions to whoever would care to listen and to those who didn't. "Crazy, crazy people!" Hortense laughed.

Truck drivers – transistor radios blaring out American Rhythm and Blues standards from their cabins – announced their presence with impatient blasts of their horns, the black smoke that their engines emitted adding to the close and choking atmosphere that hung above Kingston in a shimmering veil.

Hortense began to tap her feet. She waved to country hitch-hikers, scantily clothed in reg-jegs, who were balanced precariously upon crates of rural produce atop pick-up vehicles. They returned Hortense's greeting from their vantage point. Most of them had no personal belongings whatsoever, save the fruit they were munching, but they all shared a dream of prospering in the capital, despite not knowing where they would sleep for the night. Many of them had seen the farming lands they worked upon bought out by bauxite companies and only the fortunate few gained employment with the new corporate enterprises and the hotel chains that were being built on the north coast. Inevitably they would swell the Kingston slums for they could only offer their farming skills. Without any form of social security, the unfortunate country hitchhiker would need all his resolve and his faith to repel the immediate attractions of a life of crime.

Hearing an altercation behind her, Hortense turned around and looked at the drivers. Motorists, jostling and tooting for space with fly-encircled donkeys, bewildered goats and tug-along vendor carts, harassed and harangued each other as if they were gladiators manacled to each other a minute before they duelled. Quick-eyed and cautious pedestrians, who dared to cross the busy roads, were encouraged to do so with the utmost speed by the threat of Jamaican swear words or the manic revving of engines. Unlicensed taxi drivers kerb-crawled the streets opportunistically searching for fares. It was no embarrassment to them that their vehicles had a door missing, no visible evidence of an exhaust pipe and no front windscreen. "Taxi fe hire!" they shouted, exposing the gaps in their teeth.

Hortense smiled as she spotted a special constable adopting a rigid stance. He was wearing black pants with blue stripes and a checked shirt. He was standing on patrol outside a government building, his two foot-long truncheons dangling from his belt. Mesmerised by her surroundings, Hortense clapped her hands and smiled broadly. Suddenly she thought of David. She wondered if

David's first sight of Kingston was just as thrilling as hers. She then collected her bags from the luggage rack and hoped Cilbert would be there at the bus depot to meet her.

Parking at the Parade bus terminal in downtown Kingston, the bus driver ordered his passengers off the vehicle with an impatience that could only come from a man born in the city. "Come people, yuh t'ink me 'ave time to waste? Get off me strikin' bus before me look fe me whip! Me waan me rest before me affe drive back ah stinkin' country where yuh people shoulda stay! Me don't know why yuh come ah Kingston, becah we 'ave not'ing fe offer yuh an' de ghetto is preparing her welcome."

Burdened with three bags, Hortense offered the bus driver a lingering eye-pass as she departed. Cilbert, dressed in capacious blue trousers, a sweat-stained white Fred Perry T-shirt and a brown pork-pie hat, was waiting on the pavement. He was lipping a bottle of Guinness while darting his eyes as if wary of peril; his ready grin had departed him sometime during his studies in Kingston. Hortense briefly smiled with relief when she saw her husband but her long journey from Claremont had made her weary. "Cilbert! Don't jus' stand up der so wid ya licky licky self! Come help me wid me baggage!"

"Ya journey alright?" asked Cilbert, collecting two of Hortense's bags and offering her a kiss on the cheek.

"Nuh, mon!" Hortense replied, making sure the bus driver heard her. "Me t'ought me was gwarn to dead about six times. Me don't know how some people get dem employment."

"But yuh reach Kingston safe an' 'pon time," the bus driver riposted.

Kissing her teeth, Hortense offered a choice glare to the bus driver, then turned to Cilbert. "Come, Cilbert. Me cyan't wait to see de place where we gwarn live."

"*Don't* expect nuh palace," warned Cilbert. "It's small an' we 'ave about sixty neighbour living inna de yard. But de rent nuh too bad an' when yuh start work we coulda save ah liccle. Who knows? Mebbe widin two years we coulda forward to England." Cilbert closed his eyes for a second, his head tilted upwards. "Yes, sa.

England! Ah fine ambition."

From the bus depot, a cautious Cilbert led Hortense due west of the city. Their destination was Trenchtown. Hortense noticed that most of the downtown grocer shops were owned by people of Chinese origin and she wondered if they had to tolerate the same abuse as the Chinese family who ran a grocer's in Claremont market. Once out of the shopping area and the general hubbub of downtown Kingston, they found themselves in a bewildering network of alleyways and dusty, narrow lanes where skinny goats, scrawny chickens and fat cockroaches were fellow pedestrians. The heat seemed to grow more intense. Hortense felt her soles crunching hard-backed insects. Her white frock was now flecked with fine dust and soot that drifted from the many fires of the shanty dwellers. She noticed that Cilbert didn't strut with the same cocksure assurance he displayed in the country. He was constantly checking behind him, his eyes on permanent alert. "Hold on to ya t'ings," he advised. "Robber-mon an' all kind ah criminal der about."

Fifteen minutes later they arrived outside a two-storied stucco building of twelve apartments. It was encircled by a seven foot concrete and zinc wall. Surrounding this and other government yards, hugging the outside of perimeter walls, were squatter camps where the denizens fashioned their homes out of termite-ravaged timber, levelled oil drum cans, jagged, bitten sheets of corrugated roofing and fourth-hand bed sheets. Hortense looked on the poor wretches who lived in the shanty huts and shook her head. A bare-footed woman, three small children about her feet, was stirring a blackened pot full of banana slops over a flickering wood fire. She didn't bother to swat away the flies that were lapping around her head. An elderly, white-whiskered man, dressed only in a soiled pair of shorts, was unashamedly crawling on the dusty ground, collecting cigarette butts. Cilbert took Hortense by the arm and led her inside the government yard.

Hortense found herself in a horseshoe-shaped forecourt, at the centre of which stood a water standpipe. A few of the female residents were still taking their midday siestas in the shade offered by the perimeter wall. A young woman was breast-feeding her baby outside her front door. She was singing to her child, regarding her two-month-old son as only a mother could.

> *"Me'd rather be inna me grave an' be ah slave an' go back to me fader to be free.*
> *Oh yes, Lord. Me'd rather live poor an' clean dan live life craven an' mean.*
> *Oh yes, me Lord. Me'd rather give anyt'ing me could spare dan tell ah sufferah me cupboard bare.*
> *Oh yes, me Lord. Me sweet sweet Lord."*

Next door to the mother, an older woman was scrubbing her walls. Another head-scarfed woman was stoking a fire with strips of tyres. Beside her were the four communal toilets and four shower cubicles. Hortense, turning around on the spot and guessing that the men must be at work, commented. "Dis not too bad. De only t'ing is since we walk from de bus depot me don't see nuh green or big tree. Ah shame. Me sight nuff cacti an' acacia 'pon de narrow lanes 'pon de way here, but nuh mighty Mahoe ah stan' proud like inna country. Me gran'papa would nah like dis place at all! But me realise why dey call dis place Trenchtown. De smell from de open sewage pit dat de shanty people use nearly tek off me nose!"

Uneasy about something, Cilbert led Hortense to their ground floor apartment. Hortense nodded with approval when her shoes echoed off the tile flooring. She lifted her eyes and discovered that the apartment consisted of one room and a kitchen shared with a neighbour. There were two double beds situated against opposite walls, a pine china cabinet and two cane chairs that required re-meshing. A tired-looking, beaten up sofa was pushed against another wall.

"So, dis is it," said Cilbert matter of factly, secretly thinking of Mr DaCosta's spacious home and grounds back in Claremont. "But wid de grace ah de Most High, it'll only be ah short while we stay here. But at least we togeder at last, under we own roof. Now we cyan mek ah fine life togeder."

Closing the door, Hortense went up to Cilbert and tossed his hat to the floor. "So, Cilby," she said seductively. "Yuh don't waan to christen me 'pon me first day inna de big city? Me need ah massage becah de bus seat tough like police station bench. Yuh gwarn give me ah massage, Cilby?"

Forgetting his dislike of his new environment, Cilbert lifted Hortense off her feet and carried her to the bed. "Me had to tek ah day off from work an' dem nah pay me. But der is nuh better way of spending me free time."

Next morning, sitting together on a city bus that wound its way through the downtown area then up towards the hills that backdropped Kingston, Hortense and Cilbert were watching the bare-footed children who were stationed at traffic lights and bus stops, selling nuts, guinep and naseberries to motorists. Hortense noticed the desperate look in their eyes.

"Yuh sure dis Miss Martha is kindly?" Hortense asked. "Me never talk to ah white person before. She related to de new Queen ah England? She ah millionaire? She wear dat shiny somet'ing 'pon her head? Her face blister from de sun like dried red pepper? Yuh cyan see de blue vein inna her feet? She 'ave ah liccle flat bottom? She 'ave legs full of mighty dimple? She sweat like rainwater ah run down de trunk of de mighty Blue Mahoe after hurricane ah lick?"

Cilbert couldn't help but laugh. "Nuh, sa. Her husband is ah captain at de soldier camp up der inna de hills. Well past Stony Hill. Ah place call Newcastle me t'ink. Miss Martha is fine. When me connect her phone she give me tip to buy two drink. So she well kindly. She tell me dat she need ah cleaner to help around de house an' me tell her dat me wife soon come from de country. So she tell me to bring yuh come. So, Hortense, ah fine opportunity dis."

"How do me talk to her? Me affe call her Lady Martha? Me affe bow? Me affe wash her foot-bottom? *Nuh* way me laying down fe her husband!"

Cilbert chuckled again. "Nuh, nuh, sa. Jus' call her Miss Martha. She easy to talk to an' she nah gwarn wid high graces an' look-down-nose dat some white people love to do. She fine. Yuh will see."

Not convinced, Hortense opted to peer out of the window.
"Hmmmm."

Miss Martha's bungalow crested a hill. Hortense, already
mightily impressed by the 'palaces' as she called them, that lined
the quiet avenue, peered into the English-made motor car sitting
outside Miss Martha's white-painted, iron gates. "She mus' be ah
millionaire!"

Cilbert rang the door bell that was built into the stone gate-post
and Hortense smoothed the creases in her frock. A feint *ding-dong*
could be heard somewhere inside the house. Hortense tried to
suppress an attack of nerves. Before her was a manicured lawn that
had three young, leafless trees sprouting out of it; the tallest was no
more than head height. A croquet mallet was resting on the grass
surrounded by yellow and red balls. The lawn was framed by beds
of flowers and Hortense almost sneezed when her nose caught the
powerful scents. In the middle of the front garden was a circular
white table, shaded by a large red, white and blue umbrella. The
yellow-painted house, its width spreading out to thirty paces, was
riddled with bullet-like holes in the stone-work; Cilbert knew this
was an escape for high winds. The generous yellow and white
striped canopy ensured that the verandah was covered in shade.

Shielding the bright sunlight with her right hand, Miss Martha, an
auburn-haired woman in her late thirties, emerged from the house.
Walking with assurance she was wearing a knee-length, sleeveless
floral-patterned dress. Hortense and Cilbert straightened their
postures as she approached them. She opened the gate. "Good
morning, Cilbert! I heard the bell and thought my gardener would
answer it but he seems to be late today." Martha turned to
Hortense, offering her a warm smile and her right hand. "And this
is the delightful Hortense, I presume? I know your husband has
been missing you. Men have their requirements, Hortense, so I'm
sure Cilbert is most pleased at last to have you in Kingston."
Martha winked mischievously.

Taking hold of Martha's proffered hand, Hortense was unsure of
what to do with it. Cilbert squirmed with embarrassment as Martha
ran her eyes over Hortense. "Such rich skin," she commented

approvingly. "And nicely toned. Pretty eyes. Now I understand why Cilbert pines for you. When he connected my phone all he would ever talk about was you."

Hortense shot Cilbert a quick glance, wondering how well he knew Martha. "Come inside," urged Martha. "We'll talk on the verandah. It's nice sitting there in the morning but in the afternoon there is no escape from the sun, despite the canopy. My husband, when he was planning this house, had the front facing the wrong way. I advised him to make it face south instead of west. But what do I know? To him I'm only a woman and our common sense is habitually ignored by our men."

Trying desperately to decipher Martha's clipped English accent, Hortense also failed to detect her humour. She decided to say nothing as she was led to a chair upon the verandah. Martha went inside to fetch some drinks and Hortense took the opportunity to whisper to her husband. "Me cyan't understand ah word she say. She talk *too* fast, mon. It's like she ah talk inna foreign tongue. Don't de English talk English?"

"Nuh boder yaself. It sound strange to me when me first hear Martha talk but yuh soon get used to it."

Martha returned with a silver tray burdened with a bottle of white rum, a jug of cola, three glasses and a bowl of ice. She poured out the drinks. "Hortense, my husband always complains that all I ever do is quaff alcohol in the mornings so *don't* tell him about our morning tipple, will you."

"Er, yes, Miss Martha," Hortense replied, not sure of what Martha had said. "Me husband sometimes tickle me inna de marnin to try an' mek me laugh."

Rocking back in laughter, Martha nearly dropped her drink. Cilbert, looking very uncomfortable, sipped his rum as if he had to make it last for a week. "No, Hortense," Martha chuckled. "I don't think you gathered what I said! Oh, what the hell! Why shouldn't I enjoy my rum in the mornings while my husband plays his silly war games up in the hills. My! I don't know who is more insane? The young soldiers who perform their exercises in full uniform in this unbearable heat, or the people that demand that they should do it!"

Thinking Martha's last comment was a joke, Hortense laughed politely.

"Now, to business," Martha resumed. "Hortense, I expect you to arrive at ten o'clock; you can perform most of your chores at that time without me getting in your way. I never rise before eleven. I just expect you to keep the house respectable. My husband sometimes complains that when he has all these guests coming here for drinks, the house is not spick and span. It embarrasses him. He only wants to impress his friends who are on social terms with the governor, very boring people but I will not go into that. Cilbert swears faithfully that you are a good cook and it would be a blessing if you could cook the evening meals for us. I'm afraid I have to admit that my culinary skills are not quite up to it and my skin comes out in an awful rash if I stay in the kitchen for any length of time. It's the dreadful heat."

"Hortense ah well ably cook," interjected Cilbert, nodding and still grinning a silly grin.

"I'm sure she is," said Martha, her eyes fixed on Hortense, admiring her beauty. "Hortense. May I call you Hotty for short?"

Hortense stuttered. "Well, er. Yes, Miss Martha. Back home people did ah call me 'Fire Nettle' inna me young days but now me married everybody call me Mrs Huggins..."

"So that is settled," interrupted Martha. "I will call you Hotty. Would you like to start on Monday? My husband said he would like to give his approval to you before you start but I cannot see the logic in that. He's hardly ever here and I'll be the one you'll have to get along with. Hotty, would you care for more rum?"

"Nuh t'ank yuh, Miss Martha. Me don't finish me first glass yet. Monday alright by me."

"That is splendid," said Martha. "I can tell you it's a weight off my mind. It will present me time to socialise a bit more. My husband always says I'm cooped up in the house too much. Maybe if I had children..."

Martha trailed off and her face briefly betrayed some loss or grievance. She picked up her glass and drained half of its contents. She regained her smile. "Yes, Hotty. We will get along just fine. To be honest with you I need the company rather more than I require a house-help."

Hortense shot Cilbert a growing look of alarm. Cilbert simply smiled back, his body language betraying his self-consciousness.

Having translated what Martha expected of Hortense, Cilbert escorted his wife to Coronation market in the afternoon and there he could only admire the way she haggled for prices and conducted herself in her new environment. They lunched at a harbourside fish restaurant and Hortense took the opportunity to gaze out to sea, wondering in which direction America and England lay; exhausted, drenched teenage boys were hovering around the owners of expensive yachts in the harbour, trying to sell shells and 'pearls' they had found on the sea bed.

In the afternoon Cilbert took his wife to Kingston's craft market, an expansive, warehouse type building where retailers sold hand-made souvenirs, paintings, postcards, wooden carvings and everything else they thought would sell to a fresh visitor from abroad. After much deliberation and listening to the sales patter of two dozen retailers, Hortense purchased an African hand-carved mask.

Returning to Trenchtown in the late afternoon, Hortense found her government yard had come to life. Children were playing in the forecourt, women were singing and humming while going about their chores, the air was laced with the steam off cooking pots, transistor radios were blaring, men were playing dominoes and one young guy in a corner, who had fashioned a guitar out of old fishing lines, a sardine can and wood, was quietly strumming away putting a song together. Once Hortense had placed her shopping in her home, she set about greeting her new neighbours warmly. The men were enthusiastic to meet her, running their eyes over Hortense's lithe figure. The women were a little more cautious, regarding their menfolk from the corner of their eyes. Cilbert felt a pang of jealousy.

Hortense was soon asked if she would attend the 'lawn dance' the next Saturday in nearby Pink Lane where the giant sound system, Duke Reid the mighty Trojan, would be spinning the latest Rhythm and Blues from America. She learned of Duke Reid's 'houses of joy' – wardrobe-sized speaker boxes that could be heard by 'duppy slaves 'pon de ocean bed of de Atlantic'. Residents of the government yard spoke in awe of Duke Reid's now legendary 'microphone mon' Count Clarence. Hortense soaked all this exciting information in like a desert nomad drinking water after a long trek.

Chapter Ten

Approaching the lawn dance, Hortense, clad in a sleeveless white frock and pointed white shoes and Cilbert, sporting a short-sleeved shirt, baggy brown pants and black brogues, could both feel the quiverings of Duke Reid's sound system beneath their soles. Hortense, trying hard not to look fresh from the country, attempted to walk in the confident manner that other Trenchtown young women had perfected – a 'rockin' an' rollin' strut with the emphasis on shivering the backside on every foot-fall. Hortense couldn't quite get it right as Cilbert chuckled at her efforts. "Hortense! Stop try sway ya backside becah yuh will soon drop like ah one foot mon 'pon ah walking wire."

"We inna Trenchtown!" returned Hortense, feeling the grip of Cilbert's hand tighten. "Yuh affe do wha' de Trenchtown people do."

Over-awed, Hortense could see burly bare-backed men off-loading countless crates of beer from a Red Stripe truck. Hundreds of people milled about the lawn-dance entrance, spilling onto the street, anticipation and excitement upon their faces. Up to five thousand ravers had already paid the entrance fee and were inside the lawn dance area. Seven foot high corrugated sheeting providing the perimeter fencing. Outside, a multitude of service industries catered for the patrons. Spirals of smoke climbed into the Kingston night. Among the enterprises jostling and elbowing for space were peanut-punch vendors, sky-juice, jerk chicken and pork takeaway merchants, fresh-fruit sellers, roasted fish grillers, mobile curried goat kitchens, crushed ice retailers, nut and raisin sellers, cigarette and tobacco merchants, cannabis dealers, manesh water brewers, meat pattie outlets, fried dumpling and fish fritter fryers and Jamaica's established rum wholesalers. They all tried to out-barter each other as Kingstonian elders looked on from the other side of the street and wondered if their daughters were really attending night mass.

Deciding on a snack of fried dumpling and roast mackerel, Hortense and Cilbert joined the fifty-yard queue to gain admission as Duke Reid's 'houses of joy' could be heard all over western Kingston.

Once inside, Cilbert bought a Red Stripe beer for Hortense and himself and observed the hollering crowd. People were jiving all around them, contorting their bodies, shaking their backsides and swinging their arms to Peeling Prince Crocodile, King Bow Tie, Lord Bangarang, The Swing Duke of Chacahoula, The Mighty Mule and his Black Roosters and Louis Jordan backed by his Tympani Five. Sweat glistened on their faces as Duke Reid's 'master skankers' displayed their new dance steps to the crowd. 'Stuckies' and 'streggaes' – shanty town whores, were 'greasin' de poles' of young men – their naked thighs rubbing against the crotches in a corkscrew motion in hope of financial reward later on. Dreads smoked cannabis openly in long pipes and chalices. Other rastas, sitting in a shadowed corner, were passing to each other a 'koutchie' full of lambs bread – a variant of the cannabis plant. The smoke they emitted acted as a barrier to them and the throng who did not want to get too close. Table-shuddering games of domino were being played and provoking endless dispute. Conmen and tricksters had set up their tables with green cloths, cups, balls and playing cards; their smiles were wide and accommodating. Chinese-Jamaicans threaded through the crowd to sell their 'number' tickets. Posses of rival western Kingston communities spent their time constructing macho poses and bad-eyeing each other. Drunken and doped-up men were beaten up and robbed, then flung outside into the street, swift-footed ghetto-opportunists making off with their footwear. Baggy-suited and stetson-hatted street toughs played and posed with their German-made ratchet knives, some of them skilled enough to peel an orange with just the one hand. Duke Reid's 'rough gal bodyguards', armed with baseball bats and meat cleavers, guarded the 'houses of joy' from other jealous sound system men who might be in the crowd. Their stony expressions were uncompromising and they were kitted out in black blouses and black skirts.

Wide-eyed, Hortense turned around on the same spot, not quite believing what she was seeing. Abruptly, a fanfare sounded out from the speakers and the crowd parted as if a leper had suddenly materialised and wanted to play a game of tag. Sitting in an elaborately red and gold upholstered chair that was carried by four men dressed in black and crowned by black berets, was the thick-set figure of Duke Reid himself, the Trojan. An array of torchlight spotlit him. An oversize black cape was buttoned to his neck and fell to his feet. Upon his head was a golden coronet with fake red, gold and green stones. In his right hand he was holding a stick that had been painted gold. In his left hand was a shotgun that he pointed towards the sky. He looked down at the baying crowd as if they were his subjects.

The 'Trojan' was carried to his 'control tower' – where his American made amplifiers, decks and records were waiting for him. He stood up in his cowboyboots and gave a kingly wave to the crowd as he allowed his 'foot soldiers' to disrobe him. Gold rings decorated his fingers. Under his cape, and strapping a red-coloured waistcoat were two bandoliers of bullets criss-crossing his chest. Two silver-coloured guns rested snugly in brown leather holsters about his waist. He then aimed his shotgun into the warm Kingston night and fired a shot. The crowd went crazy. Hortense was transfixed watching the Trojan's performance.

Count Clarence, the six foot eleven master of ceremonies, picked up the microphone as the Trojan opened his gold-dusted record box with a gold-coloured key. The Count was wearing a crooked, dusty top-hat and a faded red patched-up hunting jacket. His shoes were cut away at the toes to allow them to fit and his yellow pants only tickled the top of his streaky calf muscles. Hortense thought he looked like a clown she had once seen in a picture book but Clarence looked deadly serious. "Now we ready!" he announced, surveying the chanting masses as if he was about to give the Gettysburg address. "De Duke is here! De warm up session finish! We tek it from de top to de very las' drop! An' we sound sweeter dan ah bird inna tree-top! An' while de Duke is getting ready, let me tell ya about de woe ah Miss Whiny Waist."

Count Clarence cleared his throat as the crowd hushed.

"Miss Whiny Waist ah live inna gulley near ah Salt Lane
She still feel her parents deat', it was ah grievous pain.
She never did ah learn, she never go ah school
Before she was fourteen, she bruk her virgin rule.
Four chile she 'ave by Stub Toe John
But when de fourt' did ah pop out, Stub Toe John gone.
She ah work inna restaurant to try an' survive
But her Chinee mon boss molest her like she ah wife.
Miss Whiny Waist kick de Chinee inna him face
Den she tek up her foot to mek great haste.
She gone back to her children, nuh money to feed dem
So she decide to become ah streggae, teking up all ah her hem.
Yuh see her at de dances, greasin' mon pole
Sometimes she gone ah hotel, wid ah white mon she ah roll
She nuh care if dey young or weder dem ole.
She will grine yuh ah bush an' even in de gulley
But if yuh don't waan scar yuh better pay de fee.
She nuh feel ashamed an' she demand yuh call her Miss
But nuh pounds and pence coulda mek her give yuh ah kiss."

Displaying their appreciation of Count Clarence's storytelling, bad men fired their guns into the navy-blue sky while others roared their acclaim. Hortense fell down to the turf, covering her head with her hands, thinking some kind of gang war had erupted. "Lord me Jesus! Dem ah fire 'pon each udder!" Cilbert picked her up but it took Hortense a few minutes to realise that Kingstonian acknowledgment didn't come in the form of rum toasts and a pound note slapped against the forehead. Nearby ravers stifled their chuckles with their palms and muttered under their breath, "look 'pon de fool fool country woman!"

Downing another Red Stripe to compose herself, Hortense, wanting to prove a point, led Cilbert by the hand and they proceeded to jig wildly to the sounds of the American south – raw, black, rock and roll and New Orleans 'jook joint' jazz. "Me might as well do wha' de Kingston people ah do," Hortense told herself, hardly hearing herself speak. Cilbert could only keep up with his wife for an hour before he took a breather, observing a domino game. Hortense accepted other men's offers to dance with them and jigged them to a standstill, laughing as she did so while picking up her dress to expose her thighs. Men formed a circle around her and clapped their hands, some of them wolf-whistling, some blaring their klaxons. One man even offered a wedding proposal. Hortense felt that Kingston had finally given its blessing to her. Cilbert looked on with a mixture of pride and outrage.

Upon the midnight hour, Duke Reid played a Jamaican song, a jazz infused mento tune by a singer named Wilfred Gray. It was entitled 'Bad breed neighbour ah t'ief me Sunday chicken.' The crowd went absolutely wild, demanding a play-back. The throng not only received a play-back, they also had Wilfred Gray there in person, accepting the microphone from Count Clarence; Wilfred was only five foot two and the difference in size didn't escape the Kingston audience. "*Look 'pon Goliath an' David*!" someone yelled. "*Wilfred! Where ya slingstone?*"

To riotous cheering, Wilfred burst into the chorus of his popular song. "*So me knock 'pon de door of me bad breed neighbour, chicken feders was 'pon him arms an' all over...*"

Dodging the countless empty bottles that were all over the lawn and scattered upon the street outside, a brooding Cilbert escorted Hortense back home. Once inside, Cilbert slammed the door shut.

"Me never feel so much shame inna me life!" Cilbert yelled. "Yuh forget yuh married to me? Wha' yuh t'ink yuh was doing dancing like ah blue foot wid stranger?"

Hortense innocently shrugged her shoulders. "Wha' me do wrong? Me only dancing. Me cyan't help it if ya foot tired an' yuh waan' tek ah res'. Wha' yuh expect me to do? Stan' up an' do not'ing an' look 'pon de nuh teet', dry foot people dem who ah beg money? We pay good money to go ah dance so me waan to get me enjoyment."

"Enjoyment! Dat is wha' yuh call it? *Nuh* wife ah mine will embarrass me! Yuh hear me!"

"If yuh don't like it den nex' time me will go ah dance 'pon me own. Cilbert ya too possessive."

Cilbert, becoming more enraged by Hortense's dismissive words, marched up to her, his eyes blazing. Hortense didn't back away an inch. "So wha'? Yuh come to beat me now? Who yuh t'ink yuh is? Me mudder? Yuh t'ink dat me cyan't fight mon?"

"Nuh! Yuh is me wife an' me *nah* tolerate ya behaviour. Ya carry on jus' like dem streggae women."

"So yuh t'ink me ah Jezebel? Come outta me face, Cilbert, becah yuh talk pure fart! Me foot well tired an' me waan me bed."

Unable to keep the leash on his temper, Cilbert swung a right fist that struck Hortense's left jaw. She fell to the ground, tried to get up but her legs buckled from the shock. She crawled to the bed, climbed on top of it and lay prostrate upon her back. Cilbert, immediately regretting his actions, studied his right fist before gradually releasing it. He stood rooted to the spot, his eyes shifting between Hortense and his right hand. He then went to pour himself a drink; a shot of undiluted white rum. Grimacing as the spirit scorched his throat, he then undressed to his briefs before dropping onto the spare bed.

As the roosters chorused in the dawn hour, Trenchtown mothers awoke their young sons and sent them scampering to the lawn dance site to collect as many returnable bottles as they could carry. On their way home they saw scores of women heading for church, singing as they did so. But no fowl's cry or gospel song had awoken Cilbert.

Suffering an excruciating pain in his genitals, Cilbert opened his eyes, raised his head and looked down beyond his belly button. Hortense, a bread knife in one hand that was poised over his limp penis and his testicles firmly viced in her other hand, regarded him with cold eyes. In a calm voice, almost a whisper, she swore, "lick me again an' as de Most High is me witness, me will chop off ya strikin' seedbag an' mek ya walk like t'ree leg donkey. Y'understand me? Me had to endure dat kind of tribulation from bwai when me der ah school but me woulda prefer *dead* to allow me own mon to beat me. *Try* dat again an' see which one of we mek appointment wid Dovecote cemetery first!"

Petrified, Cilbert nodded, trying to inch himself backwards. Hortense released her grip, walked to the dresser where she collected her towel and toiletries for her morning fresh and went outside, humming a tune she had heard at the lawn dance. Cilbert emitted a long sigh, closing his eyes for a long second as he did so. He would never raise a hand to his wife again.

For the next few months Hortense made it her business to get to know her neighbours. Mrs Laura Lee and her husband Kolton shared the kitchen with her, and Hortense often minded their six children. Kolton was an usher at a downtown cinema where the hard-to-please patrons were fed a continuous diet of American westerns; the screen was perforated with bullet holes and Hortense learned the proprietors were planning to display their films on a white-washed, concrete wall. Laura, renownd for her tough, unblinking negotiating skills, owned a mobile snack bar and won most of her custom on lawn dance nights.

Across the way, the broad Oliver Minott, a bicycle mechanic, lived with his wife, Babsy and their four children. Hortense noticed that Oliver cleaned his bicycle meticulously before he set off every morning, always returning from work late and was forever moaning that there was no water left to wash away the oil and grease his skin had collected during his working day. Residents nicknamed him 'Midnight Oil'.

Up on the second floor lived Bigger Knowles and his family. Bigger was a chef at an uptown hotel and he gained many friends by bringing his work home and sharing it around. Hortense soon discovered that residents of the tenement yard always complained of Bigger blocking the toilets with his 'monster shits'. "Lord bless me soul an' protect me wha' me see dis very marnin!" Mercy, the Christian woman would shriek. "Bigger's mighty bottom hole strike again! Wha' ah palava! It coming like ah mighty dam dat ah hold up river flow! Him should buil' him own strikin' toilet fe him incredible bottom!" Yielding to her nagging, Hortense escorted the virginal Mercy to church most Sundays. Hortense would never reveal to her that she overheard the single young men who lived in the yard waging bets on who would 'grine Mercy an' mek her pum-pum bawl' first.

Delroy Dyer, who worked on the docks, lived with his wife, Jaseth, two doors away from Hortense. He informed Cilbert that the deep scar upon his right shoulder was sustained following a dock-workers strike in 1956; the army was called in following the declaration of a national emergency and Delroy sustained his injury during one of the many harbour-side skirmishes. When the children were put to bed and the adults were sitting on their stoops, reflecting on their day, Delroy, who was the same age as Hortense, practised his harmonies with his friends while strumming his homemade guitar. Hortense and others were quick to offer their advice and views on Delroy's songwriting abilities. Delroy had named his group the Mighty Invincibles.

They were practising for auditions at the Carib theatre where Vere Johns held his weekly *Opportunity Hour.* If they were successful they could hear themselves being broadcast on the newly formed Jamaican Broadcasting Corporation but the competition was fierce; the last auditions attracted over a thousand wannabe Billy Eckstine's and Nat King Cole's and scuffles had broken out in the two hundred yard long queue. It was not uncommon for an artiste to finally reach the stage and then be pelted with bottles, stones, rotten coconuts, a variety of nuts and worn-out shoes before he concluded his first verse. Delroy initially had to ignore the cutting remarks from his neighbours while he rehearsed his group. "Nuh, mon! Wha' kind ah fool fool lyric is dat!" Someone might say. "Yuh nuh 'ave any sense? Yuh better go ah school an' t'ief dictionary! Becah yuh surely need it. An' de voice sound like long-belly goat ah scream when him drop down inna sewage pit! Ha Ha! About yuh waan be ah star!"

Kingsley Banton lived alone above Hortense's apartment but nobody was quite sure what he did for a living. He was never seen out of his sharp colourful clothes and his lace-up shoes were always well polished. He wore a natty hat that was angled to cover his scarred left eye. He wouldn't rise until the afternoon and when he departed to whatever business concern he had, nobody would see him until the next day. Cilbert, who was short-strawed by his neighbours to learn more about the mysterious Kingsley, went upstairs to Kingsley's apartment offering him a drink of rum. Kingsley declined but Cilbert had a glimpse of an Oriental-looking woman through a crack of a door. Cilbert, in his report to his fellow residents, guessed that Kingsley was a pimp. Oliver gave Kingsley the moniker of 'Black Drac'.

Hortense learned that Cilbert was a man of routine and habit. Finishing work early on Friday afternoons and smiling a grapefruit-wide smile, without fail he would deposit a few shillings into his bank account. "Ah very fine day, Miss." As the tiller gave him his receipt, Cilbert would mutter *"Englan'"* under his breath. He would then pay the rent, his eyes flirting with the sour-faced, toffee-skinned clerk. Disliking the rancour and bangarang of Coronation market, he would take a bus from Crossroads to Papine, where he would buy fresh fruits and snacks that he would place under napkins in a small bankra. Hortense would see him at four o'clock on the dot, sitting patiently on the ground outside Miss Martha's gates, smoking his Four Aces cigarettes. His bankra was topped up with Dragon stout and Red Stripe beer. Miss Martha, shaking her head, would continually ask Hortense why he didn't want to wait inside. "Me don't know, Miss Martha. Sometimes Cilbert too shy like."

After Hortense finished work, Cilbert, wanting to escape the city noise and air, would escort Hortense to the spacious Hope Botanical Gardens. There they would stroll arm in arm in the late afternoon sun, refreshed by the soft breezes that came down from the Blue Mountains. Cilbert would throw a penny into a fountain, making a wish while holding his wife's hand. Then he would pick out a secluded spot for a picnic, usually under the leaves of a Blue Mahoe. The beautiful scenery was a reminder to the couple of the Claremont valley. They would stay until the twilight hours, sometimes making love, sometimes just enjoying each other's company, sharing dreams of the future while gazing up at the steep-rising green hills that overlooked uptown Kingston.

Every two weeks Hortense received a letter from Jenny, informing her of all the gossip, susu and going-ons in the Claremont valley. Kwarhterleg had passed away and gone to his reward in January, 1958. A grieving Joseph, escorted by Isaac and Neville, had taken his body back to the place of his birth, Browns Town, and buried him there – Kwarhterleg's last wish. Many of Kwarhterleg's family had moved away and subsequently there were only seven mourners who watched Kwarhterleg's coffin being lowered into the ground. It was whispered that Joanne Lindus, now in her late seventies, visited Kwarhterleg's grave every night for three weeks following the burial. Neville had witnessed the pain and guilt in her eyes and he remarked, "everybody has to mek choices. Joanne made hers but leaving Kwarhterleg has haunted her every step since an' every step she will tek in dis world."

After Kwarhterleg's funeral, Joseph became even more remote to his fellow villagers, refusing to go into town on a Friday night to enjoy a beer with the new friends he had found since his story-time session. Instead he would visit Jenny, bringing with him some of the produce of his land. Amy continued to dust and clean the improvised bed where Kwarhterleg slept and sometimes forgot that she now only cooked for two.

Thankful that Amy had received him back into her life and wanting to busy himself around the house, Joseph was building a verandah as a token of his love. He had already repaired and upholstered two chairs for them to sit in. Grandpapa Neville, still walking the land straight-backed, was forever asking Joseph and Amy when Hortense or Jenny would provide his second great-grandson. Jackie had split up with her husband, who was now a chronic alcoholic; God-fearers whispered that he was possessed by a demon and had called on Isaac to perform an exorcism. Carmesha was pregnant with Levi's first child but Levi had rejected Isaac's demand that they should marry. Jenny was a bridesmaid to Mr DaCosta's daughter, Elvira, who married a young man from Treasure Beach; some alleged she was with child. Higglers in the market were claiming that Isaac had a love-child born to him by a fourteen-year-old girl who lived in Alexandria.

Jenny was ashamed of this alleged scandal involving her father-in-law and urged her husband, Jacob, to move away from Claremont and head for Kingston. There would be plenty of ministerial work for Jacob to perform in the capital, she argued. Jacob dithered and dallied, torn between his father and his new wife. And his elder brother, Levi, who he had grown to respect, counselled against the move also. Jenny, who was now teaching English at the local school, wrote to Hortense, '...*could you imagine we living together again? It will be just like the old days. If you have Jacob and myself sharing the burden of rent, then you could save more and finally forward to England. Me feel so lonesome without you in my life. Papa always looks for me but it's not the same like before. Something has been lost between us. Mama is the same old Mama. Her heart still cool like the midnight breeze. Sometimes I sit under our tree and think of all the conversations we used to have.*' Jenny always concluded her letters to Hortense by writing many kisses and '*mek sure yuh give me love to Cilbert*'.

Missing her sister's maternal-like affection since she had relocated to Kingston, Hortense presented Jenny's idea to Cilbert. Thinking of England, Cilbert quickly agreed. All Jacob had to do was to find a ministerial position in Kingston and he had the contacts to do so because he had dealt with all of Isaac's correspondence since he was ten years old.

Dusting Martha's front room one January morning in 1958, Hortense heard Martha call her from the kitchen. "I'm really in a fiddle of what we should cook for my husband's guests tonight, Hotty."

With a dust cloth draped over her right shoulder, Hortense appeared in the kitchen with her hands upon her hips. "*We?*"

"Well, er, I get your point, Hotty," Martha replied, a little taken aback by Hortense's confrontational tone.

Martha was hunting in her food cupboards, shaking her head. "I would like to offer them something quite different, a meal they can appreciate and remember. I think my husband is too polite to suggest that my beef stews are becoming tedious."

Hortense thought about it. "Why yuh nah come shopping wid me der ah market? We will decide wha' fe cook when we reach der."

"The market?" Martha asked, her face a picture of astonishment. "I have never been. It's not a place where a woman of my standing would frequent. My husband has always brought food home from the army camp – they receive British foodstuffs every week."

"Yes! An' it's tasteless! Me get sick an' tired of cooking it. Roast beef, potatoes an' blasted cabbage! An' as fe de market is nuh place fe ah woman of ya standing, yuh really mean it's nuh ah place where white women waan to go," said Hortense, now releasing her pent-up frustration with her employer who she felt couldn't do anything for herself.

Sitting down at her kitchen table, Martha was about to admonish Hortense for speaking out of turn – no employee of hers had ever been so forthright with their opinion. "Are you aware that I could quite easily dismiss you for your last remarks?" Martha said.

"Dismiss me fe telling de trut'?" Hortense dared. "Since me work here all me see yuh do is get up inna de marnin, nyam ya breakfast while yuh complain about ya husband doing dis an' dat, den yuh drive down to ah uptown bar where yuh drink liquor alone. Den yuh come back, sit down 'pon de verandah, drink ah nex' drink an' start complain dat de sun too strong. Wha' kinda life is dat?"

Dropping her head with the realisation that her life was empty, Martha replied, "you have to understand, Hotty. A white woman living here is not as free as you might think. We are not supposed to just wander down to the market on our own, we cannot just entertain the thought of attending those lawn dances that you speak of. Even drinking alone in an uptown bar is frowned upon – but I will *not* give up that."

"Rubbish yuh ah talk, Miss Martha! Wha' is der to stop yuh doing somet'ing different?"

Miss Martha raised her head and managed a smile. "What is there indeed?"

Escorting Miss Martha to Papine market, Hortense introduced her to the names and varieties of Jamaican food. Higglers looked upon the two women with amazement as Martha found the banter and characters who worked there fascinating. As Martha held onto Hortense's arm, they bought curried goat, chicken, jerk seasoning, lamb shanks, snapper fish, bream, dasheen, breadfruit, spring greens, yams, plantains, crabmeat, salted cod, okra, spinach, tamarind puree, coconut oil, varieties of herbs, avocados and mangos.

Their shopping nearly completed, Martha felt safe enough to investigate on her own and she was immediately besieged by vendors and higglers. At first alarmed, Martha backed away from the market sellers but catching sight of Hortense laughing in front of her, she bought two cups of peanut punch.

Stopping off on the way home at a rum bar, Martha couldn't contain her excitement of her shopping adventure. "My presence provoked much attention, Hotty! I felt like a Broadway star!"

Reaching home, Martha marched to her kitchen with purpose. "This time I will help, Hotty. What shall we cook?"

"Coconut chicken," suggested Hortense, who was left to carry in most of the groceries. "An' fried fish!"

Hortense showed Martha how to wash the chicken with vinegar, lemon and water. She then covered the chicken pieces with a light film of flour before frying until golden brown. Placing the chicken into an oven, Hortense displayed to Martha how to wash and prepare vegetables. When almost cooked, Hortense removed the chicken from the oven and glazed it with honey and sprinkled coconut gratings over it. She returned the chicken to the oven for another ten minutes then she dressed it with chopped coriander. "My goodness! It smells delightful," remarked Martha.

Showing Martha how to gut the fish and trim its fins, Hortense allowed Martha to season the bream with spices, salt and chilli. Lightly dusting the fish with seasoned flour, Martha fried the bream in hot oil until crispy. "Is that alright, Hotty? I fear it's too dry! My! That oil is a nuisance when it splashes upon your arm!"

"Ya doing alright, Miss Martha," laughed Hortense, enjoying herself in the role as teacher and recognising the child within Martha. "Like me said, der is not'ing to it."

"Hotty, you will stay when I serve dinner won't you? Just in case anything goes awry. I will pay you for your time. I have had a splendid day."

"Nuh worry yaself, Miss Martha. Besides, me waan some of dat chicken too!"

Miss Martha's and her husband's guests were a middle-aged white couple who lived in Constant Spring. Hortense declined Martha's invitation to join the dinner party – she still felt uncomfortable around white men. Instead, Hortense busied herself in the kitchen with the washing up while stealing glances at the reaction from those who were tasting the meal. Martha served the coconut chicken and fried bream with roasted breadfruit, yams, spring greens and spinach. The dinner was a complete success and upon receiving congratulations, Martha didn't forget to honour Hortense's involvement.

Later that night, as Martha's husband drove the guests home, Hortense was relaxing with her feet up on the verandah. She was sipping the peanut punch that Martha had earlier bought for her. "I cannot say how grateful I am," offered Martha. "My husband was so proud of me. Of course you are right about me, Hotty. I need to try different things. I have been lethargic for too long."

"Do dat mean yuh will come lawn dance wid me," laughed Hortense.

"Hotty, you might be able to teach me to cook but do you really think my husband would permit me to attend a downtown lawn dance? That would be stretching it a bit don't you think? I would be quite happy to hear of your descriptions of these colourful events. My imagination will do the rest. Hotty, raise your glass to a good day."

The two women chinked their glasses, recognising a closer understanding of each other.

It was a muggy April afternoon in 1958 when Hortense took a break from her work in Martha's house, sat in a chair upon the verandah, poured herself a shot of rum mixed with lemonade and started to read one of Jenny's letters that she didn't have time to read in the morning. She didn't notice Martha walking up the pathway, laden with shopping.

"Good afternoon, Hotty," Martha chirped, her wide-brimmed hat flapping in the breeze.

Hortense looked up in alarm, shot up out of her chair and hoped Martha might think her rum cocktail was a glass of water. "Good afternoon, Miss Martha," she greeted with a huge smile. "Yuh enjoy ya shopping ah Papine market?"

"It was a delight, Hotty. The people there are so pleasant, so colourful. I love the way they sing while they work and try to entertain the customers. My goodness! It seems that all Jamaicans want to be a Mr Bojangles. Did I tell you I saw the great man perform once on Broadway?"

"Yes, yuh did, Miss Martha," Hortense laughed. "Plenty time!"

"They even offered to carry my groceries to the car. So accommodating those Papine marketers."

Hortense guessed that the stall-holders in Papine market saw Miss Martha coming and immediately increased their prices by fifty per cent.

Martha could smell the rum. "Hotty, take your seat again and enjoy your break, don't let me stop you. Besides, I need to discuss something with you. If you could spare a moment?"

Sitting down again, Hortense gripped the arms of the chair tightly as Martha went into the kitchen to offload her shopping. She returned with a bottle of Appleton's finest, bringing a glass for herself. She topped off a suspicious Hortense's glass before she took her seat. "Now, Hotty," she began. "It seems that circumstances have upset our future plans. There is talk of independence in the air and yesterday my husband's seniors made it clear that his services may not be required for much longer."

"Wha' do yuh mean, Miss Martha?"

"Well, my dear, Hotty, it means that the British in the next year or so will gradually pull out of this blessed country. For when independence comes, my husband and his like will have no role to play. We'll have to return home."

"Dat is terrible, Miss Martha! Will yuh lose ya house an' everyt'ing?"

Martha chuckled, adoring Hortense's naivety. "Not quite, Hotty. That we can sell. We will only lose a certain dignity but we will be fine. I'm sure the British army will find some new role for my husband or perhaps they will pension him off; between you and me he is nudging fifty-eight. I'm more worried that I would have to let you go. I know it's a bit of a devil finding employment out there and I will lose more of a friend than a worker."

"Nuh worry yaself, Martha. Nuh need to look so sad. Me husband an' meself are saving to forward ah England an' me sure me cyan get ah nex' job."

Martha smiled. "And I'm sure you will do well. We have grown to love this country," she admitted. "The larger than life people, the pace of life. And I have been invited to the governor's mansion for grand dinners. By the way, he's fine. Even after independence, Jamaica will still require a governor. I suppose the only white people who will remain are those in business and the Noel Cowards and Ian Flemings of this island."

"Who is Noel Coward an' Ian Fleming?" asked Hortense.

Martha laughed again before sipping her undiluted rum. "They are both writers, Hotty, who once came here for their holidays and loved the island so much that they now reside here."

"Is dat so? Ah mon could live off wha' dem write?"

"Of course, Hotty. Their adventure in this island will continue but mine is coming to an end. It's ironic that you and Cilbert want to embark on an adventure to England. Whenever I reflect upon my years there, I remember the drabness, the hurrying and the scurrying to realise one's dream. The smog and the cold. But don't let me put you off, Hotty. It's just that I thought I would end my days here and perhaps that's why I feel a certain melancholy at returning to England."

"Me an' Cilbert don't intend to spend de res' of we days inna England. Nuh, Miss Martha. Jus' ah few years so we can save ah liccle money an' come back an' buil' ah pretty house jus' like ya own."

"That's a fine ambition, Hotty. May I propose a toast to it."

Chapter Eleven

Feeling slightly tipsy, Cilbert made his way home from a friend's yard in Denham Town. He had enjoyed a fine fish supper and quite a number of Dragon stouts, his reward for fixing a radio. He had now got used to the desperate stares of the shanty dwellers and learned to ignore the pitiful, hungry faces of young children who seemed to have forgotten how to play. There were only so many pennies he could give and those who received them never forgot the faces of their benefactors, always begging for more as Cilbert had discovered.

Walking past Second Street in Trenchtown he heard domestic disputes, barking dogs, the crackle of fires, radios tuned into Miami stations and the alto-pitched voices of yard dwellers attempting to imitate the black American trio harmony groups that were growing extremely popular. Inside the yards, children were imitating the singing adults, performing their dance steps and even bowing when they finished their songs. Their mothers laughed heartily. One over-enthusiastic child, who was taking the mickey out of his father, was cuffed upon the neck and sent to fetch a bottle of cod liver oil to 'clean out him t'roat' for being so impertinent. Smiling, Cilbert recalled what Hortense had remarked to him a few days ago. *'Every Jamaican waan to be ah Misser Bojangles.'*

Cilbert saw five ghetto toughs idling in a corner, their eyes darting from one side to the other. He quickened his pace, hoping they didn't see him but he was smartly cut off. Cilbert recognised them vaguely and produced one of his widest grins. Long ago Cilbert had learned not to carry any large amounts of cash when walking alone at night. "Me's ah poor mon dat come from de country," he said, displaying his palms. "If me coulda give yuh somet'ing den me would. An' me don't look nuh trouble."

"We *nah* look fe money," the bulkiest man replied, eyeing Cilbert from his hair-line and down to his dust-specked shoes. "We sight yuh around Trenchtown an' yuh cyan't live here so widout showing ya political colours. So who yuh intend to vote for? Which one yuh favor? PNP or JLP?"

The four other men closed in on Cilbert, forming a semi-circle.

"Me don't involve meself wid politics, sa," Cilbert replied, feigning a little misunderstanding. He stepped back a pace. "Me jus' do me liccle work to keep me family an' to keep ah roof over we head. Where me come from inna de country we don't know too much about politics."

"Dat cyan't gwarn so!" the big man riposted. "We don't like people who sit 'pon de fence. Ya eider fe one or de udder. So me ask yuh again. Which party yuh gwarn to vote for?"

Cilbert realised he had an evens chance. He felt the sweat collect around his temples and the quickening of his heartbeat. He shifted his eyes, searching for an escape route but he was surrounded. Shanty dwellers ignored the scenario as if it was simply part of a daily routine they had witnessed many times. Cilbert tried to guess from the way the thugs were dressed to what political persuasion they belonged to but found no clues. In their scuffed shoes, baggy slacks and bright-coloured T-shirts they looked like any other Trenchtown man. Cilbert recalled the vivid descriptions of political violence he had heard about; most victims never lived to tell their tales. He could sense the moistening of his palms. The fish supper was now dancing inside his stomach and he could hear every breath he took. Closing his eyes for a milisecond, he blurted out, "PNP."

Still bad-eyeing Cilbert's feet, the apparent leader of the gang, spat a thick spit of saliva and tobacco remains on the dusty ground and said in a stretched whisper, "wrrronnng mooovve, sa." He clenched his fists.

Cilbert tried to run but felt two pairs of arms grappling around his neck. His legs were kicked away from under him and his head thudded against the dusty, hard ground. Cilbert briefly opened his eyes only to see unlaced heavy boots aiming for his face. He covered up as best as he could but he heard the sickening crunch of his nose being broken. A sharp pain shooted up to his forehead and around his eyes. He tried to stem the bleeding from his nostrils, leaving his eyes exposed. A wild kick split the delicate skin between Cilbert's left eyebrow and eyelid. Blood spurted out. Cilbert could only see watery, indistinct shadows from his good eye. He heard someone say, "we know where yuh der-ya! An' we know ya pretty wife too! So yuh better support an' sponsor de JLP."

As he writhed in agony, Cilbert could hear the scampering of boots fading away. He wished he had never come to this accursed city, and then he slipped into unconsciousness.

It was Kingsley Banton who found Cilbert slumped against a shanty town wall. Not caring that Cilbert's blood was staining his 'Saturday night' shirt, Kingsley placed one of Cilbert's arms around his neck and acting as a crutch, supported Cilbert home.

Upon seeing her husband, Hortense screamed. "Dem bastard! Dem cruel bastard! Lucifer mus' be dem fader an' Jezebel der mudder. As de Most High is me witness see me don't rip open dem belly an' hang out dem liver 'pon ah shanty woman washing line!"

Hortense's histrionics alerted her neighbours and they all came to see what had occurred. Laura rushed to boil some water while Bigger Knowles bounded up the stairs to fetch his herbs. Oliver readied his bike to take Cilbert to the Jubilee hospital in downtown Kingston as Mercy comforted Hortense in a torrent of 'Lord mercy me's' and 'Hear me prayers'.

Once Laura had managed to stem the bleeding, Cilbert's body was placed in her push-cart that was now attached to Oliver's bike. Hortense, Mercy, Bigger and Kolton escorted the whimpering Cilbert to hospital.

At the Jubilee hospital reception, Hortense stood still in shock, not quite believing what was in front of her. People with gaping wounds, disfigured faces, burnt hands and a number of other appalling injuries, were laying on collapsible chairs, slumped on the blood-spotted floor and sitting against grimy walls. Flies and mosquitoes buzzed around a hanging, naked bulb. A crushed cockroach, its bodily fluids staining the wooden floor, had crawled its last crawl beneath a filthy window. Ants went about their business freely beneath the unlevel skirtings and through wall fissures. Behind the reception desk, lying prostrate in a corner, were two men. They had recently died from stab wounds and were waiting to be taken to the morgue. A single nurse was patching up whoever could be patched up; she looked utterly spent. Two doctors quickly marched by now and again, their white cloaks stained with blood. Revolting smells, not wafted away by any form of air conditioning, assaulted Hortense's nose.

Hortense turned to Bigger. "Cyan't we tek him to de university hospital?"

"Nuh, Hortense. Dat hospital is fe uptown people. We don't 'ave de right address. Trenchtown we come from."

Cilbert had to wait eight hours for treatment and when he finally emerged from the Jubilee hospital, wearing a dressing upon his nose, he had to shield his swollen eyes from the morning sun. Now conscious, he said to Hortense, "me gwarn to work every hour dat is available to me. See if me don't! An' me gwarn to save *every* penny. Me an' yuh gwarn to leave dis cursed town an' go ah England."

Writing a tearful letter to Jenny the same morning, Hortense explained to her what had befallen her husband. Too frightened to leave her yard, Hortense gave the letter to Laura to mail at the post office. Mercy, having initiated a group prayer at her church for Cilbert and Hortense, returned to the yard in the afternoon. With Laura, Mercy helped to cook the Sunday dinner for Hortense and Cilbert and it was shared out to all their new friends. Hortense was reduced to tears at the gesture and thanked them all.

Although still feeling acute pain, against well-intentioned advice, Cilbert set off for work the next day. He would never miss a working day or an overtime opportunity until he set sail for England.

Reading Hortense's letter in the empty church hall where she taught English to Claremontonian children, Jenny palmed away her tears. Only now did she recognise that her infatuation with Cilbert would never fade. She could not dismiss it. A smiling Cilbert had lodged himself in her inner vision from the first time she had blessed eyes on him and now she just had to see him, at least be close to him. "Me cyan never 'ave him but to look 'pon him every day would be ah blessing," she whispered to herself. "At least me could 'ave dat."

As soon as Jacob arrived home from his parish duties, Jenny suggested a walk in the hills to watch the sinking red sun dip below the western ranges. She told Jacob about the contents of Hortense's letter. Reaching a hill-top that offered them a spectacular view of the Claremont valley, they lay on their backs to count the stars, feeling the delicate breezes that stole in from the north coast. Jenny, who preferred to make love outdoors, seduced her husband by undressing slowly. "Me love de hillside breeze ah lick me naked skin," she grinned mischievously. "It feel so soothing." Jacob didn't need a second invitation.

Seconds after they had made love, Jenny pleaded with Jacob to start afresh in Kingston, where she would be by her sister's side. "She need me, Jacob. Hortense 'ave nuh family der ah Trenchtown an' she affe deal wid tribulation 'pon her own. Cilbert ah nearly lose him life! We might as well move becah ya fader ah scandalise himself by breeding dat young girl from Alexandria. People look 'pon me funny now an' me cyan't tek dem passing remark about ya fader's situation. Me beg yuh, Jacob. If yuh love me yuh woulda do dis t'ing fe me. Yuh know how me an' Hortense close. Me lose me one sweet brudder already. If somet'ing happen to Hortense an' me nah der to help her me would never forgive meself!"

Following many days and nights of Jenny beseeching Jacob, he finally relented and set about writing to his contacts in Kingston, enquiring about ministerial positions. He informed Isaac that he felt the Most High had need for him in Kingston. "Same way dat Jesus did ah walk among de poor an' unruly trying to save dem soul, same way I affe work. Der is plenty, plenty more soul inna Kingston to save."

Resisting the temptation to discourage his son, Isaac nodded his acceptance. He recognised that Jacob was utterly besotted with Jenny. But secretly he cursed the very existence of the Rodney family.

Chapter Twelve

Sitting upon his luggage and dabbing his forehead with a flannel, Jacob could only chuckle when a wild-haired beggar approached a pedestrian pleading for spare cash. The wayfarer shook his head before hurrying on his way but the bare-footed moocher lifted his head and said, "t'ank yuh fe considering me plea," before walking away as if he was departing the stage following a command performance. Glancing at the bus driver who had driven Jacob and Jenny from Claremont to the capital and was now putting his feet up in his cabin as he rolled a joint, Jacob laughed out loud. "Yes, Lord," he whispered. "I 'ave plenty work to do inna dis place."

Arms crossed and eyebrows angled in perfect impatience, Jenny paced up and down ten yards of the street, her eyes searching here and there. Despite the one-hundred-degree heat, no bead of sweat marked her angular face. The frosty, disapproving look that her mother offered her when she departed Claremont was still fresh in her memory, whereas the tears of her father were fading. Now in the city, she seemed to dislike the very air she breathed. Her white shoes were echoing off the concrete and she ignored the nodded greetings from people who passed her. She was wearing a smart yellow, calf-length dress and a white hat that made observers think 'wha' is dis long, well-dressed woman doing inna downtown?'

"Half-past two Hortense said," Jenny complained while glaring at her watch. "Where she der? It's t'ree ah clock now. Yuh t'ink me 'ave time to stan' up an' look 'pon tough-toe people?"

Wearing a light-blue suit with a navy-blue tie, Jacob replied, "nuh stress yaself, my love. We'll give dem anoder fifteen minutes an' if dey don't come den we will mek our own way. I 'ave de address."

"Mek we own way?" Jenny protested. "Say we get lost. Only de Most High knows wha' will happen to we wid all dese wolves an' leopards aroun'. Look 'pon dem! Me surprise dey don't chop out me liver to put inna dem cooking pot!"

Laughing, Jacob returned his gaze to the street, watching the downtown people going about their daily business. He noticed they moved quicker than the clans of the Claremont valley and seemed to carry a heavier burden upon their shoulders. "Don't start fuss, Jenny. All I see is poor people ah walk up an' down, doing dem t'ing."

Jenny primed her tongue to cuss about the beggars and vagrants she had seen since she had disembarked but before she could do so, she heard her sister's voice.

"Jenny! Jenny!"

Spinning around, Jenny saw Hortense pacing up the uneven pavement to greet her. She was waving and smiling, her sheer presence causing people to turn their heads. "Hortense Huggins," Jenny rebuked, her hands upon her hips and her humour failing to improve. She restrained her relief. "Don't yuh ever keep time! Jacob an' meself been waiting fe long time an' de people aroun' look 'pon we like dem ah craven wolf ah look 'pon ah t'ree legged sheep."

"Oh, Jenny stop ya naggy-naggy self," Hortense laughed, giving her sister a mighty hug. "Yuh always mek prize bull outta maaga calf. Always ah moan an' complain about somet'ing. Me surprise yuh never get arrested fe licking down de bus driver."

"So yuh notice how dem rude an' ungodly too? Me could nuh believe me ears. Every second word ah bad word an' if Massa God don't strike him down tonight den Him mus' ah stop lissen."

"Oh, Jenny, come here girl an' give ya liccle sister ah mighty hug."

Jenny seemed to be embarrassed as Hortense kissed her on both cheeks and squeezed the breath out of her. "Hortense yuh ah grip me too tight. Yuh waan crush me? Look how yuh crease up me nice dress! Yuh know how long it tek me to press it dis marnin? Me had to rise at four o'clock when even de big mout' rooster still ah sleep!" Jenny didn't reveal that she had longed for her sister's embrace.

"Jenny! Yuh don't change at all," remarked Hortense, releasing her cuddle. "Ya still ya cuss-cuss self. Don't ya long mout' an' busy busy tongue ever say anyt'ing else dan pure complaints?"

Almost yielding to a smile, Jenny asked, "where's Cilbert?"

"Cilbert stop off der ah bar to buy some liquor. He soon come."

Hortense then turned her attention to Jacob who had been laughing at the exchanges of the two sisters. They hugged each other warmly as Jenny searched for Cilbert.

Carrying two bags full of Red Stripe beer and Dragon stout, Cilbert approached from a side road. Jenny spotted him first. She broke out into a full grin and although feeling an urge to run, walked casually to greet him, feeling conscious that Hortense's eyes may be upon her. She didn't want Hortense to know that the fine yellow dress that Mrs Walters had made was for Cilbert's benefit. He still had that loping, feline-like strut, Jenny observed, and the promise of mischief in his dark eyes. The hat, angled to cover his left eye, made him look mysterious and sexy. "Cilbert! Long time nuh see. Yuh been looking after me sister alright? She chat off ya ears yet?" She kissed him formally upon the left cheek. Cilbert placed his hands on Jenny's shoulders and returned the kiss upon her forehead. Jenny felt a rippling, tingling sensation that electrified her body. Her skin, it seemed, became extra-sensitive and she worried that her pleasure overload might be detected.

"Of course me look after her alright," Cilbert finally answered. He took a step back. "Jenny, yuh look so elegant, lady-like. Mighty fine! Yuh mus' be keeping Mrs Walters well happy. Marriage mus' agree wid yuh."

Momentarily blushing, Jenny soon regained her composure. "Well, me ah preacher mon's wife so me affe look me bes'. Me cyan't shame Jacob an' dress like me ah penny ketcha. Nuh, sa."

Jenny and Hortense carried the drinks while Cilbert helped Jacob with the luggage. On their way to Trenchtown, Jenny stole quick, cautious glances at the stony-expressioned shanty dwellers, sometimes regretting that she had coerced Jacob into their move. But the sight and sound of Cilbert, whistling some doo-wop tune, convinced her that her move from the country was worthwhile.

Upon reaching the government yard where Hortense and Cilbert lived, Jenny found that the neighbours had been expecting her and prepared a hearty meal. Laura and Mercy had been busy in Mercy's kitchen and had cooked a soup dish over a coal fire that included pumpkins, yams, diced beef, roasted mackerel, bammy, green banana, peppers, callaloo and scallion. Jenny greeted her neighbours courteously, offering her hand and exchanging pleasantries. She thanked them warmly for the dinner but stopped short of revealing too much about herself.

Mid-way through the meal, Bigger and Kolton appeared clutching bottles of rum, a carrot cake and box juices for the children who were not shy to meet the new residents. "Good afternoon, Miss Jenny," Clifton, Kolton's seven-year-old son, said. "Yuh look so pretty inna ya yellow dress. Ya pretty like de film star Dorothy Dandridge dat me papa love but me mama don't know dat. Cyan yuh please buy me ah bicycle? If yuh smile nice to Misser Oliver he will give yuh ah discount. Misser Oliver sure like ah pretty woman! But him wife don't know dat!" Jenny could only laugh and presented Clifton with a sixpence for his cheek.

The men decided on a game of dominoes after dinner and their body language displayed that they didn't want the presence of women to talk over or interrupt their game. Hortense likened them to Miss Martha's husband's friends who after dinner would retire to a different room in the house to sip brandy, smoke Cuban cigars and play games of cards. Martha would lead her women friends to the verandah where they would gossip and comment about the latest aristocratic scandal while downing fruity, rum cocktails.

As Mercy and Laura washed up the dishes, Hortense linked arms with Jenny and took her on a tour of the government yard and the immediate area. She noticed that children felt free to run into any apartment without fear of rebuke and everybody seemed to know everybody. In one afternoon she had learned of the sexual conquests of a fifteen-year-old boy, the complete life story of

Mervin the Moocher who lived in a shanty hut outside the government yard and told in no uncertain terms that Duke Reid's sound system could 'mosh Sir Coxsone into de ground'. Jenny listened to how the Chinese shop proprietors looked upon blacks with scorn, the voting intentions and political beliefs of a dozen men and that the feisty fourteen-year-old Miss Pauline was made pregnant by a one-legged, eight-fingered card shark who lived up in the Wareika Hills. Jenny felt that the communal lifestyle she had witnessed could be a little too intimate for her but didn't relate any of her concerns to her sister. Walking with her head held high, Jenny smiled pleasantly to whomever she met and left them in no doubt of her good standing. "Praise de Lord," she would offer when parting company. "An' may He shine bright 'pon yuh."

For a first night in Kingston treat, Cilbert had acquired tickets for Jenny, Jacob, Hortense and himself for a talent show at the Carib theatre. Cilbert revealed that Delroy Dyer and his Mighty Invincibles would be appearing and it was also an opportunity for Hortense and himself to show their support to their neighbour. Although Jacob complained of tiredness and the need to rise early next morning to begin his duties with a Pentecostal church in the Red Hills district of Kingston, Jenny quickly accepted the invitation upon his behalf. "Jacob! Yuh cyan let Cilbert down! Him go outta him way to treat we. So ya coming an' don't give me nuh fuss!"

"Jenny, my love. I only t'ought yuh might be ah liccle tired an' mebbe yuh waan to res' ya sweet head," Jacob explained.

"Nuh, sa! How could me be tired when me sister an' me generous brudder-in-law offer to take we out fe de evening? It would be ungrateful to refuse."

The theatre walls were cracked and eroding. The wooden seats were hard and chipped and a single spotlight seemed to have a mind of its own, careering erratically all over the auditorium; the man operating the spotlight was toking on a huge spliff. Tobacco smoke had browned the ceiling and the aisles were full of cigarette butts, dead matches, fruit peel, nuts and soiled napkins. A partisan audience hooted in derision and threw polystyrene cups and other missiles whenever nervous-wracked harmony trios or soloists that they didn't recognise appeared on stage. Some were unable to sing their first notes, deciding that no long-held dream was worth this abuse and opting for the relative safety of backstage; Kingston comedians long ago had decided not to chance their fortune.

The Mighty Invincibles appeared on stage for their set dressed in hired sky-blue suits, white frilly shirts and black pointed shoes; their trousers and sleeves were woefully too short. They looked as uncomfortable as a group of lost English merchant sailors asking for directions in a seedy Trenchtown bar. Hortense and Cilbert leaped out of their seats to holler their approval but Delroy Dyer and his fellow band members took one long fearful look into the cursing patrons, then glanced at one another in dread and froze. The compere rushed out and smiled away the embarrassment as the crowd mocked and laughed. Jenny remained in her seat, watching the proceedings with apathy as Jacob tried to restrain a half-grin.

Leaving the theatre, Cilbert, recognising the disappointment in Hortense's face, led his party to a rum bar just off the junction of Half Way Tree. The streets were alive with ravers who were heading to a sound system lawn dance, groups of men huddled around lamp-posts and insect repellent fires who debated on everything from the size of Mr Manley's feet to the offspring of the Lost Tribe of Israel. Jenny, unsettled by the noise around her, offered a disapproving glare to the shanty town whores making their way from downtown Kingston to solicit outside Devon House – an old colonial building that had been refurbished as a restaurant and club where middle-class Jamaicans listened politely to over-smiling mento bands performing beneath the umbrella of palm leaves. Jacob and Jenny, taking in their surroundings, noticed that motorists failed to stop at traffic lights and cyclists breezed by offering words of wisdom, utter nonsense and damnation.

Taking a table upon the pavement, Cilbert paid for the drinks. Lighting his Buccaneer cigarette, he asked Jacob, "so, wha' do yuh t'ink of de big bad city?"

Jacob smiled. "Alive an' loud. I never knew Jamaican people could be so colourful."

"So many beggars," interjected Jenny. "Dem everywhere! Cyan't de government do somet'ing about dem?"

"Nuh, Jenny," answered Hortense, sipping her rum and coke. "Only de fittest ah de fittest survive. Ya get used to it."

"Jamaica *is* meking money," added Cilbert. "But de sufferahs don't see it. Profits from bauxite an' udder t'ings are banked inna foreign lands. Mostly America."

"Yuh intend to start ah family here inna Kingston?" asked Jacob, directing the question to both Hortense and Cilbert.

"Nuh, sa!" Cilbert quickly replied. "Me see some ah dem children who leave school inna Trenchtown an' all dem cyan do is stan' up 'pon street corner an' cut dem eye after people an' look trouble. Me don't even feel safe going to de picture house nuh more an' watch film." He remembered the assault he had suffered. "Bad bwai ah loiter der an' trouble decent people. Der is not'ing fe de young inna Kingston. Nuh, sa! Me an' Hortense agree dat we will 'ave children when we reach ah England. Dey will 'ave ah better chance der. Who knows? Ah son ah mine could be ah doctor or lawyer one day. Or even Prime Minister ah England!"

For a short second, Jenny gazed into Cilbert's eyes, liking the determination and conviction in them. "Jacob an' meself are t'inking de same t'ing," Jenny said.

Jacob looked perplexed at his wife. "I cyan't remember..."

Interrupting Jacob's sentence, Jenny reasoned, "but me darling, Jacob. It mek sense. It's ah blessing to come to Kingston an' serve its people inna Godly way. But der will be ah time when me waan to start ah family. An' yuh mus' waan wha' is bes' fe dem. An' England will offer dem so much more dan Jamaica."

Irritated, Jacob took a swig from his bottle of stout. Cilbert and Hortense exchanged a quick glance.

"Well, Jacob," said Cilbert, wiping his lips with the back of his right hand. "Yuh 'ave ah mighty job 'pon ya hands. Some ah de people inna Trenchtown cyan't be saved. Most of de time yuh'll be wasting ya words. Too many ah dem cyan't read. Inna Kingston der is too many people wid wooden ears an' concrete minds. An' in me opinion, yuh cyan't really blame dem. De Most High don't shine bright 'pon de people ah Trenchtown. Since me been here, me see too much sufferation. Where is de Most High when He is most needed? Dat's why nuff people turn to crime an' badness. An' de political people recognise dat an' mek use fe dem. For dey cyan't see nuh betterness. Nuh improvement inna dem lives. Dey feel de Lord God has forsaken dem. Me cyan't see how yuh cyan change dat."

Jacob slammed down his bottle in a moment of rare vexation. He caught Cilbert with an intense stare. "Yuh 'ave never been ah religious mon 'ave yuh, Cilbert? So yuh don't know of de comfort of ah good Christian life cyan give to so many people. I am *not* ignorant, Cilbert. While me der inna Claremont I get to learn about de sufferation of de people inna Kingston." Jacob raised his voice. "Yuh don't understan', Cilbert. When ah people 'ave not'ing, nuh money, nuh material t'ings, nuh roof over dem head. *Not'ing!* Den all is lef' is faith. An' dat faith lead to hope. Widout hope der will be chaos an' anarchy. So I see it as long as I provide hope, my time inna Kingston will *never* be wasted! Do yuh understan'?"

"Nuh need to get vex," cut in Jenny, smiling at her husband but her eyes still betraying her embarrassment.

"Dat is alright, Jenny," soothed Cilbert, blowing his smoke over Hortense's head. "It's true. Me nah religious but at least me nah like dem uptown people who gwarn ah Catholic church 'pon ah Sunday marnin an' ignore de beggar when dem step outta church wid der high an' mighty selves. Me like an' admire any mon who feels ah mighty passion about him beliefs. Dat is fine by me. But de downtown people need more dan passion. Me fader tell me once dat de white mon give de black slave de Bible to read. But dis was ah trap. Ah trap to mek de black mon believe dat all der suffering will be alright becah dem will get der redemption when dem dead, gwarn to heaven an' live an everlasting life full ah milk an' honey. It was ah cruel trickster trick to mek dem obedient. Jacob, yuh don't read de words an' psalms ah Solomon? Yes, me don't go to church now but when me ah bwai chile me read me Bible like everyone else. *Every* day."

Jenny leant in closer to Cilbert, impressed by his last statement.

Hortense yawned, making it clear she was becoming bored of the conversation – she had heard this issue being debated many times in the government yard.

Cilbert continued. "De mighty Solomon say." Cilbert sang in a soft whisper, closing his eyes and recalling his days of church-going. Concentration lined his forehead and a grimace tickled his cheeks. "*By de rivers ah Babylon. Where we sat down. An' where we wept, when we remembered our home land. Dey tek we away in captivity an' required from we ah song. But how cyan we sing der Lord's song when we der inna strange land.*"

Now breathing easier, Jacob controlled his temper, stood up and dismissed Cilbert with a lingering eye pass. In response, Cilbert kissed Hortense upon the cheek and gave her a hug. Jenny looked away to the traffic. "Yuh should nah twist de words ah de mighty Solomon," Jacob warned, his tone back to normal. "De song don't quite go like dat. Anyone waan ah nex' drink?" he offered, not wanting to prolong the argument.

Cilbert looked offended. He raised his voice. "*Dat* is how me grandpapa used to sing it an' him *never* wrong. De point ah de matter is, Jacob, is dat me ah look fe heaven 'pon earth. Me don't waan to suffer all me life an' den get me reward when me dead like how the white mon Bible promise. Nuh, sa! Dat is why me work so hard. Becah me waan me reward while me still alive. So me cyan enjoy it. Watch me, sa! See inna t'ree or four years when me come back from England dat me don't live inna mighty house up der ah Strawberry Hill! Hortense, one day yuh affe tek Jacob up der an' show him Miss Martha's fine mansion. When ah mon see ah house like dat, how cyan him be satisfy wid him government yard or shanty hut?"

Jacob took four strides before turning around and replying to Cilbert. "I respect ah mon wid healt'y ambition. But careful, Cilbert, fe de somet'ing dat mon love de most, cyan kill him also. De Most High is ah jealous God. Remember how de Israelites mek false idols an' Massa God get vex. When Moses come down from him mountain an' see wha' happen, Moses ketch ah rage."

"Yes, me know dat story, Jacob," replied Cilbert. "But Moses had plenty ambition. Him was ah High Priest an' did waan to challenge Pharoah power an' assert him belief of de one God. De sun God of Akhenaten."

Jacob momentarily froze, as if struck by something deep within his soul. "*Beware*! Don't talk of such t'ings, Cilbert. Becah de Most High lissen to every conversation an' cyan read every intention an' every mon's desire. My brudder believes dat too an' now he lives inna de bush."

Jenny felt her husband's words penetrate her heart and wondered if they were indirectly aimed at her. Surely he doesn't know? Jenny thought. When Jacob returned with a tray of fresh drinks, Jenny made an effort to side up to her husband and place her right arm over his shoulders. Jacob, not used to public displays of affection from his wife, began to regale his friends with anecdotes and tales about his former Claremont valley parishioners. They all laughed but underneath their happy facial expressions they all yearned for the trustworthiness and familiarity of the people they grew up with.

Preparing to leave, Cilbert downed the last of his Red Stripe bottles. "Well, Jenny, now yuh arrive mebbe me will find dinner cooked when me reach home from work."

"Yes, me love to cook," said Jenny excitedly.

Hortense looked obviously annoyed. "How cyan yuh expect dinner when some night me still ah work up der ah Miss Martha? Yuh cyan't tek up ya two hand an' cook fe yaself? Lazy ya lazy! Yuh expect woman to do everyt'ing?"

"But sometime yuh reach home before me an' instead ah cooking me somet'ing nice yuh gone off wid Miss Laura to help sell her goods. Ya first priority *is* me!"

"Cilbert, me sick an' tired ah yuh keep vexing about dis argument! Yuh know how me stay! Miss Laura one of me bes' frien' an' she help we out many time. So me help her out. So quiet ya mout', gum ya lip an' accept de situation. Remember, we live 'pon de money me mek from Miss Martha. Ya money pay de rent an' use fe saving. Remember dat."

Cilbert and Hortense kept on quarrelling until they reached

home. Jenny had discovered that the single room and kitchen apartment had been divided by three white bedsheets hanging on a length of cord. When Jenny retired to bed beneath a single pink sheet, she made sure she was nearest to the hanging bed linen. Laying on her side with Jacob snuggled up behind her, Jenny could see Cilbert's naked, silhouetted body, formed by the moonlight, moving in front of her. She found herself becoming excited and willed herself to look away. But she couldn't. Every movement of Cilbert's limbs was studied as he combed his hair before bed. By the sound of his gentle whispering and his shadowed body language, Jenny guessed that Cilbert was attempting to make up for the row he and Hortense had. Without blinking she watched Cilbert lay on top of Hortense and heard the moans and pleasures of love-making. She knew they were both naked and was surprised at their absence of inhibitions. Cilbert's silhouette was now joined with Hortense's and Jenny finally closed her eyes, dreaming that she could be the one to feel Cilbert's body pressing down upon her.

Forcing his crotch against the curve of Jenny's backside and laying a hand upon her left breast, Jacob suffered a pinch upon his penis – an indication that Jenny was not prepared to make love tonight. Jacob would discover that attempting to make love while Hortense and Cilbert were in the apartment was simply a forlorn hope. He would have to bribe Cilbert with a wink to take Hortense out for the evening or visit friends. "Wha' ah palava!" Cilbert would giggle. "Even Preacher Mon get peckish from time to time."

Jacob became very popular with the people of Trenchtown. He spoke with the same tone of voice to everyone and looked people directly in the eye from the poorest shanty-town dweller to the uptown business man. Indeed, on Saturday mornings he would rise early and tour around the roughest areas of downtown, offering words of hope and encouragement. But even the Trenchtown moochers were shocked when Jacob ventured into the 'Dungle' district of Kingston – a massive rubbish dump area where the poorest of the poor and rastafarians squirmed out a living from whatever materials and rotten foods the downtown people had no use for. The stench of human waste, multiplying insects and crippled children did not bother him. It was only the looks of resignation that kept him awake at nights. Cilbert, vividly describing the 'wild, dutty haired ones wid der blood eyes' had warned Jacob that he was laying himself open for a mugging but Jacob ignored him, remembering the counsel of his brother, Levi. Jacob would say to Cilbert, "aren't dey de people of de Most High? Don't dey deserve to hear de word of God? Ya ever see ah picture of Jesus wid short hair? Yuh forget dat Christ allowed John de Baptist to pour water over him head even though de disciples an' everyone else ah say dat John de Baptist was ah dutty, wild-haired mon? Why should de people ah de Dungle be forsaken becah dem wear dem hair long?"

Jenny found work cooking in a downtown restaurant that was frequented by many men who lived on the hustle. She soon admonished the patrons who let slip Jamaican swear words. She also constantly reminded them of their 'thank you's' and 'please's' and she was quickly accepted as a 'lovable eccentric wid country ways'. Even the bad men would greet her with, "marnin, Miss Jenny. May de Most High bless yuh 'pon dis good day." Jenny, enjoying the respect that was offered her, would bid in farewell, "don't forget to say grace before ya supper". The criminals and political thugs would lope away half-smiling and went to perform whatever badness that they had always done.

On Sunday afternoons Jenny tutored a Sunday school class set up for her by Jacob. She discovered that the children who were illiterate were also hungry. So in response Isaac used some of the collection money from his church in order to purchase food and cook large pots of beef stew for the children before their classes. Soon, the sessions became over-subscribed and parents fought each other for their children's places. Jacob's idealistic notion became unworkable and he was forced to return to just providing writing and reading lessons. Subsequently, many of the illiterate children stopped attending and this preyed on Jacob's mind.

Encouraged by their neighbours to stay in Kingston for the Christmas festivities, Hortense, Jenny and Jacob could only admire the creativity of the Trenchtown people. Tenement buildings, sidewalks and shopfronts were scrubbed and whitewashed to brighten up the environment and give it a Christmas feel. Corkscrewed orange, tangerine and avocado peels were hanging on strings from the ceilings of residents verandahs in improvised decoration. Oil lamps were hanging outside doors. Nativity paintings suddenly appeared on street walls. Only the Trenchtown rastafarians were offended with images of a white baby Jesus but most people didn't care what they thought. The soothing sound of hymns and carols echoing from all over Kingston never ceased.

On Christmas day morning, Hortense, Jenny and their spouses escorted Kolton, Oliver and their offspring to the seafront where hundreds of Trenchtown children enjoyed free boat rides in the harbour. They journeyed close to the ruins of Port Royal and the adults, pointing to the bottom of the sea, told the children about the sinful pirates who once inhabited the bay; Jacob departed the boat on groggy legs and brought up his cornmeal porridge breakfast upon the shore.

Following a communal dinner of roast pig and every kind of trimming that could be thrown in the blackened pots, everyone made their way to Hope Botanical Gardens where they clapped and cheered the marching Alpha Boys band – teenage orphans who were cared for by Catholic nuns. Indeed, graduates of the Alpha school were now making a living as top session musicians for the blossoming Kingston recording industry; entrepreneurs such as Prince Buster and Sir Coxsone, unlike the controllers of Jamaican broadcast radio, recognised the public demand for Jamaican songs and lyrics and had set up their own record labels.

Watching the Alpha Boys march by, Hortense, unable to resist the urge, grabbed Cilbert's hand and began dancing. Jenny, not wanting to make a spectacle of herself, quietly handed out leaflets advertising the sermon Isaac would present for midnight mass.

As Christmas night fell, Cilbert surprised Hortense by hailing a taxi and taking her to Hellshire Beach, a quiet strip of golden sand ten miles west of Kingston that was fringed with occasional palm and mango trees. There, under a perfect navy-blue sky where in the distance they could see the harbour lights of Kingston stretching out in a long curve, they drank from a bottle of coconut rum punch that Cilbert had prepared. "Isn't dis better dan sitting inna Jacob's church ah lissen to de same old story dat we hear when we pickney?" smiled Cilbert. "Life is fe living an' yuh affe enjoy it. De Christian way of life is all about preparing for deat'. Hortense, me heaven is inna dis world wid yuh! Let we drink to dat. Me an' yuh."

"But Jenny was so *vex*," replied Hortense. "It will tek her some time to forgive we fe nah supporting Jacob's sermon." Hortense then took in her surroundings and broke out into a glorious smile, downing a generous gulp of coconut-rum. They then made love with the gentle, frothing waves soothing and cooling their naked calves. They could both hear the music from a sound system that had set up on a beach two miles away. Under a half-moon sky that illuminated a strip of the calm waters of the Caribbean sea that stretched to the horizon, a rastafarian fisherman, paddling into shore in his red, gold and green painted canoe, observed the couple and laughed.

Hortense excitedly told Jenny of Cilbert's romantic gesture and soon after Jenny informed Hortense of her plans to return to Claremont for the New Year and visit Papa who had been sick. "Yuh nah come wid me, Hortense?" Jenny said accusingly. "Me stay inna Kingston wid yuh fe Christmas but yuh cyan't come wid me to Claremont? Selfish ya selfish!"

"Me cyan't go," answered Hortense. "Miss Martha waan me to cook dinner fe her guests 'pon New Year's Eve."

"Tell Miss Martha to learn to cook fe herself! Don't she know yuh 'ave family?"

"She been good to me an' me don't waan to let her down. An' she cyan cook fe herself! As long as me watching her."

Jenny cut her eyes at Hortense and proceeded to pack her clothes.

It was a breezy February morning in 1959 when Hortense had arrived at Miss Martha's house and found boxes, trunks and barrels filling the area of the verandah floor, ready for shipping. Miss Martha, standing in her front doorway, was watching her gardener, Jonte, perform his duties. She was sporting a wide-brimmed floppy hat and sunglasses that covered almost half her face. The flower-patterned sarong she was wearing billowed out with the wind, sometimes exposing her thighs and drawers. Hortense approached her, feeling a sadness within her heart.

"Marnin, Miss Martha. So yuh ready to go."

"Oh, morning, Hotty. Yes, paradise will soon be lost. When the breeze blows I do like to come outside and feel it on my skin. So refreshing and pleasant."

"Yes, it do feel mighty nice," agreed Hortense.

Her sunglasses masking the aim of her gaze, Martha didn't turn around and greet Hortense with a kiss like she usually did. "Do you know, Hotty, my gardener, Jonte, has been with us since the end of the war."

Hortense looked at Jonte who was bare-backed and only dressed in white shorts and sandals. The sun reflected off his bald, brown head.

"And in that length of time, Hotty," Martha continued. "He has never entered my house. When he concludes his work on a Saturday morning he waits patiently sitting down on the lawn for me to present him his wages. He doesn't even call me for it. When he first came to work for us, my husband was very strict with him, watched him like a hawk. He was perturbed about leaving Jonte and myself alone in the house. I suppose that is the fear of the white man. Jonte *is* a very attractive man. But my husband was worrying totally unnecessarily for Jonte is a quiet, withdrawn man. Very undemonstrative. He has always performed his work well and I have only felt the need to rebuke him on those rare occasions he comes in late. But after all this time he still seems afraid to look me in the eye. He has never picked up on my give-away signs. Do you understand, Hotty?"

"Yes, Miss Martha," Hortense replied with a grin. "Sometimes me wonder why yuh always tek ya breakfast 'pon de verandah. Now me know why. Jonte ah tickle ya fancy."

Martha chuckled, Hortense's candid humour a relief to her. "But why should he notice me? I am a white woman approaching middle- age and the sun withers my skin. Maybe if he had seen me in my ballet days he wouldn't have been so apathetic. Then again, perhaps Jonte has always sensed my husband's disquiet."

"Wha' are yuh getting at, Miss Martha?" Hortense asked.

"My dear, Hotty." Martha finally turned around to face Hortense. "You are so naive. And that's why I feel it is my duty just to give you a gentle warning. You will soon be in the motherland and you need to know certain peculiarities of the men there."

"Gentle warning about wha'?" Hortense wanted to know.

"I know I continually talk about the times I watched Mr Bojangles perform on Broadway. But there was definitely a sadness within his eyes, although he was smiling. A look of unfulfilled promise. Although he could dance like a dream he was never offered a leading role in a MGM musical. The nearest Mr Bojangles came to a leading lady was dancing with the seven-year-old Shirley Temple. No dancing in a ballroom or down a neon-lit, curling staircase with Ginger Rogers for Mr Bojangles. You see, Hotty, it was the white man's fear that derailed Mr Bojangles' dreams and aspirations. It's an unspoken fear. I have seen it in the way my husband regards Jonte. And as a white woman you begin to wonder where that fear comes from. You even begin to imagine... experiencing relations with a black man. They don't mind a black woman displaying their sexuality, but they have to be light-skinned to be truly accepted. Do you understand, Hotty?"

Martha's hidden gaze returned to Jonte who was bending over a flower bed, pulling out the weeds and forking the soil. His taut back muscles glistened beneath the morning sun. Hortense recalled the manner in which Martha's husband always ran his eyes over her, making her feel so uncomfortable.

Managing to restrain a grin, Hortense offered, "Miss Martha, me don't waan to speak outta place. But if yuh waan to grine Jonte, den grine him! Me sure he won't mind. Me husband tell me life is to enjoy. Look fe ya heaven 'pon earth."

Martha rocked back in laughter. "My dear, Hotty! I love the way Jamaicans can be so frank at times! You are so sweet. But, Hotty, between you and me, I know my husband has relations with a few of the, shall I say, ladies of the night. He ventures into town with his friends on a Saturday night and he returns with the scent of women on his body. The darker the better – they fascinate him. But, Hotty, even for a middle-class white lady who lives in Jamaica, there are lines etched into the sand that I cannot breach. And having any sort of relationship with a black man is one of them."

"But, Miss Martha, me still don't understand ya warning."

"From what I understand, your Cilbert is an ambitious man. But that fear of the black man still very much persists. So when you reach England, be aware of it. Don't let it break Cilbert's spirit as he attempts to better himself, for obstacles and glass ceilings will be placed in his way. It will be something your sons will have to contend with also, I should imagine."

Closing her eyes, Hortense thought of England and wondered what form these obstacles and glass ceilings would take.

Having had to listen to Hortense's and Cilbert's passionate love-making one April night in 1959, the following morning, Jenny asked Hortense if she would walk her to work. It was just before seven in the morning and vendors were pushing their carts to meet the Kingston commuters. Children, most of them dressed in khaki uniforms, were setting off for school. Higglers had already claimed their positions in Coronation market and the first road accident of the day saw a car knock over a cyclist – motorists blared their horns for someone to remove the victim and clear the road.

"Hortense, me nah waan yuh to be offended by wha' me 'ave to say," said Jenny.

"Offended by wha'?" asked Hortense.

"Well. How cyan me put dis?"

"Jenny, ya mout' tie up inna knot? Talk to me an' stop ya teasing."

"It's really about Jacob," revealed Jenny.

"Wha' about Jacob?"

"Well, when him sleeping him don't like to lissen to yuh an' Cilbert 'aving ya fun."

"'Aving fun? Yuh mean sex, Jenny? If yuh say sex de Lord God will nah strike we down wid ah t'underbolt! Me an' Cilbert married so wha' is troubling Jacob?"

Jenny had to pause to think of an answer. "Well, yuh know Jacob is ah deep religious mon. He jus' don't feel right when yuh an' Cilbert enjoying yaself. It don't boder me! But Jacob, yuh know, it mek him feel mighty embarrass."

Laughing out loud, Hortense had to stop walking to compose herself. "Wha' yuh waan we to do, Jenny? Mek love inna de courtyard an' mek everybody see? Or mebbe we shoulda gwarn to de lawn dance, strip off we garments an' grine like de world is coming to an end? Giving crowd of people ah nex' entertainment? Mebbe we should charge two dollar an' Miss Laura cyan stan' by de sidelines selling her wares."

"Jus' be ah liccle bit quieter, Hortense," asked Jenny, fretting that passers-by had heard the conversation. "Nuh mek so much blasted noise! It's ah wonder de people who live 'pon Blue Mountain don't hear ya scream."

"Me don't scream, Jenny! Yuh asking me to mek love wid ah jackfruit inna me mout' so me don't mek nuh noise? Jenny, pleasure is mighty scarce wid de life we live so when it come me 'ave to enjoy it. Tell Jacob to stop his foolishness! Me never know he is so prude-like. How does he t'ink how he come into de world?"

Later that night, before retiring to bed, Hortense whispered to Jacob, "nuh worry yaself, me will turn me volume down. De las' t'ing me waan to do is upset ah preacher mon sensibilities. An' if yuh really don't waan to hear, why yuh don't mek sweet love to Jenny an' mek her scream so dat de people 'pon Blue Mountain cyan hear."

Bewildered, Jacob looked at Jenny who was looking at her most innocent. Hortense, unable to contain her mirth, roared with laughter.

Two weeks later, Cilbert was climbing down from a telephone pylon. Collecting his tools he muttered to himself, "mon! Hot up der fe true! Now me gwarn to enjoy me birt'day tonight. Yes, sa. Me wonder if Hortense plan anyt'ing fe me? If she don't me will tek her to Devon House fe ah nice meal an' lissen to some calypso an' mento. Yes, sa. Twenty-four today!"

Wiping the sweat off his forehead he made his way down to Half Way Tree where he caught a bus back home. Upon arrival at the government yard, he spotted Hortense and Laura returning home. They were pushing a cart upon which bagfuls of groceries were catching a ride.

"Cilby!" called Hortense. "Me glad yuh reach home quick! Me buy ya favourite lamb shanks to cook tonight. Yes, mon. Gwarn inside an' tek ya res'."

Kissing Hortense upon her cheek, Cilbert smiled and said, "mebbe liccle later we cyan go fe ah drink? Yes' sa! Devon House sound good to yuh?"

Wrapping her arms around Cilbert's neck, Hortense kissed him fully on the mouth. "It would be so nice to see people wait 'pon we fe ah change."

Cilbert went to cool off his face at the standpipe as Hortense entered her home with her shopping. Someone was already cooking in the kitchen. Hortense went to investigate.

Seasoning generous portions of lamb shanks with jerk and chilli, was Jenny. Hortense dropped her bags upon the floor in disbelief. "Jenny, wha' ya doing?"

Her sleeves rolled up and her palms caked in seasoning, Jenny answered, "me know dat yuh working wid Laura today so me decide to start cook Cilbert's meal. Me only work half day today. Yuh waan help me peel de avocados?"

"Me cyan't believe dis!" shouted Hortense. "Me stop by ah market an' buy de food! It was MY treat! Now yuh gwarn an' spoil it! COME OUTTA DE KITCHEN BEFORE ME STRIKE YUH DOWN!"

"But, Hortense," replied Jenny. "When yuh finish work wid Laura yuh complain dat yuh foot so tired. So me jus' trying to help."

"Help? It's MY husband's birt'day an' ME should cook fe him 'pon him birt'day! NUHBODY ELSE!"

"But, Hortense, me don't finish yet. Yuh cyan help me."

Storming out into the courtyard, Hortense yelled Jamaican

obscenities. Jacob, who was talking with Mercy, ran back to his own house to see what the shouting was about. He and Cilbert both entered the kitchen at the same time.

"Wha' ah gwarn?" asked Cilbert. "Why Hortense run inna Laura house cussing pure bad word?"

Staring at the seasoned lamb that was now ready for frying, Jenny began to sob. "Me always try me best to help out! Me jus' waan to help but Hortense ketch ah rage. Me don't know why she ah so vex wid me. Me love me sister so much an' it pain me so to hear her cuss me like dat. Me so grateful dat she look after me since me here inna Trenchtown so me jus' ah try an' pay her back. Yuh understan', Cilbert?"

Jenny covered her face with her palms and broke down. "Jacob, see to her," said Cilbert. "Me will try an' cool Hortense's fire."

As Jacob offered Jenny a shoulder to cry on, he couldn't help but think that his wife had never been so eager to cook him a birthday treat.

Cilbert's birthday dinner was consumed in near silence. Only Jacob attempted conversation. Later that night, Cilbert took Hortense to Devon House where they drank pineapple-rum cocktails and danced to a calypso band. Jenny busied herself washing clothes, not wanting to talk with anyone. But Jacob watched her secretly, his heart disturbed about something.

Chapter Thirteen

Late June, 1960

The government yard where Hortense and Jenny lived was orange-lit by the embers of fading coal fires. Smoke from thousands of Trenchtown kitchens and improvised cooking vessels, laced with the lingering aroma of chicken, cow foot and peppers, obscured the perfect night sky; shanty dwellers would rise in the morning covered in a film of blackened ash. Tired women, humming spirituals to themselves, were hanging their washing on string lines. Men pondered their working days and how they would meet their next rent payments as they downed bottles of beer and gnawed fowl bones. Someone was complaining loudly about the lack of water inside the communal shower. The Folkes Brothers 'Oh Carolina', competing against the distant sound of a rastafarian knuckling a haunting rhythm on a Nyabinghi drum, crackled out from a bruised transistor radio that was hanging from a rusty screw. An old lady, a black scarf wrapped tightly around her head and relaxing in a tatty, uneven chair outside her home, nodded and tapped her feet in time to the music. An open Bible rested upon her lap but her eyes were closing.

Gazing lovingly at the new British passport in his hands, Cilbert, sitting on the stoop outside his home, smiled and kissed the document. Hortense, snuggling beside her husband, kissed him upon his forehead. They both felt that the Kingston night was smiling at them and that the chance to improve their lives was now within reach. "Cyan yuh believe it, Hortense? We're all British citizens! De passports say so! It's ah fine t'ing we're all going to England now becah after Independence dey will stop issue British passports." Cilbert opened the document to the first page. "An'

Misser Hugh Foot, de governor general, sign it himself. Hortense, we jus' as British as Miss Martha an' de Queen ah Englan'. Isn't dat such ah fine t'ing?"

"Me feel sorry for Oliver," said Hortense, not sharing Cilbert's joy. "De immigration office refuse him application becah Oliver 'ave ah criminal record. Him t'ief ah bicycle wheel ah few years back – ah Chinee mon expose him to de police."

Cilbert didn't seem to care about the fate of his neighbour, he only had eyes for his passport. "Too bad," he said, not looking up.

"Is dat all yuh cyan say, Cilbert? Oliver been ah good frien' to we."

"Yes, but me cyan't change de reality of de situation. Him t'ief ah bicycle one day an' now him paying fe it."

"Sometimes, Cilbert, ya narrow-minded obsession wid ya own ambition mek ya cold to ah nex' mon's tribulation. Well, at least when re reach Englan' me cyan look for Miss Martha. Me miss her deeply but me 'ave her address. She live inna place call Berkshire."

Jenny and Jacob emerged from their apartment carrying steaming mugs full of manesh water – a peppery soup. They gave one each to Hortense and Cilbert. "Well, dis time tomorrow," Jenny said. "We'll be sailing 'pon de mighty Atlantic. De same ocean we forefaders arrive from. Cyan yuh believe dat? Little we from de Claremont valley."

Looking alarmed, Jacob's eyes betrayed some dread. He tapped Cilbert upon his right shoulder and whispered, "cyan we talk? In private."

Grinning, Cilbert assumed Jacob wanted the apartment for Jenny and himself so they could make love. Cilbert stood up, placed his right arm over Jacob's shoulders and turned to Hortense. "Mon talk."

The men walked towards the stand-pipe in the middle of the yard. A squadron of mosquitoes followed them. "Nah boder yaself, Jacob," smiled Cilbert. "Hortense an' meself still 'ave to mek ah few more goodbyes so yuh cyan 'ave de place fe yaselves fe two hours or so. Every mon 'ave him needs, eehh?"

"Nuh, nuh, mon," Jacob replied, his voice tinged with

desperation. "It nah dat at all."

"Den wha' is it?"

Jacob paused and looked at the dusty ground. "I. *Don't* laugh! I am 'fraid ah de mighty ocean. I am 'fraid de ship will capsize an' we will all drown."

"Ya joking wid me," replied Cilbert.

"Nuh, mon. I mek nuh joke. I get nightmares about it fe de last few weeks. I cyan't even swim. My fader never tek me to de coast to teach me. Before I go to my bed I will pray to Massa God fe we deliverance an' to bless we ship."

"Lord wha' ah palava!" hollered Cilbert, restraining a chortle. "Why yuh never say somet'ing before? We pay £90 each fe we fare! Yuh waan to waste ya money? Look how long it tek we to save it."

Jacob felt his manliness was being interrogated. "Nuh, mon. I don't waan to waste my money. But *don't* tell Jenny about my fear. I don't waan her to say dat I am ah meek mouse."

Cilbert patted Jacob upon his back. "Nuh boder ya godly self, Jacob. Me will look after yuh. Wid de help of fire-water! Dat will calm ya nerve."

Cilbert returned to Hortense and hugged her. Jacob rinsed the evening stickiness off his face at the stand-pipe, not at all encouraged by Cilbert's words.

The next morning. nine a.m. A clear, bright sky had blessed Kingston and white birds flew above the still harbour waters. Standing in a long queue of migrating Jamaicans all wearing their best clothes, Cilbert, Jacob, Hortense and Jenny observed the busy scenes around them in wonder and dread, carrying their peeling and battered second-hand suitcases. Cussing, bare-backed men off-loaded goods from tankers, dry bulk carriers and general cargo ships. Groggy merchant sailors were reporting back for duty. The sound of cranes and other lifting mechanisms filled the air. Proud-looking Jamaican harbour pilots, sporting stained sailor hats and cheap rings on their fingers, raced here and there, some coming into port in small, questionable boats following their navigating of a vessel into open waters. Funnels discharging smoke and exhaust fumes caused Hortense to cough.

Cilbert, although linking arms with his wife, only had eyes for the passenger vessel named *The Genovese Madonna* that he would soon board. Awed by the size of the ship, Cilbert felt that his boyhood dream was now materialising before his eyes. Jacob, unsteady on his feet because of the amount of undiluted rum Cilbert had forced him to drink, observed the vessel with different feelings. To his eyes, *The Genovese Madonna* may as well have been a sea monster. Meanwhile, Jenny continually looked behind her, as if she was waiting for someone to call her back. An image of her father, to whom she bade farewell three days ago, loomed large in her mind. She wondered if she would ever see him again. Indeed, she doubted if she would ever bless her eyes on Jamaica again.

Jenny had recognised the smile that her father had only reserved for her and standing upon his plot of land, Joseph asked her, "yuh sure yuh waan to go to Englan', Jenny? Hortense is ah big woman now an' she cyan look after herself. She stop cry fe me ah long time ago an' Amy too. An' now she 'ave Cilbert. An ambitious mon."

"Jacob ambitious too," replied Jenny. "It would be ah mighty achievement to establish ah church inna Englan'."

"Yes it would," agreed Joseph. "But Jacob love dis land an' its people. So me was ah liccle surprise dat him tek dis decision."

"Didn't St Paul love him land? But him travel far an' wide to spread de gospel."

Joseph laughed. "Always de Bible student! May Kofi bless ya every step an' never forget to lift up ya head an' walk tall. Yuh is *Maroon!*"

"An' besides, Papa, Hortense will need me wid her."

Joseph fingered his chin. "Ya sure? Hortense ah big woman now. She certainly don't need her papa!"

"Yuh don't know her de way me know her. She tough like coconut shell 'pon de outside but soft like uncooked dumpling inna de inside."

Jenny embraced her father and closed her eyes, her tears dampening Joseph's rough cotton shirt. Five minutes later she stepped away, walking backwards and sideways until her father was nothing but a silhouette.

As Cilbert stepped aboard, he looked around at the other passengers, trying to keep his composure. A fear of the unknown flowed through his veins mixing with the adrenalin. He detected a certain apprehension in the eyes of his fellow countrymen and found himself tightly gripping the left hand of Hortense. Jenny searched for Hortense's right hand and clutched it eagerly as Jacob staggered behind, promising himself never to drink rum again. They were all led by a smartly dressed Italian deck officer to the cabin decks below; Cilbert had to assist Jacob down the steps of the companionways as Jenny smouldered in embarrassment. The grainy wooden beams of the interior of the ship reeked of the ocean, and Jacob fought to control what was shooting up his throat.

The cabin, containing two bunk-beds pushed against opposite walls, was four paces wide and eight strides long. The porthole offered them a view outside of seven metres above the water line. "Wha' kinda mattress dey call dis?" moaned Jenny, squeezing it with her hand. "It thin like white people lip!"

Off-loading their luggage, Cilbert, Jenny and Hortense all felt a little claustrophobic. Leaving behind Jacob crashed out on one of the bunks, they made their way back up to the passenger deck and joined others who were leaning on the railings, looking into Kingston. Nobody said much. Many shed silent tears.

Everybody dwelled on their own personal fates and feelings. Hortense recognised and felt proud that she and Jenny were the first females in their known family history to explore and see the world. She recalled her mother saying to her three days ago, "it seems all of de children of Kofi are cursed wid him curiosity an' wanderings. So it was wid sweet David. May de spirit of Kofi bless ya every step but remember where ya home is an' de people yuh come from."

Jenny's head was full of panic and apprehension. Gazing at the rising hills that backdropped Kingston, it finally struck home that she was starting life in a foreign land with a man she couldn't love. She fought to block out in her mind the cutting glare of her mother and the manner in which she crossed her arms when they parted.

"Why everyone so sad?" she asked, masking her own anxiety and guilt as she glanced at the other passengers. "Dis is de time of we life!"

An hour later, Cilbert heard Italian shouts and spotted a harbour pilot in a small boat that was attached by rope to *The Genovese Madonna*. Cilbert heard and felt the vibrations of the engines and propeller starting beneath him and could sense the ship finally moving. Hortense and Cilbert jumped up and down on the spot, waving and hollering to the crowds below. Tears were streaming down their cheeks and they hoped that their Trenchtown friends could see them. Even Jenny could not stem her sobs as Kingston, ever so gradually, reduced in size to nothing but a pale white and green haze that straddled the horizon. Hortense, surprised at her sister's display of vulnerability, for Jenny rarely revealed her emotions in public, moved with Cilbert to include her in a warm embrace. "Trus' Jacob to ketch sick," laughed Hortense. "He should be wid yuh at times like dis. It nah like him to be licky licky. Me wonder who give him de fire-water?"

Feeling the heat of Cilbert's chest upon her breasts, Jenny replied, "let him sleep it off! Me don't know how could he embarrass me so!"

Jacob had recovered by the time of the evening meal that was taken in the ship's passenger restaurant – a long hall just below the bridge. Many of the passengers had now grown accustomed to the sway and heaving of the ship and finally grasped that when *The Genovese Madonna* was riding a rogue wave, it didn't herald imminent doom. Outside, the stars shone bright and there was a chill in the air that discouraged the Jamaicans to venture on deck. The Atlantic spoke in a whisper. Moustachioed Italian waiters served heaps of pasta and mince and poured red wine into glasses. The sea air fuelling their appetites, Cilbert, Jacob and Hortense couldn't eat their meal quickly enough. In contrast, Jenny grimaced as she picked at her food with a fork. "De meat nah cooked right," she complained. "Look how it red like bauxite!"

"Stop ya fussing, Jenny," said Hortense. "Yuh better get used to it. T'ree weeks we der 'pon dis ship."

"Well, me nah eat it," asserted Jenny, slamming her fork down on the plate. "Me would complain if any of dese Italian people coulda understan' English. Yuh see de way dey look 'pon we? Dem look 'pon we like country farmer ah look 'pon hog inna truck! Me *don't* like dem. Me nah trus' dem. Fe all we know dey might poison we. An' dey 'ave dirty hand."

"Now, my love, don't get vex an' paranoid," soothed Jacob. "It's been ah very long day. I will get some more bread fe yuh."

"Nah boder yaself, Jacob," offered Cilbert. "Me will fetch it. Me waan some more ah dat mince wid de red sauce."

Rising to his feet, Cilbert made his way to the kitchen, the low ceiling only a foot above his head. Standing by a hatch where an Italian waiter was serving wine and beverages for passengers who wanted a supplement to their original servings, was an elegant, amber-skinned woman. She was wearing a burgundy-coloured pencil skirt with matching jacket. Pearls decorated her naked collarbone. Her perfect black hair had been straightened and was parted on one side. Bright red lipstick coloured her thin lips and the foundation upon her face gave the appearance of caramel-coloured porcelain. Her posture was confident and superior, like a nineteenth century Parisian courtesan. Cilbert recognised her instantly and walked over to her.

"Good evening, Almyna," Cilbert greeted, catching a strong scent of perfume. He wasn't sure if he should smile too openly.

For a short second, Almyna's eyes betrayed her astonishment but she soon regained her poise. "Well, well!" She ran her eyes over Cilbert and casually displayed the glittering wedding ring upon her left hand. "An' der was me t'inking me leaving me old life. It jus' goes to show dat yuh cyan run away from ya past, nuh matter where yuh go."

Almyna flashed a knowing smile.

"Yuh look very fine," complimented Cilbert, briefly glancing behind him to check if Hortense was observing.

"Well, t'ank yuh, Cilbert. May me say yuh look fine too, considering everyt'ing. But me see ah liccle stress aroun' ya eyes. Ya face nah so fresh nuh more. Me suppose it's de strain of adult living. Someone ah tell me yuh was living inna Trenchtown. Dey tell me it rough an' dutty down der. Mebbe dat cause de stress inna ya forehead. Yuh did look so cute as ah young bwai."

Almyna discreetly glanced at the ring on Cilbert's wedding finger. "Me married two years ago," she revealed, eager to announce her status. "To ah Misser Hubert Golding. Yuh hear about de Golding family inna Jamaica? They're very important. We get invited to dinners at de governor's mansion. Yuh mus' 'ave heard of de Goldings?"

Cilbert paused on the question, placing an index finger and thumb upon his chin, but he didn't have a clue who the Goldings were. "Nuh, Almyna. But de name ring ah bell."

"So it should," pressed Almyna. "Dem ah business family, involved wid banking, insurance an' real estate. Dey 'ave ah beautiful mansion near Port Antonio over-looking de ocean. Hubert is over der. See how him handsome!"

Almyna pointed to the tables where the first-class passengers dined. Hubert, tall and impressive in a dark suit, was of a lighter complexion than Almyna. Cilbert guessed he was a mulatto – mixed-race. Hubert's hair had also been straightened and his thinly-trimmed moustache gave him the appearance of a young Duke Ellington.

"Me really glad fe yuh, Almyna," said Cilbert, checking behind him again. Hortense had finally spotted him and made it clear with a sour glare that she wouldn't tolerate her husband socialising with one of his ex-girlfriends – especially Almyna.

"Is dat ya wife?" smiled Almyna, who knew the answer to her own question; she had made her own enquiries on return trips to Orange valley.

Cilbert nodded. Almyna rolled her eyes. "So yuh married Hortense! She very dark isn't she? Very dark. Me cyan't see not'ing but her teet'! Me never really notice it when me first see her. All me notice was how much rum punch she ah drink. Yes, Hortense was de licky licky one who made ah spectacle of herself when she start dance. *Nah* de right way fe ah lady to behave. She still ah slave to fire-water? Some people say dat addiction to fire-water cyan cause de skin to wrinkle quick time an' will mosh up ya liver. An' if she has, ya kidren will be born wid damage. She might produce cripples. But me suppose some mon 'ave dem strange fancy."

Biting his top lip, Cilbert refused to respond to Almyna's offensive remarks. "Well, Almyna, it really fine to see yuh again but me affe go now – Hortense an' me in-laws are waiting fe me."

"Go so soon? Dat nah polite, Cilbert. We born an' grow inna de same place an' dis is de first time we sight each udder fe years an' all yuh cyan do is run to ya *dark* wife? Ya 'fraid of her?"

"Nuh, nuh. It nah dat. It's jus' dat me affe look some bread, drink an' t'ing fe dem."

"Den if dat is de situation she will nah mind if we link up some time 'pon de journey. Mebbe ah drink togeder fe old time sake? After all, we *are* family." Almyna preened herself then offered a wicked grin.

By the time Almyna had constructed her next pose, Cilbert was gone, anxiety spreading across his face as he asked for more bread and tomato-flavoured mince. He would never reveal to Hortense or to anybody else that Almyna and himself were second cousins. Almyna waited for her bottle of wine, glanced at her husband who was entertaining friends and for an instant a flash of sadness revealed itself in her eyes. Then, with bottle in hand and head held high, Almyna returned to her table in a sexy strut she had long ago perfected. Knowing that Cilbert was watching her, she theatrically sat upon Hubert's lap and drained the contents of his glass. Looking on, Cilbert said to himself. "Dat girl is many t'ings but Lord me God, she know how fe *walk* an' mek any mon tek notice."

Returning to his own table, Cilbert could feel the jealousy steaming off Hortense's eyes. He tried to smile away his discomfort. Jacob, ignoring the sudden tension, accepted the bread and sliced it for Jenny. "Two slice yuh waan, me sweetheart?"

Jenny didn't hear her husband and instead placed a comforting hand on Hortense's wrist as she glared at Cilbert. Hortense's lips stiffened, her eyes staring at her meal.

"Wha' did yuh expect me to do?" asked Cilbert, spreading his arms.

"Ignore her? Me know Almyna all me life! Me never expect her to be 'pon dis ship. Anyway, she married now so *don't* t'ink dat me up to nuh good."

Twirling spaghetti around her fork, Hortense's eyes didn't leave her plate. It looked as if she might use the fork on Cilbert.

"More wine, Hortense?" Jacob offered, trying to diffuse the situation.

Hortense ignored Jacob. "Cilbert, sit down! If yuh know wha' is good fe yuh, *stay* away from dat red skin, brute of ah bitch! Look how she dress like dem blue-foot gal who stan' outside Devon House looking to sell dem tricks. An' her lipstick look like somebody sacrifice ah chicken over her mout'! Me don't know how her head cyan tek de strain of all de grease inna her hair. Yuh coulda wring out her hair an' tek de oil an' mek truck drive. An' she wear so much mek-up me surprise her cheeks don't bawl fe mercy. She look like ah Jamaican version of Coco de Clown."

Jacob almost choked on his bread as he restrained a belly laugh. Jenny caught a fit of the giggles as Cilbert didn't know whether to laugh or cry. Feeling better, Hortense accepted more wine.

The remainder of the meal was consumed in silence with Cilbert not daring to return Almyna's flirtatious glances. As Hortense downed the last of her wine; she had drank four glasses, she turned to a nervous Cilbert and demanded, "me waan talk to yuh in private, inna de cabin." She addressed Jenny. "Cyan yuh give me some time wid me husband? T'ings need to discuss."

"Of course," Jenny replied. "Jacob an' meself will mingle wid our fellow passengers. It'll be good fe dem to know der is ah minister 'pon board, ah mon of good standing."

Wiping her mouth with a serviette, Hortense stood up and departed the dining hall. She shot a wounding glance in Almyna's direction. An anxious Cilbert followed his wife, careful not to get too close to her.

Upon reaching the cabin, Hortense locked it from the inside once Cilbert had entered. "Yuh still find her tickling ya fancy?" asked Hortense, her eyes now insecure, her expression fragile.

"Of course not," lied Cilbert, trying to master his nerves.

For a moment, Hortense thought of her brother David and how he promised that he would always return to her. She recalled the strength of David's gaze and the conviction in it. She searched Cilbert's eyes for confirmation that he would never leave her. Satisfied, she walked slowly into Cilbert's embrace and they kissed and caressed each other's faces hungrily. Clothes were quickly discarded and scattered upon the floor. There was an urgency and ferocity in Hortense's love-making that Cilbert never experienced before as Hortense pressed her face against his, wanting to be utterly consumed into his body. He felt it was almost spiritual, a meeting of kindred souls.

The next morning, Cilbert accompanied his wife for a walk upon the passenger deck; a girly smile was fixed upon Hortense's face. Together they peered into the horizon, wondering what fate had in store for them. Jacob and Jenny strolled behind them, both concealing their anxiety at the absence of land. Jacob was careful to avoid straying too close to the railings. They all greeted fellow passengers warmly and paused for short conversations that were mainly about the need for Jamaican chefs and the body odour of Italian waiters. "Dem smell bad," said Jenny to a young Jamaican couple. "An' it seem dat der mudders forget to teach dem how to scrub dem fingernail!"

It was Cilbert who spotted Almyna walking towards him in her unique style, arm-in-arm with Hubert.

"Good marnin, Cilby," Almyna greeted, over-smiling. "It's good to tek in de sea breezes isn't it? May me introduce yuh to me husband, Hubert."

Hubert took off his felt hat and held it poised over his head in a formal gesture. "Good morning, Cilbert and Hortense I believe." He replaced his hat as Hortense inwardly seethed that Almyna must have spoken about her. "Isn't this a coincidence? For two people to grow up together now finding themselves upon the same ship years after they had lost touch."

"Yes it is," returned Cilbert, almost having to check himself from bowing. "May me tek dis opportunity to bless ya voyage."

"Thank you, Cilbert," smiled Hubert, recognising the

exaggerated manners of someone from Jamaican peasant stock addressing an aristocrat.

Jacob and Jenny offered their greetings, Jenny somewhat reluctantly. She couldn't conceal her animosity towards Almyna and thought the excessive display of politeness was pathetic.

"Yes, Hubert," started Almyna. "Hortense an' Jenny hail from de Claremont valley inna St Anne, nah far from where me an' Cilby born an' grow."

"A beautiful *and* bountiful part of Jamaica, by all accounts," said Hubert. "The Eden of the Caribbean."

"An' *poor* too," added Almyna. "Hortense an' Jenny are de daughters of ah mon who dey call Moonshine. Mysterious an' dark Moonshine is, an', me nuh waan to mek nuh offence, but people say him 'ave pagan ways an' underworld customs. Moonshine don't walk de ways of de Lord an' him never go ah church. His name spread far an' wide an' him come from de seed of wild Maroons. He sings in strange tongues. Some say he's in league wid de devil." Almyna concluded her sentence with a dismissive glance at Hortense.

Hortense's grip upon Cilbert's left hand tightened considerably and Hubert, embarrassed by his wife's unkind words, tried to smile away the obvious tension. "This voyage has been pleasant so far, but no doubt we will encounter more troubled waters and—"

Suddenly, a fist detonated against Almyna's left jaw, wiping her self-satisfied grin off her face and knocking her off her feet. Her back thudded against the deck and as she rolled over, she caught a strong whiff of salt. Jenny, her rage not satisfied, leapt upon Almyna like a tigress seizing its prey. Before anyone could respond, she viced Almyna's throat with her long fingers, squeezing to the absolute limit that her strength allowed. Pure hatred was within her eyes. "*Yuh ever say anyt'ing about me papa again an' as Massa God is me witness me will kill yuh. An' ya fate will be worse dan dat if yuh come near to me sister husband once more.* STAY *away from Cilbert!*" Almyna gasped and choked, her head rocking violently from side to side.

Jacob and Hubert dashed to pull Jenny off Almyna. Hubert was mindful of the threats made by someone of a Coromanty bloodline and decided against retaliation; raised in a home kept by servants and maids, Hubert had heard in bedtime stories about the 'blood-lust' and 'savagery' of the Maroons. Hortense and Cilbert looked on astonished, their mouths agape.

"Mad like dem fader!" screamed Almyna. "Jezebel pagans! Dem sister are disciples of Old Screwface!"

Ashamed of his wife's petulance and shocked at Jenny's brutality, Hubert hauled Almyna away, trying to comfort her. "Hubert! Do somet'ing about dem! Why yuh nah fight fe me? She like ah mad bull! *Pagans!*"

Rubbing the knuckles of her right fist, Jenny glanced regretfully at Hortense and marched off, tears were filling her eyes. Jacob went after her but Hortense restrained him. "Let me see to her, Jacob. Somet'ing else dan dat red skin bitch Almyna ah trouble her. Me know she anxious to mek dis trip. Nah worry yaself. She'll be alright."

Hortense found Jenny in their cabin. She was sitting on a bunk bent over, her head almost touching her knees and she was holding her face within her palms, stifling her weeping. Hortense sat beside her and placed an arm over Jenny's shoulders. "Jenny, dat was one mighty t'ump yuh give to dat red skin bitch," Hortense chuckled. "But me cyan fight me own battles now. We're nah der ah school. Yuh don't 'ave to defend me nuh more. Cilbert will never leave me fe de likes of her. She jus' jealous. So me cyan tek whatever Almyna say to me an' show de udder cheek."

"She went too far," wept Jenny. "Who she t'ink she is? Talking about Papa like dat! Me shoulda fling her overboard."

"Me feel dat way too but yuh jus' affe ignore her," counselled Hortense. "She jus' ignorant an' all becah she 'ave ah lighter complexion she go on high an' mighty like she an aristocrat. But remember wha' sweet Gran'papa Neville tell we years ago, *de higher de monkey climb, de more he get exposed*. Almyna will get expose de same way."

Jenny kept on sobbing, her wails becoming louder. "Is der somet'ing else dat ah trouble yuh, Jenny?" asked Hortense. "All of we are nervous about dis trip so mebbe it put ah strain 'pon yuh. An' me don't know wha' yuh an' Mama argue about t'ree days ago but she love yuh dearly. An' Papa too."

Moving her hands from upon her face, Jenny turned to gaze into her sister's eyes. Her lips moved to speak but no sound came out. She secretly wished they were children again, depending on each other with nobody else interfering. An' Mama didn't love *anyone*, she thought, but she kept this emotion to herself.

"Come, Jenny," urged Hortense. "Remember we promise, we don't keep anyt'ing from each udder. Not ah damn t'ing."

Palming away her tears, Jenny looked out the porthole window. There she gazed for two minutes until she said, "Hortense, me nuh sure if me love Jacob. Mebbe me shoulda stayed home."

"Now yuh cyan't really mean dat," replied Hortense. "Jacob is ah lovely mon an' yuh mean de world to him. It's ah big, big t'ing going 'pon dis trip an' all of we emotions are all over de place. Me had doubts too. But yuh will get over it. It's jus' nerves dat ah ketch yuh. Wait an' see 'til we reach Englan', everyt'ing will be alright."

Hortense kissed Jenny upon her forehead and embraced her. Jenny was about to confess something but feeling the familiarity and closeness of her sister, she closed her eyes and imagined they were back at home as children, curling up to each other in bed and listening to the hoots of the patus hidden away in the mighty Blue Mahoes.

Following the incident on deck, Cilbert led Jacob to the dining hall. Cilbert ordered a coffee for himself and an orange juice for Jacob. They sat without saying a word for ten minutes, listening to the clatter of the breakfast dishes being washed up, until Cilbert remarked, "Lord me God, ya Jenny 'ave ah fierce temper 'pon her! She t'ump like one of dem big cane cutter. Poor Almyna mus' ah wonder wha' lick her. Mon, even de mighty Sonny Liston woulda ketch 'fraid if him see Jenny inna action."

Jacob expressed a hint of pride. "Yes, mon. Jenny cyan be de most calm girl y'know, calm like de waters inna Fern Gully lake. But when she lose her temper yuh affe step inna ya shelter an' wait 'til de storm blow out. Back inna Claremont dem call Hortense 'Fire

Nettle', but dey should call Jenny 'Raging Thorn'."

"Ah fine description," Cilbert nodded. "But nex' time yuh see Hubert yuh better apologise 'pon Jenny behalf."

"Yes, yuh never know. Hubert might mek ah complaint to de captain."

They both sipped their drinks. "How is ya head?" asked Cilbert. "De rum still ah swim?"

"It'll be much better when I sight land once more."

"Well, only twenty days to go," stated Cilbert.

"Yuh sure ya frien', Lester, will be der when we arrive at Sout'ampton?"

"Of course," answered Cilbert. "Lester will nah let we down. Me know him from me university days."

"Wha' is Brixton like?" Jacob wanted to know.

"Well, Lester say it very close to de middle ah London. Plenty, plenty brick houses all over de place. An' many of we own people. Lester in him letters say de people walk so fast – if yuh t'ink Kingston people walk quick yuh don't see not'ing yet!"

"An' dis place where we will be staying, ya sure it alright? I don't waan tek Jenny to live inna run down place. Yuh know how she love complain."

"Jacob, stop boder yaself. Lester is ah mon to be trusted. Lester's brudder serve wid de Royal Air Force inna de war an' he has been inna Englan' since 1946. An' Lester been living inna Englan' since 1956, so we'll be well looked after."

"I hope so," said Jacob, not entirely convinced.

"It *will* be so," asserted Cilbert. "Ah day or two after we arrive we 'ave to forward to de labour exchange an' register we name. Jacob, yuh give any t'ought to wha' kinda job yuh waan? Becah me know yuh waan to set up ya own church but yuh cyan't do dat straight away."

Jacob paused to sip his orange juice. "I am not skilled like yuh an' I don't believe I cyan find employment inna London looking after hog! Dat is de only t'ing me cyan do apart from me service to de Most High. But I am nuh 'fraid of hard work so mebbe me will perform some labouring 'pon ah building site or wherever. But one day, mark me very words, I *will* 'ave me own church fe my own people inna London. It mus' be strange fe our brudders an' sisters inna Englan' to step inna white mon church. I feel dis is de reason de Most High place me 'pon dis earth'."

Cilbert admired the ambition in Jacob's words and they shook hands and embraced. For the first time since they had known each other they felt like brothers.

Chapter Fourteen

Three days out of Kingston. *The Genovese Madonna* steamed through the Windward straits and the passengers looking out from portside could make out the eastern Cuban shoreline shimmering in the distance. A crew member aloft in the crows-nest could see Guantanamo Bay and the masts of vessels docked there. To him they appeared like white needles bobbing in the blue yonder. Those on starboard, a few of whom were recalling the heroic deeds of the once enslaved Toussaint L'Ouverture that they had heard in story-time sessions from village elders, hoped to sight the western fringes of Haiti. But only endless glinting sea and cloudless sky met their eyes.

Two days later the Italian-made vessel weaved its way through the Turks and Caicos islands. Cilbert, mocking the protruding lumps of land that dotted this area of the Caribbean sea, wondered how the islanders could stage a cricket match. "If George Headley was batting at his brilliant best de captain of de bowling side would affe place him fielders inna de ocean! *Ha Ha*! Wha' ah fine joke!"

"George Headley was an excellent batsman," a Barbadian man agreed, adopting an English accent. He was one of only a few Barbadians on board. "But Headley can't touch the genius of Garfield Sobers. And Sobers come from Barbados. A rather *small* island."

"Damn blasted Bajee people dem!" Cilbert muttered under his breath while cutting his eyes at the suited Barbadian. "Dem t'ink dey are better dan everybody. Look at him trying to talk English an' wearing him shirt an' tie. Did Bajees ever put up resistance to de white mon? Did dey ever try an' escape from slavery? *Nuh, sa*! Dey accepted slavery too easily an' now dey try an' mimic de white mon. *Bajee uptown pussy...*"

"Oh, Cilbert, stop ya bragga an' cuss cuss," censured Hortense.

Yuh don't t'ink some Jamaican mon t'ink dem high an' mighty an' try talk de queen's English while dem ah wear dem t'ree piece suit?"

"Mebbe so," said Cilbert, raising his voice. "But we never pretend dat we *don't* come from slave!"

By the seventh day, the ship had crossed the Tropic of Cancer, a thousand miles south of Bermuda. The wind speed had picked up and the chopping seas were veined with white froth. Maverick gusts and breezes curled around the upper deck walkways, stealing through open doors and reddening crew members' noses. West Indians, viewing the blue nothingness through watering, squinted eyes, recalled childhood history lessons where they had been told that in Christopher Columbus's day, navigators dreaded to sail into unchartered waters for fear of falling over the edge of the world. Peering into the unmoving horizon, a few observers could now understand that horror.

That morning, returning from the laundry room, passing the boiler house and the engineering workshops, Hortense heard amid the general din a muffled groan from a linen cupboard. Deciding to investigate, she opened the door and there beyond the shelves, crouched in a corner, was a man dressed only in a stained vest and grubby grey chinos. His eyes were yellowed and the beard that covered his face concealed the hollows in his cheeks. The brown cloth cap he was wearing seemed too small for his head and a shanty town aroma streamed off him like emissions of rum from a kerb-side, smashed bottle. "Lord bless me gran'mama knee-bone," Hortense exclaimed. "Wha' yuh doing inside der? Yuh ah mad-mon? De sway ah de ship turn yuh into ah damn fool? Ya press banana skin inna ya eye?"

"Nuh, nuh, Miss," the man replied, looking over Hortense's shoulder to check if anybody else was around. "Me ah stowaway, Miss. Me climb up 'pon de anchor chain back inna Kingston harbour. But me t'ought de ship woulda reach Englan' after two days. An' now me hungry. *Very* hungry."

"Yuh 'ave de sense yuh was born wid?" scolded Hortense. "Yuh go ah school? Who tell yuh dat Englan' is only two day sail away? Englan' is 'pon de udder side ah de world! T'ree weeks dis journey tek. Mebbe four. Lord me God! Me see some foolish mon inna me time but yuh mus' be de king of de idiot dem."

"Me never go ah school," the man admitted, dropping his head.

"Wha' is ya name?" Hortense wanted to know.

"Bruce. Misser Bruce Clarke."

"Well, Misser Bruce Clarke," Hortense stated, her tone unforgiving. "Wha' mek yuh go on dis foolish escapade?"

"Well, Miss. Me born an' grow inna Maypen. Could nah find nuh work der so me forward to Kingston. Could nah find nuh place to live so me shack up inna de Dungle. Could nah find nuh work inna Kingston neider so me decide to tek me chance 'pon dis ship an' forward to Englan'. Plenty mon tell me de streets ah London are paved in gold. So dat is wha' me ah look for. An' if me find it me gwarn sen' it back to me poor sweet mama who cyan't walk so good."

Hortense shook her head. "People tell yuh wrong information. If yuh forward to Englan' yuh affe work hard fe every red cent." Hortense studied the pathetic demeanour of the stowaway and she remembered the story of how her own father had befriended Kwarhterleg. "Anyway, Bruce, nah worry yaself," she assured. "Me won't expose yuh to de crew. Dem cyan't understan' ah word me say anyway. Stay here an' wait 'til me come. Me will find food fe yuh but dat is all me cyan do. An' when everybody gone to dem bed me beg yuh to wash yaself. Ya smell like ah block-up Trenchtown sewer dat even de fatty cockroach dread!"

"Yes, me will do dat. T'ank yuh, Miss."

"Me name is *Mrs* Hortense Huggins."

Before Bruce could utter another thank you, the door was pulled shut and he could hear Hortense's fading steps. He retreated to his dark corner.

Returning back to her cabin, Hortense revealed to Cilbert, Jacob and Jenny what she had discovered.

"Yuh mus' report him!" shouted Cilbert. "It seem dat dis mon never work ah day in him life! Lazy him ah lazy. We scrimp an' save to board dis ship an' dis Bruce travel fe free. Why should we sponsor him an' protect him? He could be ah ginall or ah trickster."

"Yes, an' him could be dangerous," added Jenny. "Say dis Bruce get ketch an' dem find out we help him? Me don't waan to be seen as ah accomplice to ah criminal act. It will damage we reputation, especially Jacob becah he is ah preacher. When we reach Englan' dey might deport we. Sen' we back inna great shame. How yuh t'ink poor Papa will tek de news? We mus' report him to de aut'orities."

Listening quietly to the debate, Jacob recalled the days he ventured and spread the gospel in the Dungle and the solemn dignity he had found among the people there. "Bruce *is* our brudder," he asserted in a soft voice. "An' if we don't help him we are failing in our fait'. Yuh mus' help ya neighbour! So de good book say."

"Help ya neighbour?" argued Cilbert. "It was neighbours who cramp an' paralyse me inna Trenchtown! It was neighbours who t'ief we garments off we clothes-line ah nighttime. It was neighbours who t'ief Wilfred Gray's Sunday fowl! Me don't trus' nuhbody me don't know. An' if ya God don't like dat let him try live inna Trenchtown an' see how long it tek neighbours to t'ief him halo. If yuh waan to help dis Bruce den me don't waan anyt'ing to do wid it. Yuh don't hear of de saying, *kick dahg an' him will respect an' fear yuh but if yuh treat de dog kindly he will waan ya respect an' won't fear yuh.*"

"Wise words, Cilbert," concurred Jenny. "An' nor shall I help dis mon."

Jacob looked at Jenny as if he was questioning her soul. Feeling morally bereft, Jenny departed the cabin. "Me need to get some air. Too stuffy inna dis place. An' de ceiling *too* low. It mek me feel claustrophobic."

Cilbert turned to Jacob. "Dis is ya responsibility. But if t'ings go wrong, *don't* expect Massa God to come down an' help yuh." Cilbert faced his wife and searched her eyes for agreement. "Hortense, me sorry, but dat is how me feel. Yuh two decide wha' yuh affe do. Me gone to de bar to look ah rum drink."

"Yes, yuh do dat," returned Hortense. "Yuh spend more time der dan wid ya wife. Mebbe yuh tek ah fancy to dat reeking bar-mon wid de long whisker an' nuff missing teet'. Him smell like bad breat' donkey dat wander inna dutty pig pen."

"Me spend more time der becah ah liccle fire-water cyan't give me nuh argument. Dat is one t'ing me cyan't stand wid yuh, Hortense – yuh always t'ink ya right an' ya naggy naggy ways start get 'pon me nerves."

Cilbert pulled at the cabin door with force and left it swinging upon its hinges. He marched along the corridor cursing under his breath. Jacob and Hortense glanced at each other, sure in their minds they were taking the right course of action.

During subsequent meal times, Hortense, ignoring the brutal glares from Cilbert and Jenny, would slip out of the dining hall with a plastic container full of food. Bruce, afraid to emerge out of his hiding place, accepted his nourishment gratefully. Jacob visited Bruce in the evenings and upon discovering that Bruce was unable to read and write, quietly read passages of the Bible to him. Jacob also presented Bruce with two pairs of his old trousers and three shirts.

Happiest when he felt he was most needed by his own people, Jacob began to conduct prayer meetings upon the passenger deck on Sunday mornings and soon the heartfelt sound of a gospel choir could be heard in the ship's wake rising above the ripplings of a tamborine that a woman was thrashing against her thigh. Many non-church-goers attended Jacob's improvised services, including Almyna and Hubert. They believed that in displaying their presence, Massa God would grant them mercy if catastrophe blighted the voyage. Cilbert thought the whole thing was a ridiculous, hypocritical farce and spent Sunday mornings gambling with poker dice, but the onlooking Italian crew members, the vast majority of them staunch Catholics, began to warm to the Jamaicans.

On Friday and Saturday night dance nights, held in the dining hall once the tables were pushed to the walls, the Italian band, accustomed to playing instrumental versions of classical arias, were now experimenting with Jamaican ska. Their attempts never approached the heights of The Skatellites, the crack band of musicians who were hotting up the dance halls and lawns in Kingston, but the Jamaicans, starved of cultural nourishment since their boarding of the ship, turned the dining hall of *The Genovese Madonna* into a Trenchtown lawn dance. Only the first class passengers sniffed and whispered unkind comments. "Look at them downtown people!" one lady said. "We try our best to represent our country but them ghetto people force the band to play the devil's music. I've never felt so much shame!"

Fifteen days out of Kingston, the passenger vessel docked at Puerto de la Cruz in Tenerife. A number of sea-sick West Indians, observing the mountainous island from a distance, despaired as they wrongly assumed they were still in the Caribbean. Their relief was obvious when they were informed that the ship was only two hundred miles or so west from the coast of Morocco. "Me was only pretending dat me t'ought we was still inna de Caribbean sea," one man laughed. "Den why me see eye-water 'pon ya face?" another returned. Images of Humphrey Bogart's lop-sided grin, garbed in a white jacket and draining a cool cocktail in a Casablanca bar bombarded all of their minds.

Skirting the north African coast and splitting the strait of Gibraltar, *The Genovese Madonna* entered the warm waters of the Mediterranean. As the ship headed north-east through the Ligurian Sea, the passengers sensed an increased thrill and relief from their hosts who were looking forward to returning home. "Beautiful Genoa!" exclaimed one sailor to Cilbert in his stuttering English. "We'll be back in time to celebrate the feast of the Madonna della Guardia, the protector of sailors."

"Good fe yuh," half-smiled Cilbert, not impressed. He was still smarting from his latest quarrel with Hortense.

"It's a great pity you don't have the papers to walk around my beautiful city," said the sailor. "We are a very welcoming people and for hundreds of years we have seen peoples and merchants from all over the world. Many tourists make their way to the Piazza Acquaverde to see the statue of our most famous son, Christopher Columbus. His voyage to the New World was blessed by the Pope and the divine Madonna guided him herself."

Cilbert sneered and narrowed his eyes. "Columbus! Christopher damn Columbus! He was ah damn blasted liar! He discover not'ing! Der was people inna Jamaica before him. De tobacco-smoking, mild-mannered Arawaks fe one. An' all Columbus do is bring ah great evil to de island. Yes, Columbus was Old Screwface's disciple. May him soul get roasted an' nyam by de dragons of hell fe all time!"

The Italian seaman, not understanding Cilbert's sudden anger, stormed off muttering Latin obscenities.

Docking at the port of Genoa, the Jamaicans were reminded of Kingston harbour as they viewed the green-caped mountains that backdropped the city. They could see narrow, winding streets with aged, bent houses and shops and they wondered about the people who lived there. "Where are de white people palaces?" one Kingstonian asked. Bruce, who had stolen upon the passenger deck, was dismayed because there was no sight of happy men dressed in silks and robes, juggling nuggets of gold. Maybe he would witness this scenario in London, he thought.

A dozen of the first-class passengers, suited and booted, stepped ashore and spent their time strolling through the many art museums within the city, regarding paintings and sculptures as if they were seasoned art critics from the Sunday broadsheets. Others, including Hubert and Almyna, dined at fine restaurants where they attempted to impress the waiters with the small number of Italian words they had picked up from their voyage. Hubert noticed that the Genovese men were especially pleasant and complimentary to Almyna. Boosted by the lavish comments about her looks and her smooth Egyptian-like skin, Almyna giggled and underlined her Kingstonian catwalk strut whenever she bade farewell to her admirers. Hubert fumed under his thin moustache.

Following minor maintenance work and a change of crew, the ship set course to her final destination, Southampton, England. The West Indians, including those who had fallen to illness thus far, felt a growing excitement. Many of them remained on the passenger deck for the best part of the journey, all wanting to be the first to sight the shores of the Motherland. Jacob, ignoring his dread of the sea, joined them at the railings. Even those who slept in more spacious cabins joined the second-class passengers in raucous renditions of 'God Save Our Gracious Queen'.

Searching in her suitcase for her best frock, Jenny, trying to imagine how English ladies dressed, said to Hortense. "As soon as we reach Sout'ampton, me 'ave to write ah letter to Papa. Tell him we reach safely. An' Gran'papa Neville will affe stop sacrificing fowl fe we deliverance."

Jenny laughed at her own jesting and Hortense sensed that her sister had left her doubts and worries somewhere in the middle of the Atlantic. She took hold of Jenny's left hand. "Me did tell yuh everyt'ing will be alright. We're starting ah new life inna de motherland an' our children will be born *English*. Cyan yuh imagine dat?"

Embracing her sister and fantasising of the good life that the country may offer her, Jenny replied, "yes, so dey will. Cilbert will mek ah great fader an' me sure his mighty ambition an' determination will pass on to him children."

"An' Jacob will pass on him devoutness an' fait' to ya children," returned Hortense.

Jenny didn't add to Hortense's praising of Jacob.

Twenty-two days out of Kingston, *The Genovese Madonna*, under an overcast sky, skirted the Isle of Wight, bypassed the coastal town of Gosport and steamed serenely up the Solent. Yachts and other small vessels dotted the murky-green sea. In dry docks, ships were being constructed and repaired by burly men wearing boiler suits and hard hats. Looking around her, Jenny remarked. "Everyt'ing look so grey. Even de people who ah work 'pon de ships dem – grey like hurricane sky. Me never see ah cloud so broad. Don't it ever move? An' it cold! De north pole mus' be close."

Hortense found herself nodding her agreement. Cilbert, who had half-expected to be welcomed by marching bands and a jovial local mayor dressed in all his finery, stared out blankly, trying his best not to display the sense of disappointment he was feeling. He turned to look at Jacob and figure out if he shared the anti-climax.

But Jacob was no longer standing by his side. "Where Jacob gone?" he asked.

Cilbert imagined London to be much brighter, full of happy smiling people who would be fascinated to learn about Jamaicans and their traditions. He convinced himself that he would be greeted in the street and asked, 'how do you do'. In his letters, Lester had described the bustling streets of the West End and Cilbert could foresee Jamaican restaurants, bars and clubs that played Caribbean music. He chuckled to himself as he imagined white people jiving to calypso and dining on chicken, rice and peas.

Disembarking from the ship and taking her first step upon English soil, Jenny felt that she had been severed from a part of her identity and history. She couldn't help but think how out of place her father and her grandfather would be in her present surroundings. Recalling childhood suppers she remembered how her father made such a big deal if he happened to sight a 'sweaty white mon' mounted on his horse, continually swabbing his forehead with a soiled handkerchief. Now, she felt girdled by these white people, all walking so quickly, brushing past her as if they were all trying to locate misplaced cash or in need of a toilet. They appeared so grim and passed each other without offering a greeting or a nod of acknowledgement. She noticed Hortense squeezing the colour out of Cilbert's right hand.

"*Englan'*!" Cilbert exclaimed, not noticing the bemused looks from the natives. "Land of opportunity!"

Smiling nervously, Hortense glanced behind her at the sea and for a moment considered a return to the ship. She tried to summon up courage but the tears welled up in her eyes. She imagined her brother David stepping ashore in New Orleans over a decade ago but at least there had been a significant number of black people there already. In his letters to Cilbert, Lester may have eloquently described the port of Southampton and the city of London, but he failed to relate the fear and sense of loneliness upon arrival.

Not relaxing her grip on Cilbert's hand, Hortense now knew how that Chinese family felt when they first arrived in Claremont. They were ignored by almost everybody. Nobody would purchase their groceries and one night, someone set fire to their shop front. Hortense recalled the look of the Chinese mother the morning after the incident. She didn't say anything but her eyes were desperate, pleading to be accepted. From standing at her family stall, Hortense made four steps towards the Chinese woman with the intention of offering 'ah good marnin'. But sensing the eyes of other Claremontonians upon her, Hortense paused and stepped back. She now wondered if the English would treat her the same.

Anxiety written over his face, Jacob wondered if Bruce Clarke had survived his plunge into the Solent. Jacob, after failing to collect enough cash from other immigrants to secure Bruce's passage, had counselled Bruce to give himself up and perhaps the authorities would let him remain on English soil, but Bruce would not yield. "Me nah gwarn to return to Jamaica," he insisted. "Not'ing der fe me apart from de dutty Dungle! Me will tek me chances inna de sea water an' swim to de shore."

Reluctantly, Jacob led Bruce to a secluded area of the stern of the ship. There he offered Bruce a few bank notes and a fistful of change. Bruce placed his right hand upon Jacob's left shoulder in a gesture of thanks and smiled. "Pray fe me, preacher-mon? Yuh is de bes' friend me ever had."

Without hesitation, lacking style or grace, Bruce plummeted into the sea, carrying a small bundle of clothes wrapped up in a plastic bag. Jacob, his heart thumping furiously, didn't spot Bruce's head emerge above the waters until after five seconds, bobbing with the trailing wake of the ship. Jacob couldn't help but think he had helped a man to his death.

Having passed through customs without as much fuss and questions as he had expected, Cilbert saw an impressively tall black man wearing a dark blue suit, skinny red tie and a black pork-pie hat waiting by a newspaper stand. He had the ready smile and confidence of a lead singer from a doo-wop band. "Lester! Over here, sa!"

Cilbert caught a glimpse of Hubert and Almyna meeting two white men and a mixed race woman. For a short second, Almyna offered him an over-the-shoulder, regretful glance before she was led away.

Lester Hibbert swaggered to meet his old friend.

"He look like ah joy bwai," Jenny whispered to Jacob. "Like dem mon inna Trenchtown who 'ave plenty, plenty women an' even more kidren. Dey never sleep inna de same bed two nights running an' dey always ketch crab-louse 'pon der *business*."

"Don't judge by appearance, sweetheart." replied Jacob. "Give him ah chance. After all, he come down from London to greet we."

Cilbert and Lester embraced and remarked on how each other looked since their days at university. Hortense soon drew Lester's attention. "So dis is de beautiful Hortense? Well, Cilbert, yuh strike gold fe true! Nuh wonder yuh never invite me back to Claremont an' introduce me."

Hortense felt her cheeks warming as Jenny whispered into Jacob's ear, a hint of envy germinating in her mind. "Me told yuh so! Dis Lester is ah joy bwai. Me gwarn to watch him closely in case him try an' corrupt me sweet sister."

With the introductions concluded, Lester led the new arrivals to the train station. Struck by her new surroundings, Hortense marvelled at the way people queued at bus stops and taxi ranks. Everything was so orderly. Crossing the roads without motorists blaring their horns was a pleasure. She felt she was being stared at by the natives but this only encouraged her to lift her chin and walk tall. Yes! Look 'pon me people of Englan', she wanted to shout out. Me's ah proud Jamaican woman born inna Claremont where de fields an' leaf so green!

"Jacob! Jacob!" Jenny nudged her husband. "See how de white people ah look 'pon we? Don't dey ever see black people before? Dey look 'pon we like ah city mon look 'pon ah bull grining ah cow. Ungodly dem ah ungodly!"

"Everyt'ing will be alright," calmed Cilbert. "Inna Sout'ampton dem nuh used to black people. Inna London it will be different. People will come up to we an' introduce demselves. Watch an' see!"

"Haven't our people been arriving at dis port fe many years now?" queried Jacob.

"Well, dat true," answered Cilbert. "But nuh too many Jamaicans live here. Once yuh live inna area de people der get used to yuh."

"Me hope so!" remarked Jenny.

"Wha' do yuh say, Lester?" Hortense asked. "Do de people like we?"

"Well, er. Cilbert is right when him say dat de places where Jamaicans don't live, de people look 'pon we funny. But inna London we don't 'ave dat problem. Jus' ah few small minded people don't like we presence."

"Jus' ah few!" Jenny wondered. "Yuh sure it jus' ah few?"

Lester failed to answer again.

They caught the ten a.m. train from Southampton to Paddington, London. Feeling exhausted, Hortense rested her head against Cilbert's shoulder and tried to catch some sleep. Sitting opposite her with a biro poised over a notepad, Jenny peered out of the window, marvelling at the train's speed and the green countryside that flashed by. She imagined how her father would enjoy trodding the flat lands and for a moment wondered about the fate of the family donkey.

Meanwhile, Jacob was pouring over his newspaper. There was an article about Francis Chichester who had just set a new sailing time record of forty days from Plymouth to New York. Jacob chuckled at the name of Chichester's yacht, *Gypsy Moth the Second*. He wondered if the first *Gypsy Moth* had sunk in the Atlantic. Another front page lead was about an agreement between the British and French governments that work could commence soon on the Channel Tunnel. A smaller news item near the foot of the front page detailed the end of British rule in Cyprus. Jacob wondered when Jamaica would enjoy her independence.

Cilbert, studying the back page of Jacob's newspaper, couldn't wrestle his eyes from a car advertisement; a newly designed three litre Rover with all the modern appliances priced at £1,715.10. If me work hard me will get meself one of dem, he promised to himself. Yes, sa, an' when me get it me gwarn to tek ah photo of meself inna de car an' sen' it back to Trenchtown an' mek de people me know realise dat me doing well fine inna Englan'.

The train came to a halt at Paddington. Hortense got out blinking the sleep from her eyes. Seeing that she was weary, Cilbert linked

arms with his wife and took the small suitcase she was carrying.
Once Hortense's train ticket had been accepted by an unsmiling
barrier guard, Hortense saw a sobering sight. A middle-aged white
woman, wearing a headscarf and a light blue overall, was pulling a
grey metal bucket containing a mop, towards the train station's
public toilets. Her hands were protected by pink rubber gloves and
her grim expression matched her task ahead. "Cyan yuh imagine
dat?" said Hortense, pointing the woman out. "Me see some t'ings
today but dat mus' be de strangest sight of de whole day."

Cilbert looked and the cigarette in his mouth almost dropped
from his lips. An image of Miss Martha relaxing upon her verandah
came to his mind and he shook his head, blinked and gazed again at
the cleaner. "Mebbe she doing some kinda punishment," he
guessed.

Watching people going about their business, Jacob remarked, "so
much fe ah greeting! People jus' walk by yuh an' say not'ing! Nuh
manners! All me see is de same resentful faces me see inna
Sout'ampton."

"It's jus' ya imagination," returned Cilbert who forced a smile.

"Yes," Lester agreed. "Everybody catching dem train or going
'pon business. Sometimes inna London people don't 'ave nuh time
to stop an' greet people."

"Dat is *still* bad manners!" asserted Jenny. "Even in Trenchtown
people say good marnin. Me don't know how we cyan live wid ah
people so cold. Mebbe dis was ah bad idea."

Lester led the new arrivals to the bus station and the sheer weight
and noise of traffic seemed to unnerve them. They felt everybody
was watching their every move. Hortense held on tight to Cilbert's
hand and even Jenny surprised Jacob by gripping on tight to his left
hand.

Declining Lester's offer of a trip on the underground, they took
a bus to Victoria. "Lester, we jus' reach an' yuh waan to tek we
underground?" rebuked Hortense. "Me don't know how de
English live but underground is fe de dead an' where de shit ah
drop. Above ground is fe de living!"

Lester couldn't help but laugh and Hortense's jesting seemed to relax the obvious fear and tension they were all feeling.

Seated upon the top deck, Cilbert, Jacob, Hortense and Jenny enjoyed their view, not knowing which window to look out of. They all felt a lot safer upon the top deck of a bus than walking the streets. Passing Marble Arch and travelling down Park Lane, they gazed in amazement at the plush hotels and the strangely dressed men who stood outside them. "Is dat where de Queen live?" Hortense wanted to know. "An' yuh 'ave to dress like an uptown clown jus' to open door fe people? Yuh could tek der hatwear or whatever dey call it an' give it to de shanty people dem fe furniture. Everyt'ing so *big*. An' Duke Reid coulda hold ah lawn dance in some of dem car. Even de roads wide like Mr DaCosta field back inna Claremont. An de buildings! Me don't know how people cyan live so high. Mebbe dem ah learn how fe speak wid de birds. Mebbe dey t'ink dey cyan fly."

Lester pointed out the perimeter wall of Buckingham Palace and Jenny asked, "if yuh climb de wall do dey put yuh inside de Tower of London? As ah girl chile me did read about de torture inna dat wicked place. Everyt'ing so big an' frightening here! Even de roundabout we jus' pass is like ah park! Yuh could raise cows 'pon dat land an' grow scallion."

"Dat is true," concurred Jacob, feeling overwhelmed. "It kinda mek yuh feel so small. So insignificant. De first time I go to Kingston it really open me eyes. But dis place! How cyan black people live up to it? It mek yuh t'ink wha' cyan we offer dis land. Wha' is our role? How cyan we mek de English feel dat we 'ave somet'ing to offer?"

"By working hard," answered Cilbert. "After all, it's only buildings. If Jamaica had plenty money den we would 'ave buildings dat yuh see around we."

"Me disagree wid yuh, Cilbert," cut in Hortense. "Jacob right. Everyt'ing here do mek yuh feel like ah cockroach looking 'pon herd of stampeding elephants. Me eyes so full of wonder dat me cyan't blink."

"But yuh affe remember dat dey mek ah whole heap of money from de old sugar plantations," said Cilbert. "From slavery! Dat's wha' buy dem pretty buildings! Me will *never* mix sugar inna me coffee here."

"Ah mon who keep looking into de past will never realise de great future before him," said Jacob.

"Dat's one of Gran'papa Neville sayings," revealed Hortense.

Smiling, Jacob nodded. "Yes, Custos very wise."

Changing buses at Victoria bus station, they crossed Vauxhall bridge looking down at the soiled, brown waters. "Is dat where de London people tek ah doo doo?" grinned Jenny.

"Nuh, Jenny," chuckled Lester. "Dat de River Thames, broader dan any lake inna Jamaica, long like de tales from ah boring story-teller inna no-name village."

With the bus inching through the streets of south London, Cilbert was fascinated by the sight of chimneys set upon the roofs of terraced housing. He wondered if these countless places were rows upon rows of small factories and half-expected to see workmen with dirty faces and stained overalls go in and out of them. He was about to ask Lester about these strange buildings but decided against it, not wanting to sound ignorant.

Getting off the bus outside Brixton tube station, they heard the vocal strains of the Everly Brothers' 'Cathy's Clown' from a roadside cafe. Cockney shouts from the nearby market reminded Cilbert of his early days in Kingston purchasing groceries from Papine. White men went by in flat caps smoking cigarettes. A young boy was selling newspapers. The rattling sound of a train passing by over a bridge seemed to shake the ground. Advertisements were painted upon shop walls and windows. Two tramps sat in a corner at the entrance of the tube station. They caught sight of Cilbert and stretched out their hands, silently asking for money. Cilbert looked upon the vagrants and silently sighed. "De only people to acknowledge we are de damn moochers," Cilbert whispered to himself.

Jenny was comforted by the sight of more black people, most of them headscarfed women who were waiting at bus stops clutching bags of groceries or bustling through the crowds pulling shopping trolleys. Jenny thought they looked bent and ungraceful, unlike their Kingston counterparts where the poorest woman carried herself like a queen. Dem as miserable as de white people, she thought. "So dis is Brixton," she said, looking around her not impressed. "Lester, do de people of Brixton get punishment if dem bus' ah smile?"

"Nuh, Miss Jenny," Lester laughed, his over-the-top joviality making up for the grim faces around him. "It's ah working day. People going about dem business, shopping an' t'ing. Most of de men der ah work. People relax an' ready dem smile fe de weekend, an'—"

"So, Lester," interrupted Cilbert who was smarting at the fact that not one single person bid him good morning. "Yuh gwarn to tek we to where we gwarn live or yuh waan we to stan' up here so an' loiter an' talk pure fart?"

"Alright," said Lester, maintaining his smile. "Follow me. It is quite ah big house me ah tell yuh. T'ree storeys as dey say inna London. Cilbert, yuh an' Hortense 'ave yuh own room, an' Jacob an' Jenny too. Me pay ya deposit already. Pay me back when yuh cyan. De place clean but it 'ave outside toilet."

"Ah pit toilet?" Hortense asked. "Me come all de way to England to doo doo inna damn pit toilet? Even in Trenchtown me never do dat."

"Nuh, Miss Hortense. Jus' ah liccle shack inna de back yard. Me don't like outside toilet becah when winter come yuh affe brave de cold jus' fe ah piss. An' if yuh waan to shit yuh catch one mighty bitch of ah cold breeze 'pon ya bottom. Me notice some of de white people dem 'ave ah piss pot under dem bed. But me don't like sniffing me own piss when me trying to ketch sleep. Some of de new places 'ave inside toilets an' some landlords are 'aving dem built."

"So wha' is de landlord like in dis place where we gwarn to live?" asked Jacob.

"Nah too bad," answered Lester. "Ah Misser Sean Skidmore. An Irishmon. Our people get on wid dem alright. Me 'ave ah friend who live inna de basement, Misser Alfred Timoll. He come from Jamaica, Churchpen near Spanish Town. Him saving up to bring him wife an' family over. Alfred tell me him never really see Misser Skidmore. It's Misser Skidmore's wife, Mary, who run de place, collecting rent. Her mout' sometime run away wid her like Kingston taxi mon who cyan't afford new brakes, but she 'ave ah good heart. She has one daughter, name Stella. One sweet girl. She fourteen."

Walking along Coldharbour Lane, they felt hemmed in by the terraced housing which was built on both sides. They could see tower blocks in the distance. Hortense walked by studying the street's dwellings and she wondered why there was no bantering and jesting between neighbours. Almost every front door was closed, she observed. She spotted a woman scrubbing her front doorsteps and another who was cleaning her windows. Neither of them returned Hortense's smile. Hortense wondered if any of the people living here bred chickens in their back yards or pushed vendor carts to a market.

Jacob found the street cleaner than any Kingston road he had seen but he had only watched three men pass by on bicycles. Mebbe most of de people here cyan afford motor cars, he concluded. Watching a woman who was walking a dog, Jacob had to pause and look again. "Dat is very strange," he remarked. "Yuh ever see anybody walking ah dog wid some kinda rope attached to its neck?"

"Mebbe she's teking it to market," guessed Hortense. "Me don't sight nuh goat yet so mebbe de English nyam curried dahg? Dat mus' be it. Dey fat up de dahg an' den sell it. Mebbe dey cook it wid jerk, coriander an' pepper?"

"Dat is nastiness," remarked Jenny as Lester caught a fit of the giggles. "Me wonder wha' else dem nyam?"

"De English mus' be like de Bajee people dem," said Cilbert. "Yuh know Bajees, dem nyam anyt'ing including roast monkey an' fried mongoose."

Jenny still felt that everything seemed so grey and she felt a cold dampness seeping into her bones. To Jenny, the cloud above still seemed to be inert, as if Massa God was warning her of her desires. *Nuh sun shall sign 'pon ah sinner's heart*, she recalled her father-in-law telling her. The London temperature on this day was seventy-two degrees Fahrenheit. Two white men were passing by on the other side of the street wearing only T-shirts and drainpipe trousers. They only offered a furtive glance at the Jamaicans.

"Me don't know how dem white people coulda wear T-shirt an' marina?" Jenny remarked. "Don't dey know de sun nah shine bright an' warm like inna normal country? An' wha' kinda hairstyle is dat?"

"Every young white bwai waan to look like Cliff Richard," said Lester. "An yuh better get used to de cold. De first winter time me was here, me woulda gladly swapped getting up inna de marnin inna de God-cursed cold to sit beside Old Screwface an' him fire of hell. De snow did look so pretty when me see it fe de first time one marnin. But to step in it! Me never feel me toes again 'til nex' summer! Me did bawl an' bawl becah me waan to go home. An' when de wind blow inna de winter, it pass straight t'rough yuh. Believe me! It's ah wonder dat me heart never freeze over. One t'ing yuh affe do is buy plenty, plenty warm clothes an' prepare fe winter."

Hortense and Jenny both expressed their alarm. Coldharbour Lane was aptly named as far as they were concerned. Cilbert, not paying attention to the conversation, was confused by an advertisement upon a street wall. *Take Courage*, the advert advised in big red letters. Not realising Courage was a brand of beer, Cilbert guessed it was something to do with the church.

Passing Milkwood Road that ran parallel to a railway line and had rows of terraced housing stretching into the distance, they walked fearfully under a low bridge that advertised cigarettes and turned right into Herne Hill Road. The houses here were impressively tall and owned small front lawns, fronted by shaggy hedges. A few head-scarfed women wearing aprons were tending to their front gardens. Windows were open and Hortense spotted a number of people looking out of them. An old man, sitting in a white plastic chair in his front garden, was reading his newspaper. Delivery notes were left on doorsteps for milkmen and visitors were invited to wipe their feet upon rubber and bristled door-mats. Concrete steps led down to basements and concaved metal rubbish bins only added to Jenny's feeling of greyness. Jacob spotted more cyclists careering down the hill, one of them wore a white uniform and cap and in his bicycle basket he carried loaves of bread. A slow-moving milk float went the other way, its engine whining as the driver negotiated the incline.

"Dis country mus' be rich," Jacob said. "Vendors cyan afford dem own transport. Miss Laura would love one of dem. An' did yuh see de bread vendor 'pon ah bicycle? He was even wearing ah pretty uniform."

"Dis is it," smiled Lester, hoping the new arrivals would be impressed. "Ah nice place to live. In fact, ah very nice place."

Chapter Fifteen

Confidently rapping the letterbox three times, Lester adjusted his hat and readied his smile. Hortense and Jenny both stood behind their husbands as if they were expecting Old Screwface to answer. Instead, a thick-set middle-aged woman emerged. She was wearing a stained apron and a 'why did you have to interrupt my chores' look. Jenny noticed a gold cross, attached to a rope chain, nestling upon her generous cleavage as Cilbert reckoned she could be a fair challenge to the professional arm-wrestlers who hustled the bars around Kingston harbour.

"Love of the afternoon to yer, Lester," Mary Skidmore greeted. "Tell me why is it yer dress every day like yer going to yer wedding?" Mary looked over Lester's left shoulder. "And yer must be the new arrivals from Jamaica. Well, welcome to Proddy England. I don't have no time for any chit-chat and how yer do's because I'm in the back yard beating my rugs. Lester, yer know where the kitchen is so go and make these good people a pot of tea. There are biscuits in the cupboard but don't take the chocolate ones. They're for Sean and Sean loves his chocolate fingers."

Mary about-turned, left the door open and marched along the hallway, her heavy feet almost leaving imprints in the thin brown carpet.

"Well, let's go in," invited Lester, inwardly fuming at Mary's curt welcome.

Hanging from a turquoise-painted wall was a black and white framed photograph of one of the Irish Easter Rebellion leaders, Patrick Pearse. None of the Jamaicans had any idea who he was or what he did, but judging by the mahogany polished frame, they guessed he was someone of great importance to Mary and Sean.

Opposite the staring eyes of Patrick Pearse, Jenny was impressed by a framed photograph of the Pope's praying hands. Cilbert sneered at it.

They passed a white-painted door on the left hand side that had a wooden cross nailed to it. Jenny assumed it was where Mary and her family lived. Sensing the recently applied polish emitting from the staircase, they were awed by the high ceiling with its elaborate, gloss-painted beading. The staircase itself was dimly lit and had images of Christ lining the wall on the way up. "An' me t'ought it was jus' we Jamaicans who are mad wid religion," Cilbert whispered.

"Nuh, Cilbert," Jacob smiled. "De Lord has touched people all over de world."

"De kitchen is jus' straight ahead," said Lester. "Me, Jacob an' Cilbert will carry ya luggage to ya rooms. We'll soon come."

Not willing to make the first move, Jenny stood rooted to the spot. Hortense, her tiredness defeating her need to display extravagant politeness, brushed passed her sister, walked down two steps and took a chair beside a square kitchen table. She could see Mary out of a kitchen window, thrashing the life out of a rug upon a washing line. She seemed not to care about the dust that was dancing around her. "She well sturdy," observed Hortense. "Dat Miss Mary coulda tek de horns of ah mad bull."

Spotting a dull silver kettle resting upon the cooker, Hortense stood up and filled it with water. Mimicking Miss Martha, Hortense turned to Jenny. "Afternoon tea?"

"Yes please," answered Jenny, thinking that the refrigerator behind her was large enough to house a shanty town family. "Jus' de one lump."

"It's ah shame we don't 'ave any bush to place inna de tea," regretted Hortense. "Me surely need it to help me relax. Mek me sleep good. De journey from de ship really tek ah lot outta me. An' did yuh see how many people ketch sick 'pon de ship? Me wonder if yuh cyan get bush inna Englan'? Mebbe not becah de sun decide to run away from dis country."

"Hortense! Don't speak of such t'ings. We don't know if bush is illegal here. It's banned inna Jamaica so me guess it mus' be banned inna Englan'."

"Banned? Why could somet'ing be banned dat cyan provide yuh

wid ah liccle restbite an' mek yuh relax? Back inna Kingston even Miss Martha's friends did ah love it. Me used to find bush butts inna de ashtray ah marnin time an' when Miss Martha used to hold dinner party, yuh could nah even see ya way inna de front room."

Looking around at her surroundings, Jenny remarked, "Hortense, don't yuh feel strange? Me never been inside ah house dat so quiet. Inna Trenchtown yuh could hear everyt'ing dat ah gwarn. But here? It kinda spooky. Nuh radio playing, nuh children bawling, nuhbody playing ah game of domino wid all de cuss cuss. Nuhbody banging 'pon ya door selling dem wares. It *too* quiet and dis place mek me feel nervous."

"Oh, Jenny, stop ya fussing! Like Lester say everyone at work. We'll be alright. Yuh wait an' see."

Hortense's reassuring smile didn't reach her eyes.

The kettle was whistling by the time Cilbert, Lester and Jacob had returned. Lester found the mugs in a cupboard and everyone took seats around the Formica-covered kitchen table; a bowl containing fruits was placed in the middle – Jenny thought they didn't look fresh. They could all hear the repetitive *thwacks* from Mary Skidmore's carpet beater and they all read the Italic-written message hanging from a wall in a shoe-box size frame above the sink. *God Is The Unseen Guest At Every Meal. God Listens To Every Conversation. God Reads Your Every Thought.* Jenny momentarily flinched but soon regained her composure.

"As soon as yuh settle in an' find yaself employment me waan to tek yuh to de West End," offered Lester to Cilbert, showing off. "Yes, sa. Tek in de sights an' sounds of London town. Yuh 'ave plenty, plenty clubs. Some of dem dey refuse ah black mon entry but der are clubs like de Flamingo an' Roaring Twenties dat love ah black mon's presence. Jacob, yuh cyan come too. Dey even 'ave sound system here. Dis mon from Jamaica dat call himself Count Suckle..."

"Me husband is ah mon of de Lord," interrupted Jenny. "He *never* go sporting an' dem kind ah t'ing. We come over here to work hard an' live good, may Massa God bless we."

"Jenny, me cyan speak fe meself," protested Jacob.

Hortense hunted in the other cupboards for the biscuits and once she found them, shared them out. She then fell into her seat, suddenly feeling her exhaustion.

"So me guess yuh nuh waan to walk aroun' Brixton wid me," laughed Cilbert.

"Yuh mad?" returned Hortense. "Jus' tek me to me bed."

"Yes, I agree," said Jacob. "Come Jenny, mek I show yuh to our new room."

"Yuh cyan't wait 'til me finish me biscuit dem an' me mug ah tea?"

Cilbert pulled Hortense to her feet and with a massive effort, lifted her into his arms. Unsteadily, he moved along the hallway as Hortense giggled. "Cilby, yuh mek it so *obvious*. Yuh waan to christen me inna me new home, isn't it? Yuh sure ya back cyan tek de strain?"

"Cilbert," Lester called as Jenny was inwardly raging with jealousy. "Me will come fe yuh inna de marnin. Me 'ave to tek yuh an' Jacob to de labour exchange to register. Den to sign up wid de doctor so don't sleep in too late. Mek sure yuh bring ya papers."

"Alright, sa," answered Cilbert, his cheeks still warming to Hortense's teasing. "T'ank yuh fe everyt'ing."

Lester then left, leaving Jacob and Jenny in the kitchen. Jenny filled the kettle with more water, placed it on the cooker and grabbed a handful of shortcake biscuits. The dimly lit staircase still unnerved her and she didn't want to hear Cilbert and Hortense making love, even though they were in separate bedrooms. The very thought of it dismayed her.

Calling at nine o'clock the next morning, Lester found he wasn't only escorting Cilbert and Jacob to the labour exchange but Jenny and Hortense as well. Before noon, Cilbert found employment in the maintenance of outside telephone lines. Jacob accepted work as a labourer on a building site, Hortense gained a job as an early morning cleaner at County Hall and Jenny a position preparing tarts and pastries in a Lyons tea house; she had to pass a thorough medical check and a maths and English test.

During her third day in her new job, from her position in the kitchen, Jenny spotted that the waitresses were overwhelmed with orders. Showing initiative, she picked up a tray laden with Chelsea buns, a pot of tea and serviettes and intended to carry it out to the customer. Before she reached the dining area, Jenny's manager, a slim, hollow-cheeked white man in his mid-thirties, stepped in front of her.

"Where do you think you're going with that?" he asked.

"De waitresses overcome, Misser Dawkins," Jenny explained. "So me t'ought to meself dat me should bring de tray to de people who waan it instead of dem complaining."

Mr Dawkins was not impressed and leant his face towards Jenny so that his lips were only a few inches away from her forehead. "I pay you to remain in the kitchen! And remain in the kitchen you will! Now *get* back! I employ the waitresses to carry the trays in."

Her mouth primed to reply, Jenny managed to control her fury but when she arrived home, she wasted no time in telling Jacob and everyone else what had occurred. Sitting at the kitchen table, grimacing as he ate his roast beef, brussel sprouts and boiled potatoes, Cilbert could relate to Jenny's anger. On his first three working days, he had been ordered to service the phone lines in man-holes and other unsavoury locations, a dirty, grimy task. He had asked his boss why was he singled out to perform 'dese dutty tasks', and Cilbert's supervisor answered, "why do you think we need guys like you coming over here for work. You will get better opportunities when you prove yourself."

Shrugging off his supervisor's comments, Cilbert wasted no time in setting up a bank account. He promised himself to start saving for a place of his own as soon as he received his first wages. Also, the image of the Rover car pricked his mind.

By the end of his first week at work, Cilbert was simmering with frustration. Colleagues at the depot had difficulty understanding his accent and subsequently, everyone ignored him, save a Trinadadian man called Delgado.

"You have to talk slower," advised Delgado on Cilbert's sixth morning. "Your voice sound strange to them. Anyway, the manager's put you with me for your next month. You will discover that most phone lines in this country are underground, unlike the Caribbean where it's all overhead. But the wiring principles are the same so you should be alright. They will respect you if you show that you can do the work."

"Me don't mind so much dat white mon nuh understand me," replied Cilbert. "It's de monkey noises dem mek an' de funny looks. If dem carry on dem way see me don't tek me longest screwdriver an' stab ah white mon tongue!"

"Cilbert, over here you have to cool yaself," soothed Delgado. "You don't want to get sacked. Just ignore them. They'll soon get bored of winding you up. When I first came here they started on me, but now they leave me alone. Just laugh with them."

"Alright, Delgado. But me don't know if me 'ave de patience."

Working on a building site with many other West Indians, Jacob didn't have the same problems as Cilbert found on his first week. On his first day he made endless cups of teas and mixed cement. He kept his own counsel. Upon his second day, asked on what he did for a living back in Jamaica, Jacob revealed that he was a minister of the church. Immediately, Jacob's stock rose to his fellow West Indians and they sat around him during dinner breaks, asking him of news of Jamaica and if he would consider blessing their homes and christening their children.

By the end of his second week, Jacob had been promoted to a position of an electrician's mate. He worked under the stewardship of a Jamaican nicknamed Buju – Buju being the Jamaican slang for a large breadfruit.

"If yuh is ah preacher mon," Buju asked one morning. "Why yuh here 'pon building site? Where is ya church?"

"Me don't 'ave one yet," Jacob answered. "But me will. Me promise yuh dat."

"An' me will attend ya service," replied Buju. "Me hear of ah West Indian church inna nort' London but dat too far fe me an' me wife. Der is not'ing around here fe we so if yuh start church yuh should find nuff follower."

Buju had advised Jacob to enrol at night school and he began studying for a City and Guilds electrician's certificate at a college on Brixton Hill. He had trouble deciphering the tutor's broad Scouse accent and felt intimidated by his fellow white students. Pointing to Jacob seated at the back of the class, a white guy quipped, "that's what happens to you when you get an electric shock."

"An' those who laugh wid yuh will suffer ya mighty ignorance," retorted Jacob, standing up defending himself.

Aided by Cilbert's counsel and experience that he offered in the evenings following dinner, and Buju advising him at work, Jacob learned his new trade swiftly.

Disliking English cuisine and unable to find Jamaican foodstuffs in Brixton market, Jenny was introduced to a Jamaican man, Mr Campbell, who lived in Camberwell. Mr Campbell, who never revealed how he managed to obtain Caribbean food, pulled up in his large white van every Monday evening outside Jenny's home and supplied yams, green banana, canned callaloo, tinned ackee, rice, red kidney beans, plantain, ardough bread, ginger, peppers and salt fish. It wasn't much of a variety, Jenny thought, and she would have committed a crime just to sink her teeth into the amber-coloured flesh of a ripe mango, but her family felt that much closer to home whenever they ate their meals. It sure beat the roast beef, corned beef, spam meat, roast potatoes, carrots and tasteless cabbage that they consumed in their first week. Curious as to what was frying in her kitchen, even Mary Skidmore chanced a taste of fried dumpling and plantain one Saturday morning. She hated it but her daughter Stella asked Hortense for more.

Three weeks after their arrival and having paid their first rent, Mary Skidmore invited Cilbert, Jacob, Hortense and Jenny for a Sunday evening's drink in her living room. She had opened all the windows but the breezes that came through couldn't shift the lingering aroma of polish. Framed pictures of a long-haired, blue-eyed Christ decorated the walls alongside black and white photographs of rusty-haired relatives. A radiogram was placed in one corner and a mahogany-coloured piano, untold scratches upon its surface, stood by a wall. An open music book, gripped by its metal support, was propped on top of the piano alongside a

Catholic prayer pamphlet. Hanging above the mantelpiece was a velvet banner, a souvenir of the Irish town, Fermoy.

With a large wooden brush in her right hand and a comb in the other, Mary Skidmore was seated in an armchair with her seemingly petrified daughter Stella kneeling on the carpet, viced between her mother's awesome thighs. Her four guests were squeezed up in a three-seater sofa, their politeness overriding their discomfort. Mary noticed Jenny looking at the banner. "Yes, that is where I was born. On the muddy banks of the Blackwater river. A lovely place, lots of space and fresh air. More churches than you could ever count. My maiden name is O'Donahue, and my Jesus, there's a lot of us. Every time I go back I get introduced to more and more cousins. Truth of the matter is they all jump on my nerves. *Want* this *want* that. That's all I ever hear. They think I'm rich like Rockefeller."

Cilbert and Jacob chuckled but they wondered who Rockefeller was. "Do any of yer want any more whiskey?" Mary asked. "I have two more bottles in the cupboard, imported from my own country. Take it now because my offerings don't occur every day. But I think a woman must receive boarders into her home with generosity. It breeds a certain respect and understanding, don't yer agree?"

Everyone nodded but Hortense was the only one to say, "yes please," to Mary's offer. She stood up and served herself.

"I have to be honest with yer," resumed Mary, thrusting the comb into Stella's long auburn curls. "I for one am glad that you people are coming in droves to England. I tell yer why. Before you came, it was the Irish the English treated like shite. Now they treat *you* people like shite. And yer'll have to suffer that until the smelly Indians come over here in greater numbers – they'll be treated like shite. I hope the Holy Father forgives me for my thoughts but it's a relief that my folk don't get it as bad as we used to. My Sean couldn't go to a pub without some Proddy English bastard calling him names. My advice to yer is not to frequent pubs. Yer will *not* be made welcome."

"When did yuh come to Englan', Miss Mary?" Hortense asked while Cilbert and Jenny were expressing their shock at the way the conversation was developing.

"Just after the war," Mary replied. "Bomb sites all over the place. London looked like God himself decided to use his mighty right hand and finger-walk across the place. Yer had to have keen eyes about yer or yer would find yerself falling into a crater. And there was nothing to eat. I don't know how we survived on that god-forsaken ration book. *Three* eggs a week and a tiny side of beef that couldn't feed a cat, I tell yer."

"But yuh 'ave done well fe yaself," said Cilbert, looking around the room.

"Oh, yes. My Sean worked every hour available. When we first come here he worked on the train tracks throughout the night and laboured on building sites during the day. I tell yer, it was us Irish who rebuilt this Proddy country, oh yes, by the sweat of our brow and that's no lie. And are the English grateful? No bloody chance! They call us Bogtrotters and other names. And I can tell yer this, yer might work alongside them and they be all polite and smiles, but behind yer back? They'll be calling yer nigger, coon, monkey-face and sambo. Trust my words. The English are two-faced bastards, forgive my blasphemy Holy Father."

"Wha' about de local churches?" queried Jacob. "Are der any dat are...? Appropriate fe we?"

Mary laughed a horrible laugh. "Are yer joking with me, Jacob? Proddy churches infest this cursed country. My advice to yer is to sing yer praises at a Catholic church. Yer won't be made welcome in a Proddy church. No bloody chance! Yer find more integrity in Soho."

Jacob wasn't brave enough to tell her that he and his family belonged to the Anglican order, despite Jenny pinching him to do so.

Ignoring Mary's warning he escorted Jenny on the next Sunday to a church of England service in Camberwell New Street. They were immeadiately impressed by the sheer size of the church and its carved figures and interior decor. They found hymn books on their pews, sat down and looked around them. They were the only blacks in the congregation and Jenny whispered, "Lord help we!

Jacob, dis was ah very bad idea. Me don't know how yuh convince me to come wid yuh! Everybody staring at we!"

"Calm yaself, sweetheart," soothed Jacob. "We inna God's house an' everybody equal here."

Feeling like an automaton, being asked to stand up, sit down and sing, Jenny missed the handclapping, verve and excitement of a Kingston church. Even the vicar's sermon was sober, uneventful and boring, she thought. Kingston ministers were larger than life, fiery and animated, Jenny remembered and even she thought they were sometimes over the top. But this vicar? He should be confined telling his stories to children before they went to bed.

Sensing every eye upon her, Jenny refused to sing. Instead she studied the way white women were dressed. Most of them were sporting bright-coloured pencil skirts with matching, single-breasted hip-length jackets. Crowned by bonnets and hats of all shapes and sizes, Jenny felt a little better for she was similarly dressed in a sky-blue skirt and jacket with white blouse. She had to admire Jacob, garbed in his blue suit and pointed black shoes, who sang his heart out and spoke out loud every prayer

Departing the church after what Jenny and Jacob thought was a very short service – they were used to three or four hour services in Kingston – they thought it would be polite to offer their greeting to the vicar who was standing at the exit of the church. Shaking the hands of his regular flock, the vicar blatantly ignored the presence of Jacob and Jenny who were waiting in front of him.

Ushering his furious wife away, Jacob heard Jenny vent her outrage once they had returned home.

"Me cyan't believe it!" stormed Jenny. "Me will never set foot der again! How cyan ah mon of God ignore people who come to him? He made we stan' up in front of him like damn idiots. Me shoulda cuss him backside! Sometimes me wish me 'ave me sister's mout'. Miss Mary was right! Jacob, yuh better set up ya own church quick!"

Jacob decided to conduct his own services in his own room. His first congregation consisted of seven people, including his workmate Buju and his wife. News spread quickly in the local

Caribbean community and weeks later Jacob had to ask his followers for funds to enable him to hire a local hall; Mary Skidmore let it be known in plain words what she felt about 'a whole loada black Proddy worshippers trooping up her stairs'. The altar was an old school table that Jacob had acquired and his flock could only sing from two hymn books, but the verve and gusto they brought to praising their Lord soothed Jacob's soul. The only blot he felt on his heart was the absence of Cilbert. He didn't even rebuke Hortense when on one occasion he spotted her reading a letter when she was supposed to be studying the Bible.

The letter was from Miss Martha and Hortense grinned when she read it.

Dear Hotty,

Thrilled I was to learn that you have reached London safe and sound, and forgive me for my delayed reply to your letter – it was only two weeks ago that my husband and I returned from Germany. Germany was tedious to say the least. Full of miserable people who stare at the ground beneath them, so unlike Jamaican people. I'm afraid I'll soon be on the way to Hong Kong which is my husband's next post of duty. I'm looking forward to it though – the Orient and all that mystery.

Before we left for Germany I spent my days tending to my garden and reading books. Not much to do here in Berkshire – my neighbours only talk of horses and farms – and I do miss the Jamaican sun. But my husband allows me to travel to London for the weekends. I book myself in a small hotel in Kensington and go to a West End theatre or a dance show. Not sure I should be telling you this but it will surely make you giggle! At one of these shows I met a black man who offered to buy me a drink. He's a dancer! Edwin is his name and he comes from Guyana – such lithe limbs! Taking your advice about grabbing your heaven on earth, I took him back to my hotel! Can you believe that? It was so devilishly exciting and on a few occasions I didn't even bother attending a show. I would just meet Edwin outside the hotel and there we would stay all weekend. It doesn't bother me at all that I am paying for everything.

So now I venture to Hong Kong with a little sadness in my heart – I can't imagine there are any black men there! But, Hotty, the memory of Edwin and his taut body can sustain me while I'm away and who knows? Edwin might be there when I return to England.

Now I have become a demon in the kitchen, cooking varieties of dishes that my husband adores. So I thank you for that. And give my love to the rest of your family, especially Cilbert. May you all fare well in my country. When I return we'll have to share a bottle of imported overproof rum some sunny afternoon (I don't care too much for the watered-down rum that is available in England but have no fear! My husband still has his contacts in Jamaica). And when we finally meet again we can laugh like we used to.

Your friend

Martha.

Reading Martha's letter again and again, Cilbert wondered what was so funny about it as he watched Hortense collapsing in sudden giggles.

Working all the overtime available to him, Cilbert initially declined Lester's invitations to taste the London nightlife.

He couldn't shift the memory of visiting a local pub and having to wait forty-five minutes before he was served. The barman didn't acknowledge Cilbert's presence, so lifting up and dropping a glass astray upon the counter, Cilbert displayed a pound note held aloft in his hand. "Rum an' coke," he ordered.

The barman snatched the money from Cilbert's grasp offering no reply and when he served the drink, he slammed it upon the counter. Holding out his hand for the change, Cilbert had to bite his lip when he saw the barman dropping his change upon the bar three foot away from him. Cilbert downed his drink in three gulps, presented the barman with a stern eye-pass, collected his change and then stormed out.

It was a rainswept September night when Lester led Cilbert to a basement in Wardour Street in the heart of the West End. Standing at the entrance of the club was a twenty stone bouncer wearing a black jacket, bow tie and a sour expression. He recognised Lester but offered Cilbert a lingering look as the rain dripped from his hat onto his broad nose. Inside, the large single room was dimly lit and had a low ceiling. The fog of smoke stung Cilbert's eyes. Through the haze, he saw a small low stage with four rows of bolted down old cinema seats in front of it. A black jazz combo were preparing to play and Cilbert thought the drummer looked so cool in his black suit and sunglasses and gangster-style hat. The pianist was swigging from a bottle of beer as he tinkled the ivories with his other hand. The six foot five bassist's cloth cap seemed to cover his eyes and the saxophonist, dressed in a purple suit and white shoes, was tenderly wiping the mouthpiece of his instrument with a handkerchief.

Awestruck, Cilbert looked around. Men wearing mohair suits and stylish stetsons were huddled in groups of threes and fours. Seven black men dressed in American Air Force uniforms, complete with caps, were drinking and laughing in a corner. Women wearing tight, slinky sleeveless dresses and bright red lipstick sashayed by. Nobody was without a cigarette. At the back of the club, beyond the standing area, was the bar.

"Welcome to de Flamingo club," grinned Lester. "Come, mek me buy yuh ah drink."

No alcohol or spirits were on display and Lester ordered, "give me two Coca-Cola wid ah liccle somet'ing."

The generously-bosomed barmaid half-filled two glasses with coke and then she bent down beneath the counter and topped off the drinks with a hidden stash of Scotch. Cilbert looked down at her cleavage. Lester, winking at the barmaid, then paid her and said to Cilbert, "me 'ave ah liccle business to tend to. Jus' relax an' enjoy de vibe – nuff women fe yuh to look 'pon!"

Lester walked over to the American servicemen and Cilbert watched him sell cannabis to them in matchbox-sized polythene bags. Feeling nervous and excited at the same time, Cilbert took a seat on the back row, lit a cigarette and waited for the jazz musicians to play.

Half an hour later, the club was packed and Cilbert was tapping his feet and bopping his head to the sounds of cool, mellow jazz. The crowd behind him jived and hollered their approval as the sweet scent of marijuana blended with the stuffy air. As the saxophonist was performing a solo, gyrating his hips while standing on a chair, Cilbert felt the touch of a woman's palms covering his eyes. Expecting that his flirtatious glances had been acted upon from one of the many women whom he had admired at the club, Cilbert turned around sharply, readying a wide grin.

"So wha' brings yuh here," cooed Almyna, sexily dressed in a tight, strapless red dress and white pointed shoes. Her burgundy lipstick glistened under the stage lights and Cilbert could smell her perfume. Her big eyes were emphasised with mascara and her pearl necklace glowed upon her caramel skin.

"Almyna!" Cilbert managed, his surprise obvious. "Yuh look. Yuh look very nice."

"Of course," Almyna purred. "Yuh expect anyt'ing less of me?"

"Nuh, nuh, Almyna. So yuh come here often?"

"Yuh cyan say dat," answered Almyna, sitting on Cilbert's lap.

"An' ya husband is not wid yuh?" asked Cilbert, scanning the crowd.

"An' ya wife is *not* wid yuh!"

Smiling away his anxiety, Cilbert groped for his cigarettes. "Me frien' Lester tek me out fe de night. To show me de bright lights. Piccadilly Circus is really somet'ing! Me never see somet'ing quite as tall as Nelson's column. An' Chinee Town was quite ah revelation too!"

"An' finally him bring yuh to de right place."

"So, Almyna, who yuh come wid?"

"Two of me girlfrien' an' ah gentlemon." Almyna pointed to the bar. "Me husband is away in America 'pon business an' wha' he don't know cyan't boder him. Wha's ah young lady supposed to do inna foreign land? Sit down inna me yard all alone an' look 'pon de wall?"

Lighting his cigarette, Cilbert couldn't help but feel aroused by Almyna's every movement. "De band good, mon," Cilbert remarked, looking at the musicians and trying to deny his attraction for Almyna.

Almyna took a cigarette from Cilbert's packet, lit it with the lighter in Cilbert's hand and blew her smoke above his head. "So, Cilby, isn't it polite if ya offer me ah drink?"

"Yes, of course. Me forget meself. Come."

Barging through the crowd, Cilbert led Almyna to the bar. "Two Coca-Cola wid ah liccle somet'ing, please."

"Ah shame dem 'ave nuh rum," Almyna grinned.

Clinking their glasses together, Cilbert toasted, "to Orange Valley an' so many good yesterdays."

Sipping her cocktail, Almyna placed her right hand on Cilbert's shoulder. "Cilby, me waan to apologise fe me behaviour 'pon de ship. Me did hear dat yuh marry Hortense but to see yuh two togeder was ah shock fe me. But me still nah understan' why Jenny strike me down. Mebbe she 'ave some kinda feeling toward yuh too."

"Jenny? Nuh, Almyna. She jus' very protective of her sister."

"If yuh say so, Cilby. But she did ah look 'pon me like me an' her are rivals."

Cilbert shook his head.

"Cilby," Almyna continued. "Yuh remember when we were fifteen years old when it was de night of Uncle Lloyd's shelling match? All de family did crowd around de fire an' me an' yuh steal off to Walkers Wood. Yuh was very nervous, Cilby. An' yuh kept looking behind yaself, fretting dat somebody ah follow we. Me cyan remember dat night like it was yesterday."

Nodding, Cilbert recalled losing his virginity on that night.

"Dey say dat yuh never forget ya first time," Almyna resumed. "An' ya never forget ya first love."

Looking into Almyna's eyes, Cilbert realised the lasting pain he had caused by breaking up with her. Before him was no longer the confident, well dressed woman-about-town, but the innocent young country girl he had fallen in love with – cute liccle Almyna Simpson.

An hour later Cilbert escorted Almyna home to her place in Cricklewood. It was a semi-detached house complete with a garage in a tree-lined avenue. Cilbert guessed that Hubert and Almyna were the only blacks living in this street.

"Isn't dis wha' yuh dreamed of, Cilby?" teased Almyna. "Ah nice house in London wid ah front lawn? Isn't dis wha' yuh working for?"

"Yes, Almyna," Cilbert nodded. "But me waan to buil' somet'ing like dis back inna Jamaica."

"Jamaica? Me would *never* go back der. Nuh, sa. Dis is how we should live."

"Well, dat is me intention, Almyna."

"Yuh waan to come inside so me cyan offer yuh ah drink fe de road? As de white people say."

"Yes, me don't see nuh harm in dat."

Almyna led Cilbert inside and once she switched on the lights, Cilbert was mightily impressed by the flocked wallpaper, expensive furniture, mahogany coffee table, laced cushions and colourful rugs that he saw in the living room.

Before he sat on the sofa, Almyna took Cilbert's wet coat and hat and hung them up in the hallway. Cilbert studied the glass ornaments that were sitting upon the mantelpiece over the coal-fire.

Almyna returned and lit the fire. She then walked over to a large radiogram that also doubled as a drinks cabinet in a corner. Taking out a bottle of Appleton's rum and two glasses, she kicked off her shoes and joined Cilbert on the sofa.

"Where did yuh get dat?" Cilbert asked, thinking how Hortense had missed her overproof rum.

"Oh, Hubert has him contacts."

Almyna half-filled the glasses, caught Cilbert with a sexy glance and took a sip. Her burgundy lipstick smudged the glass. Cilbert watched her, realising that to deny his attraction for Almyna was futile. He downed his drink in four takes and then took the glass out of Almyna's hand and placed it on the floor with his own. They then made love in front of the coal fire upon a bear-skin rug.

Seven hours later, as Almyna slept upon the sofa, Cilbert felt a weight of guilt on his mind. Without making a noise, he laced on his shoes, donned his hat and coat and slipped out to an overcast, damp morning.

He arrived home an hour and a half later and found Hortense asleep. He quickly undressed and climbed into bed. He felt too guilty to wrap his left arm around Hortense's shoulders as he usually did and as he lay open-eyed, he asked himself silently again and again, "wha' 'ave me done?"

Awoken by Cilbert's presence, Hortense asked, "yuh rave 'til dis hour? When de lark sing inna de tree top? Wha' kinda club is dat? Was you dancing? If der was any dancing den how could yuh go widout me?"

"Calm yaself, Hortense," Cilbert said. "Der was nuh dancing. Jus' ah band playing. Yuh woulda been mighty bored. Me could nuh get ah bus home so me stop at one ah Lester frien' an' coch meself der 'til bus ah run."

"Me waan go dancing, Cilby. Promise yuh will find somewhere so me cyan dance."

"Of course, Hortense. Nuh worry yaself."

Leaning over, Cilbert kissed Hortense upon the back of her neck. His eyes still betrayed his guilt.

The following Saturday night, Lester arrived at Cilbert's home ready for another night in the West End.

"Nuh, Lester. Not tonight," Cilbert declined. "Me well tired an' me 'ave ah liccle pain inna me brain."

Lester called again the next weekend and Cilbert found it difficult to come up with another excuse. Waiting in the kitchen as Cilbert dressed, Lester spotted Jacob arriving through the front door.

"Good night, Lester," Jacob greeted. "Yuh an' Cilbert going out sporting?"

"Yes," Lester answered. "Jenny not wid yuh tonight?"

"Nuh, she's wid ah friend of hers," Jacob replied. "It look like I'm eating alone dis night."

"Why yuh don't come wid us?" asked Lester. "We cyan eat somet'ing out der 'pon street an' den tek in some cool jazz."

Jacob thought about it. "Why not? It will be an experience."

"It'll be certainly dat," grinned Lester.

Arriving at the Flamingo club at eight thirty in the evening, Cilbert, glancing anxiously around him, said, "Lester, is der an nex' club we cyan go to? Jacob don't smoke an' being inside der might trouble him chest."

"At every club der is smoke," replied Lester. "An' dis is de only one dat cater fe we."

"I will be alright," assured Jacob. "Don't worry about me. I'm looking forward to it."

They all entered the club with Cilbert looking this way and that. His worse fears were confirmed when he spotted Almyna chatting with two white women at the bar. She was wearing a yellow dress that was slit above the knee, revealing her lined stockings. Cilbert turned his back to her but Almyna had already seen him.

Walking over with a knowing smile rippling from her mouth, Almyna greeted Jacob first. "Nice to see ya once more, Jacob. Me never expected to see yuh here as yuh is ah mon of de Lord. Me guess is dat Cilby mus' ah tell yuh about it. De Flamingo club's reputation is sure growing."

"Good night, Almyna," Jacob smiled politely. "Is ya husband, Hubert here?"

"Nuh, he's away. But de last time me come here Cilby did ah look after me. He was de perfect gentlemon. Him even escort me home." Almyna then offered Cilbert a dazzling smile as Jacob regarded Cilbert with suspicion.

Grinning to mask his apprehension, Cilbert offered, "me will buy de first round. Jacob, Lester, Almyna, wha' yuh drinking?"

Cilbert took the orders and went off to the bar, leaving Almyna addressing Jacob. "So how is Jenny?" she asked. "Has she learned to cool her temper? Me wonder why she lost it dat day 'pon de ship? If anybody was gwarn to strike me down me t'ought it woulda been Hortense. But don't worry, Jacob. Dat is inna de past. Me already apologise to Cilbert fe me bahavior dat day an' now we good friends again. *Very* good friends. We were so close when we were young."

Embarrassed, Lester looked away and Jacob spotted a nervous Cilbert looking over, wondering what was being said. He quickly returned with the drinks.

Sipping her cocktail, Almyna remarked, "It's good dat two people who born an' grow togeder cyan rely 'pon each udder inna strange place. Dat kinda friendship cyan never bruk. It mek me sleep better at nighttime, y'know. Ah certain reassurance dat mek life easier inna strange land."

His temper brewing, Cilbert took hold of Almyna's arm and led her away to a corner. Jacob watched them arguing about something as Lester laughed.

Twenty minutes later, as the jazz band was jamming, Cilbert returned to Jacob's side. Exasperation was written upon Cilbert's face and sweat had dampened his temples. "Jacob, me 'ave to get out of dis place. Yuh stay here an' enjoy de music. Me going home."

Jacob watched Cilbert disappear and then Almyna stormed passed him, obviously upset. Jacob caught her arm. "Why don't yuh jus' leave him be? Cilbert's ah mon who honours him marriage. Him don't need yuh inna him life."

"Tek ya hand offa me!" roared Almyna. "An' keep ya mout' quiet becah yuh don't know not'ing! Instead of worrying about me yuh should worry about ya own wife an' who she truly desire! Now leggo me hand before me start scream. Preacher mon nuh 'ave nuh aut'ority here!"

Wondering what Almyna meant, Jacob recalled the apprehension that Cilbert displayed on their way to the club. "Mebbe dem 'aving an affair," he concluded.

"CILBERT!" screamed Almyna as she ran outside. "CILBERT!"

Aware of pedestrians looking at him, Cilbert turned around, saw the distressed figure of Almyna and walked back to her. Shaking his head, he said quietly. "Dis cyan never work, Almyna. De both of we married now. Me love Hortense now."

"But yuh mek love to me two weeks ago! Didn't dat mean not'ing to yuh? Yuh know how many times me come here hoping to see yuh? Yuh t'ink me enjoy dem American mon coming up to me an' talking to me?"

Looking into Almyna's eyes, Cilbert found them welling with tears. "Almyna, we 'ave to move on. As ah teenager me did love yuh fe true. Yes, sa! But me find Hortense an' yuh find Hubert."

"But yuh mek love to me still! Yuh did waan me an' me know yuh still waan me. SAY dat yuh don't!"

Recognising Almyna's vulnerability and need for reassurance, Cilbert reached out his arm and took hold of Almyna's left hand. "T'ings come to an end, Almyna. Me will never forget yuh. Ya right, nuhbody cyan forget dem first love. But jus' as we both leave Jamaica to mek our way inna new land, de same way we 'ave to leave each udder, mek ah new start. Y'understan'? But saying dat, Jamaica will always be in me heart an' me love it more dan me ever realise."

Letting go of Almyna's hand, Cilbert offered her a last broad smile before he turned, adjusted the hat on his head, placed his hands in his pockets and disappeared into the London night. Almyna's head dropped as she returned to the club.

Reaching home just after midnight, Jacob undressed, kissed Jenny upon her forehead and slipped into bed.

"Yuh enjoy yaself, Jacob?"

"Yes," Jacob answered. "De music was very good."

"How dis club like?"

Jacob paused, still thinking of the Almyna and Cilbert situation. "Somet'ing wrong, Jacob?"

"Nuh, Jenny. Well, yes. Me cyan't lie to yuh."

"Wha' is it?" Jenny wanted to know.

"Me see Almyna tonight. *Don't* tell Hortense."

Jenny sat up, now fully awake. "Almyna?"

"Yes. Me sorry to say dis but me t'ink Almyna an' Cilbert been 'aving an affair. But me t'ink Cilbert end it tonight. Promise me yuh won't say not'ing."

"Nuh, Jacob. Yuh t'ink me waan to see me sweet sister hurt?"

Returning to her sleeping position with her back facing Jacob, Jenny hissed, "dat red skin bitch! See me don't cuss her backside when me set eyes 'pon her. Me will box her down again!"

Remembering what Almyna had said to him that perhaps Jenny had feelings for Cilbert, Jacob closed his eyes but his troubled mind denied him sleep.

Three weeks later, on a Friday evening, Hortense was ironing Cilbert's shirts. Stretched out upon the bed was Cilbert, surrounded by unironed clothes. Barebacked, he was smoking a cigarette and tipping the ash in an ashtray upon his chest.

"So when are yuh gwarn to tek me out 'pon de town?" asked Hortense. "Since we reach London yuh don't tek me out yet. Lester tek yuh to dis Flamingo club inna de West End an' to shubeen inna Notting Hill. Me waan to check out dese places, Cilbert. Me waan to dance."

"But de West End an' Notting Hill are nuh place fe ah lady," Cilbert warned. "Blue foot girl all over de place an' dangerous people."

"Cilbert Huggins!" Hortense reprimanded. "Me walk an' talk wid people inna de most dangerous places of Trenchtown. Yuh t'ink any blue foot girl or bad-mon ever worry me?"

"Me tell yuh wha'," compromised Cilbert. "Me hear about dese Caribbean nights dem hold inna de Town Hall der ah Brixton. Me will tek yuh der. It'll be safe fe yuh. Me jus' don't waan to tek yuh somewhere inna town where de white mon fling some dutty words inna ya direction. Y'understan'?"

"Me suppose so," nodded Hortense. "But me cyan fling bad word too. Yuh t'ink dem scare me?"

The next Thursday after he had finished work, Cilbert bought Hortense a new turquoise-coloured dress and a pair of white shoes. "T'ank yuh, Cilby," said Hortense, holding the dress in front of her while looking into her bedroom mirror, "de first lady of de dance is reborn!"

The following Saturday evening, Hortense proudly wore her new outfit to the dance at Brixton Town Hall.

Hearing the jolting bassline as she approached the venue, Hortense smiled, "but, Cilby! Yuh never tell me dat dey 'ave sound system here."

"Yes, de Mighty Count Suckle," Cilbert grinned. "Nuh way as heavy as de Trojan or Downbeat but it sound sweet to me ears."

The hall was packed with West Indians and once Hortense downed a shot of Jamaican rum, mixed with coke, she happily danced to the sounds of Laurel Aitken, Strangejah Cole, Alton Ellis and Prince Buster. Feeling elated that there was a corner of the Caribbean to cling onto in Brixton, Hortense sang along to every tune she knew and even jived alongside Trinadadians when Count Suckle played calypso tunes from the likes of Lord Marvellous, King Sporty, Duke Invincible and the Earl of Pleasure.

Curried goat and other West Indian dishes were served from a hatchway in a wall. Red Stripe beer was flowing. Flags of Caribbean islands were hanging from the ceiling as Count Suckle's home-made speaker boxes, the size of wardrobes, boomed out the music. Everybody was dancing with a free abandon, shedding their fears and trepidations of starting new lives in a foreign land.

Watching Hortense as happy as he could remember her, Cilbert felt she was the only one for him. He was no longer troubled by other men admiring his wife. "Jus' ah few years den we will return," he whispered to himself. "Me owe dat to her. Lord, cyan *she* dance."

Returning home from the dance leg-weary, Hortense climbed tiredly into bed, snuggling up to her husband. Realising what she had taken for granted in Kingston, Hortense buried her face into Cilbert's chest and silently wept. "Me really enjoy meself, Cilby. But when me hear Jamaican music an' see me people all aroun' me, it mek me so sad. Me miss all de people of de government yard. Dey were like family. Over here de white mon is not too friendly. Me boss at work don't even remember me name. Him jus' come by, say good marnin an' him gone."

Looking at the ceiling, Cilbert had experienced that unwanted feeling at his workplace. He knew nothing about the social and family lives of the white men whom he worked with. Every conversation was about work and nothing more.

Cilbert placed a hand on Hortense's cheek.

"Cilby, promise me dat after t'ree years of hard work, we will return to Jamaica," pleaded Hortense, taking hold of Cilbert's hand. "Mebbe we cyan buil' ah house to where Miss Martha used to live. An' we cyan tek our stroll inna Hope Gardens an' watch de sun drop beyond de mighty mountain. Jus' like we used to do."

"Nuh boder yaself, Hortense. Jus' wait 'til we save ah money," Cilbert replied. "Of course me waan de same t'ing as yuh. It might be ah liccle more dan t'ree years but we will get der. Me promise yuh dat. Me cyan imagine teking our kidren to sail 'pon boat at Christmas time inna de harbour. Yes, sa! Ah fine ambition dat. An' we will give teas an' rum cakes to we guests 'pon ah Sunday afternoon. Yes, sa! Jus' like how Misser DaCosta used to do."

"Do yuh regret coming to Englan', Cilby?"

Cilbert took his time in answering. "Nuh, sa! Even though de people don't accept we as me t'ought an' even though some of de white mon at work despise me. An' me t'ink me 'ave to show dat me much better dan dem fe de bosses to even consider me fe promotion. Dat's how it go fe ah black mon inna dis land. But when me around London, doing me work, me see so much opportunity, so much chances. Any mon 'ave ah fine chance of meking him money. Could yuh say de same t'ing about Kingston? Nuh, sa. When me return me waan to go back wid some money, start ah business or somet'ing. An' me won't go back 'til me achieve dat. De white mon will nuh put me off."

Hortense sensed the determination in Cilbert's voice. "We will get der! See if we don't!"

Chapter Sixteen

From the second floor room of her home, Jenny, letter in hand, skipped down to the first floor to Hortense's apartment. She was about to knock for her sister but she heard vexed shouting from within. With her right fist poised two inches from the entrance, she leaned in closer and pressed her ear against a door panel. A half-grin escaped from her lips.

"Cilbert, ya always go out raving wid Lester!" Hortense ranted. "Yuh don't even tek me to town hall dance nuh more! Wha' do yuh expect me to do? Sit inna dis small, miserable room an' look 'pon de four walls? Me don't 'ave nuh radio to lissen to. Yuh promise to buy me one. An' when me go upstairs to look fe me sister an' Jacob me feel dat me start get 'pon dem nerves becah me always complain about yuh. At weekends me spend more time wid Stella dan wid yuh. Me cyan't tek it nuh more, Cilbert!"

"But Hortense," Cilbert responded. "Yuh know me saving up fe we own place. Me put money by *every* week. We cyan't afford fe both of we to go out sporting."

"Den why do me affe stay home every weekend? Why cyan't *yuh* stay home 'pon Saturday night an' stare 'pon de damp wall wid me? Yuh still waan rave when winter ah come? Look how yuh ketch sick las' year. Cough yuh ah cough all de while. Me had to drag yuh to de doctor meself becah yuh don't waan to tek time off work."

"Me alright now isn't it. Me nuh know why ya always boder yaself. Anyway, Lester 'ave many frien', an' him fix me up wid some of dem to perform private jobs, y'know, ah liccle wiring here an' der. De money is building up fe true, Hortense, an' me bank account start get fat. Me waan to maintain me contacts. Me t'ought yuh did ah waan we to return to Jamaica inna few years time?"

"Yes, me do! But *rubbish* yuh ah talk about contacts! Yuh jus' love to look 'pon dem loose girl who ah walk 'round inna dem long boot inna de West End! It seem London change yuh fe de worse! It mek ya eyes bulge out like big rat trying to ketch him breat' underneat' tight carpet! Me sick an' tired of it. An' as fe dis Lester. Wha' do him do fe earn him bread? An' why he waan yuh by him side all de while? Him ah battymon?"

"Hortense, yuh being ridiculous. Lester work here an' der. Sometimes as ah bouncer. An' him 'ave many girlfrien'. Him not ah battymon."

"Me don't see any of dese girlfrien' an' him leading yuh astray. Why don't he marry one ah dem?"

"Hortense, yuh always complain about everyt'ing. Me work hard all week an' when weekend come me jus' waan ah liccle relief. To let me hair down as dem white mon ah say at work. Not'ing wrong wid dat. We stop sporting at de West End an' spend we time at Ladbroke Grove an' Notting Hill. Lester 'ave many frien's der. But don't worry ya pretty fine head, becah me saving all de while. Soon, when we 'ave enough fe we deposit, we could move outta here an' live in we own place. Den when de time is right we will sell dat place an' move back home."

Cilbert didn't reveal to anyone his mounting frustration at work where he witnessed lesser skilled white men being promoted above him. His response was to simply work harder and accept all the overtime he was offered.

He couldn't find the courage to tell Hortense that they might well have to remain in England for longer than five years to accumulate the money they needed for their intended return to Jamaica.

"Yuh forget dat me clean an' scrub inna de marnin der ah County Hall?" reminded Hortense. "Remember me affe face de English cold before yuh get up inna de marnin. When de grass wet but nuh rain ah fall – marnin dew dis white woman at work call it. It don't pay much but at least its somet'ing. It help pay fe we food. An' besides, say we get dis new place dat ya always talk about. Will yuh stay long enough to find out where de kitchen der? Or will yuh be der 'pon street wid dat damn joy bwai, Lester? Looking 'pon dem Jezebel woman who wear skirt dat nah long enough to wrap 'round ah bleeding finger."

At this moment, Jenny decided to knock upon the door, her conscience battling with her heartfelt boost that Cilbert and Hortense were quarrelling yet again.

"Come in!" shouted Hortense.

Trying to suppress the smirk that was rippling from her mouth, Jenny entered. The room was dominated by a double bed that had layers upon layers of blankets upon it but no pillows; Cilbert had bought a pair but Hortense complained of a sore neck after a night's use. Beside the bed, a framed black and white photograph of Cilbert and Hortense on their wedding day was propped up upon a small wooden cabinet. An aged mahogany wardrobe, on top of which rested Cilbert's and Hortense's bruised suitcases, stood in a corner and Jenny always wondered how on earth Sean and Miss Mary managed to shove it up the stairs and through the door. A chest of drawers was situated near the foot of the bed with a simple wooden chair before it. A second-hand paraffin heater, covered with scrapes and indentations, sat near Hortense's side of the bed, glowing with a low heat with its strong scent filling the room. Hortense's toiletries and Cilbert's shaving equipment filled the dressing table alongside a few imported Jamaican seven-inch vinyl records that Cilbert bought for Hortense from Lester. She had nothing to play them on but Cilbert promised he would purchase a 'Dansette' record player for Christmas.

First glancing at Cilbert, who was smoking a cigarette while looking out the window, Jenny closed her eyes for a second and dreamed it was her waking up every morning with him. He was only wearing baggy grey slacks held up with braces criss-crossing his naked, v-shaped back and his brown pork-pie hat. To Jenny he seemed to exude a raw sexual aggression.

Sitting on the bed, Hortense was wrapped in her dressing gown, her feet clad in thick, men's socks. Jenny sensed an anger in her eyes and a hint of vulnerability. Mebbe dey jus' cyan't live togeder, Jenny thought.

"Mama write we ah letter," revealed Jenny. "Papa sick again. Somet'ing wrong wid him belly. It ah swell up. Him cyan't hardly walk. Gran'papa mek ah broth an' ah poultice fe him but it don't work."

Jenny glanced at Cilbert who was still pulling on his cigarette and still absently looking to the greyness outside. Hortense displayed no emotion.

"Me was talking to Jacob dis marnin," Jenny continued. "An' if we keep on saving good fe de nex' few weeks, me will go back ah Jamaica to see Papa. Me don't know ya money situation, Hortense, but me would ah really love it if yuh cyan come back wid me. Mebbe fe two weeks. Me will tek ah plane. Papa *is* sick."

"Me cyan't go," said Hortense, her expression unchanging.

"Why?"

"Becah me belly fat. Me pregnant."

Hortense turned to look at Cilbert and for a moment he froze on the spot, his cigarette poised an inch from his mouth. He then turned around, his eyes expressing shock but a smile forming within his cheeks. "Ya sure, Hortense?"

"Of course me sure! De doctor confirm it yesterday. Me t'ree mont's pregnant. Yuh don't notice dat me 'ave ah recent craving fe fried chicken an' digestive biscuits?"

"But. But. Hortense! Me t'ought dat we agree dat we will 'ave children when we get we own place?"

"Well, me pregnant," asserted Hortense. "Yuh t'ink me did it by meself? Wha' yuh expect when de both of we get peckish every night-time? Me suppose it too late fe yuh to change dem wort'less condoms dat yuh ah use. Cilbert, yuh gwarn to be ah daddy so yuh better live wid it."

Cilbert killed his cigarette in an ashtray resting on the window sill then sat beside Hortense on the bed. He cupped her cheeks with his palms and kissed her on the forehead, a huge smile spreading across his face. "He will be de most fine, bes' dressed baby in town! Yes, sa! He will 'ave everyt'ing him waan. Me swear to dis! When him grow up he could be ah doctor, teacher or even Prime Minister! Yes, sa! Me son *will* mek him mark in dis land. Nuh labouring or blue collar work fe him an' nuhbody will stop him promotion."

"Wha' mek yuh so sure dat de baby will be ah bwai?" Hortense laughed, relief and joy flushing through her.

"Me jus' know," insisted Cilbert, placing his right hand upon Hortense's stomach. "Me gwarn work even harder to provide fe him. Mek sure him ah grow up inna nice place. When him start school he will wear de cleanest white shirt an' de shiniest shoes. Yes, sa! An' he will carry him books inna one ah dem black satchel dat de uptown white bwai dem ah carry."

Observing Cilbert's delight, Jenny could see the pure love he had for his sister. She couldn't share his joy. "Me suppose congratulations is in order," she said automatically.

Unable to keep still because of his excitement, Cilbert made for the door. "Me affe tell Jacob, Miss Mary an' everybody else. We will celebrate tonight! Yes, sa. Me sure de bank manager won't bawl if me dip into me savings fe tonight. Soon come."

Jenny could only admire Cilbert's exuberance. "Hortense, yuh really an' truly mek him day. Me never seen ah happier mon." Accepting her own words, Jenny's stomach churned in desolation.

"Me did not waan to tell him becah me thought he'd be vex," revealed Hortense. "Fe ah second me was worried but Cilby's face turned to joy. Yes, Jenny, yuh gwarn to be an auntie fe ah second time."

"Mebbe yuh should come to Jamaica wid me," said Jenny. "Yuh need to eat some good food fe de baby an' mek Papa find some good herbs fe yuh so de baby grow nice an' strong inside yuh."

"*Nuh*, Jenny. De air trip might mek de pickney inside me sick. Nuh, sa, me will nah chance dat. An', Jenny, yuh cyan't go an' leave me now. Me need yuh. Nah worry yaself, Papa will be alright. Papa strong like de mountain side where him born an' grow. Now yuh affe be by me side. Yuh t'ink me coulda go anywhere if *ya* belly was fat? Nuh, sa! Me would look after yuh."

"Nuh worry yaself, Hortense. Of course me will look after yuh.

Jus' like me always do. Me will visit Papa after ya pickney born. Mebbe yuh cyan come wid me den? Gran'papa would love to see de baby, especially it if ah bwai an' he will bless him fe true."

"Ya right about dat. Yes, me will go wid yuh. Yuh know, Jenny, if me 'ave ah bwai me sure him will look like David. Mebbe Massa God is replacing de love me los'?"

Struggling to break out into a smile, Jenny replied, "yes, me sure dat is de Most High's plan."

"Mebbe He's nah such ah cruel God as Papa used to say," Hortense remarked.

"One birt' don't mek up fe everyt'ing Him done to we, Hortense."

"Oh, Jenny! Stop ya fussing! Outta me an' yuh, yuh is supposed to be de religious one."

Six months later. Wheeling home a shopping trolley along Coldharbour Lane, Hortense felt a kick from within her stomach and although she suffered a sharp, brief pain, she paused, rubbed her abdomen and smiled pleasurably. "Yes, sa! Yuh 'ave nuff energy. Yuh don't affe remind me dat ya der."

It was almost noon on a crisp, spring day. The English sun was weak, Hortense thought, but at least it now showered brightness, expelling the cold memories of damp, foggy mornings and murky, rainswept nights. She had noticed that the wintered, naked trees were now dressing themselves and the grass was now of a richer green. She grinned at children who went by on bikes, enjoying their Easter holidays. Once fearful of greeting people in the street, Hortense now waved and offered welcoming smiles to the grocer who was laying out his fruit outside his shop and Kathleen, the white woman who worked in the launderette. All seemed right with the world.

Reaching home, she made her way to the kitchen to put away her shopping; there were now a few outlets in Brixton market that sold Caribbean food – Hortense was especially pleased at the availability of sweet potato, snapper fish and cornmeal. "Anybody home? Miss Mary, Stella? Anybody waan ah cup ah tea? *Me would nah walk upon de concrete, me would nah walk upon de ground, me find meself ah liccle pony, an' ride aroun' de town."*

Hortense stretched to place canned foods inside the top cupboard. *"An de cows in de meadow go moo moo moo an' de sheep in de pastures go baa baa baa, an' de rooster, ah liccle rooster. Aaaaggghhh!"* She suffered an excruciating pain from her stomach. The tin of corn she held in her right hand fell from her grasp to the floor. Hortense bent over, holding her stomach, gritting her teeth. Then another shooting pain wracked her in agony. It felt like a knife slicing her innards from within. She screamed a harrowing scream, the tissues of her neck stretching to the limit and the rest of her body stiffened, like a ballerina's calf muscle. "CILBERRRT!"

Rushing out of their apartment, Mary Skidmore and Stella found Hortense writhing in distress upon the kitchen floor. The shopping trolley had been knocked over and two tins of baked beans were rolling towards the cupboards underneath the sink. "CILBERRRT!"

"Stella, go and call an ambulance," instructed Mary, wrapping her arms around Hortense's back and raising her from the floor. "Now, Hortense, try and take deep breaths, *don't* panic. Even the Proddy Queen of England has to go through this so don't get yerself in a frenzy."

Tears falling down her cheeks, Hortense clung onto Mary's cardigan. "Me waan. Aaaarrggghh! Me. Me waan me husband, Miss Mary. Cyan yuh call his depot fe me? Please, Miss Mary."

"Of course I will, my love. But we have to get yer to hospital, Hortense. The baby inside yer wants to take a look outside. The Lord has blessed yer baby with impatience – it's probably a boy."

"AAAAAGGGGHHHH," Hortense screamed again as another bolt of pure pain reverberated inside her.

The ambulance arrived twenty minutes later and as Hortense was wheelchaired into the emergency vehicle, Stella was standing outside her front door clutching a plastic bag full of Hortense's undergarments and night clothes. Stella presented the bag to her mother. "No, Stella," Mary declined. "Yer go with her."

"Why me, Mum? I wouldn't know what to do."

"I have things to do, Stella. Phone Hortense's family for one and try and get hold of that workaholic husband of hers. Now, go on with yer! Just offer yer hand to grip onto when she has to push. Hopefully, the entire bloody process will put yer off sex. When yer get there phone me to tell me how things are going. May the Holy Father bless her."

Apprehensive, Stella followed Hortense into the ambulance. Sirens blaring, the ambulance arrived at Kings College hospital in Camberwell within five minutes. Hortense, her waters now breaking, was wheeled straight into the delivery theatre, holding onto Stella's right hand for dear life. "Where's Cilbert? Where's Jenny?" she stuttered.

"Don't worry, Hortense, they'll be here soon."

After five and three quarter hours of labour, Hortense gave birth to a baby boy at 6.09 p.m. The infant weighed seven pounds and three ounces. Stella, examining her reddened, bruised right hand that Hortense had been gripping throughout her ordeal, sat beside the new mother feeling she had just survived a tortuous experience as well. The baby was sleeping face down upon Hortense's chest, perfectly unaware of the screaming and Jamaican curses he had provoked. Propped up by two pillows, Hortense, her hairline damp with sweat and her cheeks bloated, simply gazed lovingly at her firstborn, her pain and aches forgotten at this moment.

Her pink Lyons uniform visible under her beige mac, Jenny entered the ward with Jacob. Upon seeing her sister, Jenny quickened her step as a full smile rippled from her eyes. "Is it ah bwai? Is it ah bwai?" she asked.

Exhausted but happy, Hortense nodded.

"Gran'papa will be so pleased," said Jenny. "An' Papa too."

Looming over Hortense with his right hand poised an inch over the baby's head, Jacob, almost speaking in a whisper, offered, "do yuh waan me to bless him now, Hortense?"

Raising a huge grin, Hortense nodded again. Jacob tightly closed his eyes, placed his hand gently upon the back of the baby's head and prayed, his face a picture of concentration. *"Dear, Lord. May ya mighty right hand guide this new life. May yuh hear an' answer his call in times of need. An' may yuh protect him when peril encroaches. An' may his eyes be opened to see ya glory."*

"T'ank yuh, Jacob," appreciated Hortense. "Dat was so sweet."

The labour ward door burst open as Cilbert, still dressed in his work clothes, marched along the aisle, his expression bursting with happiness. He spotted Hortense and hot-footed towards her, banging his leg against a bed-post on his way. Laughing at his excitement, Hortense lifted her eyes to glimpse a clock hanging high on a wall. It was 7.45 p.m.

Smothering Hortense with kisses, Cilbert asked, "do me 'ave ah son? Do me 'ave ah son? De baby look so small an' sweet! Me cyan't tell if de baby ah bwai or girl, tell me Hortense! Please tell me dat me 'ave ah son. Everyt'ing alright? De baby healt'y? Yuh healt'y? Sorry me late. Cyan me pick de baby up? How small an' fine de baby look!"

Everyone collapsed in fits of giggles as Hortense carefully presented her son to her husband. "Yuh sure ya hands clean?" Hortense demanded. "An' why yuh so late?"

"Of course me hands clean," replied Cilbert, refusing to take his eyes from his firstborn. "Me only get to hear de good news when me reach back to de depot. Me rush home when me finish work an' den come here. Me never 'ave nuh time to change me clothes."

"Well, Cilby," returned Hortense. "Look 'pon ya son. Mebbe me shoulda known becah de baby did kick like ah mon wid long foot."

"I thought Hortense was gonna scream the place down," added Stella.

"Hortense, yuh mus' 'ave truly cried tough," said Cilbert. "But me did tell yuh so it would be ah bwai. Me did tell yuh so! Prophet me ah prophet."

"So what you gonna call him?" Stella wanted to know. "You said you would keep his name secret until the baby is born. Well, the baby's in your arms. So what's his name?"

Still gazing at his new son's face, Cilbert didn't answer, instead he stroked his son's face with the baby finger of his right hand. "Him look so fine!"

"Come, Cilbert, mon!" Encouraged Jacob. "Don't keep we inna suspense! Wha' is de pickney's name? I hope it is Biblical."

"Booker," Cilbert answered. "Booker T."

"Wha' kinda foolish name is dat?" argued Hortense. "Yuh cyan't give him dat name. When him go ah school de children dem will tek de mickey. Nuh, sa! De name yuh give him sound like me give birt' to ah blasted dictionary!"

Everyone laughed. "But, Hortense," Cilbert protested. "Me name him after ah great black American revolutionary. Booker T Washington! Me papa did tell me stories about dis great mon. Him raise up de black race. Famous inna America Booker T was."

"Me nah care," said Hortense. "Booker T is outta de question. Now, him middle name is David, after me sweet brudder. So, Cilbert, t'ink of somet'ing nice. Somet'ing appropriate."

"Alright, alright," nodded Cilbert. "Wha' about Marcus? Yes, mon. Marcus David Huggins."

"Wasn't he de rebel rouser who was sold fe ah bag of rice?" questioned Jenny.

"Yes, ya right, Jenny," Jacob affirmed.

"Great though de mon was," said Hortense. "But me don't waan me son to be named after ah mon wid bad luck."

"But Marcus Garvey was born inna St Anne, nah far from where *yuh* was born, Hortense," pleaded Cilbert.

"But Marcus Garvey suffer nuff tribulation inna him life," replied Hortense. "Gran'papa tell me him get boot outta America an' spend time inna jailhouse."

"Yuh cyan never satisfy," accused Cilbert. "Every name me come up wid yuh ah complain!"

"Den pick somet'ing nice," chuckled Hortense.

"We are studying American history at school," revealed Stella. "And the American Civil War. I learned that Abraham Lincoln abolished slavery. Why not name the baby after him?"

"Yes, me like dat," Hortense cooed. "Yes, Lincoln. Lincoln David Huggins. It sound important, official."

Jenny and Jacob offered concurring nods and even Cilbert expressed a certain pleasure as he whispered the name to himself.

"Alright," he said. "Lincoln David Huggins *is* me son's name. Yes, sa. It sound like de name of ah Prime Minister or somebody who win ah Nobel Prize!"

Remaining in hospital for four more nights, Hortense and Lincoln were visited by Cilbert every evening during their stay. He never paid a visit without bearing gifts. Firstly, he presented Hortense with a bunch of flowers and a box of chocolates. Then he purchased small toys and baby clothes for Lincoln. "See wha' Papa buy fe yuh," cooed Cilbert, shaking a baby rattle and showing off a pair of soft baby boots while flashing a silly smile. Not impressed, Lincoln only wanted the comfort of his mother's generous breasts. Meanwhile, Hortense, who never failed to display perfect politeness to the nurses and to those who fed her, whispered to Jenny upon her second visit, "Jenny, de people are very nice but me cyan't tek de food! Dem don't use nuh seasoning an' der food 'ave nuh flavour. It taste like soggy paper! Me beg yuh, Jenny. Bring me some Jamaican food before me shout down de hospital!"

"Alright," laughed Jenny. "Me will cook up somet'ing fe yuh every day an' bring it come inna de evenin'. But don't mek dem know dat yuh hate dem food. An' Hortense, me tell yuh fe de las' time, Lincoln *look* like Cilbert. Yuh cyan see it inna him small nose an' de twinkle inna him eye!"

"Jenny, yuh 'ave talked ah whole heap ah fart since yuh born but ya insistence dat me son look like Cilbert is de mightiest fart yuh ever talk. One of dem nasty black crow mus' ah shit inna ya eye dis marnin. It's clear to everybody dat Lincoln look like sweet David."

"Hortense Huggins! Sometime yuh so stubborn inna ya t'inking!"

"Me don't care!" replied Hortense. "When yuh write Mama, tell her Lincoln look like David. It will sweet her an' everybody else. Mek dem day."

Arriving back at home, Hortense discovered that Cilbert had bought a second-hand cot from Miss Mary. For the first few weeks of his life, Lincoln rarely slept in his own bed, instead he lay between his mother and father, sometimes listening to Hortense's gentle singing of Jamaican folk songs to help him sleep. Whenever

Jenny babysat she told Lincoln tales of fearless Maroons, great sea adventures and of the 'mighty men' who built the Panama canal. Hortense still insisted that Lincoln was the spitting image of David, and Gilbert and Jacob, not wanting to upset the new mother, agreed with her. Mary Skidmore was not so diplomatic, however. "Hortense, yer talking rubbish! I've never seen a baby boy look so much like his father. Yer should rejoice in that fact because in most Proddy families that I know of, the sons don't look like the fathers."

When Lincoln reached three months of age, Gilbert managed to purchase a pram and he insisted upon taking Lincoln for walks in nearby Ruskin Park on Sunday mornings. It wasn't as beautiful as Hope Botanical Gardens in Kingston, but at least it was an open, green space.

South London, March 1963. The snow had drifted to two feet deep against Mary Skidmore's front door. Those who dared to employ their cars found themselves slipping and sliding on the unnegotiable ice. The screeching sounds of wheelspinning added to the morning din of commuter travel. On the main roads, frustrated motorists simply abandoned their vehicles and left them to the mercy of London's most savage winter since 1947. Trains were not leaving their stations, coal trucks struggled to make their deliveries, water pipes exploded, paraffin heaters sold out, outside toilets froze over, the entire professional football programme was postponed and Gilbert found himself working sixteen-hour days to repair telephone lines. Doggedly he went out every morning, his feet clad in Wellington boots and his head covered in a black balaclava. He would walk to his depot, three miles away in Stockwell. On many occasions, his fingers were too numb to perform the intricate rewiring. He would reach home after 10 p.m., announcing his arrival by stamping his feet upon Mary's outside doormat to rid himself of the snow. A large bowl of Jamaican soup, containing yams, diced beef, peppers, dumplings and green banana, awaited him in the kitchen. After consuming his dinner he would troop wearily upstairs to see his family and more often than not, find Lincoln blissfully asleep, his mother gently rocking him beside the paraffin heater. "Inna dis cold time," Cilbert would remark. "Me never see Lincoln's eyes open. Me hope him remember who me is. Me cyan't wait 'til de sun ah shine bright inna de summer an' when de mighty Frank Worrell will lead we West Indian cricket team against de English. Everybody is excited an' talking about it, Hortense. When dey play Englan' at de Oval me planning to tek Lincoln wid me. To let him see inna de flesh heroes from our part of de world. Yes, sa. Ah great occasion dat will be."

"Are yuh ah madmon, Cilbert?" replied Hortense. "Lincoln is only ah baby. Him will never understan' wha' is happening aroun' him. Besides, de noise an' bangarang will mek him nervous an' will upset him."

"But, Hortense. It will be ah chance fe Lincoln to be surrounded by *our* people. *Our* music an' we own heroes. Inna dis country who do we 'ave to look up to? Nuhbody! Dat's why every West Indian mon me know is planning to forward to de Oval. Right about now it's de nearest t'ing we cyan show him dat is close to home an' give him ah taste of de Caribbean."

"Well, Cilbert. Yuh go to de Oval an' watch mon inna white shirt lick ah stupid red ball. But Lincoln is too young. Mebbe when him get ah liccle older."

Before Hortense finished her sentence, Cilbert, sulking in the hallway, was already pulling the bedroom door closed behind him.

One Sunday morning, Hortense denied Cilbert his custom of taking Lincoln for a walk in Ruskin Park. "But it's somet'ing me love to do," protested Cilbert, as Lincoln was enjoying a Rich Tea biscuit. "Me will wrap him up good. Lincoln cyan wear dat new bobble hat me ah buy fe him."

"*Nuh*, Cilbert!" Hortense asserted. "It *too* damn cold. It so cold me sure even Mama back home inna Jamaica feel it."

"But me don't get nuh time to spend wid me son 'pon me own," Cilbert remarked.

The couple hotly argued the matter for ten minutes until Cilbert, accepting defeat, stormed out of the room and slammed the door.

He found Jenny walking up the stairwell, a mug of cocoa held in her hands. She smiled at him. "Cilbert, yuh an' Hortense affe stop ya contention. De walls are thin here an' everybody cyan hear. Miss Mary will nah say it to ya face but she ah complain about it too. Anyway, why yuh don't let me mek yuh ah cup ah cocoa an' it might mek yuh cool off?"

"Yes, Jenny," Cilbert nodded, his anger fading.

They sat opposite each other at the kitchen table. Jenny stole glances at Cilbert whenever she brought her mug of cocoa to her lips. She sensed he was troubled as he stared vacantly through the window at the back yard. He coughed erratically, a dry chesty cough that stretched the skin upon his neck.

"Yuh know, Cilbert," Jenny started. "Argument an' contention is *not* good fe de soul. An' it's not good fe Lincoln too. Nuh pickney should affe lissen to contention. It create ah bad vibe fe ah pickney to grow. Y'understan'?"

Cilbert sipped his cocoa as he pondered Jenny's words. "It's always been de same," he coughed. "Dat is jus' how we are. We argue about stupidness, we cuss cuss each udder an' usually, Hortense get her own way."

"Yuh should nah let Hortense walk all over yuh," said Jenny. "She's always been headstrong, independent. Yuh affe stan' up fe yaself."

Injured by Jenny's implication that he was weak, Cilbert replied, "Hortense *don't* walk all over me. Me always say wha' me waan to say. But someone affe back down becah de argument will never stop."

"Is dat de way ah couple should live?" asked Jenny, lowering her voice and leaning in closer to Cilbert. "Why should yuh always back down? Hortense is not always right. Cilbert, if yuh an' Hortense carry on dis way den me don't know how ya marriage will survive. An' if dat did happen it would tear up me heart. Me promise yuh. Couples should live inna harmony. Yuh don't hear Jacob an' meself ranting an' raving at each udder."

"Hortense an' meself are very passionate people," said Cilbert. "Sometimes we say t'ings to each udder dat we don't really mean.

We always say sorry afterwards. De nex' day everyt'ing is fine."

"Is dat how yuh waan live ya full married life," questioned Jenny, her voice now a little over a whisper. "Arguments every day an' ah sorry inna de evening?"

"Of course not," replied Cilbert, now looking away from Jenny.

Rising to her feet, Jenny went to wash out her mug. On her way, she used her shoulder to nudge and close the kitchen door. She returned to her seat, feeling her heartbeat accelerate. "Me know Hortense is me sister an' me love her more dan anyt'ing in dis world. An' me waan to see her happy wid life. It pains me to see her inna contention wid yuh almost every day. De both of yuh deserve happiness but if yuh cyan find it den me an' nobody else should complain if yuh decide to go ya separate ways an' look fe happiness elsewhere. Yuh understan' wha' me ah say, Cilbert."

Rocking back in his chair, Cilbert replied, "Jenny, it's not as bad as dat. Me sorry dat de impression we give is one of bad vibes. Me promise dat we will try an' stop de cuss cuss so dat yuh don't affe worry yaself about we."

Placing his mug upon the table, Cilbert reached for Jenny's hands. "Jenny, yuh been such ah good frien' to me. Ya probably me bes' frien' in dis world, closer to me dan any of me sister or brudder an' even Lester. Me t'ank yuh fe ya concern but we'll be alright. Don't boder yaself. Me don't mean to mek yuh worry about Hortense's happiness. Mebbe when we get we own place t'ings will settle down. Dat's why me work so hard."

Leaning over, Cilbert kissed Jenny upon the cheek. He then stood up, smiling. "Where is Jacob dis marnin?" he asked.

"Oh, he's waiting at de church hall in case anybody turn up der. He did cancel de service becah of de weder but him 'fraid dat some people might still turn up."

"Yuh know, Jenny, Jacob an' meself don't agree on everyt'ing but him ah *good* mon. An honest mon. Better dan meself. Me really look up to him but *don't* tell him dat. Yes, sa. Jacob heart pure. *Don't* bruise it, Jenny."

As Cilbert walked along the hallway, Jenny heard him cough again as he climbed the stairs. She wanted to pursue him and declare her love for him but she could never do that. She had to admit to herself that indeed, Jacob was a good man, almost holy. But she didn't want to spend the rest of her life with a man who never done wrong. She wanted someone dangerous, someone to make her heart race, she still wanted Cilbert. Making love to Jacob had become a chore for her, she realised, and she wondered how much longer she could sustain her marriage. Hortense didn't even want to escort her back to Jamaica for a holiday and Jenny felt that her sister no longer needed her protection and counsel. Going back to Jamaica will give me time to t'ink, Jenny said to herself. Mebbe me need starting afresh, away from Hortense. Me jus' cyan't stan' Cilbert an' Hortense looking so good togeder!

Chapter Seventeen

South London, England
April 1963

Pulling on his Wellington boots and preparing for overtime on a Saturday morning, Cilbert coughed into his soiled, bedraggled handkerchief. The pain shooting up from his chest caused the inside wall of his throat to stretch, it felt like somebody had force-fed him with cubes of coarse peppered hay. Studying the rust-coloured mucus that Cilbert's chest had thrown up, Hortense arose from her bed, caught Cilbert with an uncompromising stare and ordered, *"right*, dat is *it*! If yuh waan go work yuh affe lick me down first! An' if me affe use me fist as God is me witness me will!"* She then marched towards the door, placing herself in front of Cilbert, her hands on her hips.

Having suffered shivering chills, high fever and chest pains in the past few weeks, Cilbert relented and threw a Wellington boot to the floor. He dropped to the bed, seemingly relieved that Hortense denied him from setting off to work. His eyes spelt resignation and exhaustion. In the next two days, Cilbert, confined to bed, weakened considerably, despite the ginger, hot honey, Irish whiskey teas and aspirins that Hortense gave him. "He'll be alright," assured Mary the next Sunday afternoon; she had poured boiling water into a bowl and tipped four capfuls of whiskey and a sprinkle of black pepper into it. Hortense added strips of ginger. Cilbert, not fully convinced of this remedy, now with a towel covering his head and too weak to resist, held his nose an inch away from the cocktail, the fumes warming his face, assaulting his nostrils and stinging his eyes. "Just a touch of the flu," Mary casually remarked while holding down Cilbert's head. "He just needs some rest and lots and lots of fluids. The whiskey will uncork his nose alright. By the time I've finished with him he'll be able to smell the Guinness brewery in Ireland."

The following Monday morning, Hortense, not wanting to wait for an evening visit from the doctor, escorted a whimpering Cilbert, who was almost drunk from his treatment of hot whiskey bowls, to the surgery. Hortense had to use all her strength and balance to keep him upright; the pavements were coated with treacherous ice and she nearly slipped into a newspaper advertisement board that head-lined how militant groups among the 25,000 Aldermaston marchers clashed with the police at Whitehall.

Examining Cilbert's chest with a stethoscope and the mucus from his cough, the doctor diagnosed pneumonia. "Wha' is dat, doctor?" Hortense queried immediately, scanning the physician's eyes for any hint of foreboding. "Ya scare me! It sound evil! He will be alright?"

Pausing before answering, the doctor replied, "most cases of pneumonia clear up by themselves but your husband is at an advanced stage from the infection. The colour of his phlegm is a tell-tale sign. You see, it's an infection of the lungs. He will have to enter hospital and receive an immediate course of antibiotics. Penicillin."

"Antibiotics! Penicillin? Wha' is dat? Yuh sure he'll be alright? Me did keep tell him to go an' see de doctor but him ah always say, 'me fine, stop fussing, Hortense'. Some mon jus' don't waan to lissen an' Cilbert is stubborn like sulking mule!"

"Antibiotics is a medicine to help clear infections. Please don't worry, Mrs Huggins. With rest and the right medication, your husband will recover."

Although the doctor displayed a certain calmness, he dialled for an ambulance to take Cilbert to the hospital for prompt attention. He turned his back to Hortense as he spoke quietly into the phone. Sitting beside Cilbert in the ambulance, Hortense held and stroked his limp right hand, gazing into his weary, half-opened eyes. There was no glint, no hunger for life, Hortense found, despite Cilbert trying to raise a smile that failed to reach his cheeks. "Nuh boder yaself, Hortense," he stammered. "Yuh t'ink dis foolish cough coulda beat me down? Nuh, sa! Watch when summer ah come! Along wid me own people me will be cheering on de mighty Frank Worrell when him ah come out to bat at de Oval. He will lick de English fe *six*! An' me will go to work wid me head lifted high. Yes, sa! Mighty Frank will show de English dat we West Indian *are* good at somet'ing. Whatever dey might say."

Returning the smile, Hortense couldn't stem the tears falling down her cheeks. Upon reaching the hospital, Cilbert received his first dose of penicillin after Hortense assured the medics that he hadn't eaten since the night before. Between her sobbing and the attacks of panic dancing in her mind, she called home. Stella, Jenny and Jacob soon joined her at the hospital, none of them quite believing the severity of Cilbert's illness. They all sensed the fear within Hortense's eyes and comforted her the best way they could.

"Cilbert *strong*," assured Jacob, embracing his sister-in-law. "Look how him recover from de beating him ah suffer inna Trenchtown."

"Cyan yuh say ah prayer fe him?" asked Hortense. "Please."

"Of course," smiled Jacob, taking Hortense's hands within his own. "*Dear Lord. May yuh protect Cilbert from any tribulation an' watch over him in his time of need. Give him the strengt' to recover an' de spirit to endure.*"

"AMEN."

Stealing fretful glances at Cilbert and finding the shadow of sickness upon his face too much to bear, Jenny had to sit down for she felt her legs would soon fail her. She closed her eyes and said her own silent prayer as the emotions raging inside her battled to be released.

By nightfall a doctor had reassured Hortense that Cilbert's condition was now stable, although he was running a high temperature and was unable to eat. He was lying perfectly still on his back, the rich, chocolate colour of his face now a dull, winter-brown. His eyes moved slowly to acknowledge his visitors and his mouth was slightly open, lips trembling, as if it would take a mighty effort for any animated conversation. His fragile breathing was hurried and his right hand rested upon Hortense's left arm. Hortense regarded him lovingly, her eyes full of compassion, her smile defiant. In contrast, behind her, Jenny could not deny the utter turmoil in her expression. She fidgeted in her seat, her eyes darting here and there, unfulfilled hope ripping her heart asunder. In her mind she heard a voice say, 'at least yuh had him, Hortense. If him dead me will never get de chance.' Shaking her head and burdened by guilt, Jenny stood up. "Hortense, it's getting late. Me affe go home now. Jacob an' Lester took Stella home four hours ago. Yuh coming wid me? Me sure Cilbert will be alright."

Only listening to Cilbert's delicate breathing and her eyes appreciating the contours of his face, Hortense didn't hear her sister. Jenny kissed Hortense upon the top of her head before departing. As she stood waiting for a bus she recalled the night of Hortense and Cilbert's wedding. She was brooding in Mr DaCosta's back yard, consumed with jealousy and anger, when Jacob found her. She admitted to him that sometimes she had 'dark thoughts' and couldn't understand why. She now realised that as far back as she could remember there was a part of her which was ungodly. She remembered one harvest night when she faked a leg injury because she just couldn't tolerate her father carrying Hortense home. She recollected her spiteful ripping of Hortense's party dress. And now she still felt cursed with loving Cilbert, despite her prayers to the Most High to release her from her lust. Feeling utterly powerless to break her infatuation, Jenny boarded the bus pulling up outside Kings College hospital with tears streaming down her cheeks. "Me mus' be de reincarnation of Jezebel," she whispered to herself. "Wha' mek me so bad-minded?"

The viral infection that rampaged through Cilbert's body proved a ferocious foe for the penicillin to battle. Nurses had to place cold flannels upon his forehead at night in an attempt to check his rising temperature. Waking up following a couple of hours of hard-fought sleep, Cilbert found himself and his pillow drenched in sweat. Now he could hardly utter a sound and he continually dreamed of his mother leaving a naked baby beside a swift-flowing stream.

Controlling her worst fears, Hortense kept rigidly to her daily routine. She would wake Lincoln at 5.15 a.m., feed him his breakfast of cornmeal, cinnamon flavoured porridge and Rich Tea biscuits before bathing him in the kitchen, using the hot water from the kettle and a large plastic bowl. She then powdered him with baby talc and anointed his skin with vaseline before dressing him in clothes that his father had bought for him. Draining the last drop of her nutmeg-flavoured tea, she would knock upon Mary's door at precisely 6 a.m., handing over a crying and bewildered Lincoln into Mary's arms. Hortense then set off to County Hall where she performed her cleaning work as diligently as she had ever done, not stopping for a conversation with anyone.

Finishing work at 10 a.m., she took a bus to Kings College hospital where she insisted upon giving Cilbert his morning 'bed wash'. There she remained until the late evening, speaking to Cilbert of their future together and the brothers and sisters they would provide for Lincoln to play with in their own house. They dreamed of playing with their children in a back garden of a big mansion up in Strawberry Hill. Cilbert, unable to answer his wife, would raise a weak smile, all the time resting his right hand upon Hortense's left arm, his bleary gaze never leaving Hortense's face.

Jenny would arrive early in the evening, bringing with her cooked Jamaican food that she hoped Cilbert would today be able to consume. Cilbert would offer Jenny a smile in a gesture of thanks but would gently shake his head. This repeated action only added to Jenny's dread, and upon their journey home, it was Hortense drying Jenny's tears upon the number 45 bus. "Nuh worry yaself, Jenny," Hortense would soothe. "Cilbert *will* shake off dis sickness. Wha' chance do dis pneumonia 'ave wid Jacob praying, Miss Mary praying, Miss Mary's priest praying an' de good will of our family? *Nuh chance*! Yuh wait an' see, Cilby will be soon up an' about like ah spring lamb who step 'pon ah dutty nail."

2nd May, 1963. Arriving at hospital at 11 a.m., Hortense found Cilbert sitting up in bed. For the first time in weeks he offered a smile that showcased his teeth and animated the fine lines upon his temples. His face was still shrouded in sickness but his gaze was keen and direct, his head movements responsive. "Yuh look ah whole heap better!" Hortense smiled.

"Cyan me read ya paper?" Cilbert asked, resisting the pain from his throat and chest, trying to impress Hortense with his new-found strength.

"So yuh feel better?" Hortense chuckled, passing over to him her edition of the *Daily Mirror*; the front page spoke of Winston Churchill's imminent retirement from politics.

"Yes, me feel ah liccle better," Cilbert answered, his voice still frail but it seemed returning to its full baritone. "De nurse tek me temperature dis marnin an' from ah 105 it drop down to 104. Dis marnin me even struggle over to de toilet. It tek de breat' outta me but me made it. *Don't* tell de nurse! Me jus' don't like using dem bed pan."

"Cilbert! Yuh know yuh affe keep ya energy! See me don't tell de doctor an' tell him to cuss yuh if yuh try dat again. Yuh mus' res' yaself."

"Stop ya naggy naggy self an' come over here an' give me ah hug."

Hortense could do nothing but smile and sat beside Cilbert upon the bed. Cilbert's embrace was weak and it was a mighty effort for him to lean into Hortense's arms. He fell back against his pillows, breathing hard but tried to disguise his obvious discomfort with a grin. He placed his right hand upon Hortense's left arm and gazed adoringly into her eyes. "Now lissen to me, Hortense. Me know me not ah perfect mon. Me impulsive, me like de bright lights, me stubborn an' sometimes me selfish. Me eyes *too* fixed 'pon de prize of ambition."

"Cilbert don't worry yaself about..."

"*Don't* interrupt me, Hortense. It affe be said. When me come outta here me gwarn to change me ways. Be more of ah family mon, spend more time wid Lincoln an' yaself. Me affe stop sporting at Notting Hill, coming home jus' as de bird dem ketch der worm. Me sure de Mangrove club cyan get along fine widout me. Lester affe find somebody else to sport wid.

"Being in here it give ah mon ah whole heap of time to t'ink. Yes, sa! When me ably me will write ah letter to me Mama. Yes, somet'ing me affe do. Let her know she ah gran'mudder. Let her know how much me love me wife. Yes, sa. Dey *will* accept yuh! Me will mek sure of dat. Sometime de boredom inside here drive me mad. Especially at night time when me cyan't sleep."

Cilbert paused, not wanting to reveal his nightmares to Hortense. "Me 'ave been very selfish," he continued. "Miss Mary tell me one time dat ah mon should nah live to work but him should work to live. Y'understan', Hortense? Do yuh understan' dat yuh was de only girl fe me? Nobody else ah compare. Nuh, sa! Fe true! Nuh matter wha' anybody might say."

Placing a hand upon Cilbert's left cheek, Hortense replied, "but yuh only working so hard to provide fe me an' Lincoln. Of course, we 'ave our fussing an' fighting an' sometimes me waan to lick yuh wid de Dutch pot, but when me wake up an' see yuh lay down beside me inna de marnin, me coulda never wish fe ah better mon. Now me tell yuh dis, *don't* let ya head swell or me will lick yuh wid de Dutch pot fe true!"

Cilbert laughed but his chuckles soon turned into coughs. "Don't excite yaself," said Hortense, patting his back. "Yuh mus' res' now. Becah me waan yuh fit an' well to tek me to de cricket inna few weeks time."

"Yuh waan watch de cricket wid me?" Cilbert wanted confirmation, leaning forward, his eyes full of excitement. "Ya coming to de Oval wid me?"

"Yes, do me 'ave to say it twice? Me cyan't understan' how grown mon get demself inna tizzy about ah mon wid stick licking ah foolish ball. But me will go wid yuh jus' fe de atmosphere. Now lay back down an res' yaself."

Cilbert did as he was told. "As me getting better now, yuh cyan bring Lincoln tomorrow? Him mus' ah wonder where him papa der."

"Yes, him do," smiled Hortense. "Sometimes inna de marnin him look over to ya side of de bed an' him 'ave ah look 'pon him face dat ah say, 'where dat big lump dis marnin?'"

"Dat is good fe know. Yuh know, Hortense, sometime me ah

wonder wid all my work an' now dis sickness if him know who me is. Me always felt dat me never really get to know me papa so me don't waan Lincoln to feel dat same feeling."

"Nuh worry yaself, Cilbert. Lincoln know who yuh is. *Definitely.* Besides, me talk about yuh all de while to him."

"Dat nice," Cilbert nodded as he opened the newspaper. "Dat nice."

There were no tears upon the number 45 bus that evening as Jenny, unable to restrain her satisfied grin, looked into her food container to confirm yet again that Cilbert had eaten solids for the first time in weeks. "We will remember dis day," said Jenny to Hortense. "Cilbert finally turning de corner. An' even de cursed snow is finally melting! Yes, sa! Massa God is smiling 'pon we. Praise His very name."

Hearing a knock upon her bedroom door at 3 a.m. the following morning, Hortense got up, checked on Lincoln who was sleeping peacefully inside his cot and answered the door. She declined to switch on the light as Mary Skidmore's frame filled the doorway. She was fingering the crucifix that was hanging around her neck and her tired eyes were smudged with tears. Her lips were quivering, mouthing words that never produced no sound, and she continually shifted the weight on each foot.

"Wha' is it? Miss Mary? Somet'ing happen to Misser Sean? Stella alright?"

Shaking her head, Mary looked down to the carpet. She now wrapped her right hand around her crucifix. "I got a call from the hospital. Cilbert died half an hour ago. Bless his soul."

Mary's head dropped into Hortense's embrace as Hortense felt her heart almost stop. Unblinking, Hortense stared out into the darkness of the passage. Her breathing ceased for six seconds and her mind exploded with memories as she and Mary clung on to each other. In split seconds, Hortense recalled the first time she had blessed her eyes upon Cilbert at Elvira's birthday night party. Then an image of her brother David's dead body being washed and anointed by her mother. David's face morphed into that of Cilbert's and it was now Hortense performing the dead rituals as a rooster's call rang in her ears. Hortense moved away from Mary's arms, her steps unsure and her gaze distant. A cold numbness coursed through Hortense's veins and her eyes refused to blink even when her head hit the mattress.

Struggling to compose herself, Mary whimpered, "oh my, Jesus! Oh my Jesus! Let me tell Jenny and Jacob, they'll know how to look after yer. I'm not much good in these situations, Hortense."

Leaving Hortense staring blankly at the sleeping Lincoln, Mary pounded up the stairs and with both fists, hammered upon Jenny's door. A minute later, Jenny, Jacob, Stella and Mary came into Hortense's room, all of them stepping as if any undue pressure might deepen Hortense's grief. Someone switched on the light and they found Hortense staring at her framed wedding photograph, tracing Cilbert's image with her right index finger. Lincoln awoke and this prompted Hortense to emerge from her trance-like state. She picked him up, held him against her shoulder and began rocking him back to sleep, walking him around the room. She failed to acknowledge the people within the room. Unsure of what to do or say, Mary slipped out to put on the kettle. Jacob sat on the bed and dropped his head in sorrow. Stella, tears free-falling down her cheeks and dribbling over her lips, walked up to Hortense, placed her arms around her and buried her head into her back.

Rooted to the spot, Jenny had to lean against a wall to remain upright. From the pit of her soul, a scream was fighting ferociously to be unleashed and Jenny fought to restrain it, the pain in her struggle displaying itself in her face. She attempted to focus her gaze upon Hortense but she only saw the accusing glare of her mother. Her breathing accelerated and she began to feel dizzy. Inching away from the wall, she fell onto Jacob's lap, burying her face into his thighs. She slammed her eyes shut, refusing to allow tears to form and this act, added to the struggle to control the escaping emotions of her soul, propelled her into unconsciousness for two minutes. Nobody noticed.

Until the alarm clock rang at 6 a.m., Hortense lay upon the bed, staring at the ceiling. She was trying to remember the 'washing of the body' rituals that as a child she had witnessed her mother perform. She comforted herself with the belief that Cilbert will finally meet David in the afterlife. Lincoln fell asleep on top of her, his head snuggled between her breasts. Stella was curled up beside Hortense, still wearing her dressing gown, her eyes raw and reddened. Jenny's head still rested upon her husband's lap, her eyes now open but the fatigue from her inner battles was visible in her utterly wracked expression. Above her, Jacob whispered prayers to himself, his lips hardly moving and his eyes closed. Empty mugs of tea and coffee littered the dressing table alongside a half-opened packet of short tea biscuits. Standing unopened was a bottle of Irish whiskey that Mary had left at 4 a.m. before retiring to her own bed, unable to cope with everyone's grief.

The next day, Hortense, accompanied by Jacob, officially identified Cilbert's body. She was allowed to wash his naked body and place blessed water, that she had obtained from Mary, into his mouth and upon his chapped lips. She maintained a dignified presence, never failing in her duties and holding her grief at bay.

Cilbert was buried in a corner of Streatham cemetery on the 11th May, 1963. Spring had finally arrived and the clouds were parting, but the snow had left puddles in its wake all over the cemetery, causing the gravediggers problems with mudslides. Grieving family and friends, including Cilbert's workmate Delgado, Lester and his brother, the Skidmore family and members of Jacob's church, had their arms stretched out to the heavens. They sang hymns and spirituals by the graveside, not caring about their muddied footwear. Jenny sprinkled rum onto the lowered coffin as Hortense looked on, her expression blank. Hortense never sang a word.

Earlier in the day, speaking to the mourners in his small church hall, Jacob spoke of a 'determined, honest mon who loved his family more than anything'. The congregation clapped as Jacob, glancing at Hortense, felt her loss and anger.

Following the service, Jacob assured Hortense, "we will keep praying for Cilbert's soul to be delivered up in heaven. Cilbert an' myself never agree 'pon everyt'ing, but I owe him ah lot. Me never forget de way him ah help me wid me studies."

No emotion showing itself upon her face, Hortense answered,

"me t'ank yuh fe ya kind words. An' yuh give ah nice sweet service. But, preacher mon. *Don't* tell me dat heaven is under de earth. *Our* heaven was 'pon earth. Being togeder! Living we life. Dat was our heaven. Yuh cyan pray if yuh waan to, but ya prayers an' Miss Mary's prayers never save me husband. Massa God *never* lissen to yuh or meself so me don't see why me shoulda talk to Him! Nuh, sa! Praise de Lord, everyone ah say. Read de Bible preacher mon ah teach, sing ya hymn out loud so Massa God cyan hear, dey insist. But when we call 'pon Him. Him ignore we. All dese so-called religious people don't really know wha' life is wort'. Me don't mean to offend yuh, Jacob, but me affe speak how me feel. An' me feel dat *ya* God has forsaken me."

Shocked by Hortense's tone, Jacob attempted to smile away his embarrassment and went to receive other mourners.

Spotting a weeping woman standing on her own away from the congregation who had encircled Cilbert's grave, Hortense, recognising her, walked slowly up to her as compassion rose in her heart. The woman was wearing a fine cut black suit and an expensive black hat. Her black shoes were now mud-brown. The tissue she was holding in her left hand was soiled with tears and mascara.

"Almyna," Hortense called. "Why yuh standing der 'pon ya own?"

Stepping back a pace, Almyna scanned the mourners through damp eyes. She spotted Jenny who was glaring at her and she decided to turn around and walk away, feeling her presence would not be tolerated.

"Almyna!" Hortense called again.

Stopping in her tracks, Almyna waited for Hortense to come to her. The two women communicated something with their eyes. There they stood for a full minute before warmly hugging each other. They remained in their embrace for the next five minutes, no words of comfort or sorrow necessary. Jenny and Jacob looked on in disbelief as the rest of the mourners wondered who this woman was. Hortense invited Almyna back to her home for the wake and Almyna reminisced about Cilbert's childhood days – memories that Hortense was eager to hear. Watching Jacob and the members of his church, Hortense whispered to Almyna, "dey t'ink dat great Massa God will come down from de sky an' mek everyt'ing alright. Well, dem foolish to believe dat." Almyna nodded but was unsure what Hortense was talking about.

"Why did yuh ask me to come here?" asked Almyna.

"Becah me don't know how me coulda be vex wid someone who truly loved Cilbert," answered Hortense. "Remember when we reached port at Sout'ampton? Almyna, me see de way yuh look 'pon Cilbert when we go our separate ways. It was de first time me really feel sorry fe yuh. Me don't know how much yuh love ya husband, Hubert, but me know how much Cilbert meant to yuh. Yuh had ah right to attend his funeral as much as everybody else."

Slightly nodding, Almyna replied, "yes. Me cyan't deny dat. Even though me spread cruel words about him. So wha' yuh gwarn do now, Hortense?"

"Carry on," Hortense replied, determination in her eyes. "Raise me son de bes' way me know how. Inna Englan'. Everybody t'inking dat me should go home, but before me do dat me affe fulfil Cilby's ambition."

Jenny let it be known in quiet conversations that Almyna had tried to prise Cilbert and Hortense apart so she could win him herself. "She 'ave ah mighty nerve coming here so!" Jenny remarked. "An' nuh shame!"

On her way out of Hortense's apartment, Almyna noticed the sideway glances aimed at her. Jacob was standing by the door and Almyna said to him, "if me was ah stranger, me would nah know who is de widow – Hortense or Jenny. Me admit dat me nuh perfect. But before yuh judge me yuh should judge ya wife."

About to reply, Jacob bit his tongue for he didn't want to provoke a scene. For the remainder of the wake, Jacob studied the body language of Jenny and found a loss within her eyes that was profound and deep. A realisation came to him that perhaps Almyna's accusations were correct.

Suffering a churning sensation in the pit of his stomach, Jacob waited to confront Jenny when all the guests had departed and

Hortense was asleep.

Sitting on her bed in her dressing gown, Jenny was braiding her hair, humming a hymn that was sang beside Cilbert's grave. The sound she emitted was like a lament. Jacob was parked on a chair beside the dressing table, still wearing his suit. Working things over in his mind, he glanced at the alarm clock upon his bedside cabinet. The time was 12.45 a.m.

"Yuh loved him, didn't yuh," Jacob said quietly.

"Loved who?" replied Jenny. "Wha' yuh talking about, Jacob."

"Cilbert."

Jenny laughed but then she saw the seriousness of Jacob's expression. "Of course me loved him – as ah friend an' ah brudder-in-law."

"NUH," Jacob raised his voice. "Yuh loved him in de Biblical sense."

"Jacob, ya being silly. Mebbe yuh drink too much rum tonight. Yuh know it don't agree wid yuh."

"DON'T PATRONISE ME!" yelled Jacob, rising to his feet and walking over to his wife.

Dropping her comb on the bed and sensing Jacob's fury, for the first time since she knew him, Jenny was scared of her husband. She backed away to the bed headrest, bringing her knees against her chest. Jacob then chuckled – a self-mocking sound. He then got up again, unscrewed a rum bottle that was resting on the dressing table, poured himself half a glass and downed it in one gulp.

"Jacob, wha' is troubling yuh?" asked Jenny, struggling to hold onto her composure.

Pulling open a drawer beneath the dressing table, Jacob took out a Bible – it had belonged to his father.

"Swear 'pon dis dat yuh never loved Cilbert!" he ordered.

Jenny flinched and struggled for words. Her lips began to tremble.

"Dey say love is blind but me de blindest of all of dem," Jacob laughed, throwing the Bible to the floor. "Me papa did ah warn me about getting involve wid ya family. An' his words were true. *True* like ya ridiculous love fe Cilbert – God rest him soul. Me wonder if him ever knew?"

Realising that it would be pointless to deny Jacob's allegations, Jenny kept quiet. Never seeing him like this before, she feared for her life.

"It all mek sense now," Jacob resumed. "It's why yuh did waan me to go to Kingston an' to Englan' too. Me was so blind. Ya even cook Cilbert him birt'day dinner one time inna Kingston an' me did ponder fe ah moment if yuh an' Cilbert had somet'ing going on. But me put it outta me mind, telling meself dat would be ridiculous."

Covering her face with her pillow, Jenny could do nothing but cry.

"*Me* should be de one bawling!" Jacob ranted. "Wha' was ya plan? To tek ya sister husband away? Wha' kinda madness is dat? Mebbe me should tell her. Hortense should not be blinded to ya wickedness!"

"NUH, JACOB," Jenny suddenly pleaded, throwing her pillow upon the bed, her tears smudged upon her face. "Nuh, Jacob. If yuh do dat me don't know wha' me should do wid meself. Me will *tek* me own life!"

"An' yuh would, too," Jacob laughed. "Ya love fe ya sister me don't doubt an' me know dat if Hortense look 'pon yuh wid scorn it will destroy yuh. An' dat is why dis palava is so hard to understan'. Knowing dat if Hortense ever found out about ya mad lust, she woulda curse yuh 'til ya grave. An' yuh woulda be an outcast. But ya still follow Hortense an' Cilbert wherever dem go."

Jacob poured himself another drink. He was now walking on unsteady legs. His lips were smirking but his eyes betrayed devastation. "Jus' de one question me waan to ask yuh, me *sweetheart*. Why did yuh marry me?"

Jenny couldn't answer.

"An' yuh cyan't even come up wid an excuse fe dat! Lord me God! Wha' kinda Jezebel me get meself involved wid? Almyna might be many t'ings, but at least she honest. Her love fe Cilbert was plain an' clear. But *yuh*! Deceitful, manipulative, plotting! Yuh really are like Anancy. Me shoulda pay more attention to ya Gran'mama Melody when she tell me ya like Anancy."

Burying her head into the mattress, Jenny sobbed, "yuh right.

But me beg yuh not to tell Hortense. Cilbert dead now."

"Yuh t'ink me bad-minded like yuh?" Jacob replied. "Hortense has lost David already an' now Cilbert. Yuh t'ink me waan to add to her grief?"

"T'ank yuh fe dat, Jacob," Jenny managed.

"Me *not* doing dis fe yuh! Fe Hortense's sake. De crazy t'ing is all she 'ave left in dis world to love is Lincoln an' yuh! Fate's cruelty mocks we sometimes."

"Me tried to fight dis t'ing me had fe Cilbert. Jacob, yuh mus' believe dat."

"Yuh asking me to believe anyt'ing yuh say? Me really don't know where we go from here. If we divorce den as ah so called preacher mon, me would lose ah certain respect even though me have plenty reason to do jus' dat. An' my papa would tell me 'I told yuh so'. But how cyan I live wid ah woman who nuh love me?"

Jacob glared at Jenny, expecting some kind of reply, his heart wanting to hear that at least she had some feelings for him. Jenny couldn't meet her husband's eyes, afraid of his expression. An expression that bore the mark of the unloved.

Filling his glass again, Jacob tottered to his side of the bed and sat down, peering out the window. Tears were falling down his cheeks. Jenny closed her eyes and imagined she was in her father's embrace.

Seven days following the funeral, Jenny found Hortense in Mary's back garden trying to get Lincoln to sleep. She was humming a spiritual that she had learned from her grandfather, enjoying the warm touch of the spring sun that shone upon her face.

"Hortense," Jenny called softly. "Ya sure yuh don't waan to come to Jamaica wid me? Papa would love to see yuh. Mama too. Me could still get yuh ah ticket 'pon de same flight. Mebbe if yuh tek Lincoln yuh cyan introduce him to Cilbert family?"

"Cilbert family?" Hortense mocked, hardening her eyebrows. "Dey never did waan me to marry him so why should me mek dem see Lincoln? An' der is not'ing inna Jamaica fe me. Cilbert is buried *here,* an' me don't waan to leave him jus' yet. Him soul might t'ink me abandon him. Nuh, sa! Jenny, yuh gwarn to Jamaica an' stop worry about me. Lincoln an' meself will be alright. Say hello to Levi an' Carmesha fe me when yuh reach."

Hortense returned to her humming as Jenny placed a comforting hand upon Hortense's left shoulder. "Me will, Hortense. But it grieves me to leave yuh like dis. Yuh ah big woman now Hortense an' yuh don't need ya big sister so much."

"Wha' do yuh mean by dat," queried Hortense.

"When me reach Jamaica me 'ave some t'inking to do of me own but don't worry about dat," answered Jenny. "Fate might lead we to different paths but me will always love yuh dearly. Me swear to dat."

Clutching Jenny's hand, Hortense managed a smile. "Jenny," she called.

"Wha' is it, Hortense."

"Do yuh t'ink dat we are cursed?"

"Wha' do yuh mean?"

"Yuh remember Papa's story about Kofi an' everybody."

"Yes."

"Well, Papa went back to him hometown an' affe bury him mama. David gone America an' when him come back deat' claim him. Now Cilby dead."

Jenny thought about it. "Nuh, Hortense. It's jus' coincidence an' bad fortune. Don't worry yaself about it."

Hortense's grip on Jenny's hand tightened. "Be careful, Jenny. Me don't waan to lose yuh. Me don't t'ink me could tek dat."

"Me will be alright. Mebbe nex' time yuh cyan come wid me an' bring Lincoln?"

"Nuh, Jenny. Me cyan't do dat! Me don't waan nuh curse inna Jamaica to trouble him. Yuh keep yaself safe."

Smiling and masking her own fears, Jenny kissed Hortense upon the forehead and released her grip. Hortense resumed her humming.

"Wha' song is dat, Hortense?"

"Yuh don't remember, Jenny? It's somet'ing Gran'papa Neville teach me to sing whenever me sad. Me used to sing it under our tree after David dead."

Jenny tried to recall the words but Hortense had already closed her eyes, concentrated her brow and began singing.

"Coromanty an' Ashanti
An dose who fished inna de sacred Oti
Crawled wid iron rattle 'pon de Atlantic
Remembering der mudders while feeling sea-sick
But der spirits never grow weary.
Fallen kins never bruk der souls
Eating chicken claw soup from dutty bowls
But der spirits never grow weary
Forced to chop down de giant silk cotton tree
Praying to Anancy to set dem free
An' der spirits never grow weary
Captained by Cudjoe an' Queen Nanny
Putting up resistance, stomping 'pon slavery
We spirits never grow weary
Dem kill Sam Sharp an' udders too
Our hand was made strong an' our resistance grew
We spirits never grow weary
De fallen will be remembered in Island Songs
Der souls above will right our wrongs
An' we spirits will never grow weary
We kidren will march into de future
Armed with Island Songs, remembering our ancestor
Nuh, sa, oh nuh
We spirits will never grow weary
So walk wid talawa, lift up ya head high
For we have survived, nuh mon cyan deny
Treasure de dead an' look to de future
For now is de time dat Massa God will deliver
Oh nuh, sa! How could we spirits ever get weary."

Tears were streaming down Jenny's face as she hugged her sister again, kissing her upon the cheek. There they remained for the next hour, immersed in their shared history while listening to the infant sounds of Lincoln who fought to claim sleep.

Chapter Eighteen

Claremont, Jamaica
July 1963

Jenny had been received warmly by her extended family and old friends. The natural mystic of rural Jamaica added to the calming North Coast breezes, soothed away her melancholy and refreshed her dormant spirit. Sights and sounds that she had taken for granted in her childhood were now a pleasure to be experienced. Upon arrival at her childhood home she ran to the Blue Mahoe tree where she and Hortense shared untold sweet and unpleasant memories. She would hike up to her father's plot and spend lazy afternoons listening to his childhood recollections beneath the palm groves. Joseph was now fit and well after receiving treatment at a Kingston hospital for his prostrate problem. Jenny found that her father was now at ease with himself, greeting everyone he met with a welcoming smile and once he began reciting old Maroon tales and legends, it was a mighty task to stop him.

The proud parents of three boys and living at Isaac's house, Carmesha and Levi wanted to know everything about London. No vivid description would satisfy their hunger. Isaac himself suffered a pride overload as Jenny informed him of Jacob's establishment of a church in Brixton. Jenny found that her father-in-law had allowed humour to enter his life and he enjoyed the company of his three grandsons. Grandpapa Neville, bedridden and bent with age, feasted his eyes upon photographs of Lincoln and couldn't thank Jenny enough for bringing the images to him. "Me 'ave made me sacrifices fe de bwai an' me curse is finally over," assured Neville. "He is de first of we family to be born inna foreign land an' his seed will grow mighty becah him 'ave t'ree winds flowing t'rough him.

De winds of Africa, Jamaica an' now Englan'. Yes, sa! Tribulation might buil' many stumbling blocks fe de bwai but Lincoln will conquer dem all. Me jus' know dat."

Riding into Claremont market square upon a donkey, Jenny laughed at the wolf whistles and admiring glances aimed at her. She bantered with the men who frequented the bars and was not shy to shout her appreciation to the bare-backed men who toiled in the fields. Forgetting Jacob in London and her guilt evaporating, Jenny felt as free as a doctor bird, her heart no longer chained to one man, the spell of her obsession finally over. One night, Joseph remarked to Amy, "it's like she come back wid ah new character? So good to see her smiling an' flinging away dat mighty intensity."

But Jenny was secretly observed from a distance by her concerned mother, Amy, who refused to believe that her daughter could be so blissful with Cilbert having passed away only nine weeks ago and Hortense still grief-stricken. Amy bided her time until one afternoon, when Jenny was idling under her favourite tree enjoying the taste of a mango and blessing her eyes upon the green, southern ranges that kissed the wispy clouds.

"Are yuh going back to ya husband?" Amy asked, her tone confrontational.

"Wha' kind of question is dat, Mama?" Jenny replied.

"Well, me real question is, why yuh look so damn pleased wid yaself when de mon of ya dreams is dead inna Englan' soil?"

Jenny paused from eating her fruit and regarded her mother as if she was a bad smell. "Mama, me know yuh don't t'ink good of me but me don't expect dem kinda nasty t'ings coming from ya mout'! Wicked yuh wicked! How could yuh ever believe dem kinda t'ing? See Massa God don't strike yuh down! Ya old an' cranky now an' mebbe ya 'fraid dat Papa will tek up him foot an' leave yuh once more. But *don't* talk dem kinda ways to me! Yuh jus' cyan't tolerate dat Papa love me more dan yuh so yuh affe talk nastiness inna me ears. Yuh cyan't tek it! Dog heart yuh ah dog heart!"

Smiling away her daughter's insults, Amy replied, "Jenny, me is ya mama. Yuh cyan't change dat. An' me know yuh. Know yuh too well. Yuh mus' t'ink dat nuhbody ah watch yuh when Hortense bring Cilbert here fe de first time. Yuh mus' ah t'ink dat nuhbody ah notice de way yuh look 'pon Cilbert at Hortense's wedding. Jenny, mebbe yuh cyan fool Papa an' Gran'papa, but yuh cyan't fool me. Me raise yuh an' come wise to ya ways."

"Yuh come wise to not'ing, Mama! Yuh did never care about me an' de foolishness yuh ah talk is jus' to spite me. Why don't yuh jus' leave me be? Becah ya heart has always been cool like mountain stream. De only t'ing yuh ever love was David an' since him dead, yuh turn into ah somebody wid nuh feeling, nuh spirit. Ah *rockstone* heart! Yuh nuh more dan ah *duppy!* Yuh forget long ago dat yuh 'ave two girl chile. So *yuh* cyan't talk to me about not'ing!"

Injured by her daughter's remarks, Amy decided to keep her tone measured. "Yes, yuh cyan accuse me of anyt'ing yuh waan. Some of it mebbe true an' some of it untrue. But Jenny, yuh should nah lie to yaself. From de first moment dat me set me eyes 'pon Cilbert at me dinner table, me see de way yuh look 'pon him, sight de way yuh respond to him an' me said to meself, 'lord 'ave mercy, dis mon capture me two daughter heart.' Yes, sa! Deny it if yuh waan to but yuh will *never* convince me. Yuh always did waan wha' Hortense did 'ave fe her own, weder it was ah dress or even ah ripe mango. Sometimes me wonder if yuh woulda hunger after Cilbert if him never did marry Hortense. Me don't tink so! De only t'ing dat is ah surprise is dat Hortense never ketch on. Lord 'ave mercy! If she ever find out..."

Raw emotion rising within her, Jenny protested, "it nah go so, Mama! It nah go so! Why yuh nah believe me?" She clenched her fist and drew it back.

Refusing to back away an inch, Amy retorted, "yes, dat is always ya way. When people touch 'pon de trut', yuh resort to violence. De las' resort of somebody who cyan't face de trut'! So wha' yuh gwarn to do? Lick down ya own cranky an' old mudder?"

Relaxing her fist, Jenny dropped her sight to the ground. Amy detected the tears forming within her daughters eyes. "Melody was right about yuh," Amy affirmed. "Jus' like Anancy yuh is. Wily, manipulative an' secretive, always putting 'pon ah false, plastic face.

Me tried to tell yuh before but yuh never did waan talk to me. Remember de time before yuh set sail to Englan'? Yuh knew dat me did ah know. Yes, sa. An' now Cilbert dead an' yuh dream shatter yuh come running home like de spoil girl yuh is. *Leaving* Hortense 'pon her own. Only caring about ya own grief. An' yuh call me ah dog-heart!"

Grasping for the lapels upon Amy's frock, Jenny could not stem her tears. Her expression was desperate. "We cyan't choose de one we love, Mama. Me tried to fight it. Mama, me waan to stay here. Start afresh. Please, Mama? Let me work wid Papa 'pon we plot. Let me jus' live ah simple life here so."

"Wha' about Jacob? Yuh marry him an' yuh affe carry de responsibility of dat. He's ah good mon. Yuh 'ave wha' most women around here would chop off der baby toe for. Count ya blessings an' love de one yuh wid! Dat is de way it ah go wid women from dese parts. We jus' get on wid it, never complaining."

"Mama," Jenny croaked, her vision becoming blurred. "Me don't love him. Me never did love him."

"Dat don't 'ave not'ing to do wid it!" Amy thundered. She regarded the now defeated expression of her daughter. "Yuh mek ya choice so yuh affe live wid it."

"But me not jus' ah wife, jus' ah woman who wait fe ah mon to ask dem to marry. Nuh! Dis is where me belong, where me born an' grow. Me waan to look after Papa when sickness ah ketch him an' when his back start bend."

"*Dat* is *my* duty to look after Joseph. Ya duty is to stan' beside Jacob. An' besides, how long yuh t'ink yuh coulda live apart from Hortense? Mebbe Hortense don't feel dat she need ya presence now, an' me guess dat is why yuh run back here. Mebbe yuh don't realise it yet, but *she* is de love of ya life. Oh yes, sa! Mebbe yuh will see it when yuh near de end. When she moved out me know it tear yuh apart. Yuh could nah sleep at all. Even when she used to stay over at Gran'papa's yuh kick up ah mighty fuss, causing all kinda contention wid me. Although Cilbert tickled ya fancy it was Hortense yuh follow when she move to Kingston. Yes, sa! It is ah fate t'ing dat yuh cyan do not'ing about. Yuh t'ink we don't talk about dis? Me, ya papa an' Gran'papa Neville? It is Hortense yuh follow when she sail to Englan'. Everybody could see how tortured yuh were widout her. Even Gran'papa Neville say so. Yuh really t'ink yuh coulda live here an' she live t'ousands an' t'ousands of miles away? Nuh, sa! Jenny, me know yuh, me raise yuh an' watch yuh. Ya place in dis world is to be close to Hortense. It has been so since David dead. Fulfil ya promise to David! Me place is to be close to Joseph an' inna Claremont. Mebbe one day yuh cyan come back here when ya back is bent an' when it's ya time to res'. But *not* yet."

Palming away her tears, Jenny realised her mother was right. She looked out to the fields behind Amy and in her inner vision saw Hortense and herself as children, riding the family donkey, laughing and joking as they went along. She could almost feel Hortense's arms wrapped around her waist, she could sense Hortense's breathing into her neck as her sister cuddled behind her at night. "Jenny, if bugaboo trouble me tonight, box de damn t'ing away from me an' stamp 'pon it's tail fe me," Hortense would jest before falling asleep.

"Alright, Mama," Jenny finally conceded, making no attempt to swab away her tears. "But if yuh ever say ah word about dis to *anyone*, me will never say ah godly word to yuh again!"

"Still defiant an' feisty even when yuh lose de argument," Amy laughed. "But yuh 'ave nuh cause fe worry. Me 'ave nuh intention of telling anyone. Besides, me 'ave Hortense to t'ink about. But me warn yuh, ya better look after her right an' be nice to Jacob. Him love yuh so much an' will do anyt'ing fe yuh. Count ya blessings, Jenny, becah fortune don't shine so bright 'pon de masses. Me t'ought dat living inna Trenchtown woulda teach yuh dat."

Struggling to hold on to her emotions, Jenny blurted out, "why yuh so cruel, Mama? Wha' did me 'ave when Papa gone? Not'ing, Mama. Yuh never love me! Me go ah school an' people cuss me. Me work 'pon de stall an' people still ah cuss me. Cilbert did talk to me first! Me t'ought dat Hortense would nah like it if me find meself ah bwai-friend'. ME WAS T'INKING OF *HER*. Why yuh so cruel to me? It was *me* who look after Hortense when David dead. *Me*!"

Pounding her fists into the grass, Jenny began shaking her head and wailing. With the reality of her mother's words striking home, Jenny was on the verge of a breakdown. She collasped to the turf in utter turmoil, masking her face with her palms, unable to stem her screams.

Taking pity upon her daughter, Amy knelt down and stroked Jenny's trembling hands. It deeply pained Amy to know that Hortense was obviously grief-stricken and to see Jenny in such a state. "We are all damaged an' marked by events dat we 'ave nuh control over," Amy said. "Me as much as anyone. Perhaps even more so. It nah nice dat me fader look 'pon me as ah girl chile an' his eyes wished fe ah son. How did me resent dat! Me still do. Everybody marked by some grievance or some unjus' t'ing dat ah happen to dem, including Carmesha, Levi an' even ya papa. Yuh love ya papa so blind but yuh never stop an' wonder why him ah give yuh so much attention. It's becah yuh look like him mudder! Hortense love yuh blind too an' she cyan't see ya Anancy-like ways. We all 'ave to accept we weaknesses an' carry on, learn to live wid cruel fate. Me never believe when ya fader say, 'He's ah cruel God'. Nuh, sa. He jus' give we test. An' everybody 'ave to pass t'rough His tests. Rich or poor. Me t'ought David's deat' would vanquish me, part of me died dat night when Isaac give we de bad news. An' ya probably right, at dat time me was not ah fit mudder, ignoring me daughters dem. Now is de time of ya test, Jenny. But yuh will get t'rough it. Me know yuh will."

Mother and daughter remained under the shade of the tree until the sun dipped below the western hills and when they returned home, linking arms, Amy felt she at last had regained her middle child.

Seven days later, Jenny was packing her suitcase. She had already bade a tearful farewell to her father and now she felt her mother's concerned eyes watching her every move. A taxi driver impatiently palmed his horn outside. As Jenny zipped up her luggage, she turned around and saw Amy standing close to her with the old family Bible held in her hands. "Jenny, tek dis."

"Mama, dat's de Bible Gran'papa give yuh. Me cyan't tek dat."

"Jenny, *tek* it. It offer yuh comfort when yuh ah girl chile, an' it might offer yuh comfort now yuh fully grown. Tek it."

Jenny knew she couldn't refuse the gift and she received the book from her mother and carefully placed it into her hand luggage. Amy smiled, kissed her daughter upon the forehead and said, "Tell Hortense we're all t'inking of her an' send we love. Mek sure yuh give her de rum. An' never forget it's not only ya papa dat love yuh. May Massa God bless ya steps."

Returning to London, Jenny accepted the hugs and kisses from Hortense as Jacob picked up her luggage without offering any welcome. Following a chicken, rice and peas dinner, Jenny played with Lincoln before climbing the stairs to her apartment where Jacob sat brooding in his chair beside the dressing table. Jenny noticed he still had the mark of the unloved within his eyes. She wondered what he would do to her but she said to herself, '*not'ing* will keep me away from me sister'.

Taking off her coat, Jenny found her Bible in her hand luggage, cautiously sat on the bed and began reading. Jacob watched her every movement. "As yuh couldn't deny ya love fe Cilbert, me cyan't deny me love fe yuh," he said. "From me ah bwai chile me 'ave watched yuh an' me 'ave never looked 'pon anybody else. It's funny, while yuh was away Hortense was talking about curses. She seems to t'ink dat becah of wha' Kofi did to de slavemaster's family, ya family has been hexed, especially de males. It's when she tell me about her paranoia dat I realised I have my own curse – loving yuh. Even t'ough wha' has happened, I realised I cyan't live widout yuh. Dat is my curse."

Jenny suffered a pang of guilt as Jacob continued. "Me main ambition now is to set up de church good an' proper. Find ah decent building an' increase numbers of de congregation. Dat is me first priority. An' as me do dat *yuh* will be by me side *every* step of de way. An' by God *yuh* learn to love me. Yuh *will* yield to sex when I need it. Nuh more excuses. Yuh will smile when we out togeder. As far as anybody else is concerned, we 'ave ah happy, blissful marriage. Yuh might t'ink dis is cruel. But yuh 'ave revealed ya hand to me – I finally know ya weakness an' yuh 'ave been exploiting my weakness since me know yuh. An' if yuh don't comply I will tell Hortense everyt'ing. Do yuh agree wid everyt'ing I say?"

Raising her eyes over the pages, Jenny stared blankly at the wall. Five minutes later she finally nodded her acceptance of Jacob's terms.

"We will start afresh," Jacob continued. "An' as yuh said. Cilbert *is* dead. An' perhaps ah liccle piece of all of us dead since we reach here. Dey say dat ah chile should not 'ave to pay fe de fader's sins. But my God. *He* meks sure we pay. Ya paying fe Joseph an' I'm paying fe my fader."

Epilogue

Norman Manley International Airport, Kingston
September, 2003

Jenny watched two male Jamaican deportees, accompanied by three British police officers, being met by the Kingston constabulary as she descended the steps of the British Airways flight. "Dey give we decent Jamaicans ah bad name," she whispered to Hortense. "If it's crack or gun dem ah deal wid, den me hope dey t'row dem inna jailhouse an' fling de key inna de deepest pit toilet dey cyan find."

Not paying attention to her sister's comments, Hortense felt the burning Kingston sun upon her head and pulled off her white cardigan. Using her right hand to shield the sun from her eyes, she looked out to a shimmering Kingston harbour in the distance and in her memories saw herself and Cilbert stepping aboard *The Genovese Madonna* over forty years ago. Now, she would not admit it to her sister or anyone else but she felt like a foreigner. "Me forget how Jamaica so hot," she smiled, masking her apprehension.

"Yuh soon get used to it again," replied Jenny.

Waiting for what seemed an eternity to collect their luggage, the now silver-haired sisters, passed through customs; caution marked Hortense's steps. "Ya sure Junior will be here to greet we?" Hortense fretted. "Me hear stories about returning Jamaicans being kidnapped an' killed by bogus taxi driver!"

"Stop fret, Hortense. Junior *will* be here."

They went through the concourse of the airport and out into the noisy, bustling forecourt where expectant families and friends jostled for room against the barrier rail, awaiting their loved ones and the chance of foreign currency. Porters, not wearing any recognisable uniforms, approached the sisters and offered to carry their luggage in hope of financial reward. "Do me know yuh?"

Hortense challenged. "How me know yuh nah run off wid me t'ings? Go'long, beggar mon an' find yaself ah proper job!"

Linking arms, Jenny whispered, "*stop* being so nervous. Come, Junior waiting fe we inna de car park."

Junior, thirty-two years old and Joseph's great grandson, had inherited the now dead Maroon's genes and he stood by his taxi, towering over everyone at an impressive six foot five. Hortense looked upon him in astonishment, her mind not quite coming to terms that she was looking at her brother David's grandson. He took their baggage and placed it in the boot of his car and watching his every move, Hortense recognised David's ready smile. She felt she was observing a ghost. "Somet'ing de matter?" Junior asked.

"Nuh, sa," Hortense replied. "Ya jus' remind me of me sweet brudder. How is ya papa, Daniel?"

"Oh, him alright. But he did withdraw himself ah liccle when de old mon Neville pass away. Ah sore loss was dat to him. Neville reach de mighty age of ninety-eight."

"Yes, me know dat, Junior," replied Hortense. "Me 'ave been away fe ah very long time but me cyan read letter!"

Weary from the nine hour flight, Jenny and Hortense napped in the back seat. Driving through Kingston, the sleeping Hortense never witnessed the Americanisation of Jamaica's capital. Advertisements for Kentucky Fried Chicken, McDonalds and Coca-Cola seemed to appear on every highway, food stores sold American rice, and the Jamaicans queueing outside the American embassy for the chance of visas seemed to be all wearing baseball caps. They stretched over two blocks with little hope expressed in their eyes. The music sounding out from Junior's car radio was laced with Hip Hop, R and B and just a small serving of reggae.

Waking up when Junior sped through Linstead, Hortense gazed out the window. She could now see the misty-cloaked hills, lush green valleys and the road-side vendors. Old, silver-bearded men with few teeth went by on donkeys and Hortense greeted them all, her feeling of trepidation now floating away. She ordered Junior to pull up and she bought some water coconuts and a jackfruit. "Yuh sure dem sweet an' fresh?" she challenged the vendor.

"Of course, Miss. Me would never sell anyt'ing stale, especially to someone old. Dat would be ah mighty disrespect."

"Ya words better ring true becah if me discover dat de fruit bad me gwarn tell me driver to turn around an' me will fling ya fruit inna ya face an' mosh up ya cart. Good day to yuh an' live good!"

"Hortense! Yuh nah easy," grinned Junior as he checked his rear view mirror and saw the vendor shaking his head and laughing. "As ah liccle bwai me hear about ya nettle tongue but me never imagine yuh still possess it now yuh head turn grey."

"Don't talk about me age!"

Following a three-hour journey, they had reached the Fish On The Mount restaurant, Levi and Carmesha's home and business. They had renovated and built extensions to Isaac's old house. Where the pig pen and the chicken coop once stood, was now a paved area for outside dining. White umbrellas shaded every round table and the tang of roasting fish flavoured the air.

David's son, Daniel, now fifty-two years old, was the first to greet Hortense and Jenny from out of the car from the crowd that had gathered. His hair was as black as the rural Jamaican night and no cares and stresses had yet to touch his forehead. Feeling overwhelmed and a little frightened, Hortense had to be cajoled out of the car. David escorted his two aunts into the house and there inside, a crying Carmesha, now into her seventies but looking much younger than Hortense and Jenny, rushed up to them both, hugging them warmly. Even Jenny could not deny her tears and the three of them remained holding one another for five minutes. No words were necessary as numerous cousins looked on, clapping happily, many of them blessing their eyes upon Hortense for the first time. "Welcome home, Hortense!" Carmesha finally said. "An', Jenny, t'ank yuh fe bringing her home."

His steps unsure but his stance upright, the grey-locked Levi emerged from an adjoining room. His heavy-lidded eyes sparkled with memories and his lips curled into a warm grin. "Nettle Tongue!" he rasped as a greeting to Hortense. "Yuh don't change at all. Yuh still 'ave fire inna ya eyes!"

Walking over to Levi, Hortense fingered his locks and caressed the bald pate upon his head. She then broke out into a knowing grin. "Levi, didn't me tell yuh dat yuh could nah live near mountain top all ya life? Dis place is magnificent! Now, me hungry! Where de food der?"

Hortense and Jenny feasted upon a mackerel and snapper dinner with ackee, bammy, breadfruit, spinach, peppers, scallion, ardough bread and rum cake. This was washed down with the finest Appleton rum, mixed with mango juice and goat's milk. Hortense was introduced to all the relations she had yet to meet and she was soon overcome at the generosity and goodwill showered upon her. She couldn't stop crying. How Cilbert would have loved this homecoming, she thought. Jenny was in deep discussion with Levi, Jacob's name surfacing time and again. They seemed to come to an agreement upon something as Levi nodded and embraced his sister-in-law.

As the sun began its descent into the western sky, Hortense, her fears and doubts of returning home for good now forgotten, helped Carmesha with the washing up. "Carmesha, before me res' me head an' go to de old house, me waan go up to de family burial plot. Yuh t'ink Junior coulda drive me?"

"Of course, Hortense. Nuh problem. Me forget dat yuh never bless ya eyes 'pon Amy an' Joseph burial plot. Junior!"

Passing through Claremont market, Hortense thought it hadn't changed much, save for a few shopfronts that advertised Jamaican rum and the tarmac road that had replaced the dusty route. But the far-off hills were specked with new houses, many of them as impressive as any she had seen back in London. Only a handful of men worked in the fields, Hortense found, and none of them were young. Goats still walked their own sure-footed paths, skinny dogs still yapped their unnecessary barks and chickens still wandered with a carefree abandon, utterly unaware of their fate. Radios tuned into the BBC's *World Service* and ghetto blasters seemed to sound out from everywhere, and Hortense wished her old bones could dance like she used to one more time. She closed her eyes and saw herself jigging at Elvira's birthday night party almost fifty years ago. "Me was de best," she whispered to herself. "Oh yes! Me was de best!"

Finally reaching Joseph's old plot of overgrown land, Hortense and Jenny climbed out of the car and gasped at the sheer natural beauty that surrounded them. For Hortense, Junior's car instantly became an unwanted intruder as she blessed her eyes upon many shades of green, browns and bright yellows. Untouched valleys, cast in lengthening shadows and ripe in mangroves, seemed to be holding on to some long-held secret and the glittering stream that sliced through the uplands, banked by sentinels of Blue Mahoe trees, only added to the mystery. The hills stretched and rose into the distance, as if they were seeking a meeting with the heavens and the natural mystic, ebbing and flowing in the gentle, Caribbean breezes, rekindled Hortense, Jenny and Carmesha's memories of their treasured past and prompted imaginings of their children's and grandchildren's great futures.

Leading Jenny and Hortense to the family burial plot, Carmesha reminisced of her years living in the misted hills. Blissful times, she thought, and such a good upbringing for her sons. Amy had been Carmesha's best friend and confidante and her death was a particularly harsh blow for her. Indeed, it was Amy who suggested that Levi and Carmesha should invest their money in a business venture to capitalise upon the returning Jamaicans from abroad. The Fish On The Mount restaurant was an instant success and it was *the* place to dine in the area.

David's grave had now been marked by a headstone and the Egyptian Ankh cross. Hortense, who had returned to the faith of her childhood, went to David's place of rest first and cleared away the leaves and dry earth that had rested upon it with her handkerchief. She then kissed the cross, closed her eyes and said a quiet prayer. Meanwhile, Jenny had dropped to her knees at her mother's last resting place, a sense of guilt probed her conscience for she had divorced Jacob a year after her mother's death. Finally meeting beside Joseph's burial plot, Hortense said to Jenny, "me suppose der ways are gone fe ever, y'know, der old customs an' traditions. Only we remember dem but soon we will join dem. An' when we pass on our ways will be forgotten too."

"Don't yuh ever regret dat Cilbert isn't bury at his place of birth?" Jenny asked.

"Nuh, sa. From de day me meet him he was talking about Englan'. Dat was his dream so he should res' der. Me know he'll be waiting fe me. Me feel bad about Jacob inna Englan' though. At me son wedding him did look so alone, so old. Me try to deny it but me feel old too. Me Island Song will soon be over."

"Oh, Hortense! Stop ya dead talk! Yuh 'ave many years left inna ya bones! An' as for Jacob, me was talking about him wid Levi. Levi will send Junior to Englan' to bring him home. For nuh matter our differences, he belongs here."

Breaking out into a smile, Hortense said, "dat's good of yuh, Jenny. Dat is good. Me still don't understan' why yuh two divorce but Jacob is ah good mon. Yuh never know? Inna de twilight of ya lives yuh might feel dat yuh waan keep each udder company?"

Returning Hortense's smile, Jenny didn't reply.

The house where Jenny and Hortense were born had also been refurbished and extended. An inside toilet had been constructed and the verandah was spacious enough for a family to eat their meals there and watch the setting sun dip beyond the western hills. The crickets in the fields still debated at night and the stars above seemed to shine brighter here than anywhere else. Joseph's ring of flowers offered welcoming colour around the house and the mambay mango tree had grown strong and fruitful, its roots creeping under the stonework at the back of the building. Once inside Jenny complained that her nephews and other relations hadn't kept the place as spick and span as they had promised while she had been away. "Stop fussing, Jenny," Hortense rebuked. "Yuh should be t'ankful dat de place wasn't burgled! It look lovely to me. Although it seem ah bit ghostly to me. So quiet."

Finally retiring to a double bed with an accommodating mattress, Jenny unpacked her old Bible and turned to the pages of Genesis. Looking on from her side of the bed, Hortense remarked, "Jenny, me really an' truly hope me pass away before yuh."

"Hortense! How cyan yuh say such ah t'ing!"

"Becah me waan to meet an' greet de angels before yuh come up an' claim dem fe yaself, talking an' nagging der ears off! As a chile yuh did always waan wha' me 'ave."

Smiling, Jenny replied, "only becah me love yuh, Hortense. Me waan to share everyt'ing wid yuh. Now res' ya head. Yuh come home an' me will look after yuh like me promise David."

Closing her eyes, Hortense found a deep comfort in her sister's words. She fell asleep with a smile on her face.

Acknowledgments

ISLAND SONGS IS DEDICATED TO MY GRANDFATHER,
LOUIS 'CHARLIE' WHEATLE, 1900-1986
– A TRUE MAROON.

I would like to thank David Shelley for displaying faith in me as well as the team at Allison & Busby. My deepest gratitude goes out to Laura Susijn who has stood by me thick and thin – the drinks will soon be on me! Leo Hollis, you're a 'producer' supreme! Thanks for your counsel, time and installing a belief in me. My appreciation goes out to the Arts Council of England for giving me support in the writing of this novel. My heartfelt thanks to my two aunts, Hermine and Lilleth, for sharing with me such vivid recollections of growing up in Jamaica in the middle of the 20th century. Much credit to my father, Alfred, for giving me such a colorful memory of his own passage from Jamaica to England in 1954. Special appreciation to my sisters, Margaret and Hope, for offering me so much understanding and compassion. Big mention to my daughter, Serena – thanks for everything. A massive shout to my sons, Marvin and Tyrone – you are Jedis now! My cousins, Jackie, Debbie, Gary, Junior, Sharon, I have not forgotten you. Shout-outs to all the Wheatle's out there – I didn't realize there were so many! Special mention to those living in Old Harbour, St Catherine, where they serve the tastiest fish and bammy on the island. And big up to those dwelling in Papine, Kingston – I may be biased but Papine has *the* best market in Kingston. Respect to all those who have supported me during my writing career, especially the fan who came into the Index Book Store in Brixton whilst I was performing a signing and presented to me a chocolate herb bar!

"Jamaicans have such a range of words describing phenomena so neatly and I think this is a testimony to their combativeness...they are a breed apart, in my estimation of any people."

Walter Rodney – lecturer, political activist.

Readers' Notes

When I was twelve years of age and living in a children's home in a quiet corner of Surrey, I wanted to know about the circumstances that had led me to living in care since I was four. At the time I didn't know my parents full names or even what nationality they were. My housemother informed me that for a reading of my file, my social worker had to be present. I waited a week and when that huge file was opened, thick as two hardback copies of *War and Peace*, the most startling thing that I learned was that I had four older sisters and one brother, all on my mother's side. Unfortunately, the file didn't say where they were.

I went to my bed that night asking one question: how could my mother love and care for her other children but not me? The question stayed with me for years and years, and as I went through the journey of my life, I discovered that this question is not just posed by people who grew up in council care. I have met people from all walks of life and have found that a son may feel that his father has no time for him but adores his sister, or a daughter can be convinced that her mother doesn't love her but loves her brother.

I explored this theme in my novel *East of Acre Lane* but I wanted to examine it further in *Island Songs*. Of course, great authors before me have written about this subject matter. *East of Eden* by John Steinbeck and *The Thorn Birds* by Coleen McCulloch are just two examples.

It was when I made a pilgrimage to Bob Marley's birthplace, a tiny village called Nine Mile in the garden parish of Jamaica, St Anne, that I found I had my setting for my 'big love epic'. The rich green colours, the still jackfruit trees, perfect sky and the beautiful hills just demanded for someone to set a story there.

When I sat down to sketch the characters, I had in my mind two brothers who would be the main protagonists. I decided they would have a Cain and Abel-like relationship with one favoured and adored by the father and the other despised. What changed my mind was Jamaican women. Within my own family, the women are full of life, colour, complexity, feistiness and great spirit. In my opinion it is the Jamaican women who keep families together, Jamaican women who have made the greater sacrifices. With that in mind, Augustine and Clement came to be Hortense and Jenny. It was also handy because it allowed me to revive these characters from *East of Acre Lane*.

Most of my research involved me talking to my two aunts, Hermine and Lilleth. They made me roar with laughter as they described childhood scenes of them living in the 'bush'. What made it even more entertaining and fascinating was the turn of phrase they used with their thick Jamaican accents. I felt that the beautiful way they spoke had to be included in the dialogue and hoped that readers would get a sense of that as they read the book. For me, the way Jamaican women speak is an essential element of their character.

One of the first scenes I wrote for *Island Songs* was the Atlantic passage: Hortense, Cilbert, Jacob and Jenny's journey to England from Jamaica. It was my father, Alfred, who offered his memories and insights for this piece during a long-distance telephone call from his home in Jamaica. He himself had a similar trip when he first came to England in 1954, and it was his recollections about stowaways and how they jumped overboard moments before the ship reached port that caught my imagination. Even more entertaining were my father's memories about seeing central London for the first time. If I'm ever accused of being a plagiarist then I will only hold my hand up if my father is pointing the finger!

With all the characters assembled I had a crisis of confidence. How could a man get inside the minds of two women? I have trouble understanding just one. So before I set pen to paper I talked to as many women as I could. The stories I collected seemed to be concentrated on one theme: the man I decided to go for turned out to be a bastard. 'He was always a bit of a rogue but I thought I could change him.' This fascinated me. Why are women always attracted to men with danger signals on them? Why do many women take for granted the kind of man who would treat them like a queen and never break their heart? Many women say this isn't true but let me put forward some evidence. Sean Connery's portrayal of James Bond is often voted as the best and sexiest Bond. His portrayal of Bond also treated women appallingly, yet women love it. Whilst George Lazenby, who offered a more vulnerable James Bond, displaying Bond falling in love, is often voted the worst Bond ever. Why is this?

It's for the reason above that I sketched Cilbert, another character that I parachuted in from *East of Acre Lane,* as a bit of a rogue, yet Almyna, Hortense and even Jenny lust after him. Of course, Jacob, although he is devoted to Jenny and would never willingly hurt her in any way, is betrayed. You might think this is unfair, but I ask a question to you women out there if you have finished the book: if you had to choose between wayward Cilbert and God-fearing Jacob for a wild night out, full of promise and passion, who would you choose? Be honest now!

Religion has always been a central part of Jamaican family life and I didn't see how I could write a Jamaican 'epic' that didn't include it. When I visit the countryside of Jamaica there is no more beautiful sight than a Sunday morning when families, dressed in their Sunday best, walk from their homes through the bush to their immaculately kept church. But deep-held beliefs with Jamaican folk has its contradictions. For example, living in Brixton in the late 1970s and early 1980s, I witnessed many friends being forced out of their homes because they had decided to follow rastafarian doctrine and had dreadlocked their hair. Some parents saw it as blasphemy. I wanted to explore where this rasta phenomenon first took hold, and that is why I introduced Levi. To sketch his character I talked to rasta elders in Jamaica and Brixton.

Also, I wanted to examine loss of faith. It is something I have experienced when I was a child and it affected me deeply. I remember, feeling at my lowest ebb when I was about thirteen, I went to see my local Catholic priest. Naively, I asked him if I could live in the church because living in a children's home was a hell for me. He smiled and blessed me. An hour later he called the relevant authorities and I was taken back to the children's home. I never returned to any church again until the christening of my first son. It wasn't a Catholic church.

People have different reactions when they have faced tragedy. Some embrace religion as it gives them comfort in their darkest hour. But some, like Hortense in *Island Songs*, utterly reject it, just like I did. My struggle still continues to this day. Seeing so many bad things happening in the world makes me ask: why, if there really is an all powerful good God, does He allow so much tragedy to happen?

For someone who didn't know what it was like to grow up in a family, observing family life was a fascination for me. When I left the children's home and headed for Brixton in 1977, I always wanted to be invited by my new friends to their homes just to see how they interacted, fell out, made up with each other, and how mothers would show their love or fathers display to their sons how to be a man. Of course, I never revealed to my friends what I was up to, but I discovered that some parents were not even aware that one of their offspring felt they were being neglected, unloved or biased against. *Island Songs* and *East of Acre Lane* are, I guess, the study paper of all my watching and listening.

Alex Wheatle
South London, November 2005

Books that influenced the writing of *Island Songs*
East of Eden, John Steinbeck
The Thorn Birds, Colleen McCulloch
Sula, Toni Morrison
The Color Purple, Alice Walker
Catch A Fire – The Life and Times Of Bob Marley, Timothy White

Music Artists listened to while writing *Island Songs*
(I find it impossible to write without a musical backdrop)
Bob Marley & The Wailers, *The Studio One Sessions*
Leroy Sibbles & The Heptones, *At Studio One*
Alton Ellis, *The Rock Steady Hits*
The Skatellites, *Perfect Ska* – the best instrumental band ever to come out of Jamaica
Curtis Mayfield & The Impressions, *The Early Years*
Slim Smith, *At Studio One*
Pat Kelly & The Techniques, *At Treasure Isle/Duke Reid*

Great People born in St Anne
Bob Marley
Burning Spear
Marcus Garvey

Names
Hortense – named after the great Jamaican vocalist *Hortense Ellis.*
Jenny – the name of one of my partner's aunts.
Cilbert – a friend I used to play cricket with – an excellent batsman.
Almyna – Myna, my mother's nickname, used by those who know her very well.
Hubert – there are about three or four Huberts and Herberts in my family on my father's side.
Amy – An aunt on my father's side. She looked after me so well on my first trip to Jamaica in 1987.
Carmesha – a student who lodged at my aunt Lilleth's home in Kingston while studying at the University of the West Indies. On

my 2001 trip to Jamaica, Carmesha spent hours braiding my son's hair and took him out dancing, showing him the dancehalls of Kingston.

Odd Fact

In *Island Songs*, my Claremont Valley is fictional, based on the bountiful lands surrounding Nine Mile. But there is a real Claremont in the parish of St Anne that I passed through one day on a country bus. So my apologies to the real Claremontonians if you feel that I have taken liberties with the geography of your area.